D0040156

HEAVEN'S WAGER

HEAVEN'S WAGER

TED DEKKER

W PUBLISHING GROUP™

www.wpublishinggroup.com

A Division of Thomas Nelson, Inc.
www.ThomasNelson.com

Heaven's Wager © 2000 by Ted Dekker. All rights reserved. No portion of this book may be reproduced, stored in a retrieval system, or transmitted in any form or by any means—electronic, mechanical, photocopy, recording, or other—except for brief quotations in printed reviews, without the prior permission of the publisher.

This book is a work of fiction. Names, characters, places, and incidents are the product of the author's imagination or are used fictitiously. Any resemblance to real persons, living or dead, or to events or locales is entirely coincidental.

Library of Congress Cataloging-in-Publication Data

Dekker, Theodore R., 1962–

    Heaven's wager / by Theodore R. Dekker.

        p. cm. — (The martyr's song series ; bk. 1)

    ISBN 0-8499-4241-1

    1. Providence and government of God—Fiction. 2. Good and evil—Fiction. 3. Revenge—Fiction. I. Title.

PS3554.E43 H42 2000

813'.6—dc21   00-043461

                                                       CIP

Printed in the United States of America

03 04 05 06 07 PHX 16 15 14 13 12

For LeeAnn, my wife,
without whose love I
would be only a shadow
of myself. I will never
forget the day you saw heaven.

1

Present Day

An overhead fan swished through the afternoon heat above Padre Francis Cadione's head, squeaking once every rotation, but otherwise not a sound disturbed the silence in the small, dimly lit room. A strong smell of lemon oil mixed with pipe smoke lingered in the air. The windows on either side of the ancient desk reached tall and narrow to the ceiling and cast an amber light across the oak floor.

Some described the furnishings as gothic. Cadione preferred to think of his office as merely atmospheric. Which was fitting. He was a man of the church, and the church was all about atmosphere.

But the visitor sitting with folded hands in the burgundy guest chair had brought his own atmosphere with him. It spread like an aura of heavy perfume that dispensed with the nostrils and made straight for the spine. The man had been sitting there for less than a minute now, smiling like a banshee as though he alone knew some great secret, and already Padre Cadione felt oddly out of balance. One of the visitor's legs swung over the other like a hypnotizing pendulum. His blue eyes held their gaze on the priest's, refusing to release the connection.

The padre shifted his eyes, reached for his black pipe, and clicked its stem gently along his teeth. The small gesture of habit brought a familiar easiness. A thin tendril of tobacco smoke rose lazily past his bushy eyebrows before meeting wafts of fan-air and then scattering. He crossed his legs and realized the moment he had done so that he'd inadvertently matched the visitor's posture.

Relax, Francis. You're seeing things now. He's just a man sitting there. A man not as easily impressed as others, perhaps, but a mere man nonetheless.

"So then, my friend. You seem to be in good spirits."

"Good spirits? And what do you mean by good spirits, Padre?"

The man's gentle voice seemed to carry that strange aura with it—the one that had tingled the padre's spine. It was as though their roles had become confused. Spun around by that old ceiling fan whacking away up there.

Padre Cadione drew at the pipe and released the smoke through his lips. He spoke through the haze. Atmosphere. It was all about atmosphere.

"I only meant you seem to be pretty happy with life, despite your . . . adversity. Nothing more."

"Adversity?" The man's left brow arched. The smile below his blue eyes broadened slightly. "Adversity is a relative term, isn't it? It seems to me that if someone is *happy,* as you say, his circumstances cannot be adequately described as *adverse.* No?"

Cadione wasn't sure if the man actually wanted an answer. The question felt more like a reprimand—as if this man had risen above mere happiness and now schooled those foolish mortals who still struggled with the simple pursuit of it.

"But you are right. I am in very good spirits," the man said.

Cadione cleared his throat and smiled. "Yes, I can see that."

Thing of it was, this man was not just happy. He literally seemed thrilled with whatever had gotten under his skin. Not drugs—surely not.

The visitor sat there cross-legged, staring at him with those deep blue eyes, wearing an inviting smile. Daring him, it seemed. *Come on, Padre, do your thing. Tell me about God. Tell me about goodness and happiness and about how nothing really matters but knowing God. Tell me, tell me, tell me, baby. Tell me.*

The priest felt a small, nervous grin cross his face. That was the other thing about this man's brand of happiness. It seemed infectious, if a tad presumptuous.

Either way, the man was waiting, and Cadione could not just sit there forever contemplating matters. He owed this man something. He was, after all, a man of God, employed to shed light. Or at least to point the way to the light switch.

"Being certain of one's place in life does indeed bring one happiness," Cadione said.

"I knew you could understand, Padre! You have no idea how good it is to speak to someone who really understands. Sometimes I feel like I'm ready to burst and no one around me understands. You do understand, don't you?"

"Yes." Cadione nodded instinctively, grinning, still surprised by the man's passion.

"Exactly! People like you and I may have all the wealth in the world, but it's this other thing that is really the magic of life."

"Yes."

"Nothing compares. Nothing at all. Am I right?"

"Yes." A small chuckle escaped Cadione's lips. Goodness, he was starting to feel as though he were being led into a trap with this long string of *yeses.* There could be no doubting the man's sincerity. Or his passion, for that matter. On the other hand, the man might very well have lost his reason. Become eccentric, even senile. Cadione had seen it happen to plenty of people in the man's social strata.

The visitor leaned forward with a sparkle in his eyes. He spoke in a hushed voice now. "Have you ever seen it, Padre?"

"Seen what?" He knew he sounded far too much like a young boy sitting wide eyed at the instruction of a wise father, but Cadione was powerless to stop himself.

"The great reality behind all things." The man lifted his eyes past Cadione to a painting of God's hand reaching out to a man's on the wall behind. "The hand of God." He nodded at the painting, and the priest twisted in his seat.

"God's hand? Yes, I see it every day. Everywhere I look."

"Yes, of course. But I mean really *see*, Padre? Have you actually seen him *do* things? Not something you believe he *might* have done. Like, *Lookie there, I do believe God has opened up a parking spot near the door for us, Honey.* But have you really seen God do something before your eyes?"

The man's exuberance reignited the tingle in Cadione's spine. If the man had lost his sensibilities, perhaps he had found something better. Of course, even if God did have his fingers down here on Earth stirring the pot, people couldn't just open their eyes and *see* it. He pictured a large thumb and forefinger picking up a car and moving it to allow a van easy parking.

"Actually, I can't say that I have."

"Well, I know someone who has. I know someone who *does.*"

A silence settled. The visitor stared at him with those piercing baby blues. But the eyes were not the eyes of a madman. Padre Cadione drew on the pipe, but it had lost its fire and he was rewarded with nothing but stale air.

"You do, huh?"

"I do." The man leaned back again, smiling softly. "And I have seen. Would you like to see, Padre?"

There was a magic in the man's words. A mystery that spoke of truth. He swallowed and leaned back, once again matching the visitor's posture. It occurred to him that he had not actually responded to the man's question.

"It might change your world," the man said.

"Yes. I'm sorry, I was . . . uh . . ."

"Well then." The man drew a deep breath and crossed his legs once again. "Open your mind, my friend. Wide open. Can you do that?"

"Yes . . . Yes, I suppose."

"Good. I have a story for you."

The visitor took another deep breath, thoroughly satisfied with himself, it seemed, and he began.

2

The city was Littleton, a suburb of Denver. The neighborhood was best known as Belaire, an upper-middle-class spread of homes carefully spaced along black streets that snaked between bright green lawns. The street was named Kiowa after the Indians who'd long ago called the plains their own. The home, a two-story stucco topped with a red ceramic tile roof—affectionately called the Windsor by the developer—was the most luxurious model offered in the subdivision. The man standing at the front door was Kent Anthony, the holder of the hefty mortgage on this little corner of the American dream.

In his left hand, a dozen fresh-cut red roses moved to a gentle breeze, starkly accenting the black, double-breasted suit that hung from his narrow shoulders. He stood a lanky six feet, maybe six-two with shoes. Blond hair covered his head, close cropped above the collar. His eyes sparkled blue above a sharp nose; his smooth complexion cast the illusion that he was ten years younger than his true age. Any woman might see him and think he looked like a million bucks.

But today was different. Today Kent was *feeling* like a million bucks because today Kent had actually *earned* a million bucks. Or maybe several million bucks.

The corners of his mouth lifted, and he pressed the illuminated doorbell. His heart began to race, standing right there on his front porch waiting for the large colonial door to swing open. The magnitude of his accomplishment once again rolled through his mind and sent a shudder through his bones. He, Kent Anthony, had managed what only one in ten thousand managed to achieve, according to the good people in the census bureau.

And he had done it by age thirty-six, coming from perhaps the most unlikely beginnings imaginable, starting at absolute zero. The skinny, poverty-stricken child from Botany Street who had promised his father that he would make it, no matter what the cost, had just made good on that promise. He had stretched his boundaries to the snapping point a thousand times in the last twenty years and now . . . Well, now he would stand tall and proud in the family annals. And to be truthful, he could hardly stand the pleasure of it all.

The door suddenly swung in and Kent started. Gloria stood there, her mouth parted in surprise, her hazel eyes wide. A yellow summer dress with small blue flowers settled graciously over her slender figure. A queen fit for a prince. That would be him.

"Kent!"

He spread his arms and smiled wide. Her eyes shifted to the hand holding the roses, and she caught her breath. The breeze swept past him and lifted her hair, as if invited by that gasp.

"Oh, Honey!"

He proudly offered her the bouquet and bowed slightly. In that moment, watching her strain with delight, the breeze lifting blonde strands of hair away from her slender neck, Kent felt as though his heart might burst. He did not wait for her to speak again but stepped through the threshold and embraced her. He wrapped his long arms around her waist and lifted her to meet his kiss. She returned the affection passionately and then squealed with laughter, steadying the roses behind him.

"Am I a man who keeps his word, or am I not?"

"Careful, dear! The roses. What on Earth has possessed you? It's the middle of the day!"

"*You* have possessed me," Kent growled. He set her down and pecked her cheek once more for good measure. He spun from her and bowed in mock chivalry.

She lifted the roses and studied them with sparkling eyes. "They're beautiful! Really, what's the occasion?"

Kent peeled off his coat and tossed it over the stair banister. "The occasion is you. The occasion is us. Where's Spencer? I want him to hear this."

Gloria grinned and called down the hall. "Spencer! Someone's here to see you."

A voice called from the hallway. "Who?" Spencer slid around the corner in his stocking feet. His eyes popped wide. "Dad?" The boy ran up to him.

"Hi, Tiger." Kent bent and swept Spencer from his feet in a great bear hug. "You good?"

"Sure."

Spencer wrapped his arms around his father's neck and squeezed tight. Kent set the ten-year-old down and faced them both. They stood there, picture perfect, mother and child, five-three and four-three, his flesh and blood. Behind them a dozen family pictures and as many portraits graced the entryway wall. Snapshots of the last twelve years: Spencer as a baby in powder blue; Gloria holding Spencer in front of the first apartment, lovely lime-green walls surrounded by wilting flowers; the three of them in dwelling number two's living room—a real house this time—grinning ear to ear as if the old brown sofa on which they sat was really the latest style instead of a ten-dollar afterthought purchased at some stranger's garage sale. Then the largest picture, taken two years earlier, just after they had purchased this home—house number three if you counted the apartment.

Kent saw them all in a glance, and he immediately thought a new picture would go up now. But on a different wall. A different home. A much bigger home. He glanced at Gloria and winked. Her eyes grew as if she'd guessed something.

He leaned down to his son. "Spencer, I have some very important news. Something very good has just happened to us. Do you know what it is?"

Spencer glanced at his mother with questioning eyes. He nimbly swept blond bangs from his forehead and stared up at Kent. For a moment they stood, silent.

Then his son spoke in a thin voice. "You finished?"

"And what is *finished* supposed to mean? Finished what, boy?"

"The program?"

Kent shot Gloria a wink. "Smart boy we have here. And what does that mean, Spencer?"

"Money?"

"You actually finished?" Gloria asked, stunned. "It passed?"

Kent released his son's shoulder and pumped a fist through the air. "You bet it did! This morning."

He stood tall and feigned an official announcement. "My friends, the Advanced Funds Processing System, the brainchild of one Kent Anthony, has passed all tests with flying colors. The Advanced Funds Processing System not only works, it works perfectly!"

Spencer grinned wide and whooped.

Gloria glowed proudly, reached up on her tippytoes, and kissed Kent on his chin. "Splendid job, Sir Anthony."

Kent bowed and then leapt for the living room. A catwalk spanned the two-story ceiling above; he ran under it toward the cream leather furniture. He cleared the sofa in a single bound and dropped to one knee, pumping that arm again as if he'd just caught a touchdown pass. "Yes! Yes, yes, *yes!*"

The Spanish-style interior lay immaculate about him, the way Gloria insisted it remain. Large ceramic tile ran past a breakfast bar and into the kitchen to his right. A potted palm draped over the entertainment center to his left. Directly before him, above a fireplace not yet used, stood a tall painting of Christ supporting a sagging, forsaken man holding a hammer and spikes. *Forgiven,* it was called.

He whirled to them. "Do you have any idea what this means? Let me tell you what this means."

Spencer squealed around the sofa and jumped on his knee, nearly knocking Kent to his back. Gloria vaulted the same cream leather sofa, barefooted, her yellow dress flying. She ended on her knees in the cushions, smiling wide, waiting, winking at Spencer, who had watched her make the leap.

Kent felt a fresh surge of affection seize his heart. Boy, he loved her! "This means that your father has just changed the way banks process funds." He paused, thinking about that. "Let me put it another way. Your father has just saved Niponbank millions of dollars in operating costs." He thrust a finger into the air and popped his eyes wide. "No, wait! Did I say millions of dollars? No, that would be in one year. Over the long haul, *hundreds* of millions of dollars! And do you know what big banks do for people who save them hundreds of millions of dollars?"

He stared into his son's bright eyes and answered his own question quickly before Spencer beat him to it. "They give them a few of those millions, that's what they do!"

"They've approved the bonus?" Gloria asked.

"Borst put the paperwork through this morning." He turned to the side and pumped his arm again. "Yes! Yes, yes, yes!"

Spencer slid off his knee, flopped backward on the couch, and kicked his legs into the air. "Yahoo! Does this mean we get to go to Disneyland?"

They laughed. Kent stood and stepped toward Gloria. "You bet it does." He plucked one of the roses still gripped in her hand and held it out at arm's length. "It also means we will celebrate tonight." He winked at his wife again and began to dance with the rose extended, as if it were his partner. "Wine . . ." He closed his eyes and lifted his chin. "Music . . ." He spread his arms wide and twirled once on his toes. "Exquisite food . . ."

"Lobster!" Spencer said.

"The biggest lobster you can imagine. From the tank," Kent returned and kissed the rose. Gloria laughed and wiped her eyes.

"Of course, this does mean a few small changes in our plans," Kent said, still holding up the red bud. "I have to fly to Miami this weekend. Borst wants me to make the announcement to the board at the annual meeting. It seems that my career as a celebrity has already begun."

"This weekend?" Gloria lifted an eyebrow.

"Yes, I know. Our anniversary. But not to worry, my queen. Your prince will be leaving Friday and returning Saturday. And then we will celebrate our twelfth like we have never dreamt of celebrating."

His eyes sparkled mischievously, and he turned to Spencer. "Excuse me, sire. But would Sunday or Monday suit you best for a ride on the Matterhorn?"

His son's eyes bulged. "The Matterhorn?" He gasped. "Disneyland?"

Gloria giggled. "And just how are we supposed to get to California by Sunday if you're going to Miami?"

Kent looked at Spencer, sucking a quick breath, feigning shock. "Your mother's right. It will have to be Monday, sire. Because I do fear there is no carriage that will take us to Paris in time for Sunday's games."

He let the statement stand. For a moment only the breeze sounded, flipping the kitchen curtains.

Then it came. "Paris?" Gloria's voice wavered slightly.

Kent turned his head toward her and winked. "But of course, my queen. It is, after all, the city of love. And I hear Mickey has set up shop to boot."

"You are taking us to *Paris?*" Gloria demanded, still unbelieving. The giggle had fled, chased away by true shock. "Paris, France? Can—can we *do* that?"

Kent smiled. "My dear, we can do anything now." He lifted a fist of victory into the air.

"Paris!"

Then the Anthonys let restraint fly out the window, and pandemonium broke out in the living room. Spencer hooted and unsuccessfully attempted to vault the couch as his parents had. He sprawled to a tumble. Gloria rushed Kent and shrieked, not so much in shock, but because shrieking fit the mood just now. Kent hugged his wife around the waist and swung her in circles.

It was a good day. A very good day.

3

They sat there, the three of them, Gloria, Helen, and Spencer, in Helen's living room, on overstuffed green chairs, the way they sat every Thursday morning, preparing to begin their knocking. Gloria's right leg draped over her left, swinging lightly. She held folded hands on her lap and watched grandmother and grandson engage each other with sparkling eyes.

The fact that Spencer could join them came as one of the small blessings of homeschooling. She had questioned whether a boy Spencer's age would find a prayer meeting engaging, but Helen had insisted. "Children have better spiritual vision than you might think," she'd said. It only took one meeting with Helen for Spencer to agree.

At age sixty-four, Gloria's mother, Helen Crane, possessed one of the most sensitive spirits harbored in the souls of mankind. But, then, knowing her story of the years before Gloria's birth, even the most dimwitted soul would at least suspect why. She'd been to hell and back, Gloria thought, in ways very few could imagine, much less actually experience. Helen's was a story that could fill an entire volume. Suffice it to say that it had deposited her here with a crystal-clear wit and a damaged body, neither of which was noticeable at first glance. It was when she spoke that one would first hear her wit. And it was when she walked, with her limp, that others might wonder what she had endured to weaken those legs so.

Gloria's father had died when she was very young, leaving Mother alone to find solace with God. And nothing seemed to bring her that solace like the hours she spent shuffling about the house, hounding heaven, drawing near to the throne. The shuffling used to be pacing, an insistent pacing that actually began many years ago while Gloria was still a child. Gloria would often kneel on the sofa, combing the knots from her doll's hair, watching her mother step across worn carpet with lifted hands, smiling to the sky.

"I am an intercessor," Helen told her young daughter. "I speak with God."

And God spoke to her, Gloria thought. More so lately, it seemed.

Helen sat flat footed, rocking slowly in the overstuffed green rocker, her hands resting on the chair's worn arms. A perpetual smile bunched soft cheeks. Her hazel eyes glistened like jewels set in her face, which was lightly dusted with powder but otherwise free of makeup. Her silver hair curled to her ears and down to her neck. She was not as thin as she had been in her early years, but she carried the additional fifteen pounds well. The dresses her mother wore were partly responsible. She could not remember ever seeing her mother wear slacks. Today the dress was a white summer shirtwaist sprinkled with light blue roses that flowed in soft pleats to her knees.

Gloria glanced at her son, who sat with his legs crossed under him the way he always sat, Indian style. He was telling his grandmother about the upcoming trip to Disneyland with wide eyes, stumbling over his words. She smiled. They had finalized the plans last evening at Antonio's while dining on steak and lobster. Kent would leave for Miami Friday morning and return Saturday in time to catch a 6 P.M. flight to Paris. The short-notice tickets had cost the world, but the fact had only put a broader smile on her husband's face. They would arrive in France on Monday, check into some classy hotel called the Lapier, catch their breath while feasting on impossibly expensive foods, and rest for the next day's adventure. Kent was finally about to live his childhood dream, and he was setting about it with a vengeance.

Of course, Kent's success did not come without its price. It required focus, and something was bound to give in favor of that focus. In Kent's case it was his faith in God, which had never been his strong suit anyway. Within three years of their marriage, Kent's faith left him. Entirely. There was no longer room in his heart for a faith in the unseen. He was too busy chasing things he *could* see. It wasn't just an apathy—Kent did not do apathy. He either did or he did not do. It was either all out or not at all. And God became not at all.

Four years ago, just after Spencer had turned six, Helen had come to Gloria, nearly frantic. "We need to begin," she'd said.

"Begin what?" Gloria had asked.

"Begin the knocking."

"Knocking?"

"Yes, knocking—on heaven's door. For Kent's soul."

For Helen it was always either knocking or hounding.

So they had begun their Thursday morning knocking sessions then. The door to Kent's heart had not opened yet, but through it all Gloria and Spencer had peeked into heaven with Helen. What they saw had them scrambling out of bed every Thursday morning, without fail, to go to Grandma's.

And now here they were again.

"Delightful!" Helen said, flashing a smile at Gloria. "That sounds positively wonderful. I had no idea there was more than one Disneyland."

"Heavens, Mother," Gloria said. "There's been more than one Disney park for years now. You really need to get out more."

"No, thank you. No, no. I get out quite enough, thank you." She said it with a grin, but her tone rang with sincerity. "My being a stranger in that world out there is just fine by me."

"I'm sure it is. But you don't have to sequester yourself."

"Who said I was sequestering myself? I don't even know what sequestering means, for goodness' sake. And what does this have to do with my not knowing about a Disneyland in Paris, anyway?"

"Nothing. You were the one who brought up being a stranger. I'm just balancing things out a bit, that's all." God knew Helen could use a little balance in her life.

Her mother's eyes sparkled. She grinned softly, taking up the challenge. "Balance? Things are already out of balance, Honey. Upside down out of balance. You take one hundred pounds of Christian meat, and I guarantee you that ninety-eight of those pounds are sucking up to the world. It's tipping the scale right over, love." She reached up and pulled at the wrinkly skin on her neck. Nasty habit.

"Maybe, but you really don't have to use words like *sucking* to describe it. That's what I'm talking about. And how many times have I told you not to pull on your neck like that?"

Dramatics aside, Helen was right, of course, and Gloria took no offense. If anything, she warmed to her mother's indictments of society.

"It's just flesh, Gloria. See?" Helen pinched the loose skin on her arms and pulled, sampling several patches. "See, just skin. Flesh for the fire. It's what's tipping the scales the wrong way."

"Yes, but as long as you live in this world, there's no need to walk around pulling your skin in public. People don't like it." If she didn't know better, she would guess her mother senile at times.

"Well, this isn't public, for one thing, dear." Helen turned to Spencer, who sat watching the discussion with an amused smile. "It's family. Isn't that right, Spencer?"

She turned back to Gloria. "And for another thing, maybe if Christians went around pulling their skin or some such thing, people would actually know they were Christians. God knows you can't tell now. Maybe we should change our name to the Skinpullers and walk around yanking on our skin in public. That would set us apart."

Silence settled around the preposterous suggestion.

Spencer was the first to laugh, as if a dam had broken in his chest. Then Gloria, shaking her head at the ridiculous image, and finally Mother, after glancing back and forth, obviously trying to understand what was so funny. Gloria could not tell if Helen's laughter was motivated by her own skin-pulling or by their infectious cackling. Either way, the three of them had a good, long hoot.

Helen brought them back to a semblance of control, still smiling. "Well, there's more to my suggestion than what you might guess, Gloria. We laugh now, but in the end it will not seem so strange. It's this ridiculous walking around pretending not to be different that will seem crazy. I suspect a lot of heads will be banging the walls of hell in regret someday."

Gloria nodded and wiped her eyes. "Yes, you're probably right, Mother. But you do have a way with images."

Helen turned to Spencer. "Yes, now where were we when your mother so delicately diverted our discussion, Spencer?"

"Disneyland. We're going to Euro Disney in Paris," Spencer answered with a smile and a sideways glance at Gloria.

"Of course. Disneyland. Now Spencer, what do you suppose would be more fun for a day, Euro Disney or heaven?"

The sincerity descended like a heavy wool blanket.

It was perhaps the way Helen said *heaven*. As if it were a cake you could eat. That's how it was with Helen. A few words, and the hush would fall. Gloria could feel her heart tighten with anticipation. Sometimes it would begin with just a look, or a lifted finger, as if to say, Okay, let us begin. Well, now it had begun again, and Gloria sighed.

Spencer's mouth drifted into a smile. "Heaven!"

Helen lifted an eyebrow. "Why heaven?"

Most children would stutter at such a question, maybe answer with repeated words learned from their parents or Sunday school teachers. Basically meaningless words for a child, like, "To worship God." Or, "'Cause Jesus died on the cross."

But not Spencer.

"In heaven . . . I think we'll be able to do . . . anything," he said.

"I think we will too," Helen said, perfectly serious. She sighed. "Well, we'll see soon enough. Today it will have to be Paris and Disneyland. Tomorrow maybe heaven. If we're so fortunate."

The room fell silent, and Helen closed her eyes slowly. Another sign.

The sound of her own breathing rose and fell in Gloria's ears. She closed her eyes and saw pinpricks in a sea of black. Her mind climbed to another consciousness. *Oh, God. Hear my son's cry. Open our eyes. Draw our hearts. Bring us into your presence.*

For a few minutes Gloria sat in the silence, displacing small thoughts and drawing her mind to the unseen. A tear gently ripped opened in heaven for her then, like a thin fracture in a wall, allowing shafts of light to filter through. In her mind's eye, she stepped into the light and let it wash warm over her chest.

The knocking started with a prayer from Helen. Gloria opened her eyes and saw that her mother had lifted her hands toward the ceiling. Her chin was raised, and her lips moved around a smile. She was asking God for Kent's soul.

For thirty minutes they prayed like that, taking turns calling on God to hear their cry, show his mercy, send word.

Near the end, Helen rose and fetched herself a glass of lemonade. She got hot, praying to heaven, she said. Being up there with all those creatures of light made her warm all over. So she invariably broke for the lemonade or ice tea at some point.

Sometimes Gloria joined her, but today she did not want to break. Today the presence was very strong, as if that crack had frozen open and continued to pour light into her chest. Which was rather unusual, because usually the tear opened and closed, allowing only bursts of light through. A thoughtful consideration by the gatekeepers, she had once decided. So as not to overwhelm the mortals with too much at once.

Thoughts of Paris had long fled, and now Gloria basked in thoughts of the unseen. Thoughts of floating, like Spencer had said. Like the pinpricks of light in the dark of her eyes. Or maybe like a bird, but in outer space, streaking through a red nebula, wide mouthed and laughing. She would give her life for it, in a heartbeat. Thinking of it now, her pulse thickened. Sweat began to bead on her forehead. Raw desire began to well up within her, as it often did. To touch *him*, to see the Creator. Watch him create. Be loved with that same power.

Helen once told her that touching God might be like touching a thick shaft of lightning, but one filled with pleasure. It might very well kill you, she said, but at least you'd die with a smile on your face. She'd chuckled and shook her head.

Her mother seated herself, slurped the lemonade for a few seconds, and set the clinking glass beside her chair. Helen sighed, and Gloria closed her eyes, thinking, *Now, where was I?*

It was then, in that moment of regularity, that the tear in heaven gaped wide, opening as it never had. They had prayed together every Thursday, every week, every month, every year for five years, and never before had Gloria even come close to feeling and seeing and hearing what she did then.

She would later think that it is when contemplating inexplicable times such as these that men say, *He is sovereign. He will do as he wills. He will come through a virgin; he will speak from a bush; he will wrestle with a man. He is God. Who can know the mind of the Lord? Amen.* And it is the end of the matter.

But it is not the end of the matter if *you* are the virgin Mary, or if *you* hear him from a bush like Moses, or if *you* wrestle with God as did Jacob. Then it is only the beginning.

It happened suddenly, without the slightest warning. As if a dam holding the light back had broken, sending volumes of the stuff cascading down in torrents. One second trickles of power, feathering just so, like lapping waves, and the next a flood that seemed to pound into the small living room and blow away the walls.

Gloria gasped and jerked upright. Two other audible heaves filled the room, and she knew that Spencer and Helen saw it as well.

The buzzing started in her feet and ran through her bones, as if her heels had been plugged into a socket and the juice cranked up. It swept up her spine, right into her skull, and hummed. She gripped the chair's padded arms to keep her hands still from their trembling.

Oh, God! she cried, only she didn't actually cry it, because her mouth had frozen wide. Her throat had seized. A soft moan came out. "Uhhhh . . ." And in that moment, with the light pouring into her skull, rattling her bones, she knew that nothing—absolutely nothing—could ever compare to this feeling.

Her heart slammed in her chest, thumping loudly in the silence, threatening to tear itself free. Tears spilled from her eyes in small rivulets before she even had time to cry. It was that kind of power.

Then Gloria began to sob. She didn't know why exactly—only that she was weeping and shaking. Terrified, yet desperate for more at once. As if her body craved more but could not contain this much pleasure in one shot. Undone.

Far away, laughter echoed. Gloria caught her breath, drawn to the sound. It came from the light, and it grew—the sound of a child's laughter. Long strings of giggles, relentlessly robbing the breath from the child. Suddenly Gloria ached to be with the child, laughing. Because there in the light, captured in a singular union of raw power and a child's unrestrained giggles, lay eternal bliss. Ecstasy. Maybe the very fabric from which energy was first conceived.

Heaven.

She knew it all in a flash.

The light vanished suddenly. Like a tractor beam pulled back into itself.

Gloria sat arched for a brief moment and then collapsed into the chair's soft cushions, her mind spinning through a lingering buzz. *Oh, God, oh, God, oh, God, I love you! Please.* She could not say the appropriate words. Perhaps there were no appropriate words. She moaned softly and went limp.

No one spoke for several long minutes. It was not until then that Gloria even remembered Helen and Spencer. When she did, it took another minute to reorient herself and begin seeing things again.

Helen sat with her face tilted to the ceiling, her hands pressed to her temples.

Gloria turned to her son. Spencer was shaking. His eyes were still closed, his hands lay on his lap, palms up, and he shook like a leaf. Giggling. With his mouth spread wide and his cheeks bunched and his face red. Giggling like that child in the light. The sight was perhaps the most perfect image she had ever witnessed.

"Jesus," her mother's soft voice groaned. "Oh, dear Jesus!"

Gloria squeezed the chair just to make sure she was not floating, because for a moment she wondered if she'd actually been taken from the chair and set on a cloud.

She looked at her mother again. Helen had clenched shut her eyes and lifted her chin so that the skin on her neck stretched taught. Her face rose ashen to the ceiling and Gloria saw then that her mother was crying. Not crying and smiling like Spencer. But crying with a face painted in horror.

"Mom?" she asked, suddenly worried.

"Oh, God! Oh, God, please. Please, no!" Helen's fingers dug deep into the chair arms. Her face grimaced as though she were enduring the extracting of a bullet without an anesthetic.

"Mother! What's wrong?" Gloria sat straight, memories of the incredible laughter dimmed by this sight before her. "Stop it, Mother!"

Helen's muscles seemed to tense at the command. She did not stop it. "Oh, please God, no! Not now. Please, please, please . . ."

From her vantage, Gloria could see the roof of her mother's mouth, surrounded by white dentures, like a pink canyon bordered by towering pearl cliffs. A groan broke from Helen's throat like moaning wind from a deep, black cavern. A chill descended Gloria's neck. She could not mistake the expression worn by Helen now—it was the face of agony.

"Nooooo!" The sound reminded Gloria of a woman in childbirth. "Noooo . . ."

"Mother! Stop it right now! You're frightening me!" She jumped up from the chair and rushed over to Helen. Up close she saw that her mother's whole face held a slight tremor. She dropped to her knee and grabbed her mother's arm.

"Mother!"

Helen's eyes snapped open, staring at the ceiling. The moan ran out of air. Her eyes skipped over the white plaster above. She mumbled softly. "What have you shown me? What have you shown me?"

She must have found herself then, because she suddenly clamped her mouth shut and dropped her head.

For a moment they stared at each other with wide eyes.

"Mom, are you okay?"

Helen swallowed and looked over to Spencer, who was now watching intently. "Yes. Yes, I am. Sit down, my dear." She shooed Gloria back to her seat. "Go sit down. You're making me nervous." Helen was obviously scrambling for reorientation, and the words came out with less than her usual authority.

Gloria stood, stunned. "Well, you scared the living daylights out of me." She retreated to her chair, trembling slightly.

When she faced Helen again, her mother was crying, her head buried in her hands. "What *is* it, Mother?"

Helen shook her head, sniffed loudly, and straightened. "Nothing, Honey. Nothing."

But it was not *nothing;* Gloria knew that.

Helen wiped her eyes and tried to smile. "Did you hear the laughter?"

Gloria glanced at her son, who was nodding already. "Yes. It was . . . it was incredible."

Spencer grinned at her. "Yeah. I heard the laughter."

They held stares, momentarily lost in the memory of that laughter, smiling silly again.

The contentment came back like a warm fog.

They sat silently for a while, numbed by what had happened. Then Helen joined them in their smiling, but she could not hide the shadows that crossed her face. Still, the laughter consumed Gloria.

At some point a small thought ran through her mind. The thought that they were leaving for Paris soon—to celebrate. But it seemed like a fleeting, inconsequential detail, like the memory that she'd brushed her teeth that morning. Too much was happening here to think of Paris.

4

Across town, Kent, light-footed and as carefree as he could remember feeling, walked up the broad steps leading to Denver's main branch of the multinational banking conglomerate Niponbank. It was an old, historic building with a face-lift of gigantic proportions. Although sections of the original wood-frame structure could still be seen on the back half of the bank, the front half appeared as grand and as modern as any contemporary building. It was the bank's way of compromising with elements in the city who did not want the building torn down. The stairway flared at street level and narrowed as it ascended, funneling patrons to three wide glass doors. Behind him eight lanes of Thursday morning's traffic bustled and blared obnoxiously, but the sound came as an anchor of familiarity, and today familiarity was good.

He smiled and smacked through the glass doors.

"Morning, Kent."

He nodded to Zak, the ever present security guard who meandered about the main lobby during business hours. "Morning, Zak. Beautiful day, isn't it?"

"Yes sir. It surely is."

Kent walked across the marble floor, nodding at several tellers who caught his eye. "Morning."

"Morning."

Mornings all around. The long row of tellers readied for business to his left. A dozen offices with picture windows now sat half-staffed on his right. Hushed tones carried through the lobby. High heels clacked along the floor to his right and he turned, half expecting to see Sidney Beech. But then, she'd already left with the others for the bank's annual conference in Miami, hadn't she? Instead it was Mary, a teller he'd met once or twice. She stepped by with a smile. Her perfume followed her in musty swirls, and Kent pulled the scent into his nostrils. Gardenia blossoms.

A dozen circular pedestals stood parallel to the long banking counter, each offering a variety of forms and golden pens to fill them out. A twenty-foot brass replica of a sailing yacht hovered five feet off the floor at the foyer's center. From a distance it appeared to be supported on a single, one-inch gold pipe under its hull. But closer inspection revealed the thin steel cables running to the ceiling. Nevertheless, the effect was stunning. Any lingering thoughts of the building's historic preservation evaporated with one look around the lobby. The architects had pretty much gutted this part of the building and started over. It was a masterpiece in design.

Kent stepped forward, toward the gaping hall opposite the entrance. There the marble floor ended, and a thick teal carpet ran into the administration wing. A large sea gull hung on the wall above the hall.

Today it all came to him like a welcoming balm. The sights, the smells, the sounds all said one word: *Success.* And today success was his.

He'd come a long way from the poor-white-trash suburbs of Kansas City. It had been the worst of all worlds—bland and boring. In most neighborhoods you either had the colors of wealth or the crimes of poverty, both of which at least introduced their own variety of spice to a boy's life. But not on Botany Street. Botany Street boasted nothing but boxy manufactured homes sporting brown lawns only occasionally greened by manual sprinklers. That was it. There were never any parades on Botany Street. There were never any fights or accidents or car chases. To a household, the neighbors along Botany Street owed their humble existence to the government. The neighborhood was a prison of sorts. Not one with bars and inmates, of course. But one to which you were sentenced with the drudgery of plowing through each day, burdened with the dogged knowledge that, even though you weren't running around stealing and killing, you were about as useful to society as those who did. Your worthless state of existence meant you would have to park your rear end here on Stupid Street and hook up to the government's mighty feeding tube. And everyone knew that those on the dole were a worthless lot.

Kent had often thought that the gangs across town had it better. Never mind that their purpose in life was to wreak as much havoc as possible without going to prison; at least they had a purpose, which was more than he could say about those on Botany Street. *Stupid Street.*

His candid observations had started during the third grade, when he'd made the decision that he was going to be Jesse Owens one day. Jesse Owens didn't need a basketball court or a big business or even a soccer ball to make the big bucks. All Jesse Owens needed were his two legs, and Kent had a pair of those. It was on his runs beyond Botany Street that Kent began to see the rest of the world. Within the year he had arrived at two conclusions. First, although he enjoyed running more than anything else in his little world, he was not cut out to be Jesse Owens. He could run long, but he could not run fast or jump far or any of the other things that Jesse Owens did.

The second thing he figured out was that he had to get off Botany Street. No matter what the cost, he and his family had to get out.

But then, as a first-generation immigrant whose parents had begged their passage to America during the Second World War, his father had never had the opportunity, much less the means to leave Botany Street.

Oh, he'd talked about it enough, all the time in fact. Sitting on the shredded brown lounger after a long day shoveling coal, in front of a black-and-white television that managed one fuzzy channel. On a good day he might have a generic beer on his lap. "I tell you, Buckwheat (his dad always called him Buckwheat), I swear I'll take us out of here one day. My folks didn't come two thousand miles on a boat to live like rabbits in someone's play box. No sir." And for a while Kent had believed him.

But his dad had never managed that journey beyond Botany Street. By the time Kent was in sixth grade he knew that if he ever wanted a life remotely similar to Jesse Owens's or even the average American's, for that matter, it would be solely up to him. And from what he could see there were only two ways to acquire a ticket for the train leaving their miserable station in life. The one ticket was pure, unsolicited fortune—winning the lottery, say, or finding a bag of cash—a prospect he quickly decided was preposterous. And the other ticket was high achievement. Super high achievement. The kind of achievement that landed people Super Bowl rings, or championship belts, or in his case, scholarships.

Beginning in grade seven he divided the sum total of his time between three pursuits. Surviving—that would be eating and sleeping and washing behind the ears now and then; running, which he still did every single day; and studying. For several hours each night he read everything he could get his spindly fingers on. In tenth grade he got a library card to the Kansas City Municipal Library, a building he figured had about every book ever written about anything. Never mind that it was a five-mile run from Botany Street; he enjoyed running anyway.

It all paid off for him one afternoon, three months after his father's death, in a single white envelope sticking out of their mail slot. He'd torn the letter out with trembling fingers, and there it was: a full academic scholarship to Colorado State University. He was leaving Stupid Street!

Some came to characterize him as a genius during his six years of higher education. In reality, his success was due much more to long hard hours with his nose in the books than to overactive gray matter.

The sweet smell of success. Yes indeed, and today, finally, success was his.

Kent walked into the hall. The back foyer was empty when he entered. Normally Norma would be sitting at the switchboard, punching buttons. Beyond her station the wide hall continued to a series of administrative divisions, each housing a suite of offices. At the hall's end, an elevator rose to three additional floors of the same. Floors four through twenty were serviced by a different elevator used by the tenants.

Kent's eyes fixed on the first door, ahead to his right, shadowed in the hall's fluorescent light. Bold, white antique letters labeled the division: Information Systems Division. Behind that door lay a small reception room and four offices. The spawning ground for Advanced Funds Processing System. His life. The division could have been placed anywhere—in a basement bunker, for all that mattered. It had little to do with the Denver branch specifically and was in fact only one of a dozen similar divisions hammering out the bank's software across the globe. Part of Niponbank's decentralization policy.

Kent walked quickly down the hall and opened the door.

His four coworkers stood in the small lobby outside of their offices, waiting for him.

"Kent! It's about time you joined us, boy!" Markus Borst beamed. His boss held a champagne glass brimming with amber liquid. A large, hooked nose gave him the appearance of a penguin. A bald penguin at that.

The redhead, Todd Brice, pushed his oversized torso from the sofa and grinned wide. "It's about time, Kent." The kid was a fool.

Betty, the department secretary, and Mary Quinn held champagne glasses they now raised to him. Red and yellow crepe paper hung in ribbons from the ceiling.

He dropped his case and laughed. He could not remember the last time the five of them had celebrated. There had been the occasional birthday cake, of course, but nothing deserving of champagne—especially not at nine o'clock in the morning.

Betty winked one of those fake black lashes. "Congratulations, Kent." Her white-blonde hair was piled a little higher than usual. She handed him a glass.

"Ladies and gentlemen," Borst announced, lifting his own glass. "Now that we are all here, I would like to propose a toast, if I may."

"Here, here," Mary chimed in.

"To AFPS, then. May she live long and prosper."

A chorus of "Here, here!s" rumbled, and together they sipped.

"And to Kent," Mary said, "who we all know made this happen!"

Another chorus of "Here, here!s," and another round of sips. Kent grinned and glanced at the light glaring off Borst's balding head.

"Gee, thanks, guys. But you know I couldn't have done it without you." It was a lie, but a good lie, he thought. In reality he could have done it easily without them. In half the time, possibly. "You guys are the best. Here's to success." He lifted his glass.

"Success," they agreed.

Borst downed the rest of his drink and set it on the coffee table with a satisfied sigh. "I say we close her down at noon today," he said. "We have a big weekend coming up. I'm not sure how much sleep we'll be getting in Miami."

Todd lifted his glass again. "To knocking off at noon," he said and threw back the balance of his drink.

Mary and Betty followed suit, mumbling agreement.

"Betty has all of your plane tickets to the Miami conference," Borst stated. "And for Pete's sake, try not to be late. If you miss the flight, you're on your own. Kent will be giving the address since he obviously knows the program as well as any of us, but I want each of you to be prepared to summarize the essentials. If things go as well as we expect, you may very well be mobbed with questions this weekend. And please, leave any mention of program bugs out of your comments for now. We don't really have any to speak of at this point, and we don't need to muddy the waters yet. Make sense?"

The man was handling himself with more authority than was customary. No one responded.

"Good, then. If you have any questions, I'll be in my office." Borst nodded theatrically and retreated to the first door on the right. Kent swallowed the last of his champagne. *That's it, Borst, go to your office and do what you always do. Nothing. Do absolutely nothing.*

"Kent." He lowered his empty glass and found Mary at his elbow, smiling brightly. Most would tag Mary as chunky, but she carried her weight well. Her brown hair was rather stringy, which did not help her image, but a clear complexion saved her from a much worse characterization. In any case, she could write basic code well enough, which was why Borst had hired her. Problem was, AFPS did not consist of much ordinary code.

"Morning, Mary."

"I just wanted to thank you for bringing us all here. I know how hard you've worked for this, and I think you deserve every bit of what you have coming."

Kent smiled. *Brown-nosing, are we, Mary?* He wouldn't put it past her, despite the innocent round eyes she now flashed up at him. She went with the flow, this one.

"Well, thanks, Mary." He patted the hand at his elbow. "You're too kind. Really."

Then Todd was there at his other elbow, as if the two had held a conference and decided that he would soon hold the keys to their futures. Time to switch their attention from the bald bossman to the rising star.

"Fantastic job, Kent!" Todd lifted his glass, which was empty, and threw it back anyway. By the looks of it, Todd had a few hidden vices.

Kent's mind flashed back to the two-year stint during graduate studies when he himself had taken to nipping at the bottle during late nights hovering over the keyboard. It was an absurd dichotomy, really. A top honors student who had found his brilliance through impeccable discipline, now slowly yielding to the lure of the bottle. A near drowning on one of his late-night runs had halted his slippery slide back to Stupid Street. It had been midwinter, and unable to muscle through a programming routine, he'd gone for a jog with half a bottle of tequila sloshing in his gut. He had misjudged a pier on the lake for a jogging path and run right off it into freezing waters. The paramedics told him if he'd not been in such good shape, he would have drowned. It was the last time he'd touched the stuff.

Kent blinked and smiled at Todd. "Thanks. Well, I've got some work to finish, so I'll see you guys tomorrow, right?"

"Bright 'n' early."

"Bright 'n' early." He nodded, and they stepped aside as though on strings. Kent walked past them to the first door on the left, across from the one through which Borst had disappeared.

This was going to be all right, he thought. Very much all right.

ᴄᴏᴗᴗ

Helen hobbled along beside her daughter in the park, eyeing the ducks waddling beside the pond, nearly as graceful as she. Walking was a thing mostly of the past for her wounded legs. Oh, she could manage about fifty yards without resting up for a while, but that was definitely it. Gloria had persuaded her to see an orthopedic doctor a year earlier, and the quack had recommended surgery. A knee replacement or some such ridiculous thing. They actually wanted to cut her open!

She'd managed a few hours of sleep last night, but otherwise it was mostly praying and wondering. Wondering about that little eye-opener God had decided to grace her with.

"It is lovely here, don't you think?" Helen asked casually. But she did not feel any loveliness at all just now.

"Yes, it is." Her daughter turned to the skating bowl in time to see Spencer fly above the concrete wall, make a grab for his skateboard in some insane inverted move, and streak back down, out of sight. She shook her head and looked back at the pond.

"I swear, that boy's gonna kill himself."

"Oh lighten up, Gloria. He's a boy, for goodness' sake. Let him live life while he's young. One day he'll wake up and find that his body doesn't fly as well as it used to. Until then, let him fly. Who knows? Maybe it brings him closer to heaven."

Gloria smiled and tossed a stick toward one of the ducks swaying its way in search of easy pickings. "You have the strangest way of putting things, Mom."

"Yes, and do you find me wrong?"

"No, not often. Although some of your analogies do stretch the mind." She reached an arm around her mother and squeezed, chuckling.

"You remember that time you suggested Pastor Madison take the cross off the church wall and carry it on his back for a week? Told him if the idea sounded silly it was only because he had not seen death up close and personal. Really, Mother! Poor fellow."

Helen smiled at the memory. Fact of it was, few Christians knew the cost of discipleship. It would have been a fine object lesson. "Yes, well, Bill's a fine pastor. He knows me now. And if he doesn't, he does a fine job pretending as though he does."

She guided her daughter by the elbow down the path. "So you leave tomorrow, then?"

"No, Saturday. We leave Saturday."

"Yes, Saturday. You leave Saturday." The air seemed to have grown stuffy, and Helen drew a deliberate breath. She stopped and looked around for a bench. The closest sat twenty yards away, surrounded by white ducks.

Gloria's voice spoke softly at her elbow. "You okay, Mother?"

Suddenly Helen was not okay. The vision strung through her mind, and she closed her eyes for a moment. Her chest felt stuffed with cotton. She swallowed hard and turned away from her daughter.

"Mother?" A cool hand encircled her biceps.

Helen fought back a flood of tears and narrowly succeeded. When she spoke, her voice warbled a bit. "You know that things are not what they seem, Gloria. You know that, don't you?"

"Yes. I know that."

"We look around here, and we see all sorts of drama unfolding about us—people marrying and divorcing and getting rich and running off to Paris."

"Mother . . ."

"And all along, the drama unfolding in the spirit world is hardly noticed but no less real. In fact, it is the real story. We just tend to forget that because we cannot see it."

"Yes."

"There are a lot of opposites in life, you know. The first will be last, and the last, first." Gloria knew this well, but Helen felt compelled to say it all, just the same. To speak like this to her only daughter. "A man finds the whole world but loses his soul. A man who loses his life finds it. A seed dies, and fruit is born. It is the way of God. You know that, don't you? I've taught you that."

"Yes, you have, and yes, I do know that. What's wrong, Mother? Why are you crying?"

"I am not crying, Honey." She faced Gloria for the first time and saw her raised eyebrows. "Do you see me weeping and wailing?" But her throat was aching terribly now, and she thought she might fall apart right here on the path.

She took a few steps into the grass and cleared her throat. "Death brings life. In many ways, you and I are already dead, Gloria. You know that, don't you?"

"Mother, you *are* crying." Her daughter turned her around as if she were a child. "You're trying not to, but I can hear it in your voice. What's wrong?"

"What would you think if I were to die, Gloria?"

Gloria's mouth parted to speak, but she said nothing. Her hazel eyes stared wide. When she did find her voice, the words came shaky.

"What do you mean?"

"Well, it's a simple enough question. If I were to pass on—die—and you buried me, what would you think?"

"That's ridiculous! How can you speak to me like that? You're nowhere near dying. You shouldn't think such thoughts."

The tension provided Helen with a wave of resolve that seemed to lighten her emotion for the moment. "No, but *if*, Gloria. If a truckdriver missed his brakes and knocked my head off my shoulders—what would you think?"

"That's terrible! I would feel terrible. How can you say such a thing? Goodness! How do you think I would feel?"

She looked directly at her daughter for a few seconds. "I didn't say *feel*, Honey. I said *think*. What would you suppose had happened?"

"I would suppose that a drunken truckdriver had killed my mother, that's what I'd think."

"Well, then you would think like a child, Gloria." She turned away and feigned a little disgust. "Humor me in my old age, dear. At least pretend that you believe what I've taught you."

Her daughter did not respond. Helen cast a sideways glance and saw that she had made the connection. "Mother, there is no end to you."

"No. No, I suppose there isn't, is there. But humor me. Please, darling."

Gloria sighed, but it was not a sigh of resignation—it was a sigh that comes when the truth has settled. "All right. I would think that you had been taken from this world. I would think that in your death, you had found life. Eternal life with God."

"Yes, and you would be right." Helen turned to face Gloria and nodded. "And what might that be like?"

Gloria blinked and turned to the pond, lost in a hazy stare. "It would be . . ." She paused, and a smile curved her lips ever so slowly. ". . . like what we saw yesterday. Laughing with God." Her eyes grew wide, and she faced Helen.

"So, then, would you want me to find that?"

Her daughter's eyebrows narrowed in question for a fleeting moment, and then she nodded slowly. "Yes. Yes, I suppose I would."

"Even if finding it meant losing this life?"

"Yes. I suppose so."

Helen smiled and drew a deep, satisfied breath. "Good."

She stepped close to Gloria, put her arms around her daughter's waist, and pulled her close. "I love you, Sweetheart," she said and rested her cheek on her daughter's shoulder.

"I love you too."

They held each other for a long moment.

"Mother?"

"Yes?"

"You're not going to die, are you?"

"Someday, I hope. The sooner the better. Either way, our worlds are about to change, Gloria. Everything is turning inside out."

5

Kent woke at 6 A.M. on Friday, instantly alert. His plane departed at nine, which gave them two hours to dress and make their way to the airport. He flung the sheets aside and swung his legs to the floor. Beside him, Gloria moaned softly and rolled over.

"Up and at 'em, Sweetheart. I've got a plane to catch."

Gloria grunted an acknowledgment and lay still, milking the waning seconds for the last of sleep, no doubt.

Kent walked under the arch into their spacious bathroom and doused his head under the tap. Fifteen minutes later he emerged, half dressed, expecting to make a trip to the kitchen to ask Gloria about his socks. But he was spared the jaunt downstairs—he would not find Gloria down there because she was still in bed with an arm draped over her face.

"Gloria? We have to leave, Sweetheart. I thought you were up."

She rolled toward him and sat up groggily. "Oh, goodness! I feel like a freight train hit me."

Her complexion looked rather peaked, at that. He sat beside her and ran a finger under her chin. "You look pale. Are you okay?"

She nodded. "Stomach's a bit upset."

"Maybe you have a touch of the flu," Kent offered. He rested a hand on her knee. "Why don't you take it easy. I can get to the airport alone."

"I wanted to take you."

"Don't worry about it. You rest up. We have a big trip tomorrow." He stood. "The twelve-hour flu has been making the rounds at the office. Who knows? Maybe I brought it home. Do you know where my navy silk socks are?"

Gloria motioned to the door. "In the dryer. Honestly, Honey, I'm fine. You sure you don't want me to take you?"

He turned and gave her a wink. "Yes, I'm sure. What's a trip to some lousy airport? We have Paris to think about. Get some rest—I'll be fine." Kent bounded down the steps to the laundry room and rummaged around until he found the socks. He heard the clinking in the kitchen and knew then that Gloria had followed him down.

When he rounded the refrigerator, Gloria was scooping grounds into the coffee machine, her pink housecoat swishing at her ankles. He slid up behind her and slipped his arms around her waist. "Really, Honey. I have this handled."

She dismissed the comment with a flip of her wrist. "No. I'm feeling better already. It was probably that asparagus I ate last night. You want some coffee? The least I can do is send you away with a decent breakfast."

He kissed her on the neck. "I'd love some coffee and toast. Thank you, Sweetheart."

They ate together on the dinette set, Kent neatly dressed, Spencer rubbing sleep from his eyes, Gloria looking like she had risen from her coffin for the occasion. Coffee gurgled, porcelain clinked, forks clattered. Kent eyed Gloria, ignoring the concern that whispered through his skull.

"So, you have tennis today?"

She nodded. "One o'clock. I play Betsy Maher in the quarterfinals." She lifted a white cup to her lips and sipped. "Assuming I'm feeling better."

Kent smiled gently. "You'll be fine, Honey. I can't remember the last time you missed a match. In fact, I can't remember the last time you missed anything due to illness." Kent chuckled and bit into his toast. "Man, I remember the first time we played tennis. You remember that?"

His wife smiled. "How could I forget with your reminding me every few months."

Kent turned to Spencer. "You should've seen her, Spencer. Miss Hotshot with her tennis scholarship trying to take on a runner. She might have been able to place the ball where she wanted, but I ran her into the ground. She wouldn't stop. And I knew she was getting tired after the fourth set, because I could barely stand up and she was over there wobbling on her feet. I'd never seen anybody so competitive." He glanced at Gloria. Some color had come back into her face.

"Until she puked."

"Gross, Dad!"

"Don't look at me. Look at your mother."

Gloria just smiled. "Don't forget to tell him who won, dear."

"Yes, your mother did whip me good that day—before she puked, that is. I think I fell in love with her then, while she was bent over by the far net post."

"Gross!" Spencer giggled.

"Fell in love, ha! As I remember it, you were head over heels for some other thing in a skirt at the time."

"Perhaps. But it all began between us then."

"Well, it took you long enough to come around. We didn't even date until you were out of school."

"Yes, and look at where we are today, dear." He stood, slid his dish into the sink, and returned to kiss her on the cheek. Her skin was warm. "I think it was worth the wait, don't you?"

She smiled. "If you insist."

Twenty minutes later, Kent stood by the front door and saluted them, packed bags in hand. "Okay, you guys have the itinerary, right? I'll see you at five o'clock tomorrow night. We have a plane to catch at six. And remember to pack the camera, Honey. This is one trip that's going down in Anthony family history."

Gloria walked to him, still wrapped in her pink bathrobe. "You take care of yourself, my prince," she said and kissed him gently on the cheek. "I love you." For a moment he looked into those sparkling hazel eyes and smiled.

He bent and kissed her forehead. "And I love you. More than you could possibly know, Sweetheart."

"See you, Dad," Spencer said sheepishly. He walked over and put a flimsy arm around his father's waist.

Kent ruffled his hair. "See you, Chief. You take care of Mommy, you hear?" He kissed him on the forehead.

"I will."

He left them standing at the door, his son under his wife's arm. There was a connection between those two he could never entirely grasp. A knowing glint in their eyes that sapped his power, made him blink. It had been painfully obvious yesterday around the dinner table. But he had just made them rich; it was to be expected, he supposed. They kept exchanging glances, and when he'd finally asked them about it, they'd just shrugged.

Man, he loved them.

The flight from Denver International to Miami was an eventful one. At least for Kent Anthony it was eventful, if for no other reason than because every waking moment had become eventful. He had become a new man. And now in the DC-9 cabin, even his peers recognized him in a new light. Five others from Niponbank's Denver branch were making the belated trip to Florida for the conference. He'd meandered about the aisle, talking to all of them. And all of them had looked at him with a twinkle in their eyes. A glint of jealousy, perhaps. Or a spark of hope for their own careers. *Someday, if I'm so lucky, I will be in your shoes, Kent,* they would be thinking. Of course, there was always the possibility that the glint was actually light—a reflection from the oval windows lining the fuselage.

His boss, Markus Borst, sat three rows up with his shiny bald spot poking just above the seat like an island of sand in a black sea. Borst had worn a toupee over that bald spot all last year, discarding it only after the underhanded comments had driven him to hide for long days with a DO NOT DISTURB sign on his closed door. What the superior did behind that door, Kent could not fathom. He was certainly not breaking records for coordinating software design, as his title suggested. And when he did emerge from his cave, he did little but look over Kent's shoulder and wish he'd thought of this, or mumble about how he could have done that.

And now, within the week Borst could very well be working for him. Kent ran a finger under his collar and stretched his neck. The red tie had been a good choice. It accented the navy suit well, he thought. The perfect attire for meeting the real powerhouses in the bank's upper echelon. They would have heard about him by now, of course. Young man, firm grip, broad shoulders, brilliant mind. From the western United States. He's got the stuff.

An image of a podium facing a thousand executives around dinner tables formed in his mind. He was at the microphone. *Well, it wasn't so difficult once I constructed the advanced timing paradigm. Of course, it's all a matter of perspective. Brilliance is a function more of the destination than of the journey, and let me assure you, my friends, we have arrived at a destination never before imagined, much less traveled.* The conference hall would shake under thunderous applause. He would hold up his hand then, not emphatically but as a slight gesture. It did not take much to command.

Not so long ago, a man named Gates—Bill Gates—introduced an operating system that changed the world of computing. Today Niponbank is introducing the Advanced Funds Processing System, and it will change the world of banking. Now they would be standing, pounding their hands together. Of course, he wouldn't take direct responsibility for the work. But they would understand, just the same. At least those at the top would understand.

Beside him Will Thompson cleared his throat. "Hey, Kent. You ever wonder why some people move up the ladder so quickly and others stay put their whole careers? I mean people with the same basic skills?"

Kent looked at the forty-year-old loan manager, wondering again how the man had finagled his way on this trip. Will insisted that his boss, already in Miami, needed him to explain some innovative ideas they had been working on to some higher-ups. But Kent didn't know Will to have an innovative bone in his body. His colleague's black hair was speckled with gray, and a pair of gold-rimmed glasses sat on his nose. Yellow suspenders rode over a white shirt in good East Coast fashion. If he considered anyone at the bank a friend, it was Will.

"Hmm?"

"No, really. Look at us. I still remember the first day you skipped into the bank, what, seven years ago?" He chuckled and sipped at the martini on his tray. "You were as green as they come, man. Hair all slicked back, ready to set the office on fire. Not that I was any more experienced. I think I had a whole week on you. But we came in at the bottom, and now look at us. Making triple digits, and still climbing. And then you take someone like Tony Milkins. He came six months or so after you and he's what? A teller." Will chuckled again and sipped his drink.

Kent shrugged. "Some want it more. It all comes down to the price you're willing to pay. You and I put our dues in, worked long hours, got the right education. Shoot, if I were to sit down and calculate the time and energy I've put into making it this far, it would scare most college kids right out of school and into boot camp."

"No kidding." Will sipped again. "Then there's a few like Borst. You look at them and wonder how in God's name they ever sneaked in. You'd think his old man owned the bank."

Kent smiled and looked out the window, thinking he'd have to be careful what he said now. One day it would be him that people like Will talked about. True enough, Markus Borst was misplaced in his position, but even those well suited for their positions bore the brunt of professional criticism from the lower ranks.

"So, I guess you'll be moving up now," Will said. Kent glanced at him, noting a hint of jealousy there.

Will caught the look and laughed it off. "No, well done, my friend." He lifted a finger and raised his brows. "But watch your back. I'm right behind you."

"Sure," Kent returned with a smile.

But he was thinking that even Will knew that the notion of Will doing any such thing was an absurd little piece of nonsense. The loan manager could look forward to nothing but slipping into eventual obscurity, like a million other loan managers throughout the world. Loan managers simply did not become household names like Bill Gates or Steve Jobs. Not that it was Will's fault, really. Most people were not properly equipped; they simply did not know how to work hard enough. That was Will's problem.

It suddenly occurred to Kent that he'd just come full circle on the man. He thought of Will in the same way that Will thought of Tony Milkins. A slacker. A friendly enough slacker, but a dope nonetheless. And if Will was a slouch, then people like Tony Milkins were slugs. Ham-and-eggers. Good enough to collect a few bills here and there, but never cut out to spend them.

"Just watch your back too, Will," Kent said. "Because Tony Milkins is right there."

His friend laughed and Kent joined him, wondering if the man had caught his offhanded dig. Not yet, he guessed.

The plane touched down with a squeal of rubber, and Kent's pulse accelerated a notch. They deplaned, found their luggage, and caught two cabs to the Hyatt Regency in downtown Miami.

A porter dressed in maroon, with a tall captain's hat and a nametag that read "Pedro Gonzalas" quickly loaded their bags on a cart and led them through a spacious foyer toward the front desk. To their left, a large fountain splashed over marble mermaids in a blue pool. Palm trees grew in a perfect circle around the water, their leaves rustling in the conditioned air. Most of the guests walking about had come for the conference. Left their branches across the globe to gather in dark suits and gloat over how much money they were all making. A group of Asians laughed around a smoking table, and Kent guessed by their demeanor that they might be near the top. Important men. Or at the very least, thinking themselves important. Some of his future peers, perhaps. Like the short, white-haired one drawing most of the attention, sipping an amber drink. A man of power. Filthy rich. Two hundred and fifty dollars a night for a hotel like this would come out of his tip fund.

"Now *this* place is first class," Todd said beside him.

"That's Niponbank for you," Borst agreed. "Nothing but the best. I think they took the whole hotel. What do you think *that* cost?"

"Geez. Enough. You think we'll have open access to those little refrigerators in the rooms?"

Mary turned to Todd with a raised brow. "Of course we will. What, you think they lock them up for the programming staff? Keep their minds clear?"

"No. I know they'll be open. I mean free. You think we'll have to pay for what we take?"

Borst chuckled. "Don't be a moron, Todd. They cover the entire trip, and you're worried about free booze in little bottles. I'm sure there'll be plenty to drink at the reception. Besides, you need to keep your head clear, boy. We're not here for a party. Isn't that right, Kent?"

Kent wanted to step away from the group, disassociate himself from their small talk. They sounded more like a boy scout troop than programmers who had just changed history. He glanced around, suddenly embarrassed and hoping they had not been overheard.

"That's right," he offered and drifted a few feet to his left. If he was lucky, the onlookers wouldn't put him with this group of clowns.

They'd come to the long, cherrywood check-in counter, and Kent stepped up to a Hispanic dark-haired woman, who smiled cordially. "Welcome to the Hyatt," she said. "How may I help you?"

Well, I have just become rather important, you see, and I am wondering if you have a suite . . .

He terminated the thought. *Get a grip, man.* He smiled despite himself. "Yes, my name is Kent Anthony. I believe you have a reservation for me. I'm with the Niponbank group."

She nodded and punched a few keys. Kent leaned on the counter and looked back toward the men laughing in the lounge chairs. Several were shaking hands now, as if congratulating themselves on a job well done. *Excellent year, Mr. Bridges. Stunning profits. By the way, have you caught wind of the young man from Denver?*

The programmer? Isn't he here somewhere? Brilliant, I've heard.

"Excuse me, sir."

Kent blinked and turned back to the counter. It was the check-in clerk. The pretty dark-haired one. "Kent Anthony, correct?" she asked.

"Yes."

"We have a message for you, sir." She reached under the counter and pulled a red envelope out. Kent's pulse spiked. It was starting already then. Someone other than the bonehead troop under Borst's command had sent him a message. They had not sent it to Borst; they had addressed it to him.

"It's marked urgent," she said and handed it to him.

Kent took the envelope, flipped it open, and withdrew a slip of paper. He scanned the typed note.

At first the words did not create meaning in his mind. They just sat there in a long string. Then they made some sense, but he thought they had made a mistake. That they had given him the wrong message. That this was not *his* Gloria to which the note referred. Couldn't be.

His eyes were halfway through the note for the second time when the heat came, like a scalding liquid searing through his veins from the top of his head right down his spine. His jaw fell slack, and his hand began to quiver.

"Are you all right, sir?" a voice asked. Maybe the clerk's.

Kent read the note again.

KENT ANTHONY:

YOUR WIFE GLORIA ANTHONY IS IN DENVER MEMORIAL HOSPITAL STOP
COMPLICATIONS OF UNDIAGNOSED NATURE STOP
CONDITION DETERIORATING QUICKLY STOP
PLEASE RETURN IMMEDIATELY STOP
END MESSAGE

Now that quiver had become a quake, and Kent felt panic edge up his throat. He whirled around to face Borst, who had missed the moment entirely. "Markus." His voice wavered.

The man turned, smiling at something Betty had just said. His lips flattened the moment he laid eyes on Kent. "What is it?"

Yes indeed! What was it? Leave these in power about him to their excesses before he'd had a chance to help them understand who he was? Leave the party in Borst's hands? Good grief! It was a preposterous notion!

Surely Gloria would be fine. Just fine.

Please return immediately, the message read. And this was Gloria.

"I have to go. I have to return to Denver." Even as he said it, he wanted to pull the words back. How could he leave now? This was the pinnacle. The men laughing over there by the fountain were about to change his life forever. He had just flown two thousand miles to meet them. He had just worked *five years* to meet them!

"I'm sorry. You'll have to take the meeting for me." He shoved the note at his boss and stumbled past him, suddenly furious at this stroke of fate.

"Great timing, Gloria," he muttered through clenched teeth, and immediately regretted the sentiment.

His bags were still on the cart, he realized, but then he didn't care where his bags were. Besides, he would be right back. By tomorrow morning, perhaps. No, tomorrow evening was the Paris trip. Maybe on the way to Paris then.

Okay, Buckwheat. Settle down. Nothing has happened here. Just a little glitch. A bug. She's only in the hospital.

Kent boarded a Yellow Cab and left the bustle at Miami's Hyatt Regency behind. Gloria would be okay. Had to be. She was in good hands. And what was one conference? A dread fell into Kent's gut, and he swallowed.

This had not been in the plans. Not at all.

6

The waiting room in Denver Memorial's ICU wing was decorated in a rust color, but in Helen's mind it was red and she wondered why they would choose the color of blood.

Helen gripped pastor Bill Madison's arm at the elbow and steered the much larger man toward the window. If anybody could understand, it would be the young, dark-haired Greek who had attracted her to the Community Church in the first place ten years earlier. He had been fresh out of seminary then—not a day over twenty-five and bubbling with love for God. Somewhere in there the church bureaucracy had tempered his passion. But Pastor Madison had never been confused about his beliefs.

He had arrived in the night sometime, but she could not remember precisely when because things were fuzzy now. They were all exhausted, that much was clear, and her knees throbbed with a dull pain. She had to sit. Behind them, Spencer sat like a lump on one of the blood-rust waiting chairs.

Helen knew her strained voice betrayed her anxiety, but given the circumstances, she hardly cared. "No. I'm not telling you I *think* I've seen this. I'm telling you I *did* see this." She squeezed hard, as if that might help him understand. "You hear me?"

Bill's dark eyes widened, but she didn't know if it came from her announcement or her squeezing. "What do you mean, you *saw* this?" he asked.

"I mean I *saw* this!" She stretched a shaking arm toward the swinging doors. "I saw my daughter in there, on that bed, that's what I saw." The anger came back as she recalled her vision, and she shook with it.

He eyed her with a raised brow, skeptical to the bone, she saw. "Come on, Helen. We all have impressions now and then. This is not a time to stretch perceptions."

"You are questioning my judgment then? You think I did not see what I say I saw?"

"I'm just saying that we shouldn't rush to conclusions at times like these. This is a time for caution, wouldn't you say? I know things are difficult, but—"

"Caution? What does caution have to do with the fact that my daughter is in there spread on the table? I saw it, I'm telling you! I don't know why I saw it or what God could possibly mean by showing it to me, but I saw it, Pastor. Every last detail."

He glanced about the room and steered her toward the window. "Okay, keep your voice down, Helen." A thin trail of sweat leaked past his temple. "When did you see this?"

"Two days ago."

"You saw all of this two days ago?"

"Isn't that what I just said?" she demanded.

"Yes." He turned from her and sat on the windowsill. His hands were shaking. Helen stood by the window.

"Look, Helen. I know you see things differently than most—"

"Don't even start, Pastor. I don't want to hear it. Not now. It would be insensitive."

"Well, I'm trying to be sensitive, Helen. And I'm thinking of the boy over there. No need to bury his mother just yet."

Helen looked toward Spencer, who sat, chin on palms, legs swinging under the chair. Dark circles looped under his bloodshot eyes. Through the night he'd slept a fitful hour, at most.

"I'm not *burying* my daughter, Bill. I am confiding in you. I saw this, and it terrifies me that it is precisely what I saw."

He did not respond to that.

She stared out the window and folded her hands. "The fact is I like it even less than you. It's gnawed at me like a cancer since that first moment. I can't seem to wrap my mind around this one, Bill." A lump rose to her throat. "I can't understand why God is doing this thing. And you would think *I* should know, of all people."

His hand reached out and rested on her shoulder. The gesture brought a sliver of comfort. "And how can you be certain it is God?"

"It doesn't matter. It is God by default. What he allows, he does."

"Maybe, but only if he is truly God. Omnipotent. All powerful. And if so, it is for him to decide why he would do such a thing."

"Yes, I *know* that, Bill! But it's my daughter in there hooked up to a machine!" She lowered her head, confused and angry at the emotions boiling up within her.

"I'm very sorry, Helen." Bill's voice sounded strained.

They remained silent for a few long moments, face to face with the impossibilities of the matter. Helen wasn't sure what she expected from him. Certainly not a pithy statement of inspiration. *Now, now there, Helen. Everything will be just fine. You'll see. Just trust in the Lord.* Heavens! She really ought to know. She'd been here before, facing the threat of death like this.

"So then, you saw more?" Bill was speaking. "Did you see her die?"

She shook her head. "No, I did not see her die."

She heard him swallow. "We should pray then," he said.

Helen tried to still her emotions. "I did not see her death, but I did see more, Bill."

He didn't answer right away. When he did, his voice came haltingly. "What . . . what did you see?"

She shook her head. "I can't say, really. I . . . I don't know."

"If you saw it, how could you not know?"

She closed her eyes, suddenly wishing she had said nothing to the man. She could hardly expect him to understand. "It was . . . hazy. Even when we see we don't always see crystal clear. Humanity has managed to dim our spiritual eyesight. But you already know that, don't you, Bill?"

He did not respond immediately, possibly offended at her condescension. "Yes," he finally offered in a weak voice.

"I'm sorry, Pastor. This is rather difficult for me. She is my daughter."

"Then let's pray, Helen. We will pray to our Father."

She nodded, and he began to pray. But her head was clogged with sorrow, and she barely heard his words.

~~~

Kent browsed through the trinkets in the airport gift shop, passing time, relaxing for the first time since he'd read that message eight hours earlier. He'd caught a connection to Chicago and now meandered through the concourse, waiting for the 3 A.M. redeye flight that would take him to Denver.

He bent over and wound up a toy monkey wielding small gold cymbals. The primate strutted noisily across the makeshift platform, banging its instrument and grinning obnoxiously. *Clang-ka-ching, clang-ka-ching.* Kent smiled despite the foolishness of it all. Spencer would get a kick out of the creature. For all of ten minutes possibly. Then it would end up on his closet floor, hidden under a thousand other ten-minute toys. Ten minutes for twenty dollars. It was skyway robbery.

On the other hand, it was Spencer's face grinning there for ten minutes, and the image of those lips curved in delight brought a small smile to his own.

And it was not like they didn't have the money. These were the kinds of things that were purchased by either totally irresponsible people, or people who did not bother with price. People like Tom Cruise or Kevin Costner. Or Bill Gates. He would have to get used to the idea. *You wanna live a part, you'd better start playing that part. Build it, and they will come.*

Kent tucked the monkey under his arm and sauntered over to the grown-up female trinkets neatly arranged against the wall beside racks of *I love Chicago* sweaters. Where Gloria had picked up her fascination with expensive crystal, he did not know. And now it would no longer matter, either. They were going to be rich.

He picked up a beveled cross, intricately carved with roses and bearing the words "In his death we have life." It would be perfect. He imagined her lying in some hospital bed, propped up, her green eyes beaming at the sight of the gift in his hand. *I love you, Honey.*

Kent made his way to the checkout counter and purchased the gifts.

He might as well make the best of the situation. He would call Borst the minute he got home—make sure Bonehead and his troop were not blowing things down there in Miami. Meanwhile he would stay by Gloria's side in her illness. It was his place.

And soon they would be on the plane to Paris anyway. Surely she would be able to travel. A sudden spike of panic ran up his spine. And what if the illness was more serious than just some severe case of food poisoning? They would have to cancel Paris.

But that had not happened, had it? He'd read once that 99 percent of people's fears never materialize. A man who internalized that truth could add ten years to his life.

Kent eased himself into a chair and glanced at the flight board. His plane left in two hours. Might as well catch some sleep. He sank deep and closed his eyes.

⤸⤷

Spencer sat next to Helen, across from the pastor, trying to be brave. But his chest and throat and eyes were not cooperating. They kept aching and knotting and leaking. His mom had gone upstairs after seeing Dad off, saying something about lying down. Two hours and an exhaustive run through his computer games later, Spencer had called through the house only to hear her weak moan from the master bedroom. His mom was still in bed at ten o'clock. He'd knocked and entered without waiting for an answer. She lay on her side, curled into a ball like a roly-poly, groaning. Her face reminded him of a mummy on the Discovery Channel— all stretched and white.

Spencer had run for the phone and called Grandma. During the fifteen minutes it took her to reach their house he had knelt by his mother's bed, begging her to answer him. Then he had cried hard. But Mother was not answering in anything more than the occasional moan. She just lay there and held her stomach.

Grandma had arrived then, rambling on about food poisoning and ordering him around as if she knew exactly what had to be done in situations like this. But no matter how she tried to seem in control, Grandma had been a basket case.

They had literally dragged his mom to the car, and Grandma had driven her to the emergency room. Dark blue blotches spotted her skin, and he wondered how food poisoning could bring out spots the size of silver dollars. Then Spencer had overheard one of the nurses talking to an aide. She said the spots were from internal bleeding. The patient's organs were bleeding.

"I'm scared," he said in a thin, wobbly voice.

Helen took his hand and lifted it to her lips. "Don't be, Spencer. Be sad, but don't be afraid," she said, but she said it with mist in her eyes, and he knew that she was terrified too.

She pulled his head to her shoulder, and he cried there for a while. Dad was supposed to be here by now. He'd called from the airport at six o'clock and told the nurse he was catching a 9 P.M. flight with an impossible interminable layover in Chicago that wouldn't put him into Denver until 6 A.M. Well, now it was seven o'clock, and he had not arrived.

They had started putting in tubes and doing other things to Mom last night. That was when he first started thinking things were not just bad. They were terrible. When he asked Grandma why Mom was puffing up like that, she'd said that the doctors were flooding her body with antibiotics. They were trying to kill the bacteria.

"What bacteria?"

"Mommy has bacterial meningitis, Honey," Grandma had said.

A boulder had lodged in his throat then. 'Cause that sounded bad. "What does that mean? Will she die?"

"Do not think of death, Spencer," Grandma said gently. "Think of life. God will give Gloria more life than she's ever had. You will see that, I promise. Your mother will be fine. I know what happens here. It is painful now, but it will soon be better. Much better."

"So she will be okay?"

His grandmother looked off to the double swinging doors behind which the doctors attended his mom, and she started to cry again.

"We will pray that she will be, Spencer," Pastor Madison said.

Then the tears burst from Spencer's eyes, and he thought his throat might tear apart. He threw his arms around Grandma and buried his face in her shoulder. For an hour he could not stop. Just couldn't. Then he remembered that his mother was not dead, and that helped a little.

When he lifted his head he saw that Grandma was talking. Muttering with eyes closed and face strained. Her cheeks were wet and streaked. She was talking to God. Only she wasn't smiling like she usually did when she talked to him.

A door slammed, and Spencer started. He lifted his head. Dad was there, standing at the door, looking white and ragged, but here.

Spencer scrambled to his feet and ran for his father, feeling suddenly very heavy. He wanted to yell out to him, but his throat was clogged again, so he just collided with him and felt himself lifted into safe arms.

Then he began to cry again.

⌒⌒

The moment Kent slammed through the waiting room door he knew something was wrong. Very wrong.

It was in their posture, his son's and Helen's, bent over with red eyes. Spencer ran for him, and he snatched the boy to his chest.

"Everything will be all right, Spence," he muttered. But the boy's hot tears on his neck said differently, and he set him down with trembling hands.

Helen rose to her feet as he approached. "What's wrong?" he demanded.

"She has bacterial meningitis, Kent."

"Bacterial meningitis?" So that would mean what? Surgery? Or worse? Something like dialysis to grace each waking day. "How is she?" He swallowed, seeing more in those old wise eyes than he cared to see.

"Not good." She took his hand and smiled empathetically. A tear slipped down her cheek. "I'm sorry, Kent."

Now the warning bells went off—every one of them, all at once. He spun from her and ran for the swinging doors on numb legs. The sign above read "ICU." The ringing lodged in his ears, muting ordinary sounds.

Everything will be fine, Kent. Get a grip, man. His heart hammered in his ears. *Please, Gloria, please be all right. I'm here for you. I love you, Honey. Please be all right.*

He gazed around and saw white. White doors and white walls and white smocks. The smell of medicine flooded his nostrils. A penicillin-alcohol odor.

"May I help you?"

The voice came from his right, and he turned to see a figure standing behind a counter. The nurses station. She was dressed in white. His mind began to soothe his panic a bit. *See now, everything will be just fine. That's a nurse; this is a hospital. Just a hospital where they make people better. With enough technology to make your head spin.*

"May I help you?" the nurse asked again.

Kent blinked. "Yes, could you tell me where I can find Gloria Anthony? I'm her husband." He swallowed against the dryness of cotton balls seemingly stuffed in his throat.

The nurse came into better focus now, and he saw that her nametag read "Marie." She was blonde, like Gloria—about the same size. But she did not have Gloria's smile. In fact she was frowning, and Kent fought the sudden urge to reach over there and slap those lips up. *Listen lady! I'm here for my wife. Now quit looking at me like you're the Grim Reaper and take me to her!*

Marie's dark eyes looked across the hall. Kent followed the look. Two doctors bent over a hospital bed behind a large, reinforced viewing window. He made for the room without waiting for permission.

"Excuse me, sir! You cannot go in there! Sir—"

He shut her out then. Once Gloria saw him, once he looked into her beautiful hazel eyes, this madness would all end. Kent's heart rose. *Oh, Gloria . . . Sweetheart. Everything will be just fine. Please, Gloria, Honey.*

Four faces popped into his mind's eye, suddenly, simultaneously, with a brutality that made him catch himself, midstride, halfway to the room. The first was that of the wench back there with dark eyes. Grim Reaper's bride. The second was Spencer's. He saw that little face again, and it was not just worried. It was crushed. The third was Helen's sweet smiling face, but not smiling. Not at all. Wrinkled with lines of grief maybe, but not smiling. He wasn't sure he'd ever seen it that way.

One of the doctors had moved, and he saw the fourth face through the window, lying there on that bed. Only he did not recognize this face at first. It lay still, stark white under the bright lights overhead. A round, blue corrugated tube had been fed into the mouth, and an oxygen line hung from the nostrils. Purple blotches discolored the skin. The face was bloated like a pumpkin.

Kent blinked and set his foot down. But he did not move forward. Could not move forward.

Bile rose into his throat, and he swallowed hard. What this one face here could possibly have to do with the others he could not fathom. He did not know this face. Had never seen a face in such agony, so distorted in pain.

And then he did know this face. The simple truth tore through his mind like an ingot of lead crashing through his skull.

This was Gloria on the bed!

His heart was suddenly smashing against his rib cage, desperate to be out. His jaw fell slowly. A high-pitched screaming set off in his mind, denouncing this madness. Cursing this idiocy. This was no more Gloria than some body pulled from a mass grave in a war zone. How dare he be so sure? How dare he stand here frozen like some puppet when all the while everything was just fine? There had been a mistake, that was all. He should run over there and settle this.

Problem was, Kent could not move. Sweat leaked from his pores, and he began to breathe in ragged lurches. *No!* Spencer was out in the lobby, his ten-year-old boy who desperately needed Mommy. This could not be Gloria! He needed her! Sweet, innocent Gloria with a mouth that tasted of honey. Not . . . not this!

The doctor reached down and pulled the white sheet over the bloated face.

And why? Why did that fool pull that sheet like that?

A grunt echoed down the hall—his grunt.

Then Kent began to move again. In four long bounds he was at the door. Someone yelled from behind, but it meant nothing to him. He gripped the silver knob and yanked hard.

The door would not budge. *Turn, then! Turn the fool thing!* He turned the knob and pulled. Now the door swung open to him, and he staggered back. In the same moment he saw the name on a chart beside the door.

Gloria Anthony.

Kent began to moan softly.

The bed was there, and he reached it in two steps. He shoved aside a white-coated doctor. People began to shout, but he could not make out their words. Now he only wanted one thing. To pull back that white sheet and prove they had the wrong woman.

A hand grabbed his wrist, and he snarled. He twisted angrily and smashed the man into the wall. "No!" he shouted. An IV pole toppled and crashed to the floor. An amber monitor spit sparks and blinked to black, but these details occurred in the distant, dark horizon of Kent's mind. He was fixated on the still, white form on the hospital bed.

Kent gripped the sheet and ripped it from the body.

A *whoosh!* sounded as the sheet floated free and then slowly settled to the ground. Kent froze. A naked, pale body laced with purple veins and blotches the size of apples lay lifeless before him. It was bloated, like a pumped-up doll, with tubes still forcing mouth and throat open.

It was Gloria.

Like a shaft of barbed iron the certainty pierced right through him. He staggered back one step, swooning badly.

The world faded from him then. He was faintly aware that he was spinning and then running. Smashing into the door, facefirst. He could not feel the pain, but he could hear the crunch when his nose broke on impact with the wooden door. He was dead, possibly. But he couldn't be dead because his heart was on fire, sending flames right up his throat.

Then he lurched past the door somehow, pelting for the swinging ICU entry, bleeding red down his shirt, suffocating. He banged through the doors, just as the first wail broke from his throat. A cry to the Supreme Being who might have had his hand in this.

"Oh, God! Oh, Gauwwwd!"

To his right, Spencer and Helen stood wide eyed, but he barely saw them. Warm blood ran over his lips, and it gave him a strange, fleeting comfort. The gutturals blared from his spread mouth, refusing to retreat. He could not stop to breathe. Back there his wife had just died.

"Oh, God! Oh, Gauwwwd!"

Kent fled through the halls, his face white and red, wailing in long deathly moans, turning every head as he ran.

A dozen startled onlookers stood aside when he broke into the parking lot, dripping blood and slobbering and gasping. The wails had run out of air, and he managed to smother them. Cars sat, fuzzy through tears, and he staggered for them.

Kent made it all the way to his silver Lexus before the futility of his flight struck him down. He slammed his fist against the hood, maybe breaking another bone there. Then he slid down the driver's door to the hot asphalt and pulled his knees to his chest.

He hugged his legs, devastated, sobbing, muttering. "Oh, God. Oh, God. Oh, God!"

But he did not feel God.

He just felt his chest exploding.

7

Kent Anthony held Spencer on his lap and gently stroked his arm. The fan whirled high above, and an old Celine Dion CD played softly, nudging the afternoon on. His son's breathing rose and fell with his own, creating a kind of cadence to help Celine in her crooning. He could not tell if Spencer was awake— they had hardly moved in over an hour. But this sitting and holding and just being alive had become the new Anthony home signature in the week or so since Gloria's sudden death.

The first day had been like a freight train smashing into his chest, over and over and over. After sobbing for some time by the Lexus he had suddenly realized that little Spencer needed him now. The poor boy would be devastated. His mother had just been snatched from him. Kent had stumbled back to the waiting room to find Helen and Spencer holding each other, crying. He'd joined them in their tears. An hour later they had driven from the hospital, dead silent and stunned.

Helen had left them in the living room and made sandwiches for lunch. The phone had rung off the hook. Gloria's church partners calling to give their condolences. None of the calls were from Kent's associates.

Kent blinked at the thought. He shifted Spencer's head so he could reach a glass of tea sitting by the couch. It was one good thing about the church, he supposed. Friends came easily. It was the *only* good thing about the church. That and their attending to the dead. Kent's mind drifted back to the funeral earlier that week. They had managed to mix some gladness into the event, and for that he was thankful, although the smiles of those around him never did spread to his own face. Still it made for a manageable ordeal. Otherwise he might have broken down, a wreck on that front pew. An image rolled through his mind: a slobbering man, dressed in black and writhing on the pew while a hundred stoic faces sang with raised hymnals. Might as well toss him in the hole as well.

A tear slipped from the corner of his right eye. They would not stop, these tears. He swallowed.

Helen and two of her old friends had sung something about the other side at the funeral. Now *there* was a religious case. Helen. After setting sandwiches before them that first day, she had excused herself and left. When she returned three hours later, she looked like a new woman. The smile had returned, her red eyes had whitened, and a buoyancy lightened her step. She had taken Spencer in her arms and hugged him dear. Then she had gripped Kent's arm and smiled warmly, knowingly. And that was it. If she experienced any more sorrow over her daughter's death, she hid it well. The fact had burned resentment into Kent's gut. Of course, he could not complain about the care she had shown them over the last ten days, busying herself with cooking and cleaning and handling the phone while Kent and Spencer floated around the house like two dead ghosts.

She was on her way to collect Spencer now. She had made the suggestion that the boy visit her for a few hours today. Kent had agreed, although the thought of being alone in the house for an afternoon brought a dread to his chest.

He ran his fingers through his son's blond hair. Now it would be him and Spencer, alone in a house that suddenly seemed too big. Too empty. Two weeks ago he had described their next house to Gloria while they dined on steak and lobster at Antonio's. The house would be twice the size of their current one, he'd told her. With gold faucets and an indoor tennis court. They could afford that now. "Imagine that, Gloria. Playing on your own air-conditioned court." His wife had smiled wide.

In his mind's eyes he saw her leaning into a forehand, her short white skirt swishing as she pivoted, and a lump rose in his throat.

He lay his head back and moaned softly. He felt trapped in an impossible nightmare. What madman had decided that it was time for his wife to die? If there was a God, he knew how to inflict pain exceptionally well. Tears blurred Kent's vision, but he held himself in check. He had to maintain some semblance of strength, for Spencer if not for himself. But it was all lunacy. How had he grown so dependent on her? Why was it that her passing had left him so dead inside?

The doctor had patiently explained bacterial meningitis to him a dozen times.

Evidently the beast lingered in over half of the population, hiding behind some cranial mucous membrane that held it at bay. Occasionally—very rarely—the stuff got past the membrane and into the bloodstream. If not caught immediately it tended to rampage its way through the body, eating up organs. In Gloria's case the disease had already set its claws into her by the time she got to the hospital. Eighteen hours later she had died.

He'd replayed that scene a thousand times. If he'd taken her to the hospital Friday morning instead of traipsing off for glory, she might be alive today.

The monkey and the cross he'd purchased as gifts still lay in his travel bag upstairs, absurd little trinkets that mocked him every time he remembered them. *"Lookie here, Spencer. Look what Daddy bought you!"*

"What is it?"

"It's a stupid monkey to help you remember Mommy's death. See, it's smiling and clapping 'cause Mom's in heaven." Gag!

And the crystal cross . . . He would smash it as soon as he built up the resolve to open that bag. The doorbell rang, and Spencer lifted his head. "Grandma?"

"Probably," Kent said, running the back of his wrist across his eyes. "Why don't you go check?"

Spencer hopped off his lap and loped for the front door. Kent shook his head and sniffed. *Get a grip, old boy. You've handled everything thrown your way for years. You can handle this.*

"Hello, Kent," Helen called, entering the room at Spencer's leading. She smiled. She was wearing a dress. A yellow dress that struck a chord of familiarity in Kent. It was the kind of dress Gloria might have worn. "How are we doing this afternoon?"

How do you think, you old kook? We've just lost our hearts, but otherwise we are just peachy. "Fine," he said.

"Yes, well I don't believe you, but it's good to see that you're making an attempt." She paused, seeing right through him, it seemed. He made no attempt to rise. Helen's eyes held his for a moment. "I'm praying for you, Kent. Things will begin to change now. In the end, they will be better. You will see."

He wanted to tell her that she could keep her prayers. That of course things would get better, because anything would be better than this. That she was an old, eccentric fossil and should keep her theories of how things would go to herself. Share them with some other cross-stitchers from the dark ages. But he hardly had the energy, much less the stomach, for the words.

"Yeah," he said. "You taking Spencer?" Of course she was. They both knew it.

"Yes." She turned to the boy and laid a hand on his shoulder. "You ready?"

Spencer glanced back at his father. "I'll see you soon, Dad. You okay?"

The question nearly had him blubbering. He did not want the boy to go. His heart swelled for his son, and he swallowed. "Sure, Spencer. I love you, son."

Spencer ran around the couch and hugged his neck. "It's okay, Dad. I'll be back soon. I promise."

"I know." He patted the boy's back. "Have fun."

A soft *clunk* signaled their departure through the front door. As if on cue, Celine ceased her crooning on the CD player.

Now it was just his breathing and the fan. He lifted the glass of ice tea, thankful for the tinkle of its ice.

He would sell the house now. Buy a new one, not so large. Scrap the tennis court. Put in a gym for Spencer instead.

The tall picture of Jesus holding a denim-clad man with blood on his hands stood to Kent's right. *Forgiven,* the artist had called it. They said that Jesus died for man. How could anyone follow a faith so obsessed with death? That was God, they said. Jesus was God, and he'd come to Earth to die. Then he'd asked his followers to climb on their crosses as well. So they'd made as their emblem a familiar symbol of execution, the cross, and in the beginning most of them died.

Today Jesus might have been put to death by lethal injection. An image of a needle reared in Kent's mind, and he cringed, thinking of all the needles Gloria must have endured. *Come die for me, Gloria.* It was insane.

And to think that Gloria had been so enraptured with Christianity, as if she actually expected to meet Christ someday. To climb up on that cross and float to the heavens with him. Well, now she had her chance, he supposed. Only she hadn't floated anywhere. She'd been lowered a good eight feet into red clay.

An empty hopelessness settled on Kent, and he sat there and let it hurt.

He would have to go back to work, of course. The office had sent him a bouquet of flowers, but they had made no other contact. He thought about the Miami meeting and the announcement of his program. Funny how something so important now seemed so distant. His pulse picked up at the thought. Why had they not called to tell him about the meeting?

Respect, he quickly decided. You don't just call a man who has lost his wife and segue into office talk. At least he had a bright career ahead of him. Although, without Gloria it hardly seemed bright. That would change with time.

Kent let the thoughts circle in his mind as they had endlessly for days now. Nothing seemed to fit. Everything felt loose. He could not latch on to anything offering that spark of hope that had propelled him so forcefully for years.

He leaned back and stared at the ceiling. For the moment his eyes were dry. Stinging dry.

⌒⌒⌒

Spencer sat in his favorite green chair across from Grandma Helen with his legs crossed Indian style. He'd pulled on his white X-Games skateboard T-shirt and his beige cargo pants that morning because he loved skateboarding and he thought Mom would want him to keep doing the things he loved most. Although he hadn't actually hopped on the board yet. It had been a long time since he'd gone more than a week without taking to the street on a board.

Then again, things had changed a week ago, hadn't they? Changed forever. His dad had lost his way, it seemed. The house had become big and quiet. Their schedule had changed, or gone away, mostly. His heart hurt most of the time now.

Spencer ran his fingers through blond curls and rested his chin on his palms. This hadn't changed though. The room smelled of fresh-baked bread. The faint scent of roses drifted by—Grandma's perfume. The brown carpet lay beneath them exactly as it had two weeks ago; the overstuffed chairs had not been moved; sparkling china with little blue flowers still lined an antique-looking cabinet on the wall. A hundred knickknacks, mostly white porcelain painted with accents of blue and red and yellow, sat in groupings around the room and on the walls.

The large case Grandma called a hutch hugged the wall leading to the kitchen. Its engraved lead-glass doors rested closed, distorting his vision of its contents, but he could see well enough. A small crystal bottle, maybe five inches high, stood in the middle of the top shelf. The contents looked almost black to him. Maybe maroon or red, although he'd never been good with all those weird names of colors. Grandma had once told him that nothing in the hutch mattered to her much, except that one crystal bottle. It, she said, symbolized the greatest power on earth. The power of love. And a tear had come to her eye as she said it. When he had asked her what was in the bottle, she had just turned her head, all choked up.

The large picture of Jesus rested quietly on the wall to their right. The Son of God was spread on a cross, a crown of thorns responsible for the thin trails of red on his cheek. He stared directly at Spencer with sad blue eyes, and at the moment, Spencer didn't know what to think about that.

"Spencer."

He turned to face Grandma, sitting across from him, smiling gently. A knowing glint shone in those hazel eyes. She held a glass of ice tea in both hands comfortably.

"Are you okay, Honey?"

Spencer nodded, suddenly feeling strangely at home. Mom wasn't here, of course, but everything else was. "I think so."

Helen tilted her head and shook it slowly, empathy rich in her eyes. "Oh, my poor child. I'm so sorry." A tear slipped down her cheek, and she let it fall. She sniffed once.

"But this will pass, son. Sooner than you know."

"Yeah, that's what everybody says." A lump rose in his throat, and he swallowed. He didn't want to cry. Not now.

"I've wanted to talk to you ever since Gloria left us," Helen said, now with a hint of authority. She had something to say, and Spencer's heart suddenly felt lighter in anticipation. When Grandma had something to say, it was best to listen.

"You know when Lazarus died, Jesus wept. In fact, right now God is weeping." She looked off to the window opened bright to the afternoon clouds. "I hear it sometimes. I heard it on that first day, after Gloria died. It about killed me to hear him weeping like that, you know, but it also gave me comfort."

"I heard laughter," Spencer said.

"Yes, laughter. But weeping too, at once. Over the souls of men. Over the pain of man. Over loss. He lost his son, you know." She looked into his eyes. "And there weren't doctors clamoring to save him, either. There was a mob beating him and spitting in his face and . . ." She didn't finish the sentence.

Spencer imagined a red-faced man with bulging veins spraying spit into that face on the painting over there. Jesus' face. The image struck him as odd.

"People don't often realize it, but God suffers more in the span of each breath than any man or woman in the worst period of history," Helen said.

Surprisingly, the notion came to Spencer like a balm. Maybe because his own hurt seemed small in the face of it. "But can't God make all that go away?" he asked.

"Sure he could, and he is, as we speak. But he allows us to choose on our own between loving him and rejecting him. As long as he gives us that choice, he will be rejected by some. By most. And that brings him pain."

"That's funny. I've never imaged God as suffering. Or as hurting."

"Read the old prophets. Read Jeremiah or Ezekiel. Images of God wailing and weeping are commonplace. We just choose to ignore that part of reality in our churches today."

She smiled again, staring out of that window. "On the other hand, some will choose to love him of their own choosing. And that love, my child, is worth the greatest suffering imaginable to God. That is why he created us, for those few of us who would love him."

She paused and directed her gaze to him again. "Like your mother."

Now a mischievous glint lit his grandmother's face. She sipped at her tea, and he saw a tremble in her hand. She leaned forward slightly. "Now, that's a sight, Spencer," she said in hushed voice.

Spencer's palms began to sweat. "What is?"

"The other side." She was grinning now like a child unable to contain a secret.

"The other side of this pain and suffering. The realm of God." She let it drop without offering more. Spencer blinked, wanting her to continue, knowing that she would—had to.

Helen hesitated only a moment before dropping the question she had brought him here to ask. "Do you want to see, son?"

Spencer's heart jumped in his chest and his fingers tingled cold. *Want to see?* He swallowed. "See?" he asked, and his voice cracked.

She gripped the arms of her chair and leaned forward. "Do you want to see what it's like on the other side?" She spoke hushed, eagerly, quickly. "Do you want to know why death has its end? Why Jesus said, 'Let the dead bury the dead'? It will help, child."

Suddenly his chest felt thick again, and an ache rose through his throat. "Yes," he said. "Can I see that?"

Grandma Helen's mouth split into a broad smile. "Yes! Actually you would've been able to see it that first day, I think, but I had to wait until after the funeral, see? I had to let you mourn some. But for some reason things have changed, Spencer. He is allowing us to see."

The room was heavy with the unseen. Spencer could feel it, and goose flesh raised on his shoulders. A tear slipped from his eye, but it was a good tear. A strangely welcomed tear. Helen held his gaze for a moment and then took a quick sip of her tea.

She looked back at him. "Are you ready?"

He wasn't sure what *ready* was, but he nodded anyway, feeling desperate now. Eager.

"Close your eyes, Spencer."

He did.

It came immediately, like a rush of wind and light. A whirlwind in his mind, or maybe not just in his mind—he didn't know. His breath left him completely, but that didn't matter, because the wind filled his chest with enough oxygen to last a lifetime. Or so it felt.

The darkness behind his eyelids was suddenly full of lights. Souls. People. Angels. Streaking brightly across the horizon. Then hovering, then streaking and looping and twisting. He gasped and felt his mouth stretch open.

It struck him that the lights were not just shooting about randomly, but they flew in a perfect symmetry. Across the whole of space, as if they were putting on a show. Then he knew they *were* putting on a show. For him!

Like a million Blue Angels jets, streaking, hair-raising, perfect, like a billion ballerinas, leaping in stunning unison. But it was their sound that made little Spencer's heart feel like exploding. Because every single one of them—one billion souls strong—were screaming.

Screaming with laughter.

Long, ecstatic peals of barely controlled laughter. And above it all, one voice laughed—soft, yet loud and unmistakably clear. It was his mom's voice. Gloria was up there with them. Beside herself with joy in this display.

Then, in a flash, her whole face filled his mind, or maybe all of space. Her head tilted back slightly, and her mouth opened. She was laughing with delight, as he had never seen anyone laugh. Tears streamed over bunched cheeks, and her eyes sparkled bright. The sight did two things to Spencer at once, with crushing finality. It washed some of that joy and desire into his own chest, so that he burst into tears and laughter. And it made him want to be there. Like he had never wanted anything in his whole life. A desperate craving to be there.

The whole vision lasted maybe two seconds.

And then it was gone.

Spencer slumped in his chair like a blubbering, laughing, raggedy doll.

When Grandma Helen finally took him home two hours later, the world seemed like a strange new place to him. As if it were a dream world and the one he'd seen in Grandma's house was the real one. But he knew with settling certainty that this world, with trees and houses and his dad's Lexus parked in the driveway, was indeed very real.

It made him sad again, because in this world his mom was dead.

8

Week Four

Kent punched the numbers again, hoping that this time, Borst would be in his office. In the last two weeks he'd left three messages for his supervisor, and the man had yet to return a call. He had called the first week and left word with Betty that he would be taking two or three weeks off to collect himself, put things in order.

"Of course," she'd said. "I'll pass it right on. Do what you need to do. I'm sure everyone will understand. Our hearts are with you."

"Thank you. And could you ask Borst to give me a call?"

"Sure."

That had been seventeen days ago. Goodness, it had not been *he* who'd passed on. The least they could do was return a call. His life was in enough disarray. It had taken all of two weeks for him to take the first steps back to reality. Back to the realization that aside from Spencer, and actually because of Spencer, his career was now everything.

And now Borst was avoiding him.

The phone rang three times before Betty's voice crackled in his ear. "Nipon-bank Information Systems; this is Betty."

"Betty. Hi. This is—"

"Kent! How are you?" She sounded normal enough. Her reaction came as a small wave of relief.

"Okay, actually. I'm doing better. Listen, I really need to speak with Borst. I know he must be busy, but do you think you could patch me through for a minute?" It was a lie, of course. He knew nothing of the kind. Borst had not had a busy day in his life.

She hesitated. "Uh, sure, Kent. Let me see if he's in." A butterfly took flight in his belly at her tone. Borst was always *in*. If not in his office then in the john, reading some Grisham novel. *Let me check?* Who did they think he was?

Betty came back on. "Just a minute, Kent. Let me put you through."

The line broke into Barry Manilow's "I Write the Songs." The music brought a cloud to Kent's heart. That was one of the problems with mourning; it came and left without regard for circumstances.

"Kent!" Borst's voice sounded forced. Kent imagined the man sitting behind that big screen in his office, overdressed in that navy three-piece he liked to wear. "How are you doing, Kent?"

"Fine."

"Good. We've been worried about you. I'm sorry about what happened. I had a niece who died once." Borst did not elaborate, possibly because he'd suddenly realized how stupid that sounded. *Don't forget your pet ferret, Monkey Brains. It died too, didn't it? Must've been devastating!*

"Yeah. It's tough," Kent said. "I'm sorry for taking so much time off here, but—"

"No, it's fine. Really. You take all the time you need. Not that we don't need you here, but we understand." He was speaking quickly. "Believe me, it's no problem."

"Thanks, but I think the best thing now is to get back to work. I'll be in on Monday." It was Friday. That gave him a weekend to set his mind in the right frame. "Besides, there are a few clarifications I need to make on the funds processing system." That should spark a comment on the Miami conference. Surely the reception to AFPS had been favorable. Why was Borst not slobbering about it?

"Sure," his supervisor said, rather anemically. "Yeah, Monday's good."

Kent could not contain his curiosity any longer. "So, what did they say to AFPS?" he asked as nonchalantly as possible.

"Oh, they loved it. It was a real smash, Kent. I wish you could have been there. It's everything we hoped for. Maybe more."

Of course! He'd known it all along. "So did the board make any mention of it?" Kent asked.

"Yes. Yes, they did. In fact, they've already implemented it. System wide."

The revelation brought Kent to his feet. His chair clattered to the floor behind him. "What? How? I should have been told. There are some things —"

"We didn't think it would be right to bother you. You know with the missis dying and all. But don't worry; it's been working exactly as we designed it to work."

We *nothing, Bucko. It was my program; you should have waited for me!* At least it was working. "So it was a big hit, huh?" He retrieved his chair and sat down.

"Very big. It was the buzz of the conference."

Kent squeezed his eyes and gripped his fist tight, exhilarated. Suddenly he wanted to be back. He imagined walking into the bank on Monday, a dozen suits thumping his back with congratulations.

"Good. Okay, I'll see you Monday, Markus. It'll be good to get back."

"Well, it'll be good to have you back too, Kent."

He thought about telling the man about the changes he'd made to the program before leaving for Miami but decided they could wait the weekend. Besides, he rather liked the idea of being the only man who really knew the inner workings of AFPS. A little power never hurt anybody.

Kent hung up, feeling decent for the first time since Gloria's death. It was settled, then. On Monday he would reenter his skyrocketing career. It would breathe new life into him.

∽∾

Monday morning came slow for Kent. He and Spencer had spent the weekend at the zoo and Elitch Gardens amusement park. Both the animals and the mobs of people served to distract them from their sorrow for a time. Helen had dragged them off to church on Sunday. Actually, Spencer had not needed dragging. In fact, it might be more accurate to say that *Spencer* had dragged him off to church—with Helen's full endorsement, of course. Pastor Bill Madison had lectured them on the power of God, which only served to annoy Kent immensely. Sitting in the pew, he'd thought about the power of death. And then his mind had drifted to the bank. Monday was on his mind.

And now Monday was here.

The arrangements had gone smoothly. Helen would watch Spencer at her place on Monday and Tuesday. Linda, one of Helen's buddies from church, would watch him Wednesday morning at the house. Spencer insisted he could finish off his home-school curriculum on his own this year. Next year he might attend the public school.

Kent rose a full hour ahead of schedule, anxious and not knowing exactly why.

He showered, dressed in navy slacks and a starched white shirt, and changed ties three times before settling on a red silk Countess Mara. He then sat at the kitchen table, drinking coffee and watching the clock. The bank opened at eight, but he would walk in at ten after. Seemed appropriate. Make a statement, although he was not sure why he needed to make a statement. Or even what that statement would be. Possibly he relished the image of walking through the bank after everyone else had arrived, nodding to their smiles of consolation; acknowledging their words of congratulations. He dismissed the notion. If anything, he felt like sneaking in and avoiding the predictable shows of sympathy. Still, some form of congratulations would be in order.

A hundred scenarios ran through his mind, followed by a healthy dose of self-correction for letting the thoughts occupy him at all. In the end he blamed it all on his stressed mental state. Some psychiatrists suggested that men bent upon success became more attached to their work than to their spouses. Married to their jobs. He doubted he'd ever gone to such extremes, but the notion seemed somewhat attractive now. After all, Gloria was gone. So then, possibly he was having first-date jitters.

Kent scoffed at the idea and stood from the table. Enough blather. Time to go.

He climbed behind the wheel of the silver Lexus and drove to the bank. The butterflies rose in his stomach when the renovated office complex, now bearing the name Niponbank, loomed on the corner of Fifth and Grand. A thousand times he'd approached the old, red-brick building in the Lexus, barely aware of the downtown maze through which he drove. Hardly noticing his stopping and starting at lights as he closed in on the twenty-story structure, sitting there like an oversized fire station.

Now every movement became acute. A newsman ran on about inflation over the stereo. Cars streamed by, completely lost to the fact that he was reentering their world after a three-week absence. Pedestrians wandered in abstract directions with intent, but otherwise aimless. He wondered if any of them had lost someone recently. If so, no one would know. The world was moving ahead, full stride, with or without him.

The light just before the bank remained red for an inordinate period. Two full minutes, at least. In that time he watched eighteen people ascend or descend the sweeping steps leading to the bank's main floor. Probably tenants from the upper stories.

The car behind him honked, and he started. The light had turned. He motored across the intersection and swung the Lexus into the side parking lot. Familiar cars sat in their customary slots. With one last look in the mirror, his pulse now drumming steadily, Kent eased out of the sedan. He snatched his brief-case from the backseat and strode for the main entry.

Like walking up to a dream date on prom night. Good grief!

Long, polished, white steps rose like piano keys to the brass-framed glass doors. The year-old face-lift suited the building. He grabbed the brass handrail and clicked up the steps. With a final tingle at the base of his spine, he pushed through the entry.

The three-story lobby loomed spacious and plush, and Kent paused just inside the doors. The tall brass yacht hovered ahead, stately and magnificent, seemingly supported by that one thin shaft. Sidney Beech, the branch's assistant vice president, clacked along the marble floor, thirty feet from Kent. She saw him, gave him a friendly nod, and continued her walk toward the glass-enclosed offices along the right wall. Two personal bankers he recognized as Ted and Maurice talked idly by the president's office door. A dozen stuffed maroon guest chairs sat in small groupings, waiting in perfect symmetry for patrons who would descend on the bank at nine.

To Kent's left, the gray-flecked floor ran up to a long row of teller stations. During peak hours, fifteen tellers would be shuffling bills across the long, hunter-green counter. Now, seven busied themselves for the opening.

Kent stepped forward toward the gaping hall opposite him where the marble floor ended and the teal carpet ran into the administration wing. The large seagull that hung on the wall above the hall seemed to be eyeing him.

Zak, the white-haired security guard, stood idly to Kent's right, looking important and doing exactly what he had done for five years now: nothing. He had seen it all a thousand times, but coming in now, it struck him as though new. Like a déjà vu. *I've been here before, haven't I? Yes, of course.* At any moment a call would come. Someone would notice that Kent Anthony had just entered the building. The man responsible for the new processing system. The man whose wife had just died. Then they would all know he had arrived.

But the call did not come.

And that bothered him a little. He stepped onto the carpet and swallowed, thinking maybe they had not seen him. And, after all, these front-lobby workers were not as close to his world as the rest. Back in the administration sections they referred to those who worked out in the large foyer as the *handlers*. But it was them, the *processors*, who really made banking work—everyone knew that.

Kent breathed deeply once, walked straight down the hall, and opened the door to his little corner of the world.

Betty Smythe was there at her desk on the left—bleached, poofy-white hair and all. She had a tube of bright red lipstick cocked and ready to apply, one inch from pursed lips already too red for Kent's taste. Immediately her face went a shade whiter, and she blinked. Which was how he supposed some people might respond to a waking of the dead. Only it was not he who had died.

"Hi, Betty," he said.

"Kent!" Now she collected herself, jerked that red stick to her lap, and squirmed on the seat. "You're back."

"Yes, Betty. I'm back."

He'd always thought that Borst's decision to hire Betty had been motivated by the size of her bra rather than the size of her brain, and looking at her now he was sure of it. He glanced about the reception area. Beyond the blue armchairs the hall sat vacant. All four oak office doors were shut. A fleeting picture of the black nameplates flashed through his mind. Borst, Anthony, Brice, Quinn. It had been the same for three years now.

"So how are things going?" he asked absently.

"Fine," she said, fiddling with the latch on her purse. "I don't know what to say about your wife. I'm so sorry."

"Don't say anything." She had not mentioned AFPS yet. He turned and smiled at her. "Really, I'll be fine." So much for the blaring reception.

Kent walked to the first door on the left and entered his office. The overhead fluorescent stuttered white over his black workstation, tidy as he had left it. He closed the door and set the briefcase down.

Well now, here he was. At home once again. Three computer monitors rested on the corner station, each displaying the same exotic-fish screensaver in unison. His high-back leather chair butted up to the keyboard.

Kent reached for his neck and loosened his collar. He slid into his chair and touched the mouse. The screens jumped to life as one. A large three-dimensional insignia reading "Advanced Funds Processing System" rolled out on the screen like a carpet inviting entry. "Welcome to the bank," the last of it read. Indeed, with this little baby, an operator had access to the bank in ways many a criminal would only dream of through fitful sleep.

He dropped into his chair, punched in his customary access code, and dropped a finger on the ENTER key. The screen went black for a moment. Then large yellow letters suddenly popped up: ACCESS DENIED.

He grunted and keyed in the password again, sure he had not forgotten his own son's name: SPENCER.

ACCESS DENIED, the screen read again. Borst must have changed the code in his absence. Of course! They had integrated the program already. In doing so, they would need to set a primary access password, which would automatically delete the old.

Kent hesitated at the door to his office, thinking again that he had been in the office for a full five minutes now and not one word of congratulations. Borst's closed door was directly across the hall. He should walk in and let the man bring him up to speed. Or perhaps he should make an appearance in Todd's or Mary's office first. The two junior programmers would know what was up.

At the last moment he decided to check in on Will Thompson in the loan department instead. Will would know the buzz, and he was disconnected.

He found Will at his desk, one floor up, bent over his monitor, adjusting the focus.

"Need any help with that?" Kent asked, grinning.

Will looked up, surprised. "Kent! You're back!" He extended a quick hand. "When did you get back? Gee, I'm sorry."

"Ten minutes ago." Kent reached down and twisted a knob behind the monitor. The menu on the screen immediately jumped into clear view.

Will smirked and sat down. "Thanks man. I always could count on you. So, you okay? I wasn't sure I'd ever see you back here."

Kent sat in a guest chair and shrugged. "I'm hanging in there. It's good to be back to work. Keep me distracted, maybe."

The loan officer lifted an eyebrow. "So, you're okay with it all?"

Kent looked at his friend, not sure what he was asking. "It's not like I have a lot of choice in the matter, Will. What's done is done."

"Yeah. You're right. I just thought that on top of your wife's death and all, you might see things differently." The room suddenly seemed deathly quiet. It struck Kent then that something was amiss. And like Betty, Will had not congratulated him. A thin chill snaked down his spine.

"See what differently?" he asked.

Will stared at him. "You . . . you've talked to Borst, right?"

Kent shook his head. Yes indeed, something was very much amiss, and it wasn't sounding good. "No."

"You're kidding, right? You haven't heard a thing?"

"About what? What are you talking about?"

"Oh, Kent . . ." His friend winced. "I'm sorry, man. You've got to talk to Borst."

That did it. Kent stood abruptly and strode from the room, ignoring a call from Will. His gut turned in lazy circles down the elevator. He stepped into the computer wing and walked right past a wide-eyed Betty to the back offices where Todd and Mary would be diligently at work.

He smacked through Todd's door first.

"Hey, Todd."

The redhead started and shoved his chair back. "Kent! You're back!"

A stranger sat in a chair to the junior programmer's right, and the sight caught Kent off guard for a moment. The man rose with Todd and smiled. He stood as tall as Kent, he wore his hair short, and his eyes were the greenest Kent had ever seen. Like two emerald marbles. A starched white shirt rested, crisp, on broad shoulders. The man stuck his hand out, and Kent removed his eyes from him without taking it.

Todd stood slack-jawed. A button on his green shirt had popped open, revealing a hairy white belly. The programmer's eyes looked at him like black holes, filled to the brim with guilt.

"I'm back. So, tell me what's up, Todd. What's happening here that I don't know about?"

"Ah, Kent, this is Cliff Monroe. I'm showing him the ropes." He motioned to the man beside him. "He's new to our staff."

"Good for you, Cliff. Answer my question, Todd. What's changed?"

"What do you mean?" The junior programmer lifted his shoulders in an attempt to look casual. The motion widened the shirt's gap at his belly, and Kent dismissed the sudden impulse to reach in there and yank some hair.

Kent swallowed. "Nothing changed while I was out, then?"

"What do you mean?" Todd shrugged again, his eyes bugging.

Kent grunted in disgust, impatient with the spineless greenhorn. He turned and stepped across the hall to Mary's office. He pushed the door open. Mary sat at her desk with her phone pressed to her ear, facing away from the door, talking. She turned around slowly, her eyes round.

As if, Honey! You knew I was coming. Probably having an important discussion with a dial tone. Fitting partner.

Kent shut the door firmly and strode for Borst's door, his spine now tingling right up to his skull. The man sat stiffly in his chair, his three-piece suit tight, sweat beading his brow. His bald spot shone as if he'd oiled it. His large, hooked nose glistened like some shiny Christmas bulb. The superior made a magnanimous effort to show shock when Kent barged in.

"Kent! You made it back!"

Of course I made it back, you witless fool, he almost replied. Instead he said, "Yes," and plopped down in one of Borst's tweed guest chairs. "I called you on Friday, remember. So who's the new employee?"

"Cliff? Yes, he's a transfer from Dallas. An excellent programmer, from what I hear." The middle-aged man flicked his tongue across thick lips and ran a hand through what hair he had. "So. How's the missis?"

The room lapsed into silence. The missis? Gloria? Borst must have realized his blunder, because a stupid grin crossed his face, and he went red.

Kent spoke before the man could cover his error, hot with anger. "The missis is dead, remember, Markus? It's why I've been gone for three weeks. You see, there's an office across the hall that has my name on it. And for five years now, I've been working there. Or had you forgotten that as well?"

Borst turned beet red now, and not from embarrassment, Kent guessed. He continued before the man could recover. "So how did the AFPS presentation go, Markus?" He forced a smile. "Are we on top?" He meant, am *I* on top, but he was sure that Borst would catch the drift.

The phone rang shrilly on the desk. Borst glared at Kent for a moment and then snatched it up, listening.

"Yes . . . yes put him through."

Kent sat back and crossed his legs, aware that his heart was pounding. The other man straightened his tie and sat upright, attentive for whoever was about to address him on the phone. He turned from Kent and spoke. "Yes, Mr. Wong . . . Yes, thank you, sir."

Mr. Wong? Borst was thanking *the* Mr. Wong?

"I'd be delighted." He turned and faced Kent purposefully. "Yes, I'm tied up with a luncheon on the East Coast Wednesday, but I could fly to Tokyo on Thursday." Kent knew that something very awful was happening here. He was now sweating badly, despite the air conditioning.

"I'd be delighted," Borst said. "Yes, it did take a lot, but I had a good crew on it as well . . . Yes, thank you. Good-bye."

He dropped the phone in its cradle and stared at Kent for a long moment. When he finally spoke, it came out rehearsed. "Come on, Kent. Surely you didn't expect all of the glory on this, did you? It's my department."

Kent swallowed, suddenly fearing the worst. But that would be virtually impossible.

"What did you do?" His voice sounded scratchy.

"Nothing. I'm just implementing the program. That's all. It is *my* program."

Kent began to tremble slightly. "Okay, let's back up here. In Miami I was set to introduce AFPS to the convention. You remember that, right?" He was sounding condescending, but he could not help himself.

Borst nodded once and frowned.

"But I got called away, right? My wife was dying. You with me here?"

This time Borst did not acknowledge.

"So I asked you to wing it for me. And I'm assuming you did. Now, surely somewhere in there you mentioned my name, right? Gave credit where credit was due?"

Borst had frozen like ice.

Kent scooted forward on his seat, steaming. "Don't tell me you stole all the credit for AFPS, Markus. Just tell me you didn't!"

The division supervisor sat with an ashen face. "This is *my* division, Kent. That means that the work out of here is *my* responsibility. You work for me." He went red as he spoke. "Or did *you* forget *that* simple fact?"

"You put the paperwork through! This has always been my bonus! We've discussed it a thousand times! You left me out?!"

"No. You're in there. So is Todd, and so is Mary."

"Todd and Mary?" Kent blurted incredulously. "You put my name in small print along with Todd's and Mary's?" And he knew Borst had done exactly that.

He shoved an arm toward the door. "They're junior programmers, Markus! They write code that I give them to write. AFPS is *my* code!" He nearly shouted now, boring down on the supervisor with a straining neck.

"I designed it from scratch. Did you tell them that? It was *my* brainchild! I wrote 80 percent of the functioning code, for Pete's sake! You yourself wrote a measly 5 percent, most of which I trashed."

That last comment pushed Borst over the edge. The veins on his neck bulged. "You hold your tongue, mister! This is my department. I was responsible for the design and implementation of AFPS. I will hire and fire who I see fit. And for your information, I have been allotted a twenty-five-thousand-dollar spiff for the design engineer of my choice. I was going to give that to you, Kent. But you are rapidly changing my mind!"

Now something deep in Kent's mind snapped, and his vision swam. For the first time in his life he felt like killing someone. He breathed deeply twice to stabilize the tremor in his bones. When he spoke, he did so through clenched teeth.

"Twenty-five thousand dollars!" he ground out. "There was a performance spiff on that program, Markus. Ten percent of the savings to the company over ten years. It's worth millions!"

Borst blinked and sat back. He knew it, of course. They had discussed it on a dozen occasions. And now he meant to claim it all as his. The man did not respond.

The rage came like a boiling volcano, right up through Kent's chest and into his skull. Blind rage. He could still see, but things were suddenly fuzzy. He knew he was erupting, knew Borst could see it all—his red face, his trembling lips, his bulging eyes.

Gripping his hands into fists, Kent suddenly knew that he would fight Borst to his death. He had just lost his wife; he was not about to give up his own livelihood. He would use every means at his disposal to claim his due. And in the process he would bury this spineless pimp before him.

The thought brought a sterling cool to his bones, and he let it filter through his body for a moment. He stood, still glaring angrily. "You're a spineless worm, Borst. And you're stealing my work for your own."

They held stares for a full ten seconds. Borst refused to speak.

"What's the new code?" Kent demanded.

Borst pursed his lips, silent.

Kent spun from the man, exited the office with a bang, and stormed down to Todd's office. He shoved the door open.

"Todd!" The junior started. "What's the new AFPS access code?"

Todd seemed to shrink into his chair. "M-B-A-O-K," he said.

Kent left without thanking him.

He needed a rest. He needed to think. He grabbed his briefcase and walked angrily past Betty's desk without acknowledging her. This time one of the tellers called a greeting to him as he rushed through the towering lobby, but he ignored the distant call and slammed through the tall glass doors.

9

The madness of it all descended upon Kent one block from the bank. It was then that a burning realization of his loss sank into his gut. If Borst pulled this off—which, judging by the call from Wong, he was doing just splendidly—he would effectively strip Kent of everything. Millions of dollars. That hook-nosed imbecile in there was casually intercepting his life's work.

Kent's chest flushed with a wave of panic. It was impossible! He'd kill anybody who tried to steal what was his. Shove a gun in the guy's mouth and blow his brains out, maybe. Good grief! What was he thinking? He could hardly shoot a prairie dog, much less another man. On the other hand, maybe Borst had just given up his right to life.

And what of Spencer? They would be virtually broke. All the boasting of Euro Disney and yachts and beachfront homes would prove him a fool. An image of that grinning monkey from the Chicago airport clapped its cymbals through his mind. *Clang-ka-ching, clang-ka-ching.*

Kent snatched up his cell phone and punched seven digits. A receptionist answered after two rings. "Warren Law Offices."

"Hi. This is Kent Anthony." His voice wavered, and he cleared his throat. "Is Dennis in?"

"Just a minute. Let me see if he's available."

The line remained silent for a minute before his old college roommate's voice filled his ear. "Hello, Kent. Goodness, it's been awhile. How you doing, man?"

"Hey, Dennis. Actually, not so good. I've got some problems. I need a good attorney. You have some time?"

"You okay, buddy? You don't sound so good."

"Well, like I said, I've got some problems. Can I meet with you?"

"Sure. Absolutely. Let's see . . ." Kent heard the faint flip of paper through the receiver. "How about Thursday afternoon?"

"No, Dennis. I mean now. Today."

Dennis held his reply for a second. "Pretty short notice, buddy. I'm booked solid. It can't wait?"

Kent did not respond. A sudden surge of emotions had taken hold of his throat.

"Hold on. Let me see if I can reschedule my lunch." The phone clicked to hold music.

Two minutes later Dennis came back on. "Okay, buddy. You owe me for this. How about Pelicans at twelve sharp? I already have reservations."

"Good. Thanks, Dennis. It means a lot."

"You mind me asking what this is about?"

"It's employment related. I just got screwed out of a major bonus. I mean major, as in millions."

Static sounded. "Millions?" Dennis Warren's voice cracked. "What kind of bonus is worth millions? I didn't know you were in that kind of money, Kent."

"Yeah, well, I won't be if we don't act quick. I'll give you the whole story at lunch."

"Twelve o'clock then. And make sure you have your employment file with you. I'll need that."

Kent pulled back into traffic, feeling a small surge of confidence. This wasn't the first time he'd faced an obstacle. He glanced at the clock on the dash. Nine o'clock. He'd have to burn three hours. He could retrieve a copy of his employment agreement from the house—that would take an hour if he stretched things.

"God, help me," he muttered. But that was stupid, because he didn't believe in God. But maybe there was a Satan and his number had come up on Satan's big spinning wheel: *Time to go after Kent. After him, lads!*

Ridiculous.

~∾~

Pelicans Grill bustled with a lunch crowd willing to pay thirty bucks for the privilege of eyeing Denver's skyline while feasting. Kent sat by the picture window, overlooking Interstate 25, and stared at his plate, thinking he really should at least finish the veal. Apart from a dip from the mashed potatoes and a corner sawed off the meat, his lunch sat untouched. And that after an hour at the table.

Dennis sat dressed smartly in a black tailored suit, cut with care to hang just so on his well-muscled frame. The jet-black mustache and deep tan fit his Greek heritage. By the Rolex on his wrist and the large emerald ring on his right forefinger, Kent's college roomy had obviously done just fine for himself. He had listened to Kent's tale with complete rapture, biting at his steak aggressively and *humphing* at all the right junctures. The man had just heard of Gloria's death for the first time, and the announcement had brought his fork clattering to his plate. He stared at Kent, frozen, his mouth slightly agape.

"You're kidding?" he stammered, wide eyed. Of course he had known Gloria. Had met her at their wedding, three years after college, when they were both just getting started. "Oh, Kent, I'm so sorry."

"Yeah. It all happened so quickly, you know. I can barely believe it's happened half the time."

Dennis wiped his mouth and swallowed. "It's hard to believe." He shook his head. "If there's anything I can do, buddy. Anything at all."

"Just help me get my money, Dennis."

His friend shook his head. "It's incredible how these things can come out of nowhere. You heard about Lacy, right?"

Lacy? A bell clanged to life in Kent's mind. "Lacy?" he asked.

"Lacy Cartwright. You dated her for two years in college. Remember her?"

Of course he remembered Lacy. They had broken up three months before graduation. She was ready for marriage, and the thought had frightened him clean out of love. Last he'd heard she had married some guy from the East Coast the same year he and Gloria had married.

"Sure," he said.

"She lost her husband a couple years ago to cancer. It was quick from what I heard. Just like that. You didn't get the announcement? Last I heard she'd moved to Boulder."

"No." Kent shook his head. Not surprising, really. After the way he'd cut her off, Lacy wouldn't dream of reintroducing herself at *any* juncture, much less at her husband's funeral. She was as principled as they came.

"So what do you think about the case?" Kent asked, shifting the conversation back to the legal matter. Dennis crossed his legs and leaned back. "Well . . ." He sucked at his teeth and let his tongue wander about his mouth for a moment, thinking. "It really depends on the employment contract you signed. You brought it with you?"

Kent nodded, withdrew the document from his briefcase, and handed it to him.

Dennis flipped through the pages, scanning the paragraphs quickly, mumbling something about boilerplate jargon. "I'll have to read this more carefully at the office but . . . Here we go: Statement of Propriety."

He read quickly, and Kent nibbled on a cold pea.

The attorney flopped the document on the table. "Pretty standard agreement. They own everything, of course. But you do have recourse. Two ways to look at this." He held up two fingers. "One, you can fight these guys regardless of this agreement. Just take them to court and claim that you signed this document without full knowledge."

"Why? Is it a bad document?" Kent interrupted.

"Depends. For you, in your situation, yes. I'd say so. By signing it you basically agreed to forfeit all natural rights to proprietary property, regardless of how it materialized. You also specifically agreed to press no claims for compensation not specifically drawn under contract. Meaning, unless you have a contract that stipulates you are due 10 percent of the savings generated by this . . . what is it?"

"AFPS."

"AFPS . . . it's up to the company to decide if you are entitled to the money."

Kent's heart began to palpitate. "And who in the company decides these things?"

"That's what I was going to ask you. Immediately, it would be your superior."

"Borst?"

Dennis nodded. "You can go over his head, of course. Who above him knows of the work you put into this thing?" Kent sat back, feeling heavy. "Price Bentley. He's the branch president. I sat in a dozen meetings with him and Borst. He has to know that the man is about as bright as mud. Can't I bring in coworkers?"

"If you want to sue, sure. But by their reactions, it sounds to me like they might be more on Borst's side than yours. Sounds like the guy was doing some fast talking while you were out. Your best bet is probably to go straight to the bank president and appeal your case. Either way you're going to need strong support from the inside. If they all side with Borst, we're going to have to prove a conspiracy, and that, my friend, is near impossible."

Kent let the words soak in slowly. "So basically either I gain favor with one of Borst's superiors and work internally, or I'm screwed. That about it?"

"Well, like I said, I really need to read this thing through, but, barring any hidden clauses, I'd say that's the bottom line. Now, we can always sue. But without someone backing up your story, you might as well throw your money to the wind."

Kent smiled courageously. But his mind was already on Price Bentley's face. He cursed himself for not taking more time to befriend upper management. Then again, they'd hired him as a programmer, not as a court jester. And program he had, the best piece of software the banking industry had seen in ten years.

"So I go back there and start making friends," he said, looking out the picture window to the cars flowing below. From the corner of his eye he saw Dennis nod. He nodded with him. Surely old Price was smart enough to know who deserved credit for AFPS. But the idea that another man held the power to grant or deny his future sat like lead in his gut.

10

Kent walked straight to Price Bentley's office on Tuesday morning before bothering with Borst.

He'd spent Monday afternoon and evening chewing his fingernails, which was a problem because he had no fingernails to speak of. Spencer had wanted to eat chicken in the park for dinner, but Kent had no stomach for pretending to enjoy life on a park bench. "Go ahead, son. Just stay away from any strangers."

The night had proved fitful. A sickening dread had settled on him like a human-sized sticky flysheet, and no matter what twists and turns he put his mind through, he could not shake it free. To make matters worse, he'd awakened at three in the morning, breathless with panic and then furious as thoughts of Borst filtered into his waking mind. He'd spent an hour tossing and turning only to finally throw the covers across the room and swing from bed. The next few hours had been maddening.

By the time the first light filtered through the windows, he had dressed in his best suit and downed three cups of coffee. Helen had collected Spencer at seven and had given Kent a raised eyebrow. It might have been his palms, wet with sweat. Or the black under his eyes. But knowing her, she had probably seen right into his mind and picked through the mess there.

He had nearly hit a yellow Mustang at the red light just before the bank because his eyes were on those sweeping steps ahead and not on the traffic signal. His was the first car in the lot, and he decided to park on the far row in favor of being seen early. Finally, at eight sharp, he'd climbed from the Lexus, swept his damp, blond locks back into place, and headed for the wide doors.

He ran into Sidney Beech around the corner from the president's office. "Hi, Kent," she said. Her long face, accentuated by short brown hair, now looked even longer under raised brows. "I saw you yesterday. Are you okay? I'm so sorry about what happened."

He knew Sidney only casually, but her voice now came like warm milk to his cold tremoring bones. If his mission was to win friends and influence the smug suits, a favorable word with the assistant vice president couldn't hurt. He spread his mouth in a genuine smile.

"Thank you, Sidney." He reached for her hand and grasped it, wondering how much would be too much. "Thank you so much. Yes. Yes, I'm doing better. Thank you."

An odd glint in her eye made him blink, and he released her hand. Was she single? Yes, he thought she was single. The left corner of her lip lifted a hair. "That's good to hear, Kent. If there's anything I can do, just let me know."

"Yes, I will. Listen, do you know what Mr. Bentley's schedule is today? There's a rather important issue that I—"

"Actually, you might catch him now. I know he has an eight-thirty with the board, but I just saw him walk into his office."

Kent glanced in the direction of the president's office. "Great. Thank you, Sidney. You're so kind."

He left, thinking he had overdone it with her, maybe. But then, maybe not. Politics had never been his strong suit. Either way, the exchange had given him a sensibility that took the edge off the manic craziness that had gripped him all night.

True to Sidney's words, Price Bentley sat in his office alone, sorting through a stack of mail. Rumor had it that Price weighed his salary: 250. Only his salary came in thousands of U.S. dollars, not pounds. The large man sat in a gray pin-striped suit. Despite being partially obscured by a layer of thick flesh, his collar looked crisp, possibly supported by cardboard or plastic within its folds. The man's head looked like a plump tomato atop a can. He looked up at Kent and smiled. "Kent! Kent Anthony. Come on in. Sit down. To what do I owe this pleasure?" The president did not rise but continued flipping through the stack.

If the man knew of Gloria's passing, he was not going there. Kent stepped to an overstuffed blue guest chair and sat. The room seemed warm.

"Thank you, sir. Do you have a minute?"

"Sure." The bank president leaned back, crossed his legs, and propped his chin on a hand. "I have a few minutes. How can I help you?"

The man's eyes glistened round and gray. "Well, it's about AFPS," Kent started.

"Yes. Congratulations. Fine work you guys put together back there. I'm sorry you couldn't be at the conference, but it went over with quite a splash. Excellent job!"

Kent smiled and nodded. "That's what I heard. Thank you." He hesitated. How could he say this without sounding like a whiner? *But sir, his blue ribbon was bigger than my blue ribbon.* He hated whiners with a passion. Only this was not about blue ribbons, was it? Not even close.

"Sir, it seems there's been a mistake somewhere."

Bentley's brows scrunched. "Oh? How's that?" He seemed concerned. That was good. Kent picked up steam.

"The Advanced Funds Processing System was my brainchild, sir, five years ago. In fact, I showed you my rough diagrams once. Do you remember?"

"No, I can't say that I do. But that doesn't mean you didn't. I see a thousand submissions a year. And I'm aware that you had an awful lot to do with the system's development. Excellent job."

"Thank you." So far so good. "Actually, I wrote 90 percent of the code for the program." Kent leaned back for the first time. He settled into the chair. "I put a hundred hours a week into its development for over five years. Borst oversaw parts of the process, but for the most part he let me run it."

The president sat still, not catching Kent's drift yet. Unless he was choosing to ignore it. Kent gave him a second to offer a comment and then continued when none came.

"I worked those hours for all those years with my eye set on a goal, sir. And now it seems that Borst has decided that I do not deserve that goal." There. How could he be any clearer?

The president stared at him, unblinking, impossible to read. Heat rose through Kent's back. Everything now sat on those blind scales of justice, waiting for a verdict. Only these scales were not blind at all. They possessed flat gray eyes, screwed into that tomato head across the desk.

Silence settled thick. Kent thought he should continue—throw in some lighthearted political jargon, maybe shift the subject, now having planted his seed. But his mind had gone blank. He became aware that his palms were sweating.

Bentley suddenly spread his jowls in a grin, and he chuckled once with pursed lips. Still not sure what the man could possibly be thinking, Kent chuckled once with him. It seemed natural enough.

"The savings bonus?" the president asked, and he was either very conde-scending or genuinely surprised. Kent begged for the latter, but now the heat was sending little tingles over his skull.

"Yes," he answered, and cleared his throat.

Bentley chuckled again, and his jowls bounced over his collar with each chuckle. "You actually thought that you had a substantial bonus coming, didn't you?"

The breath left Kent as if he'd been gut-punched.

"Those saving spiffs are hardly for non-management personnel, Kent. Surely you realized that. Management, yes. And this one will be substantial indeed. I can see why you might be slobbering over it. But you have to pay your dues. You can't just expect to be handed a million dollars because you did most of the work."

Kent might have lost his judgment there, on the spot—reached over and slapped Fat-Boy's jowls. But waves of confusion fixed him rigid except for a blink-ing in his eyes. Niponbank had always boasted of its Savings Bonus Program, and everyone knew that it was aimed at the ordinary worker. A dozen documents clearly stated so. Last year a teller had come up with an idea that earned him a hundred thousand dollars.

"That's not how the employment manual lays the program out," Kent said, still too shocked to be angry. Surely the president didn't think he could get away with *this* line of argument. They would fry his behind in court!

Bentley's lips fell flat. "Now, you listen to me, Anthony. I don't give a rat's tushy what you think the employment manual says. In this branch, that bonus goes to the management. You work for Borst. Borst works for me." The words came out like bullets from a silenced pistol.

The president took one hard breath. "What work you did for the bank, you did on our time, at our request, and for it we paid you well over a hundred thou-sand dollars a year. That's it. You hear me? You even think about fighting this, and I promise you we will bury you." The large man said it, shaking.

Kent felt his mouth drop during the diatribe. This was impossible! "You can't do that!" he protested. "You can't just rip my bonus off because . . ." And sud-denly Kent knew precisely what he was up against. Bentley was in on it. He stood to receive huge sums of money from the bonus. He and Borst were in on this together. Which made it a conspiracy of sorts.

The man was glaring at him, daring him to say more. So he did.

"Listen!" He bit the word off with as much intensity as Bentley had used. "You know as well as I do that if I had been in Miami, I would have made that presentation, and I would be receiving most if not all of the bonus." A lump of self-pity rose to join the bitterness, and he trembled. "But I wasn't, was I? Because I had to rush home to tend to my wife, who was dying. So instead, you and Borst put your slimy heads together and decided to steal my bonus! What was it?" Kent wagged his head, mocking. 'Oh, poor little Anthony. His wife is dying. But at least he'll be distracted while we stab him in the back and strip him naked!' Is that about it, Bentley?"

The bank president's reaction was immediate. His eyes widened, and he drew an unsteady breath. "You speak like that to me in my own office? One more word out of you, and I'll have you on the street by day's end!"

But Kent had lost his political good sense entirely. "You have no right to do any of this, Bentley! That is my bonus you are stealing. People go to jail for theft in this country. Or is that news to you, as well?"

"Out! Get out!"

"I'll take this to the top. You understand me? And if I go down, you're going down with me. So don't even think about trying to cut me out. Everyone knew that the programming was my code."

"You might be surprised what everyone knew," Bentley shot back. He had forsaken that professional sheen, and Kent felt a spike of satisfaction for it.

"Yes, of course. You will bribe them all, I suppose?" he sneered.

The room went quiet again. When Bentley spoke again, it was low and stern, but the tremor was unmistakable. "Get out of my office, Anthony. I have a meeting in a few minutes. If it's all right with you, I need to prepare a few notes."

Kent stared the man down for a moment. "Actually, nothing is okay with me just now, sir. But then, you already know that, don't you?" He stood and walked behind the chair before turning back.

"And if you try to take my job from me I will personally sue you to the highest heaven. Your bonus may be an internal matter, but there are state laws that deal with employment. Don't even think about stripping me of my income."

He turned to the door and left Bentley sitting with big jowls and squinty eyes, like Jabba the Hut.

It was not until he heard the door close behind him that Kent fully realized how badly it had just gone for him. Then it crashed on him like a block of concrete, and a sick droning obscured his thoughts. He struck for the public restrooms across the lobby.

What had he done? He had to call Dennis. All of his worst fears had just come to life. It was a prospect he could not stomach. *Would* not stomach. Walking across the lobby, he suddenly felt like he was pushing through a steam bath. More than anything he'd ever wanted, possibly even more than the money itself, Kent wanted out of this nightmare. Go back three weeks and check back into Miami's Hyatt Regency. This time when they handed him the note it would have a different name on it. *I'm sorry, you have the wrong party,* he'd say. *I am not Ken Blatherly. My name's Kent. Kent Anthony. And I'm here to become a millionaire.*

Ignoring a young man he recognized as one of the tellers, Kent bent over the sink and threw water on his flushed face. He stood, watched the water drip down his face, and strode for the public phone in the corner, not bothering to wipe his face. Water spotted his starched shirt, but he couldn't care less. Just let Dennis be in. Please let him be in.

The young teller walked out, his eyes wide.

Kent punched the number.

"Warren Law Offices," the female voice came.

"Dennis in?" Silence. "Is Dennis in?"

"Who's calling?"

"Kent."

"May I tell him what it is regarding?"

"Just tell him it's Kent. Kent Anthony."

"Please hold."

No new thoughts formed in the silence. His mind was dipping into numbness.

"Kent! How's it going?"

Kent told him. He said it all in a long run-on sentence that ended with, "Then he threw me out."

"What do you mean, threw you out?"

"Told me to get out."

Silence again.

"Okay, buddy. Listen to me, okay?" Those were sweet words because they came from a friend. A friend who had something to say. That would be good, wouldn't it?

"I know this may sound impossible right now, but this is not over, you hear me? What he did in there, what Bentley just did, changes things. I'm not saying it hands us the case, but it gives us some pretty decent ammo. Obviously the political approach is dead. You pretty much slaughtered that. But you also managed to give us a fairly strong case."

Kent felt like crying. Just sitting down and crying.

"But I need you to do something for me, buddy. Okay? I need you to walk back to your office, sit down at your desk, and work the day out as if nothing at all happened. If we're lucky, they will fire you. And if they fire you, we'll slap the biggest unlawful discharge suit on them the state has ever seen. But if they don't fire you, I need you to continue working in good faith. We can't give them cause to release you. They might consider your confrontation this morning as insubordination, but there were no witnesses, right?"

"Right."

"So then you work as if you did nothing but go to Bentley's office and deliver some paper clips. You hear me? Can you do that?"

Kent wasn't sure he could, actually. The thought of seeing Borst and company back there made him swallow. On the other hand, he had to keep his options open. He had a mortgage and a car payment and groceries to think about. And he had Spencer.

"Yes, I can do that," he replied. "You really think we have something here?"

"It may be messy and take awhile. But yes, I do."

"Okay. Okay. Thanks, Dennis. I owe you."

"Don't worry. There'll be a bill if things go our way."

Kent tried to chuckle with his friend. It came out like a cough.

He hung up, straightened himself in front of the mirror, and let his eyes clear. Ten minutes later, he left the restroom and strode for the administrative offices, clenching his jaw. He'd been through hell already. There could be nowhere but up from here.

Nowhere but straight up.

✦

Helen shuffled over the groove a dozen years of pacing had worn in her bedroom carpet along the length of the double French doors leading to her second-story balcony. It was her prayer closet. Her prayer groove. The place from which she most often broke through to the heavens. In better days she would think nothing of staying on her feet, pacing for hours at a stretch. But now her worn legs limited her to a plodding twenty minutes, tops. Then she would be forced to retreat to her bed or to the rocker.

She wore a long, pink housecoat that swayed around her bare feet. Her hair rested in tangles; bags darkened her eyes; her mouth had found frowning acceptable these days. Despite her understanding of a few things, the fact that her daughter was now gone did not rest easily. It was one thing to peek into the heavens and hear the laughter there. It was another thing altogether to be stuck here, yearning for that laughter. Or even the sweet reprimanding voice of her dear Gloria, instructing her on the finer points of manners.

She pulled at her skin and smiled briefly. *Skinpullers.* Gloria was right, it was a ridiculous name.

It was most often the memories that brought floods of tears to her eyes. But in the end she supposed that it was all right, this weeping. After all, Jesus himself had wept.

Five feet to the right, her white-lace-canopy bed waited with sheets already pulled back. Beside it, a clay bowl filled with red potpourri sent wafts of cinnamon across the room. The ceiling fan clicked overhead, barely moving the air in its lazy circles. Helen reached the end of her groove and turned back, eyeing that bed. Now it was on her left.

But she was not headed there just yet, despite the midnight hour. Not until she broke through here, in her groove. She could feel it in her spirit—or more accurately, her spirit *wanted* to feel something. It wanted to be spoken to. Soothed by the balm from heaven. Which usually meant that heaven wanted to soothe her. Speak to her. It was how God drew mortals, she'd decided once. He spoke desire into willing hearts. Which actually came first, the desire or the willing, was sort of like the chicken or the egg scenario. In the end a rather ridiculous exercise best left to theologians.

In either case, Helen knew to trust her senses, and her senses suggested she intercede now—intercede until she found what peace her spirit sought. If for no other reason than she knew of no other way. The problem began when her eyes had been opened to that scene in the heavens before Gloria's death. She had seen her daughter lying on the hospital bed, and that had sent her over a cliff of sorts.

Oh, she had recovered quickly enough, but it was the rest of the vision that had plagued her night and day over the last few weeks.

Helen closed her eyes and paced by feel, ignoring the dull pain in her knees, subconsciously stepping off the seven paces from end to end. Her mind drifted back to the meeting with Pastor Madison earlier that afternoon. He had said nothing more about their conversation at the hospital. But when she walked into his office today and plopped down in the guest chair facing him, he'd stared her straight through. She knew then that he had not so easily shaken her claim at having seen more.

"How you doing, Bill?" she'd asked.

He did not bother answering. "So, what's happening, Helen?"

"I don't know, Pastor. That's what I came to find out. You tell me."

He smiled and nodded at her immediate response. "Come on, Helen. You are as much a pastor to me as I am to anybody here. You made some pretty strong statements at the hospital."

"Yes. Well, it hasn't gotten any better. And you are wrong if you think that I do not need you to pastor me. I am nearly lost on this one, Bill."

"And I am *completely* lost, Helen. We can't have the blind leading the blind, now, can we?"

"No. But you have been placed in your office with a gifting that comes from God. Use it. Pastor me. And don't pretend that you are a mere clergyman without supernatural guidance—we have enough of those to fill the world's graveyards as it is."

The large Greek smiled and folded his hands on his oak desk. He presented a perfectly stately image, sitting there all dressed in black with a red tie, surrounded by bookshelves stuffed with expensive-looking books.

"Okay, Helen. But you can't expect me to see the way you see. Tell me what you saw."

"I already told you what I saw."

"You told me that you saw Gloria lying in the hospital. That's all you told me. Except that you saw more. So what did you see?"

She sighed. "I was praying with Gloria and Spencer, and we were taken to a place. In our minds or our spirits—I don't know how these things actually work. But I was given a bird's-eye view of Gloria's hospital room two days before she died. I saw everything, right down to the green pen in the attending physician's coat."

She said it with a firm jaw, steeling herself against emotion. She'd had enough sorrow to finish the year out, she thought.

Pastor Madison shook his head slowly. "It just seems incredible. I mean . . . I've never heard of such vivid precognition."

"This was not *pre* anything. This was as real as if I were there."

"Yes, but it happened *before*. That would make it *pre*. A vision of what is to happen."

"God is not bound by time, young man. You should know that. I was there. Maybe in spirit only, but I was there. It is not my job to understand how I was there; I leave that to the more learned in the church. But understanding does not necessarily change an experience. It merely explains it."

"I don't mean to argue with you, Helen. I'm not the enemy here."

Helen closed her eyes for a moment. The pastor was right, of course. He might very well be her only ally in all of this. She would be wise to choose her words with more care.

"Yes. I'm sorry. It's just . . . maddening, you know." Memories of Gloria clogged her mind, and she cleared her throat. "I'm afraid I'm not entirely myself these days."

"But you are yourself, Helen." His deep voice came soothingly. A pastor's voice. "You are a woman who has lost her daughter. If you were not frustrated and angry, I might worry."

She looked up at him and smiled. Now he was indeed pastoring her, and it felt like it should—comforting. She should have come here a week ago.

"You said you saw something else, Helen. What was the rest?"

"I can't tell you, Bill. Not because I don't want to, but because I have only seen glimpses that make no sense. And I've felt things. It is the feelings mostly that bother me, and those are hard to explain. Like God is whispering to my heart but I can't see or hear his words. Not yet."

"I see. Then tell me how it feels."

She looked past his shoulder to a long string of green books with a German-looking name stamped in gold foil across each spine: knowledge.

"Questions? Step right up! We have the answers. Yes, ma'am. You in the yellow dress."

"Yes. Why does God kill the innocent?"

"Well, now. That depends on what you mean by kill. Or by innocent—"

"I mean kill! Dead. Head against the rocks. And innocent. Plain innocent!"

"Helen?"

She looked back at Bill. "Tell you how it feels? It feels like those whispers to the heart. Like you've just walked into a dark dungeon. You've just seen one skull, and the hair on your neck stands on end, and you know there must be more. But you see, that's where it all gets fuzzy. Because I don't know if it's God's dungeon or Satan's dungeon. I mean, you would think it was Satan's. Who ever would think of God having a dungeon. But there are others peering into this dark space, as well. Angels. God himself. And there is the sound of running feet—running away. But I know that the skull there on the black earth is Gloria's. I do know that. And I know it's all part of a plan. It's all part of the running feet. That's the thing. You see, my daughter was sacrificed."

Helen paused and drew her breath carefully, noting that it had grown short. "There are some more things, but they would not make any sense right now." She looked up at him with heavy eyes.

"And this does?"

She shrugged. "You asked for it."

Pastor Madison looked at her with wide eyes. "And I don't think you can be so sure that your daughter was sacrificed. God does not work like that."

"You don't think so? Well, it's one thing to read about how God butchered a thousand nasty Amalekites long ago, but when the object of his ax is your own daughter's neck, the blindfolds go on, do they?"

Bill sat back without removing his eyes from hers. His dark brows were pulled together, creating furrows above the bridge of his nose. He'd stopped shepherding, she thought. Not that she blamed him. She had stopped bleating.

"It's okay, Bill. I don't really understand it, either. Not yet. But I would like you to pray with me. Pray *for* me. I'm a part of this, and it's not yet finished; that much I do know. It is all just beginning. Now you're a part of it. I need you, Pastor."

"Yes," he said. "Of course I will. But I want you to at least consider the possibility that you are misreading these images." He held up his hand. "I know it's not in your nature to do so, Helen. But so far all that has happened is that your daughter has died. I'm not minimizing the trauma of her death, not at all. In fact that very trauma may be initiating all of this. Can you at least understand my line of thinking?" His eyebrows lifted hopefully.

She nodded and smiled, thinking he might very well be the one who was misunderstanding here; he appeared to have missed the point entirely. "Yes, I can. Any psychiatrist in his right mind would tell me the same." She stood then. "But you are wrong, Bill. Gloria's death is not the only thing that has happened. They are rather frantic in the heavens, I think. And there is more to come. It is *this* for which I need your prayers. That and possibly my sanity. But I assure you, young man. I have not lost it yet."

She had walked out then.

He had called two hours later and told her he was praying. It was a good thing, she thought. He was a good man, and she liked him.

Helen let the memory drift away and brought her mind back to the present. Lack of understanding seemed as valuable to God as understanding. It required man to dip into the black hole of faith. But dipping into the hole was pretty much like walking through the dungeon at times.

She tilted her head back and breathed to the ceiling. "Oh God, do not keep silent; be not quiet, oh God, be not still." She quoted the Psalms as she often did in prayer. It was a kind of praying that seemed to fit her new life. "I am worn out calling for help; my throat is parched. My eyes fail looking for my God."

Yes indeed. In its own way, God's silence was as powerful as his presence. If for no reason other than it nudged you toward that hole. Taking the plunge was another matter. That took faith. Believing God was present when he felt absent.

She closed her eyes and moaned at the ceiling. "God, where have you gone?"

I have gone nowhere.

The voice spoke quietly in her spirit, but loudly enough to make her stop halfway down her groove.

Pray, daughter. Pray until it is over.

Now Helen began to tremble slightly. She sidestepped to the bed and sat heavily. "Over?" she vocalized

Pray for him and trust me.

"But it is so difficult when I cannot see."

Then remember the times when you have seen. And pray for him.

"Yes, I will."

The voice fell silent.

A wave of warmth swept through Helen's bones. She stretched her arms for the ceiling and tilted her head back. How could she have ever doubted this? This being who breathed through her now? "Oh, God, forgive me!"

Her chest swelled, and tears spilled from her eyes, unchecked. She opened her mouth and groaned—begging forgiveness, uttering words of love, trying to contain the emotions burning in her throat.

Helen sank to the mattress twenty minutes later, thoroughly content, unable to rid her face of its broad smile. How could she have possibly questioned? She would have to tell the pastor in the morning. It was all painfully obvious now.

An hour later, all of that changed.

Because an hour later, half an hour after she'd fallen into the sweetest sleep she could imagine, God spoke to her again. Showed her something new. But this time it did not feel like a soothing breath sweeping though her bones. This time it felt like a bucket of molten lead poured down her neck.

A scream woke her, filling her mind like a blaring klaxon that jerked her from the dream. It was not until she'd bolted up in bed and sat rigid that she realized the scream was coming from her own mouth.

"God, noooooo! Noooo! Noo—"

She caught her breath mid-wail. God no *what?* Why was she drenched in sweat? Why was her heart racing like a runaway locomotive?

The vision came back to her like a flood.

Then she knew why she had awakened screaming. She moaned, suddenly terrified again.

Darkness crowded her, and she glanced around the room for references, for some sense to dash this madness. Her wardrobe materialized against the far wall. The French doors glowed with moonlight. Reality settled in. But with it, the stark vision she had just witnessed.

Helen dropped to her back and breathed again, pulling in long, desperate breaths. "God, why, God? You can't!"

But she knew he could. Knew he would.

It took her three full hours to find a fitful sleep again and then only after changing her pillowcase twice. She thought it might be the wetness from her tears that kept her from sleep. But in the end she knew it was just the terror.

God was dealing in terror.

11

Kent dragged himself to the bank Wednesday morning, gritting his teeth in a muddle of humiliation and anger. He'd managed his way back to his office yesterday after the Bentley fiasco—fortunately without encountering a soul. For two hours he'd tried to work—and failed miserably. At eleven he'd left, brushing past Betty, mumbling something about an appointment. He had not returned.

Today he entered through the front door, but only because of his attorney's insistence that he maintain normalcy—act like nothing under the sun was bothering him when actually he was falling apart inside. He hurried through the lobby with his head down, fiddling with his third button as if something about it required his full attention. One of the tellers called out his name, but he pretended not to hear it. The button was far too consuming.

He rested his hand on the door to the Information Systems suite and closed his eyes. *Okay, Kent. Just do what needs to be done.* He pushed his way in.

Betty stared at him uncomfortably. Oversized fake black lashes shielded her eyes from the fluorescents. He had an urge to pluck one of them off. Then when she batted her eyes, there would be only one lash fanning the reception room; the room was too small for two anyway.

He nodded. "Morning."

"Morning," she returned, and her voice cracked.

"Borst in?"

"He's in Phoenix today. He'll be back tomorrow."

Thank God for small favors.

Kent walked into his office and closed himself in. Ten minutes later he came to the grinding conclusion that he could not work. Just couldn't. He could pretend to work and play Dennis Warren's game if it would reward him with a fat settlement. But with the door closed, pretending felt absurd.

He punched up a game of solitaire and found it dreadfully boring after the second hand. He tried to call Dennis but learned from the little bimbo at the law offices' front desk that he was in court.

When the knock on the door sounded at ten, it came as a relief. A kind of put-me-out-of-my-misery relief. Kent punched the dormant solitaire game off his screen. "Come in," he called and adjusted his tie knot out of habit.

The new transfer walked in and shut the door. Cliff Monroe. All crisp and clean and charged to climb the ladder. He smiled wide and stuck out his hand—the same hand that Kent had ignored two days earlier.

"Hi, Kent. It's a pleasure to meet you. I've heard a lot about you." His pineapple-eating smile covered the full spectrum—a genuine ear-to-ear grin. "Sorry about the other day."

Kent took the hand and blushed at the memory of *the other day.* "Not your fault. I should apologize. Not the best first impression, I guess."

Cliff must have taken Kent's tone as an invitation to sit, because he grabbed a chair and plopped down. His eyes flashed a brilliant green. "No, it wasn't a problem, really. From what I've picked up between the lines, if you know what I mean, you had every reason to be upset."

Kent straightened. "You know what's going on?" Cliff was still wearing that grin. His teeth seemed inordinately white, like his shirt. "Let's put it this way, I know that Kent Anthony was primarily responsible for the creation of AFPS—I knew that while I was still in Dallas. That's where I transferred in from. I guess the boys upstairs decided that you could use another decent programmer. It's not permanent yet, but believe me, I hope it becomes permanent because I love this place. Even if I don't have my own office yet." Somewhere in that long preamble Cliff had lost his grin. He pressed on before Kent could refocus him. "Yes sir, I would absolutely love to move to the mountains here in Denver. I figure I can crack code during the week, make some decent dough, and the slopes will be mine on the weekends. Do you snowboard?"

The oversized kid was a piece of work. Kent just stared at the programmer for a moment. He'd heard of this type: all brain when it came to the keyboard, and all brawn when it came to the weekends. He smiled for the first time that day.

Cliff joined him with a face-splitting grin of his own, and Kent had an inkling that the kid knew exactly what he was doing.

"I've skied a day or two in my time," he said.

"Great, we can go sometime." The new transfer's face dropped long. "Sorry about what happened to your wife. I mean, I heard about that. It must be hard."

"Uh-huh. So what do you know besides the fact that I was responsible for AFPS?"

"I know that things got a bit topsy-turvy at the convention. Your name was somehow bypassed in all the fuss. Sounds like Borst grabbed all the glory." Cliff grinned again.

Kent blinked and decided not to join him. "Yeah, well you may think that's a cheesy let's-all-have-a-grin-about-it affair, but the fact is, Borst not only got the glory, he's getting all the money as well."

The kid nodded. "Yeah, I know."

That set Kent back. The kid knew that as well? "And you don't have a problem with that?"

"Sure I do. I also have a problem with the fact that the slopes are two hours away. I came to Denver thinking the resorts are out everybody's backdoor, you know. But unless we can find a way to move mountains, I think we're both kinda stuck."

Yes, indeed, Cliff was no dummy. Probably one of those kids who started punching up computer code while they were still in diapers. "We'll see."

"Well, if you need my help, just ask." Cliff shrugged. "I know I will."

"You will what?"

"Need help. From you. My responsibility is to dig into the code and look for weaknesses. I've found the first three already."

"Look for weaknesses, huh? And what makes you think there are any weaknesses? What three?"

"Todd, Mary, and Borst." That grin wrinkled the kid's face again.

Kent could hardly help himself this time. He chuckled. Cliff was looking more and more like an ally. Another small gift from God, possibly. He'd tell Dennis about this one.

He nodded. "You're all right, Cliff. But I wouldn't be saying that too loudly around here, if I were you. You know what they say about power. It corrupts. And by the sound of things, Borst has found himself a load of power lately."

Cliff winked. "Not to worry, Kent. I'm on it already. You got my vote."

"Thanks."

"Now seriously, I do have a few questions. Do you mind running me through a few routines?"

The kid was a walking paradox. At first glance, clean cut and ready to brown-nose the closest executive, but something entirely different under the starch. A snowboarder. Spencer would get a kick out of this.

"Sure. What do you want to know?"

They spent the rest of the morning and the first afternoon hour plowing through code. Kent's instincts proved correct: Cliff was a regular programming prodigy. Not as fluent or precise as Kent, but as close to him as anybody he'd met. And likable to boot. He'd set up shop down the hall in an office that had served as the suite's overflow room before his arrival. He retreated there shortly after one.

Kent stared at the door after Cliff's departure. What now? He picked up the phone and began to dial Dennis Warren's number. But then he remembered that the attorney was in court. He dropped the phone in its cradle. Maybe he should talk to Will Thompson upstairs. Recruit the loan officer's support on the matter of the missing bonus. That would mean walking past Betty again, of course, and he could hardly stand the thought. Unless she was taking a late lunch.

Kent shut his computer down, grabbed his briefcase, and headed out.

Unfortunately, Betty was back from lunch, unwittingly transferring blush from her well-oiled face to her phone's mouthpiece while gabbing with only heaven knew who. Some other lady who had absolutely no clue about banking. Her beautician perhaps.

Kent didn't bother reporting his plans. He found Will upstairs, banging on his monitor again. "You need some help there, young man?"

Will jerked up. "Kent!" He sat back and nodded in a bouncing motion.

"You still having problems with that monitor?"

"Every time you come by, it seems. The thing keeps winking off on me. I need to inadvertently push it off the desk and requisition a new one. Maybe a twenty-one incher."

"Yeah, that'll definitely push the loans right along. The bigger the better."

Will conducted a few more of his nods and smiled. "So I heard that you had a run-in with Bentley yesterday," he said.

Kent sat calmly in the guest chair facing Will, ignoring the heat suddenly washing over his shoulders. "And how did you know that?"

"This is a small city we work in, Kent. Complete with built-in, free-flowing lines of communication. Things get around."

Good night! Who else knew? If big-mouth here knew, the whole world would soon hear. Probably already had. Kent glanced around the room and caught a pair of eyes resting on him from the far side. He shifted his eyes back to Will.

"So what did you hear?"

"I heard that you walked in there and demanded to be named employee of the month for your part in the AFPS development. They said you were screaming about it."

The heat spread right down Kent's spine. *Employee of the month?* That lousy imbecile! I could . . ." He bit off the rest and closed his eyes. They weren't messing around, then. He had become their fool. The poor fellow in administration who wanted a bigger pat on the back.

"You didn't actually scream at—"

"You're darned right I screamed at that jerk!" Kent said. "But not about some lousy employee-of-the-month parking space." He breathed heavily and tried to calm his pulse. "People are actually buying that?"

"I don't buy it." Will sat back and glanced around. "Keep your voice down, man."

"What's everybody else saying?"

"I don't know. They're saying that anyone who screams at Bentley about employee-of-the-month status has got a screw loose, to be sure." A slight grin crossed the loan officer's face. "They're saying that if anybody should get employee of the month it should be the whole department because AFPS came from the department."

Something popped in Kent's mind, as if someone had tossed a depth charge in there and run for cover. *Kaboom!* He stood to his feet. At least he *wanted* to stand to his feet. His efforts resulted in more of a lurch. The room swam dizzily.

He had to get to Dennis! This was not good!

"I've got to go," he mumbled. "I'm late."

Will leaned forward. "Kent, sit down for heaven's sake! It's not a big deal. Everybody knows you were the real brains behind AFPS, man. Lighten up."

Kent bent for his case and strode deliberately from the desk. He only wanted one thing now. Out. Just out, out, out.

If there had been a fire escape in the hall, he might have taken it in favor of chancing a face-to-face encounter with another employee. But there was no fire escape. And there *was* another person in the elevator. She might have been Miss America, for all he knew, because he refused to make eye contact. He pressed into the corner, praying for the moments to pass quickly.

The backdoor released him to the alley, and tears blurred his vision before the latch slammed home. He bellowed angrily, instinctively. The roar echoed, and he spun his head, wondering if anyone had heard or seen this grown man carrying on. The alley lay dark and empty both ways. A large diesel engine growled nearby— an earthmover, perhaps, breaking ground on someone's dream.

Kent felt very small. Very, very, very small. Small enough to die.

⌒⌒

While Kent was dying at work, Helen was doing her best to forget the images that had visited her the previous night. But she was not doing so good.

She stirred the pitcher of ice tea slowly, listening to Spencer hum "Jesus, Lover of My Soul" in the other room. All of their lives seemed to hinge on that song, she thought, remembering how Spencer's grandfather had loved to sing it in his mellow, baritone voice. From grandfather to grandson. Ice clinked in the tea, and she began to sing softly with him. "Jesus, Lover of my soul . . ."

If the boy only knew.

Well, today he would know a little more. Enough for things to brighten.

She hobbled past Spencer, who sat, as usual, cross-legged on the floor, then she eased into her worn green rocker. A small glass bottle sat in the hutch, ancient and red, glaring at her with its history. It held its secrets, that glass vile, secrets that brought a chill to her spine still. She swallowed and shifted her eyes. Now the picture of the cross with Jesus spread out, dying on its beams, stared directly at her, and she kept up with the boy in a wobbly soprano. ". . . Let me to thy bosom fly . . ." She would have to hold it together now—in front of the boy at least. She would have to trust as she had never trusted. As long as she could keep her eyes off the scales of justice that had found their way into her mind, she would do fine. As long as she could trust that God's scales were working, even though her own tipped, lopsided, in her mind, she would make it.

Funny how so many saw that cross as a bridge over the gulf between God and man—between heaven and earth—and yet how few took the time to cross it. No pun there, just a small nugget of truth. How many were busy looking for another way across? How many Christians avoided the death of God? Take up your cross daily, he'd said. Now, there was a paradox.

"Spencer."

"Yes, Grandma?" He looked up from the Legos that had held his attention for the last half-hour. He'd built a spaceship, she saw. Fitting.

She looked around the room, thinking of how best to tell him. "Did your father talk to you last night?"

Spencer nodded. "Sure."

"About his job?"

Spencer looked up at her curiously. "How did you know that?"

"I didn't know. That's why I asked. But I did know he was having . . . complications at work."

"Yeah, that's what he said. Did he tell you about it?"

"No. But I wanted to help you understand some things today about your father."

Spencer let the Lego pieces lie on the floor and sat up, interested. "He's having a hard time."

"Yes he is, isn't he?" She let silence settle for a few seconds. "Spencer, how long do you think we've been praying for your father to see the light?"

"A long time."

"Five years. Five years of beating on the brass heavens. Then they cracked. You remember that? Almost three weeks ago?"

The boy nodded, wide eyed now. "With Mom." Spencer scrambled to his feet and climbed into "his" chair opposite Grandma. The air suddenly felt charged.

"It seems that our prayers have caused quite a stir in the heavens. You should know, Spencer, that everything happening with your father is by design."

The boy tilted his head slightly, thinking that through. "Mom's death?"

The boy was not missing a beat here. "It has its purpose."

"What purpose could God have in letting Mom die?"

"Let me ask you, which is greater in regard to your mother's death? *Her* pleasure or your father's sorrow?" She suddenly wanted to throw her own grief on the scales and withdraw the question. But that was not her part here—she at least knew that.

He looked at her for a moment, thinking. The corner of his mouth twitched and then lifted to a small sheepish grin. "Mom's pleasure?" he said.

"By a long shot, Honey. You remember that. And no matter what else happens to your father, you remember that a hundred thousand eyes are peering down on him from the heavens, watching what he will do. Anything can happen at any time, and everything happens for a purpose. Can you understand that?"

Spencer nodded, his eyes round with eagerness.

"You ever hear of a man named C. S. Lewis? He once wrote, 'There is no neutral ground in the universe: every square inch, every split second, is claimed by God and counter claimed by Satan.' It's like that with your father, Spencer. Do you believe that?"

Spencer closed his mouth and swallowed. "Yes. Sometimes it's hard to know . . ."

"But you do believe it, don't you?"

"Yes. I believe it."

"And why do you believe it, Spencer?"

He looked at her, and his eyes shone like jewels. "Because I've seen heaven," he said. "And I know that things are not what people think they are."

Her feelings for the boy boiled to the surface, and she felt a lump rise in her throat. Such a tender face under those blue eyes. He had Gloria's face. *Oh, my God, my God. What could you possibly be thinking?* Her chest felt like it might explode with grief, looking at the boy.

She felt a tear slip from her eye. "Come here, Honey," she said.

The boy came and sat on the arm of her chair. She took his hand and kissed it gently then pulled him onto her lap. "I love you, my child. I love you so dearly."

He blushed and turned to kiss her forehead. "I love you too, Grandma."

She looked into his eyes. "You are blessed, Spencer. We have just begun, I think. And you have such a precious part to play. Savor it for me, will you?"

"I will, Grandma."

"Promise?"

"Promise."

For a long time, Helen held her grandson, rocking in the chair in silence. Remarkably, he let her—seemed to relish the embrace. Tears were soon flowing freely down her face and wetting her blouse. She did not want the boy to see her cry, but she could not stop herself. Her life was being shredded, for God's sake.

Quite literally.

12

Kent slumped into a dead sleep sometime past midnight Wednesday, with visions of vultures circling lazily through his dreams. He woke late and scrambled to dress for work. The thought of returning to the den of thieves made him sick just now, but he had not seen his way past Dennis Warren's suggestion that he at least maintain his status of employment with the bank. And he had not succeeded in making contact with the attorney the previous afternoon, despite a dozen attempts. His lawyer's bimbo was developing a dislike for him, he thought.

And now it was morning. Which meant it was time to go back to the bank. Back to hell. Maybe today he would wash Borst's feet. Give him a good rubdown, perhaps. Congratulate him for making employee of the month. *Jolly good, sir.* Good grief!

"Dad."

Kent looked up from the edge of the bed, where he'd just pulled on his last sock. Spencer stood in the bedroom doorway, fully dressed. His hair lay in a tangled web, but then the boy was going nowhere today.

"Hey, Spencer."

His son walked in and sat next to him. "You're up late," the boy observed.

"Yeah. I slept in."

Spencer suddenly put an arm over his shoulder and squeezed him gently. "I love you, Dad."

The show of affection brought a heaviness to Kent's chest. "I love you too, son."

They sat together, still and quiet for a moment.

"You know that Mom is okay, don't you?" Spencer looked up. "She's in heaven, Dad. With God. She's laughing up there."

Kent blinked at that. "Sure, son. But we're down here. There's no heaven down here."

"Sometimes there is," Spencer said.

Kent ruffled the boy's hair and smiled. "Heaven on earth. You're right. Sometimes there is." He stood and fed his tie around his collar. "Like when your mother and I got married. Now *there* was some heaven. Or like when I first bought the Lexus. You remember when I came home with the Lexus, Spencer?"

"I'm not talking about that kind of heaven."

Kent walked to the mirror on the wall, not wanting this conversation now. Now he wanted to tear Borst's throat out. He saw his eyebrows furrow in the mirror. Beyond, Spencer's reflection stared back at him. This was his boy on the bed, eyes round, legs hanging limp almost to the ground.

"C'mon, Spencer. You know I don't see things the way you do. I know you want what's best for Mom, but she's just gone. Now it's you and me, buddy. And we will find our own way."

"Yeah, I know."

That's right, son. Let it go.

"But maybe we should follow Mom's way."

Kent closed his eyes and clenched his jaw. Mom's way? And what was Mom's way? Mom's way was death. *Yeah, well, why don't we all just die and go to heaven?*

He pulled his tie tight and turned back to Spencer. "We don't live in a fantasy world; we live in a real world where people actually die, and when they die it's the end. Six feet under. Game's over. And there's no use pretending otherwise."

"What about God?"

The doorbell chimed in the foyer. That would be Linda, the sitter Helen had arranged for, coming to watch Spencer for the day. Kent turned for the door.

"Why don't you just believe in God?"

Kent stopped and turned back toward Spencer. "I do believe in God. I just have a broader concept, that's all."

"But God loves you, Dad. I think he's trying to get your attention."

Kent swung around, his gut suddenly churning. He wanted to say, *Don't be so simplistic, Spencer. Don't be so stupid!* Wanted to shout that. If what was happening in his life had anything at all to do with some white-bearded scribe in the sky, then God was getting senile in his old age. It was time for someone with a little more compassion to take over.

Kent turned back to the door without responding.

"He won't let you go, Dad. He loves you too much," Spencer said softly.

Kent whirled, suddenly furious. His words came before he could stop them. "I don't care about your God, Spencer! Just shut up!"

He spun around and steamed for the front door, knowing he had crossed a line. He pulled open the door and glared at the brunette baby-sitter who stood on the front steps.

She shoved out her hand. "Mr. Anthony?"

"Yes." Kent heard Spencer pad up behind him, and he wanted to turn to the boy and beg his forgiveness. Linda was staring at him with bright gray eyes, and he diverted his gaze past her to the street. *Spencer, my dear son, I love you so much. I could never hurt a hair on your head. Never. Never, never!*

He should turn now and hold the boy. Spencer was all he had left. Kent swallowed and stepped past her. "Take care of him," he instructed without shaking her hand. "He knows the rules."

Every bone in Kent's body ached to spin and run back to Spencer. Yet he trudged forward to the Lexus waiting in the driveway. He saw his son from the corner of his eye when he slammed the door shut. The boy stood in the doorway with limp arms.

Kent roared down the street, thinking he had just stooped as low as he had ever stooped. Might as well have licked some concrete while he was down there. Why the subject of God sent him into such a tailspin he could hardly fathom. Death usually seemed to bring people to their knees, begging the man upstairs for some understanding. But Gloria's death seemed to have planted a root of bitterness in his heart. Maybe because she had died so violently despite her faith. And his mother-in-law Helen's prayers had ended where all prayers end: in her own gray matter.

He arrived at the red-brick bank filled with foreboding from its first sighting, ten blocks earlier. He would call Dennis again today—find out how quickly they could get a suit filed. Maybe then he could leave.

Kent made his way to the alley behind the bank. There was no way he would step through those fancy swinging doors up front and risk running into fat-boy Bentley. The rear entrance would do just fine for the balance of his tenure, thank you. He stepped down the dingy alley.

White fingers of steam rose from a sewer grate halfway down the narrow passage.

Garbage lay strewn beside the dumpster, as if the whole cage had been tipped and then righted again. Some homeless vagrant too eager for his own good. Kent pulled a ring of keys from his pocket and found the silver one he'd been issued for the door a year earlier after complaining he needed longer access. Since then he'd come and gone as he pleased, often working late into the night. The memory sat in his mind now, mocking.

How many hours had he given to the bank? Thousands at least. Tens of thousands, all for Borst and Fat-Boy. If Spencer's God was somehow actually involved in the world, it was as a tormentor. *Let's see which of them we can get to scream the loudest today.* Kent pushed the key into the slot.

A whisper rasped on the wind behind him. "You ain't seen nothin' yet, you sicko." Kent whirled.

Nothing!

His heart pumped hard. The dumpster sat still; the alley gaped on either side, empty to the streets, white strands of steam lifted lazily from the grate. But he had heard it, clear as day. *You ain't seen nothin' yet, you sicko!*

The stress was getting to him. Kent turned to the gray-steel fire door and reinserted the key with an unsteady hand.

To his left, a movement caught his eyes, and he jerked his head that way. A man wearing a torn red Hawaiian shirt and filthy slacks that had possibly once been blue leaned against the dumpster, staring at him. The sight frightened Kent badly, and his hand froze on the key. Not three seconds ago, he would have sworn the alley was empty.

"Life sucks," the man said, and then lifted a brown bag to his lips and took a slug from a hidden bottle. He did not remove his eyes from Kent's. Scattered patches of scraggly hair hung off his neck. His lumpy nose shined red and big.

"Life really *sssssucksss!*" He grinned now, and his teeth were jagged yellow. He cackled and lifted the brown bag.

Kent watched the vagrant take another slug. He yanked on the door and stepped in quickly. Something was haunting him; his mind was bending. *Get a grip, Kent. You're losing your grip.*

The door swooshed shut, and suddenly the hall was pitch dark. He groped the wall, found the switch, and flipped it up. The long fluorescent tubes stuttered to white, illuminating the empty hall. Long and empty like the prospects facing his life now. Bleak, white, long, empty.

Life sucks.

Kent forced himself to the end and out to the main corridor. Somehow he had embarked on a roller coaster, swooping up and down and around sharp curves at breakneck speed, intent on throwing him to his death. Some thrill ride from hell, and he wasn't being allowed to disembark. Each hour was rolling into the next, each day full of new twists and turns. They say that when it rains, it pours. Yes, well, it was pouring all right. Fire and brimstone.

Betty was gone when he stepped into the Information Systems suites, probably to the john to apply yet another layer of mascara to her foot-long fake lashes. She'd always fancied herself to be half her age with twice the life. Kent slipped into his office and closed the door quietly. *Here we go then.* He sat and tried to still the buzzing in his head.

For a full minute Kent stared at the exotic fish making their predictable sweeps across the three monitors. It was not until then that it occurred to him that he still gripped his briefcase. He dropped it on the floor and picked up the phone.

It took five minutes for the cranky secretary at Dennis Warren's office to finally put him through, and then only after Kent's threat to call back repeatedly every three minutes if she didn't tell Dennis this very minute that he was on the phone.

Dennis came on. "Kent. How goes it, my friend? Go easy on my girls."

"She was giving me lip. Shouldn't give lip to customers, Dennis. Bad business."

"You're not a customer. Not yet, Kent." A chuckle. "When you get a bill, you'll be a customer. So what's up?"

Kent chose to ignore the jab. "Nothing. Unless you call sitting in an office doing nothing for eight hours while everybody around you has their ear to the wall, listening for your *nothing,* something. It's falling apart here, Dennis. The whole bank knows."

"Lighten up, buddy."

"We have to move forward, Dennis! I'm not sure how long I can do this."

A long silence filled his ear, which was rather uncharacteristic of his friend, who never seemed at a loss for words. Now Dennis was suddenly silent. Breathing, actually. Breathing heavily. When he spoke his voice sounded scratchy.

"We can move forward on this as soon as you are positive, Kent."

"Positive? About what? I *am* positive! They think I've lost my mind around here! Do you understand that? They think I'm off the deep end, for goodness' sake! We're going to bury these guys, if it's the last thing we do!" He let the statement settle, wondering if his voice had carried out to the hall. "Right?"

A chuckle crackled on the phone. "Oh, we'll be doing some burying, all right. But what about you, Kent?" Now Dennis was speaking around short breaths, pausing after each phrase to pull at the air. "Are you positive about where you stand?" A breath. "You can't go soft halfway through." A breath. Another breath. Kent scrunched his eyebrows.

The attorney continued. "It's not like God's going to reach down and hand you answers, you know. You decide to go one way, you go all the way that way. Right to the end, and screw them all if they need their crutch!" A series of breaths. "Right, Kent? Isn't that right?"

Kent furrowed his brow. "What are you talking about? Who's talking about going soft halfway? I'm saying we bury them, man! Screw 'em all to the wall." He let the comment about the crutch go. Something was confused there.

"That's right, Kent," the attorney's voice rasped. "You do whatever it takes. This is life and death. You win, it's life; you lose, it's death."

"I hear you, man. And what I'm saying here is that, by the looks of things, I'm already a dead man. We have to move now."

"You do things their way and you end up getting buried. Like some fool martyr." A ragged pause. "Look at Gloria."

Gloria? Kent felt his pulse rise in agreement with his attorney. He understood what Dennis was doing now. And it was brilliant. The man was reaching out to him; connecting with him emotionally; drawing the battle lines.

"Yes," he said. And Dennis was saying that the bank and God were on the same side. They both wanted to do some burying. Only God was really fate, and fate had already done its burying with Gloria. Now the bank was having its go. With him.

The hair lifted on the nape of his neck. "Yes. Well, they're not going to bury me, Dennis. Not unless they kill me first."

The phone sat unspeaking in his palm for a few seconds before Dennis came on again. "No. Killing is against the rules. But there are other ways."

"Well, I'm not actually suggesting killing anybody, Dennis. It's just a figure of speech. But I hear you. I hear you loud and clear. And I'm ready. When can we get this ball rolling?"

This time the phone went dead for a long time.

"Dennis? Hello?"

"No," Dennis returned. His voice was distant, like an echo on the phone now. "I don't think you are ready. I don't think you are ready at all, my fine friend. Perhaps this afternoon you will be ready."

The phone clicked. Kent held it to his ear, stunned. This afternoon? What in the world did this afternoon have to do with anything? A sudden panic rose to his throat. What was going on? What in—

The phone began burping loudly in his ear. An electronic voice came on and told him in a roundabout way that holding a dead phone to the ear was a rather unbrilliant thing to do.

He dropped the receiver in its cradle.

Yes indeed, the roller coaster from hell. *After him, lads! After him!*

Now what? What was he supposed to do in this cursed place? Sit and stare at fish while Borst sat across the hall, planning how to spend his forthcoming fortune?

Cliff poked his head in once and offered a "Good morning" around that pineapple-eating grin of his. Kent forced a small smile and mumbled the same.

"You keep your nose clean, now. You hear?" Cliff said.

"Always. Clean's my middle name," he returned. He tried to find some levity in his own irony, but he could not.

"Okay. Just hang in there. Things will look up if you hang in there."

When Kent looked up, Cliff had pulled out. The door clicked shut. Now what did *he* know? Like some father offering sound wisdom. *Hang in there, son. Here, come sit on my lap.*

He tried to imagine Cliff catching air on a snowboard. The image came hard. Now Spencer, there was someone who could catch air. Only it was on a skateboard.

Kent spent an hour running through e-mail and idiotic bank memoranda. Most of it went to the trash with a click. He expected that at any moment one of the others would pop in and say something, but no one did, and the fact began to wear on him. He heard their muffled voices on several occasions, but they seemed to be ignoring him wholesale. Maybe they didn't know he'd come in. Or more likely they were embarrassed for him. *Did you hear about Kent and Bentley? Yeah, he's really flipped, huh? Poor guy. Lost his wife—that's what did it. For sure.*

Several times he contemplated calling Dennis back—asking him what he'd meant about this afternoon. But the memory of the man's voice echoing in the receiver made him postpone the call.

He called up AFPS and entered the new password: MBAOK. The familiar icon ran across the screen, and he let it cycle through a few times before entering the system. A program like this would be worth millions to any large bank. He should just download the source code and take it on the road. It was his, after all.

But that was the problem. It was not his. At least, not legally.

Kent was startled by the sudden buzz of his phone. Dennis, possibly. Calling to apologize about that ludicrous exchange. He glanced at the caller ID.

It was Betty. And he was in no mood to discuss office business. He let the phone buzz annoyingly. It finally fell silent after a dozen persistent burps. What was her problem?

A fist pounded on his door, and he swung around. Betty stood in the door frame, stricken white. "You have a call," she said, and he thought she might be ill. "It's urgent. I'll put it through again."

She pulled the door closed. Kent stared after her.

The phone blared again. This time Kent whirled and snatched up the receiver. "Hello."

"Hello, Mr. Anthony?" It was a female voice. A soft, shaky female voice.

"Yes, this is Kent Anthony."

A pause. "Mr. Anthony, I'm afraid there's been an accident. Do you have a son named Spencer Anthony?"

Kent rose to his feet. His hands went cold on the receiver. "Yes."

"He was hit by a car, Mr. Anthony. He's at Denver Memorial. You should come quickly."

Adrenaline flooded Kent's bloodstream like boiling ice. Goose flesh prickled down his shoulders. "Is . . . Is he okay?"

"He's . . ." A sick pause. "I'm sorry. I can't . . ."

"Just tell me! Is my son okay?"

"He died in the ambulance, Mr. Anthony. I'm sorry . . ."

For a moment the world stood still. He didn't know if the woman said more. If she did, he did not hear it because a buzzing had erupted in his skull again.

The phone slipped from his grasp and thudded on the carpet. Spencer? His Spencer!? Dead?

He stood rooted to the floor, his right hand still up by his ear where the receiver had been, his mouth limp and gaping. The terror came in waves then, spreading down his arms and legs like fire.

Kent whirled to the door. It was shut. Wait a minute, this could have been one of those voices! He was going mad, wasn't he? And now the voices of madness had touched him where they knew he would be hurt most. Tried to yank his heart out.

He died in the ambulance, the voice had said. An image of Spencer's blond head lying cockeyed on an ambulance gurney flashed through his mind. His boy's arms jiggled as the medical van bounced over potholes.

He staggered for the door and pulled it open, barely conscious of his movements. Betty sat at her desk, still white. And then Kent knew that it had been a real voice.

Blackness washed through his mind, and he lost his sensibilities. The days leading up to this one had weakened them badly. Now they simply fell away, like windblown chaff.

He groaned, unabashed, oblivious to the doors suddenly cracking around him for a view of the commotion. A small part of his mind knew that he was lumbering through the hall, hands hanging limp, moaning like some retarded hunchback, but the realization hung like some tiny inconsequential detail on the black horizon. Everything else was just buzzing and black.

Kent stumbled through the hall door, on autopilot now. He was halfway to the main lobby when the cruelty of it all crashed into his brain and he began to gasp in ragged pulls like a stranded fish gulping on the rocks. Spencer's sweet, innocent face hung in his mind. Then Gloria's swollen body, still blotched and purple.

He lifted his hands to his temples and fell into an unsteady jog. He wanted to stop. Stop the groaning, stop the pain, stop the madness. Just stop.

But it all came like a flood now, and instead of stopping he began to sob. Like a man possessed, Kent ran straight through the main lobby, gripping the hair at his temples, wailing loudly.

For a moment, banking stopped cold.

Twelve tellers turned as one and stared, startled. Zak, the security guard, brought his hand to the butt of his shiny new .38, for the first time, possibly.

Kent burst through the swinging doors, leapt down the concrete steps, and tore around the corner. He slammed into the car, hardly knowing it was his.

Spencer! No, no, no! Please, not Spencer!

His son's face loomed tender and grinning in Kent's mind. His blond bangs hung before his blue eyes. The boy flipped his head back, and Kent felt a wave of dizziness at the ache in his own chest.

The door to his Lexus was not opening easily, and he frantically fumbled with a wad of keys, dropping them once and banging his head on the mirror as he retrieved them. But he did not feel any pain from the gash above his left eye. It bled warm blood down his cheek, and that felt strangely comforting.

Then he was in his car and somehow screaming through the streets with his horn blaring, wiping frantically at his eyes to clear his vision.

He felt barely conscious now. All he noticed were the pain and blackness that crashed through his mind. He wove in and out of traffic, banging on the wheel, trying to dislodge the pain. But when he squealed to a stop at the hospital and met a wide-eyed paramedic head on, bent on restraining him, uttering consolations, he knew it made little difference.

Spencer was dead.

Somewhere in the confusion, a well-meaning man in a white coat told him that his son, Spencer, had been struck by a car from behind. A hit-and-run. One of the neighbors found him sprawled on the sidewalk, halfway to the park, with a broken back. Spencer couldn't have known what hit him, he said. Kent screamed back at the man, told him he should try letting a car snap *his* spine at forty miles an hour and see how that felt.

He stumbled into the room where they had left Spencer's little body lying on a gurney. He was still in his shorts, bare chested and blond. They had worked with his body, but at first glance Kent saw that his son's torso rested at an odd angle to his hips. He imagined that body snapping in two, folding over, and he threw up on the gray linoleum floor. He lurched forward to the body, hazy now. Then he touched his son's white skin and rested his cheek on his still rib cage and wept.

It felt as though a white-hot iron had been pulled from the fires of hell and stamped on his mind. No one deserved this. *No one.* That was the tattoo.

The pain burned so strongly that Kent lost himself to it. They later told him that he'd ranted and raved and cursed—mostly cursed—for over an hour. But he could remember none of it. They gave him a sedative, they said, and he went to sleep. On the floor, in the corner, curled up like a fetus.

But that was not how he remembered things. He just remembered that most of him died that day. And he remembered that branding iron burning in his skull.

13

Week Six

Helen Crane piloted the ancient, pale yellow Ford Pinto through a perfectly mani-cured suburbia, struck by the gross facade. Like a huge plastic Barbie-doll set care-fully constructed on the ground to cover a reeking cesspool beneath. Made to cover these dungeons down here.

It felt strange driving through the world. Lonely. As if she were dreaming and the houses rising above green lawns were from another planet—because she knew what was really here, and it resembled something much closer to a sewer than this picture-perfect neighborhood.

That was the problem with holing yourself up in prayer for a week and hav-ing your eyes opened. You saw things with more clarity. And God was making her see things more clearly these days, just as he'd done with Elisha's servant. Drawing her into this huge drama unfolding behind the eyes of mortals. She played the intercessor—the one mortal allowed to glimpse both worlds so that she could pray. She knew that. And pray she had, nearly nonstop for ten days now.

But it was just the beginning. She knew that just as she would know the turn-ing of the leaves signaled the coming of autumn. More was to follow. A whole season.

She was starting to accept God's judgment in the matter. Much like a house-wife might accept her husband's leadership—with a plastic smile to avoid con-frontation. Of course, this was God, not some man brimming with weaknesses. Still, she could not let him so easily off the hook for what he had done. Or at the very least, allowed—which, given his power, was the same thing. Her time seemed to be divided equally between two realities. The reality in which she cried pitifully, chastising God for this mad plan, begging for relief, and the reality in which she bowed and shook and wept, humbled to have heard God's voice at all.

Chastising God was foolishness, of course. Utter nonsense. Humans had no right to blame their difficulties on God, as if he knew precisely what he was doing when he breathed galaxies into existence but was slipping now in his dealings with the beings on planet Earth.

On the other hand, it was God himself, in all of his wisdom, who had created man with such a fickle mind. Believing one day, doubting the next; loving one moment, forgetting within the hour. Mankind.

"Oh God, deliver us from ourselves," she muttered and turned the corner leading toward Kent's.

She no longer struggled with the believing, as most did. But the loving . . . Sometimes she wondered about the loving. If human nature was a magnet, then self-gratification was steel, clinging stubbornly. And loving . . . loving was like wood, refusing to stick to the magnet no matter how much pressure was applied. Well, like it or not she was still human. Even after all she had been through before this mess. Yes indeed, Kent here was a *saint* compared to what she had been.

"Why are you taking us here, Father? Where does this road end? What have you not shown me?"

In the five weeks since she'd first seen the heavens open, together with Gloria and Spencer, she had seen a glimpse of the light every day. But only on three occasions had she seen specific visions of the business up there. That first one when she had learned of this whole mess. The second showing Spencer's death. And a third, a week ago, just after Spencer had joined his mother.

Each time she had been allowed to see a little more. She had seen Gloria laughing. And she had seen Spencer as well, laughing. She didn't know if they laughed all the time—it seemed the pleasure of it would wear thin. Then again, wearing thin would require time, and there was no time in heaven, was there? And actually it had not been one big laughter up there. Not every moment was filled with laughter, if indeed there even were such things as moments on the other side. Twice in the last vision she had seen both Spencer and Gloria lying still, neither laughing nor speaking but hanging limp and quivering, their eyes fixed on something she could not see. Wallowing in pleasure. Then the laughter came again, on the tail of the moment. A laughter of delight and ecstasy, not of humor. In fact, there was nothing funny about the business her daughter and grandson were up to in the heavens.

It was the business of raw pleasure. If she had not seen that, she might very well have gone mad.

Helen blinked and turned onto Kent's street. His two-story rose like a tomb, isolated against the bleak, gray sky.

In her last vision, Helen had caught a glimpse of this thing's magnitude, and it had left her stunned. She had seen it in the distance, beyond the space occupied by Gloria and Spencer, and for only a brief moment. A million, perhaps a billion creatures were gathered there. And where was *there?* There was the whole sky, although it seemed impossible. They had come together in two halves, as though on cosmic bleachers peering down on a single field. Or was it a dungeon? It was the only way Helen could translate the vision.

An endless sea of angelic creatures shone white on the right, clamoring for a view of the field below. They appeared in many forms, indescribable and unlike anything she had imagined.

On the left, pitch blackness created a void in space filled only with the red and yellow of countless flickering eyes. The potent stench of vomit had drifted from them, and she had blanched, right there, on the green chair in her living room.

Then she saw the object of their fixed attention. It was a man on the field below, running, pumping his arms full tilt, like some kind of gladiator fleeing from a lion. Only there was no lion. There was nothing. Then the heavens faded, and she saw that it was Kent and he was sprinting through a park, crying.

She had gone to him that afternoon and offered him comfort, which he'd promptly rejected. She had also asked him where he'd been at ten that morning, the time of her vision.

"I went for a run," he'd said.

Helen pulled into the drive and parked the Pinto.

Kent answered the door after the third buzz. By the rings under his eyes the man had not been sleeping. His hair lay in blond tangles, and his normally bright blue eyes peered through drooping lids, hazed over.

"Hello, Kent," Helen offered with a smile.

"Hello." He left the door open and headed for the living room. Helen let herself in and closed the door. When she walked under the catwalk he had already seated himself in the overstuffed beige rocker.

The odor of day-old dishrags hung in the air. Perhaps week-old dishrags. The same music he had played for days crooned melancholically through the darkened living room. Celine someone-or-other, he had told her. Dion. Celine Dion, and it wasn't a tape; it was a CD, like the initials of her name. CD.

She scanned the unkempt room. The miniblinds were closed, and she blinked to adjust her eyesight. A pile of dishes rose above the breakfast bar to her right. The television throbbed silently with colors to her left. Pizza boxes lay strewn on a coffee table cluttered with beer bottles. If he permitted, she would do some cleaning before she left.

Something else had changed in the main room. Her eyes rested on the mantel above the fireplace. The large framed picture called *Forgiven* was missing. It had been of Jesus, holding a denim-clad killer who held a hammer and nails in his hand that dripped with blood. A faint, white outline showed its vacancy.

She slid onto the couch. Kent was not being so easily wooed. *Father, open his eyes. Let him feel your love.*

Kent glanced at her as if he'd heard the thought. "So, what do you want, Helen?"

"I want you to be better, Kent. You doing okay?"

"Do I look like I'm doing okay, Helen?"

"No, actually you look like you just returned from hell." She smiled genuinely, feeling a sudden surge of empathy for the man. "I know there's little I can say to comfort you, Kent. But I thought you might like some company. Just someone to be here."

He eyed her with drooping eyes and sipped at a drink in his left hand. "Well, you think wrong, Helen. If I needed company, you think I'd be in here watching silent pictures on the tube?"

She nodded. "What people need to do and what they actually do are rarely even remotely similar, Kent. And yes, I do think that even if you did need company, you would be in here watching the tube and listening to that dreadful music."

He shifted his stare, ignoring her.

"But your situation is not so unique. Most people in your position would do the same thing."

"And what do *you* know about my position?" he said. "That's asinine! How many people do you know who've lost their wife and their son in the same month? Don't talk about what you do not know!"

Helen felt her lips flatten. She suddenly wanted very much to walk over there and slap his face. Give him a dose of her own history. How dare he spout off as if he were the sole bearer of pain!

She bit her tongue and swallowed.

On the other hand, he did have a point. Not in her being clueless to loss; God knew nothing could be further from the truth. But in his assertion that few suffered so much loss in such a short time. At least in this country. In another time, in another place, such loss would not be uncommon at all. But in America today, loss was hardly in vogue.

Father, give me grace. Give me patience. Give me love for him.

"You are right. I spoke too quickly," she said. "Do you mind if I do a little cleaning in the kitchen?"

He shrugged, and she took that as a *Help yourself.* So she did. "You have any other music?" she asked, rising. "Something upbeat?"

He just *humphed.*

Helen opened the blinds and dug into the dishes, praying as she worked. He rose momentarily and put on some contemporary pop music she could not identify. She let the music play and hummed with the tunes when the choruses repeated themselves.

It took her an hour to return the kitchen to the spotless condition in which Gloria had kept it. She replaced the dishrags responsible for the mildew odor with fresh ones, wondering how long they would remain clean. A day at most.

Helen returned to the living room, thinking she should say what she had come to say and leave. He was obviously not in the mood to receive any comfort. Certainly not from her.

She glanced at the ceiling and imagined the cosmic bleachers, crowded with eager onlookers, unrestrained by time. She stood behind the couch and studied the man like one of those heavenly creatures might study him. He sat dejected. No, not dejected. Dejected would be characterized by a pouting frown, perhaps. Not this vision of death sagging on the chair before her. He looked suicidal, devastated, unraveled like a hemp rope chewed by a dog.

"I cleaned the kitchen," she said. "You can at least move around in there without knocking things over now."

He looked at her, and his Adam's apple bobbed. Maybe her voice reminded him of Gloria—she hadn't considered that.

"Anyway. Is there anything else I can do for you while I'm here?"

Kent shook his head, barely.

She started then. "You know, Kent, you remind me of someone I know who lost his son. Much like you did, actually."

He ignored her.

She considered leaving without finishing. *Are you sure, Father? Perhaps it is too soon. The poor soul looks like a worm near death.*

God did not respond. She hadn't really expected him to.

"He was crazy about that boy, you know. They were inseparable, did everything together. But the boy was not so—what shall I say—becoming. Not the best looking. Of course, it meant nothing at all to his father." She dismissed the thought with a wave. "Nothing at all. But others began to ridicule him. Then not just ridicule, but flatly reject. They grew to hate him. And the more they hated him, the more his father loved him, if that was possible."

Helen smiled sweetly. Kent looked at her with mild interest now. She continued.

"The boy was murdered by some of his own peers. It about killed the father. Reminds me of you. Anyway, they caught the one who killed his son. Caught him red-handed with the weapon in his hand. He was homeless and uncaring—headed for a life behind bars. But the father did not press charges. Said one life had been taken already. His son's. Instead, he offered love for the one who'd killed his son."

She looked at Kent's eyes for a sign of recognition. They stared into her own, blank. "The unexpected affection nearly broke the young killer's heart. He went to the father and begged his forgiveness. And do you know what the father did?"

Kent did not respond.

"The father loved the killer as his own son. Adopted him." She paused. "Can you believe that?"

Kent's lip lifted in a snarl. "I'd kill the kid." He took a swig from that drink of his.

"Actually, the father had already lost one son. To crucifixion. He wasn't about to let another be crucified."

He sat there like a lump on a log, his eyes half closed and his lower lip sagging. If he understood the meaning behind her words, he did not show it.

"God the Father, God the Son. You know how that feels, don't you? And yet you have murdered him in your own heart. Murdered the son. In fact, the last time I was in here, there was a picture of you above the fireplace." She motioned to the whitewashed wall where the picture had hung. "You were the one holding the hammer and nails. Looks like you got tired of looking at yourself."

She grinned.

"Anyway. Now he wants to adopt you. He loves you. More than you could ever know. And he knows how this all feels. He's been here. Does that make sense to you?"

Kent still did not respond. He blinked and closed his mouth, but she wasn't about to start interpreting his gestures. She simply wanted to plant this seed and leave.

For a moment she thought that he might actually be feeling sorrow. But then she saw his jaw muscles knot up, and she knew better.

"Think about it, Kent. Open your heart." Helen turned from him and walked toward the door, wondering if that was it.

It was.

"Good-bye, Kent," she said, and walked out the door.

She suddenly felt exhilarated. She realized that her heart was pounding simply from the excitement of this message she had delivered.

Her Pinto sat on the driveway, dumb and yellow. She withdrew her keys and approached the car door. But she didn't want to drive.

She wanted to walk. Really walk. An absurd notion—she had been on her feet enough already, and her knees were sore.

The notion stopped her three feet from the car, jingling the keys in her hands. She could not walk, of course. Helen glanced back to the front door. It remained closed. The sky above hung blue in its arches. A beautiful day for a walk.

She wanted to walk.

Helen turned to her left and walked to the street. She would walk. Just to the end of the block. Granted, her knees were not what they once were, but they would hold her that far if she walked slowly. She hummed to herself and eased down the sidewalk.

⁓⁓

Kent saw the door swing shut, and its slam rang like a gong in his mind. He did not move except to swivel his head from the entry. But his eyes stayed wide open, and his fingers were trembling.

Desperation swept in like a thick wave, and on its face rose a wall of sorrow that took his breath away. His throat tightened to an impossible ache, and he grunted to release the tension in the muscles. The wave engulfed him, refusing to sweep by alone, carrying him in its folds.

Then Kent's shoulders began to shake, and the sobs came hard. The ache worked on his chest like a vise, and he was suddenly unsure if it was sorrow or desire now squeezing the breath out of him.

Spencer was right.

Oh, God! Spencer was right!

The admission erupted from his mind, and Kent felt his mouth yawning in a breathless cry. The words came out audibly, in a strained croak.

"Oh, God!" He clenched his eyes. Had to—they were burning. "Oh, God!"

The words brought a wash of comfort, like a soothing anesthetic to his heart. He said it again. "Oh, God."

Kent sat in the wave for a long time, strangely relishing each moment of its respite, aching for more and more. Losing himself there, in the deepest sorrow, and in the balm of comfort.

He recalled a scene that played on the walls of his mind like an old, eight-millimeter film. It was Gloria and Spencer, dancing in the living room, late one evening. They held hands and twirled in circles and sang about streets that were golden. His camera eye zoomed to their faces. They gazed at each other in rapture. He had discarded the moment with a chuckle then, but now it came like the sugar of life. And he knew that somewhere in that exchange lay the purpose of living.

The memory brought a new flood of tears.

When Kent finally stood and looked about the living room, it was dusk. Spent, he trudged into the kitchen and opened the refrigerator without bothering to turn on the lights. He pulled out a day-old pizza, slid onto a barstool, and nibbled on the soggy crust for a few minutes.

A mirror glared at him from the shadowed wall. It showed a man with sagging cheeks and red eyes, his hair disheveled, wearing the face of death. He stopped his chewing and stared, wondering if that could be him. But he knew immediately that it was. There was the new Kent—a broken, discarded fool.

He turned his back to the mirror and ate part of the cold pizza before tossing it and retiring before the television. Kent fell asleep two hours later to the monotones of some Spanish soccer commentator.

The alarm clock's green analog numbers read 11 A.M. when his eyes flickered open the following morning. By noon he had managed a shower and clean clothes. He had also managed a conclusion.

It was time to move on.

Only six days had passed since Spencer's death. Four weeks to the day since Gloria's passing. Their deaths had left him with no one. But that was just it— there was no one left to mourn with. Except Helen. And Helen was from another planet. That left only him, and he could not live with himself. Not just himself.

He would have to find death quickly, or go off and find some life.

Killing himself had a certain appeal—a kind of final justice to the madness. He had mulled over the idea for long hours in recent days. If he did kill himself, it would be with an overdose of some intoxicating drug; he'd already concluded that after discarding a hundred other options. Might as well go out flying high.

On the other hand, something else was brewing in his head, something set off by Helen's words. This God business. The memory lingered like a fog in his mind, present but muddled. The emotions had nearly destroyed him. A sort of high he could not remember having felt.

He remembered thinking, just before falling asleep the night before, that it might have been his love for Spencer that triggered the emotions. Yes, that would be it. Because he was desperate for his son. Would give anything—everything— to give him life. How incredible that one little life could mean so much. Six billion people crawling over the globe, and in the end, the death of one ten-year-old boy caused him to ache so badly.

Kent left the house, squinting in the bright sunlight.

It was time to move on.

Yes, that was the conclusion.

But it was really no conclusion at all, was it? Move on to *what?* Working at the bank carried as much appeal as a barefooted trek across the Sahara. He hadn't had contact with any of his coworkers for a week now. How could he possibly face Borst? Or worse, fat-boy Bentley? They no doubt carried on, soaking in acclamations of a superb job, reaping his rewards while he sat dead in the water, surrounded by two floating bodies. If he had even a single violent bone in his body he'd take that nine-millimeter pistol his uncle had given him for his thirtieth birthday and walk on down to that bank. Play postal worker for a day. Deliver some good will.

He could sue, of course—fire a few legal projectiles their way. But the thought of suing with Dennis Warren's assistance now brought a sickness to his gut. For one thing, Dennis had gone off to lala land that last day. His attorney's words still rumbled through his mind: *I don't think you are ready. I don't think you are ready at all, my fine friend. Perhaps this afternoon you will be ready.*

This afternoon? Then Spencer had died.

No, Dennis was out of the question, Kent concluded. If he did sue the bank, it would be with another attorney.

That left finding another job, a thought that sickened him even more than the notion of suing. But at least he would be able to continue paying the bills. A lawsuit might very well suck him dry.

Either way, he should probably talk to Helen again. Go back for some of the comfort she seemed to have a handle on. God. Maybe Spencer was right after all. Kent felt a knot rise to his throat, and he cursed under his breath. He wasn't sure he could stomach too many more of these emotional surges.

The day passed in a haze, divided between the park and the house, but at least Kent was thinking again. It was a start. Yes, it was time to move on.

14

The vision came to Kent that night in the early morning hours, like a shaft of black through the shadows of his mind.

Or maybe it wasn't a vision. Maybe he was actually there.

He stood in the alley behind the bank. Steam rose from the grate; the dumpster lay tipped on its side, reeking foul, and Kent was watching that vagrant slurping at his bagged bottle. Only now he wasn't tipping the bag back. He was sticking a long, pink tongue down the bottle's neck and using it like a straw. It was the kind of thing you might expect in a dream. So yes, it must have been a vision. A dream.

The vagrant no longer wore faded clothes but a black tuxedo with shiny shoes and a pressed shirt. Downright respectable. Except for the straggly hairs growing off his chin and neck. It appeared as though the man was attempting to cover up a dozen red warts, but the long strands of hair only emphasized them, and that certainly was not respectable. That and the tongue trick.

The vagrant-turned-respectable-citizen was rambling on about how lucky Kent was with his fancy car and big-time job. Kent interrupted the prattling with the most obvious of points.

"I'm no better off than you, old man."

"Old man?" The vagrant licked his lips wet with that long pink tongue. "You think I'm old? How old do I look to you, fella?"

"It's just an expression."

"Well, you are right. I am old. Quite old, actually. And I have learned a few things in my time." He grinned and snaked his tongue into the bottle again without removing his eyes from Kent.

Kent furrowed his brow. "How do you do that?" he asked.

The tongue pulled out quickly. "Do what?"

"Make your tongue do that?"

The vagrant chuckled and fingered one of the warts under his chin. "It's one of the things I've learned over the years, boy. Anybody can do it. You just have to stretch your tongue for a long time. See?" He did it again, and Kent shuddered.

The man pulled his tongue back into his mouth and spoke again. "You ever see those tribal people who stretch their necks a foot high? It's like that. You just stretch things."

A chill seemed to have descended into the alley. The white steam from the grate ran along the ground, and Kent was thinking he should get on in to work. Finish up some programming.

But that was just it. He didn't want to walk through that door. In fact, now that he thought about it, something very bad had happened in there. He just couldn't quite remember what.

"So what's keeping you, boy?" The man peered at the door. "Go on in. Take your millions."

"Huh? That's what you think?" Kent replied. "You think people like me make millions slaving away for some huge bank? Not even close, old man."

The grin left the vagrant's face, and his lips twitched. "You think I am stupid? You call me old man, and yet you talk as though I know nothing? You are a blathering idiot!"

Kent stepped back, surprised by the sudden show of anger. "Relax, man. I don't remember calling you a fool."

"Might as well have, you imbecile!"

"Look, I really didn't mean to offend you. I'm no better off than you, anyway. There's no need to be offended here."

"And if you think you're no better off than me, then you're really a fool. Furthermore, the fact that you're not yet even thinking of doing what I would do in your place proves you are a moronic idiot!"

Kent furrowed his brows, taken aback by the vagrant's audacity.

"Look. I don't know what you think you would do, but people like me just don't make that kind of money."

"People *like* you? Or *you?* How much have *you* made?"

"Well that's really none of your . . ."

"Just tell me, you fool," the man said. "How much money have you rightfully made in that cement box over there?"

"How much . . . rightfully?"

"Of course. How much?"

Kent paused, thinking about that word. *Rightfully.* Rightfully he had made the bonuses due from AFPS. Millions. But that hardly counted as income. And it was certainly no business of this weirdo, anyway.

A sly grin lifted the vagrant's lips. He tilted his head slightly and narrowed his eyes. "Come on, Kent. It's really not that difficult, is it?"

Kent blinked at the man. "How do you know my name?"

"Oh, I know things. I've been around, like I said. I'm not the fool you might think. I say you've made millions, boy. And I say you take your millions."

"Millions? It's not like I can just waltz into the vault and take a few million."

"No. But you have a key, now, don't you?"

"A key? Don't be stupid, man. A key to this door has nothing to do with the vault. Besides, you obviously know nothing about security. You don't just walk into a bank and steal a penny, much less a million."

"Stop calling me stupid, you spineless idiot! Stop it, stop it, stop it!"

Kent's heart slammed in his chest.

The vagrant barely moved now. He glared at Kent, and his voice growled low. "Not that key, you fool. The key in your head. The backdoor to that software. You have the only backdoor code. They don't even know it exists."

The alley grew still. Deadly still. It occurred to Kent that he had stopped breathing.

"I won't tell. I promise," the man said through his grin. He opened his mouth wide and began to cackle. The sound of his laughter bounced off the tall brick walls.

Kent jumped back, stunned.

That mouth widened, showing a black hole at the back of the vagrant's throat. His tongue snaked like a long road leading into the darkness. It grew like a vortex and swallowed the alley in echoing chuckles.

Kent bolted upright.

Silence crashed in on him. Darkness met his wide eyes. Wet sheets stuck to his stomach. His chest thumped like an Indian war drum.

He sat in bed, wide awake, paralyzed by the thought that had awakened him so rudely. The images of the vagrant quickly dwindled to oblivion, overshadowed by the singular concept he'd dropped in Kent's mind. Not a soul had known of the backdoor he'd programmed into AFPS that last week. He'd meant to tell Borst in Miami, complete documentation on it as soon as they returned. That was before.

ROOSTER.

That was the code he'd temporarily assigned to the security entry. With it, any authorized banking official could enter the system through an untraceable handle, tackle any security issue, and leave without affecting normal operations. Of course, not just any banking official would be authorized. Only one or two, perhaps. The president and vice president, who would have to guard the code in the strictest confidence. Under lock and key.

Kent swung his legs from the bed and stared into darkness. Outlines of the room's furniture began to take vague shape. The realization of ROOSTER's significance ballooned in his mind like a mushroom cloud. If the bank had not discovered the backdoor, then it would still be open to anyone with the code.

And he had the code. The vagrant's key.

ROOSTER.

What could an operator accomplish with ROOSTER? Anything. Anything at all with the right skills. Software engineering skills. The kind of skills that he himself possessed with perhaps greater mastery than anyone he knew. Certainly within the context of AFPS. He'd *written* the code, for heaven's sake!

Kent pushed himself from the bed, quaking. He glanced at the clock: 2 A.M. The bank would be deserted, of course. He had to know if they'd found ROOSTER during the program's initial implementation. Knowing Borst, they had not.

He went for the closet and stopped at the door. What was he thinking? He couldn't go down there now. The alarm company would have a record of his entry at two in the morning. How would that look? No. Out of the question.

Kent turned for the bathroom. He had to think this through. *Slow down, boy.* Halfway to the bathroom he spun back to the bedroom. He didn't need to use the bathroom. *Get a grip, man.*

On the bed again he began to think clearly for the first time. The fact of the matter was that if they had overlooked ROOSTER, he could enter AFPS and create a link with any bank on the federal reserve system. Of course, what he could do once he was there was another matter altogether.

He couldn't very well take anything. For starters, it was a federal crime. People grew old in prison for white-collar crime. And he was no criminal. Not to mention the simple fact that banks did not just let money walk without tracing it.

Each dollar was accounted for. Accounts were balanced, transactions verified.

Kent crossed his legs on the bed and hugged a pillow. On the other hand, in implementing AFPS prematurely, without his help, Borst not only had inadvertently opened his flank but he had left the barn door open on a billion accounts throughout the world. Kent felt a chill run through his veins. Niponbank's accounts alone numbered nearly one hundred million worldwide. Personal accounts, business accounts, federal accounts—and they were all there, accessible through ROOSTER.

He could waltz right into Borst's personal account if he so desired. Leave nasty messages on his bank statements. Scare the fool right into the arms of God. Ha! Kent smiled. A thin sheen of sweat covered his upper lip, and he drew an arm over his mouth.

He imagined Bentley's eyes when he opened a statement and, instead of that hundred-thousand-dollar bonus, found a notice of an overdraft. He would stiffen like a board. Maybe go purple and keel over dead.

Kent blinked and shook the thoughts from his head. Absurd. The whole notion was absurd.

Then again, everything in his life had become absurd. He had lost his resolve to live. Why not go for a piece of glory, pull off the crime of the century, steal a wad from the bank that had screwed him? It might give him a reason to live again. He'd lost a lot in the recent past. Taking a little back had a ring of justice.

Of course, doing it without getting caught would be nearly impossible. *Nearly* impossible. But it *could* be done—given enough planning. *Imagine!*

Kent did that. He imagined. Till dawn brought shape and color to his surroundings he imagined, wide eyed, with his legs bunched and a pillow under his chin. Sleep was out of the question. Because the more he thought about it, the more he realized that if ROOSTER still lived, he could be a wealthy man. Filthy rich. Start a new life. Make some of his own justice. Risk life in prison, to be sure, but life nonetheless. The alternative of plodding along the corporate trail again struck him more like a slow death. And he'd had enough of death.

It was Wednesday. Today he would go to the bank and casually find out if the ROOSTER still lived. If it did . . .

A chill ran right through Kent's bones. It was indeed time to move on. And what of Helen's little guilt trip? This God business? It would have to wait, of course. If the mighty red ROOSTER lived, he had himself a banquet to plan.

15

Kent drove past the bank at eight-thirty, parked on a side street, and walked briskly toward the back alley. It occurred to him that the vagrant might be there, hiding in the dim light. The thought spiked his pulse. He pulled up at the entrance and peered around the brick wall, blinking against an image of a long pink tongue poking through the neck of a bottle. But the alley appeared empty except for that dumpster, which had been emptied. Kent made straight for the rear door and slipped into the bank. He breathed once deeply, checked his tie, and strode for the Information Systems suite.

Betty's eyes popped when he opened the door and stepped in. He smiled and dipped his head, purposefully courteous. "Morning, Betty."

Her mouth opened, but no sound come out.

"What's the matter? Cat got your tongue? Borst in?"

She nodded. "Good morning. Yes."

"Good morning," he repeated and walked for Borst's office.

He tapped on the door and stepped in at the sound of a muffled call. Borst sat behind his desk, all dressed up in a new dark brown suit. The toupee had made a comeback, covering his bald spot with slick black hair. Jet black. Bright red suspenders rounded out the look.

Borst's eyes bulged out, and he bolted from his seat as though an electrode had juiced him there. The suspenders pulled his slacks snug into his crotch when he straightened. He looked like a clown.

"Good morning, Borst." This would have to go smoothly. Easy now. Step by step. "I'm back. I assume that I do still work here, right?"

The man blinked and licked pink lips. "Good night, Kent! You scared me. I had no idea you planned on coming in this morning. We didn't hear from you." His lips twitched to a grin. "Yes. Sure you still work here. Have a seat. How are you?"

"Actually, I'd like ten minutes to get situated. That okay?"

"Sure. I leave for Phoenix at noon." The man's eyebrows lifted. "You here to stay, then?"

Kent turned from the door. "Give me a few minutes. We'll talk then." He pulled the door closed and saw that Borst was already reaching for the phone. Reporting in to Bossman, no doubt. Kent's heart pounded.

Did they know?

Of course not. How could they know of a dream? He had done nothing yet.

Kent nodded at an oogle-eyed Betty and slid into his office. He locked the door. The exotic yellow fish still grazed placidly on his screen. His fingers trembled badly when he lowered them to the keyboard, and he squeezed them into fists.

Okay, settle down, man. All you're doing is checking on a piece of your own code. Nothing wrong with that.

The plan was simple. If ROOSTER remained intact, he would go in there and suck up to Borst. Buy himself some time to think this out. If they had closed ROOSTER down, he would resign.

A touch on the mouse made the fish wink off. A dozen icons hung suspended against a deep blue underwater oceanscape. Kent drew the mouse over the red-and-blue AFPS icon to an explorer icon. Entry into the system would be tracked—at least any entry through the doors of which they were aware. And if he was lucky they had not expanded their security measures to cut off his terminal completely.

His heart thumping loudly in the room's silence, Kent flew through the menus to a hidden folder requiring his own password for entry. He punched it in. The contents sprang to life. He scrolled down and scanned for the file in which he'd placed ROOSTER. The list ran by too quickly, and he repeated the scan, reading more methodically. *Come on, baby. You have to be here.*

And then it *was* there, throbbing in his vision: MISC. He dragged the mouse over the name and double-clicked.

The screen snapped to black. Kent caught his breath, aware that his legs trembled slightly now. He was on his toes under the desk, and he lowered his heels to settle the quaking. *Come on, baby.*

The monitor flashed white, riddled with black letters and symbols. Code. Kent exhaled loudly. ROOSTER's code! A living, viable, untraceable hook into the funds processing system, right here at his fingertips.

He stared at it without moving for a minute, awash with relief that he'd had the foresight to add this final whistle to the package. It wasn't pretty. No colors or boxes yet. Just raw code. But now another question: Would it still link to the system? Kent suddenly felt the heat of panic wash down his back. What if they had found it and left the code but removed its hook into the system?

He hit a key and entered a single word: RUN. A new line immediately appeared, asking for a password. He entered the name. R-O-O-S-T-E-R.

The screen darkened for a second and then popped up with the familiar blue menu he'd worked from for so many years. Kent blinked at the screen. He was in AFPS! Beyond security. From here he could do what he wished without the knowledge of another living soul.

In the right hands, it was a security measure in itself, designed to deal with sabotage and viruses. In the wrong hands it was a way into the bank's vaults. Or worse, a way into every account tied to the bank.

Kent backed out quickly, handling the mouse with a sweating palm. He watched the menus retrace their steps to the deep blue ocean scene, then he lowered his hands to his lap. Even now, short of dusting for prints, Borst could not discover that anyone had even touched this computer, much less peeked up the bank's skirt.

He breathed deeply and stood. It was insane. These crazy thoughts of stealing money would be the end of him. Preposterous. They would bury him. He thought suddenly of Spencer and lifted a hand to his brow. It was all madness.

Either way, he now had his answer.

A fist pounded on the door, and Kent bolted a full foot off the carpet. He spun to the computer and scanned the keyboard. No, there was no trace. Relax. *Relax, relax!*

"Who is it?" he called.

"Cliff."

Cliff. Better than Borst. Kent let him in. "Sorry, I didn't know it was locked," he lied.

"What are you doing in here, Kent?" The new recruit smiled. "Anything I should know about?" He nudged Kent as if they shared an understanding.

"Yeah, right." Kent willed his heart to settle. He sat and crossed his legs. "So what can I do for you?"

"Nothing. Betty just told me you were back. I figured you needed a welcome." The grin straightened. "I heard what happened. You know . . . to your son. I can hardly imagine. Are you okay?"

"Actually, I'm not sure what okay means anymore, but I'm ready to get back to work, if that's what you mean."

"I'm sure it'll take some time. Maybe getting your mind on work is the best way to pass it. And speaking of work, I've dug pretty deep since you were last here." He smiled again. "You'd be proud of me. I've found things I'm sure only you know about."

A chill broke over Kent's crown at the words. *ROOSTER?* "Yeah? Like what?"

"Like links to the Chinese banking codes that are still inactive. Now, that's what I call foresight, man."

"Well, it *is* a global system, Cliff. So what else have you dug up with that long snout of yours?"

"A few anecdotal notes buried in the code—things like that. *Borst has the brain of sausage.*" He grinned wide.

"Good night, you found *that?* That *was* buried. I should probably pull it out."

"No, leave it in. He'll never find it."

They nodded, smiling.

"Anything else?" Kent asked.

"That's it so far. Well, it's good to have you back." Cliff stood and walked to the door. "After you get settled I have some code to run by you. You up for that?"

"Sure."

The younger man slapped the wall and disappeared. Now, that was close. Or was it? Actually, the chances of Cliff or anybody finding ROOSTER would be akin to picking a particular grain of sand from a bucket full of the stuff. Either way, he'd have to keep an eye on the man.

Kent settled his nerves with a few long pulls of air and walked into Borst's office.

"Have a seat, Kent."

Kent sat.

"We weren't sure we'd see you again."

Yeah, I'll bet. You and your pal Bentley both. "Well to be honest, I wasn't so sure myself. So, how were things in my absence?" he asked, thinking the question stupid but unable to think of a better way to begin this sucking-up thing to which he had now committed himself.

"Fine, Kent. Just fine. Boy, you've been through hell, huh?"

Kent nodded. "Life can deal some pretty nasty blows." He suddenly despised being here. He should stand now and walk away from this foolishness.

"But I'm back. I need to work, Markus." *That's right, get personal with him. Appeal to his need for friendship.* "I need it bad. All I really have left is my career. I miss work here. Can you understand that?" His voice came soft and sensitive.

"Yes. Makes sense." The man had taken the bait. He paused and shifted his eyes. "Look, Kent. I'm sorry about the misunderstanding about AFPS. I just . . ."

"No. You don't need to say anything. These things happen. And I apologize for blowing up the way I did. It was totally uncalled-for." *Gag. If you only knew, you slimeball.*

Borst nodded, delighted behind that controlled smile, no doubt. "Well, we all got a bit off line, I think. Perhaps it's best we just put the incident behind us."

Kent crossed his legs. The sweat was drying cold on his neck. "You're right. Water under the bridge. So how is AFPS these days?"

Markus brightened. "In a word? Incredible. We put together a doozie, Kent. They're already saying that it will save a third of the manpower the old system used. Price has estimated the overall savings to the bank at over twenty million annually."

Price? First-name basis now. Partners in crime. Probably had dinner together every night. "Great. That's great. No bugs?"

"Sure. Plenty. But they're minor. Actually, you'd probably be best suited to start working on them." The Information Systems supervisor had honestly fooled himself into full ownership of the system, Kent thought.

The man shifted the conversation back to what was apparently his favorite topic these days: money. "Hey, I still haven't allocated that twenty-five-thousand-dollar bonus," he said with a glint in his eyes. "At least not all of it. I'm giving Betty, Todd, and Mary five thousand each. But that leaves ten thousand. You need any spare change these days, Kent?" He jerked his brows high a few times. "Hmm?"

Kent nearly lost the charade then. Came within a gnat's whisker of leaping over the cherrywood desk and strangling his boss. For a few seconds he could not respond. The other *three?* Betty was getting a five-thousand-dollar spiff too? But that was just fine, of course, because he, Kent Anthony, the creator of said program, was to get double that. Yes sir! A whopping ten grand. And Borst? What would bug-eyed Borst's cut be? Oh, well, Borst was the main man. He would get 10 percent of the savings for ten years. A mere fifteen, twenty million. Chump change.

Sounded like a good, round number. Twenty million.

"Sure," Kent said. "Who couldn't use ten thousand dollars? I could cut my Lexus payment in half." That last comment slipped out before he could reign it back. He hoped Borst did not catch his cynicism.

"Good. It's yours. I'll talk to Price this afternoon."

"I thought you were going to Phoenix today."

"Yes. We are. I'll talk to Price on the plane."

It was an unstoppable freight train with those two. Kent swallowed his anger. "Thank you." He stood. "Well, I guess I should get started. I want to talk to the others—you know, make sure there are no misunderstandings."

"Good. Splendid idea. It's good to have you back."

Kent turned at the door. "One more thing, Markus. I kind of blew it with Bentley the other day. You wouldn't mind putting in a word for me, would you? It was just a bad week." He swallowed deliberately and was surprised at the sudden emotion that accompanied it. They said the grief would last a year, gradually easing. Evidently he was still in the stage where it could be set off with a mere swallow.

"Sure, Kent. Consider it done. And don't worry. He and I are rather tight these days."

Yes, I'll bet you are, Kent thought. He left before the revulsion had him doing something silly, like throwing up on the man's carpet.

✿✿✿

Pastor Bill Madison parked his gray Chevy on the street and strode up to Helen's door. She had sounded different on the phone. Almost excited. At least peachy. Like someone who had just been handed some very good news. Or like someone who had flipped their lid.

Given the last few weeks' events, he feared the latter. But then this was Helen, here. With Helen you could never know. The New Testament characterized followers of Christ as peculiar. Well, Helen was just that. One of very few he would consider peculiar in their faith. Which was in itself strange when he got right down and thought about it. Perhaps they should all be rather unusual; Christ certainly was.

She had asked him to pray, and he had indeed prayed. But not simply because of her request. Something was happening here. He might not have the spiritual eyes that Helen claimed to possess, but he could sense things. Discernment, some called it. A spiritual gift. The ability to look at a situation and sense its spiritual origins. Like, *This face sends chills up my spine; it must be evil.* Not that he always operated in the most accurate mode of discernment. He had once felt chills peck at his heart, looking at a strange, alien-looking face on the television screen. To him it looked downright demonic. Then his son had informed him that it was a closeup of a friendly little creature found in the Amazon. One of God's creatures.

That had confused him a little. But this thing with Helen—it was more than just a weird face on the boob tube. It was an aura that followed her around in much the same way he imagined an aura might have followed Elisha or Elijah around.

He rang the doorbell. The door swung in immediately, as if Helen had awaited his arrival with her hand on the knob.

"Come in, Pastor." She wore a yellow dress, tube socks, and running shoes, a ridiculous sight for one who had trouble walking even around the house.

"Thank you, Helen." Bill stepped in and closed the door, glancing at her legs. The musty scent of roses hung in the air. The old lady's perfume was everywhere. She left him for the living room, smiling.

"Is everything all right?" he asked, following.

She did not respond directly but walked across the carpet humming her anthem, "Jesus, Lover of My Soul." She had told him once that the song summed it all up. It made death worthwhile. Bill stopped behind her large, green easy chair, fixated on the sight of Helen walking. She was seemingly oblivious to him.

"Are you okay?"

"Shhhh." She hushed him and lifted both hands, still pacing back and forth. Her eyes rested closed. "You hear that, Bill?"

Bill cocked his head and listened, but he heard nothing. Except her faint humming. "Hear what?"

"The laughter. Do you hear that laughter?"

He tried to hear laughter, but he heard only her soprano hum. *Let me to Thy bosom fly . . .* And he smelled roses.

"You might have to open your heart a little, but it's there, Pastor—very faint, like the breeze blowing through trees."

He tried again, closing his eyes this time, feeling a little foolish. If one of the deacons knew he was over at Helen Crane's house listening for laughter with her, they might very well begin the search for a new shepherd. After hearing nothing but Helen for a few moments, he gave up and looked at her.

Helen suddenly stopped her pacing and opened her eyes. She giggled and lowered her hands. "It's okay, Pastor. I didn't really expect you to hear anything. It's like that around here. Some days it's silent. And then some days he opens up my ears to the laughter and I want to walk around the house kissing things. Just kissing everything. Like today. Would you like some tea?"

"Yes, that would be nice."

She shuffled toward the kitchen. She had her socks pulled up to midcalf. A red Reebok logo splashed across the heel of her shoes. Bill swallowed and eased around the chair. She might very well have lost it, he thought. He sat on the green chair.

Helen emerged from the kitchen holding two glasses of tea. "So, you're thinking that my elevator is no longer climbing to the top floor, am I right?" She smiled.

"Actually, I had given it some thought." He grinned and chuckled once. "But these days, it's hard to differentiate between strangeness and craziness." He lost the grin. "They thought Jesus was crazy."

"Yes, I know." She handed him the drink and sat. "And we would think the same today."

"Tell me," Bill said, "did you see Spencer's death in all of this?"

"Yes."

"When?"

"The night after we last talked, a week or so ago. When we talked, I knew there would be more skulls in the dungeon. I could feel it in my spine. But I never really expected it to be Spencer's skull lying there on the ground. It nearly killed me, you know."

"So this is really happening, then." He said it calmly, but he found himself trembling with the thought. "This whole thing is really happening. I mean . . . orchestrated."

"You have put two people in the dirt. You should know. Looked real enough to me."

"Fine, I'll grant you that. It's just hard to swallow this business about you knowing about their deaths beforehand. Maybe if I could see into the heavens like you can, it would be easier."

"It's not everybody's place to see things so clearly, Pastor. We all have our place. If the whole world saw things clearly our churches would be flooded. The nation would flock to the cross en masse. What faith would that require? We might as well be puppets."

"Yes, well, I'm not so sure having full churches would be so bad."

"And I'm not so sure the deaths of my daughter and grandson were so necessary. But when I hear their laughter, when I'm allowed to peek to the other side, it all makes sense. That's when I want to walk around and start kissing things."

He smiled at her expression. In many ways they were very similar, he and Helen. "So then . . ." He paused, collecting his thoughts.

"Yes?"

"In my office last week you told me you'd had a vision in which you heard the sound of running feet in a dungeon. To whom do the running feet in your dungeon belong?" He glanced at her feet, clad in those white Reeboks. "You?"

She laughed. "No." She suddenly tilted her head, thinking. "At least I had not considered it. But no, I don't think so. I think the running feet belong to Kent."

"Kent?"

"He's the player in this game. I mean, we're all players, but he is the runner."

"Kent's the runner. And where is Kent running?"

"Kent is running from God."

"This is all about Kent?"

She nodded. "And about you and me and Gloria and Spencer. Who knows? This might very well be about the whole world. I don't know everything. Sometimes I know nothing. That's why I called you over today. Today I know some things."

"I see." He looked at her feet absently. "And why are you wearing running shoes, Helen? You walking more these days?"

"With my knees?" She wiggled her feet on the carpet. "No, they just feel good. I've got this itching to be young again, I guess." She stared out the window behind Bill. "It seems to ease the pain in my heart, you know."

Helen sipped quietly at the glass, and then set it down. "I've been called to intercede for Kent, Pastor."

He did not respond. She was an intercessor. It made sense.

"Intercede without ceasing. Eight hours a day."

"You spend eight hours a day praying for Kent?"

"Yes. And I will do so until it is over."

"Until *what* is over, Helen?"

She looked at him directly. "Until this game is over."

He studied her, looking for any sign of insincerity. He could see none. "So now it's a game? I'm not sure God plays games."

She shrugged. "Choose your own words, then. I have been called to pray until it is over."

Bill shook his head with disbelief. "This is unbelievable. I feel like we've been transported back to some Old Testament story."

"You think? This is nothing. You should read Revelation. Things get really strange later."

The sense of her words struck at him. He'd never thought of history in those terms. There had always been biblical history, the time of burning bushes and talking donkeys and tongues of fire. And there was the present—the time of normalcy. What if Helen's peculiar view behind the scenes was really just an unusual peek at the way things really were? And what if he was being allowed to peek into this extraordinary "normalcy" for a change?

They sat and talked for a long while after that. But Helen did not manage to shed any more light on his questions. He concluded it was because she herself knew little more. She was seeing through a glass dimly. But she was indeed seeing.

And if she was right, this drama of hers—this game—It was indeed all just beginning.

16

Lacy Cartwright leaned back in the lounge chair on her balcony, drinking coffee, enjoying the cool morning breeze. It was ten o'clock. Having a day off midweek had its advantages, she thought, and one of them was the quiet, out here under a bright blue Boulder sky while everyone else worked. She glanced over her body, thankful for the warmth of sun on her skin. Just last week Jeff Duncan had called her petite. Heavens! She was thin, maybe, and not an inch over five-three, but petite? Her coworker at the bank had said it with a glint in his eye, and she had suspected then that the man had a crush on her. But it had been under two years since her husband's death. She was not ready to engage a man.

The breeze feathered her face, and she lifted a hand to sweep the blonde strands behind her ear. Her hair rested on her shoulders in lazy curls, framing hazel eyes that smiled. A thin sheen of suntan oil glistened on her pale belly between a white halter top and jean shorts. Some women seemed to relish baking in the sun—lived for it even. Goodness! A picture of a hot dog sizzling on a grill popped into her mind, and she let it hang there for a moment. Its red skin suddenly split, and the image fizzled.

Lacy turned her head and studied the distant clouds looming black toward the southeast. Denver had had its share of weather lately, and it appeared the area was in for a little more. Which was another reason she liked it up here in Boulder more than in the big city. In Denver, if you weren't dealing with weather, you were dealing with smog. Or at the very least, traffic, which was worse than either. She ought to know—she'd spent most of her life down there.

But not anymore. After John's death two years earlier she had upped and moved here. Started a new career as a teller and busied herself with the monumental task of ridding her chest of its ache. She'd done it all well, she thought. Now she could get on with the more substantive issues of starting over. Like lying out in the sun, waiting for the UV rays to split her skin like that hot dog. Goodness!

A high-pitched squeal jerked her mind from its reflections. She spun toward the sliding glass door and realized the awful sound was coming from her condo. As if a pig had gotten its snout caught in a door and was protesting. But of course there were no pigs in there, squealing or not. There was, however, a washing machine, and if she wasn't mistaken, the sound was actually coming from the laundry room, where she had started a load of whites fifteen minutes ago.

The sound suddenly jumped an octave and wailed like a siren. Lacy scrambled from the lounger and ran for the laundry room. It would be just her luck that old Mrs. Potters next door was jabbing at the oversized nine-one-one numbers on her trusty pink telephone at this very moment.

Lacy saw the soapy water before she reached the door, and her pulse spiked, midstride. Not that she'd never seen soapy water before—saw it all the time, but never bubbling under a door like some kind of monster foaming at its mouth. She felt the wet seep between her toes through the navy carpet a good five feet from the door. She let out a yelp and tiptoed to the door. This was not good.

The door swung in over an inch of gray water. The washing machine rocked madly, squealing, and Lacy dove for the control knob. Her palm smashed it in, which under normal conditions would have killed the thing right then. But evidently things were no longer normal in this room, because the boxy old machine just kept rocking and wailing.

The plug! She had to pull the plug. One of those big fat plugs behind the contraption. Water bubbled over the top of the washer and ran down to the floor in streams. Frantic now, Lacy flopped belly-down on the shaking appliance and dove for the back. The plug stuck stubbornly. She squirmed over the lid so that her feet dangled, all too aware of the water soaking her clothes. She put her full weight into the next tug. The plug came free, sending her flying backward, off the dying machine and to the floor like a fish spilled from a net.

She struggled from the floor, grateful for the ringing silence. In all the commotion her hair had attracted enough water to leave it dripping. She gazed about, and her stomach knotted at the sight. A pig stuck in the door might have been better.

Before John died this would all have been different. She would simply call the precinct and have him run by to take care of things. For her it would be a quick shower and then perhaps off to lunch.

But that was before. Before the cancer had ravaged his body and sent him to the grave exactly two months before he would have made sergeant. An image of her late husband all decked out in those navy blues and shiny brass buttons drifted through her mind. He was smiling, because he had always smiled. A good man. A perfect cop. The only man she could imagine herself with. Ever.

Lacy bent over her oak dinette table half an hour later, the phone book spread yellow before her, a paper towel protecting the phone from her blackened fingers. Her attempt at messing with gears under the machine had proved futile. A lazy voice filled her ear.

"Frank," it drawled. Frank was chewing gum by the sounds of his rhythmic smacking. He'd obviously slept through the etiquette portion of his plumber-school training.

"Hi, Frank. This is Lacy Cartwright. I'm guessing you're a certified Goldtech technician, right?"

"Yes, ma'am. What can I do for you?" *Smack, smack.* She swallowed.

"Well, I have a problem out here, Frank. The water pump on my washing machine somehow got stuck open and flooded the floor. I need it repaired."

"Stuck open, huh?" A hint of amusement rang in the man's voice. "And what model number are we talking about?"

"J-28," she said, ready for the question.

"Well, you see? Now there's a problem, because J-28s don't get stuck open. J-28s use pumps operated on a normally closed solenoid, and if anything, they get stuck closed. You hear any sounds when this machine went belly up?"

"It squealed."

"It squealed, huh? I'll bet it squealed." He chuckled. "Yes, ma'am, they sure know how to squeal, them Monroe pumps." The phone went silent. Lacy was wondering where they had found Frank. Seemed to know pumps, all right. But maybe his own pump was not reaching the wellhead.

When he did not offer any further comment, she spoke. "So what do I do?"

"Well, you need a new pump, Miss Cartwright."

Another short silence. "Can you install a new pump for me?"

"Sure, I can. It's not a question of *can*, ma'am. I've been putting in new pumps for ten years." An edge had come to his voice midsentence. She lifted her eyes and caught her reflection in the dining room mirror. Her blonde hair had dried in tangles.

"The problem is, we don't have any Monroe pumps in stock today. So you see, even if I wanted to come out there, which I couldn't do for three days anyway, I couldn't do it because I don't have anything to do it with." He chuckled again.

Lacy blinked. She suddenly wasn't sure she even *wanted* Frank to fix her washing machine. "Is it hard?"

"Is what hard?"

"Do you think I could replace the pump?"

"Any idiot could replace that pump, Miss." *Evidently.* "Three bolts and a few wires, and you're in and out before you know it. I could do it with a blindfold on. In fact, I *have* done it with a blindfold on." *Good for you, Frankie.* "But, like I said, Honey. We have no pumps."

"Where else can I get a pump?"

"Nowhere. At least nowhere in Boulder. You go to the manufacturer in Denver, they might sell you one."

Denver? She gazed out the window to those ominous clouds in the southeast. It would be an hour there, another hour in traffic regardless of where it was, and an hour back. It would blow her day completely. She glanced at the clock. Eleven. On the other hand, her day was already blown. And she couldn't very well wait a week for Frankie to come out and walk around her condo with a blindfold on while he did his thing.

"Well, lady, I can't sit here all day."

Lacy started. "I'm sorry. Yes, I think I'll try Monroe. Do you have the number?"

Thirty minutes later she was in the car, headed for the freeway, with the old J-28 pump in a box beside her. Frank had been right. Once she managed to tip the washer enough to prop it up with a footstool and slide under it, removing the little beast had not been so bad. She had even closed her eyes once while loosening a bolt, wondering what possessed a man to try such a thing.

Lacy pulled onto the freeway, struck by how easily the course of her day had changed. One minute lying in attempted bliss, the next diving into soapy gray water.

Goodness.

～～～

The week had flown past, skipping across the peaks of Kent's nerves like a wind-surfer pushed by a gale-force wind. It was the wind of imagination, and it kept his eyes wide and burning. By the end of that first day Kent knew what he was going to do with a certainty that brought fire to his bones.

He was going to rob the bank blind.

Literally. He was going to take every penny he had coming. All twenty million of it. And the bank would remain as blind as a bat through it all. He sat there at his desk, exhilarated by the idea, his fingers frozen over the keyboard as his mind spun.

He tried in vain to concentrate on Cliff's questions about why he'd chosen this routine or where he could find that link. And that was a problem, because now more than ever, fitting back into the bank as Joe Smooth Employee took on significance. The way he saw it, he already had some ground to make up; some kissing up to do. Walking around the bank with a big red sign reading "Here walks the man who screamed at Bentley over employee of the month parking" would not do. He would have to concentrate on being normal again. On fitting in with the other fools who actually believed they were somehow important in this nine-to-five funny farm. There was the small matter of his having lost a wife and son, but he would just have to bite his tongue on that one, wouldn't he? Just try not to bleed all over the place. He would have to rein in his mind, control his thoughts. For the sake of ROOSTER.

But his thoughts kept sliding off to other things.

Things like what he would do with twenty million dollars. Things like how he could hide twenty million dollars. Things like how he could *steal* twenty million dollars. The details flew by, dizzying in his analytical mind. A hundred sordid details—each one spawning another hundred, it seemed.

First, he would have to decide from where to take the money. Using ROOSTER he could take it from almost anywhere. But, of course, *anywhere* would not do. It would have to come from a place where twenty million would not be quickly missed. No matter how untraceable the transaction itself might be, its net result would be nearly impossible to hide. Nearly.

Then he would have to decide where to put the money. He would never actually have the physical bills—the coin—but even a ledger balance of twenty million was enough to generate at least interest. And that kind of interest was not something he needed. If the money ever turned up missing, the FBI would be all over it like stink on sewer. He would have to find a way to lie at the bottom of that sewer.

He'd have to plan the actual execution of the theft very carefully, of course. Couldn't very well be caught downloading twenty million dollars. "What are those large balances on your screen, Kent?"

"Oh, nothing. Actually, that's my bonus from AFPS, if you must know. I'm just taking an early withdrawal."

He would also have to find a way to exit his current life. Couldn't be a millionaire and work for Borst. Had no ring of justice to him. And this whole thing was really about justice. Not just with his job but with life in general. He had climbed the ladder like a good boy for twenty years only to be dropped back on his tail in the space of thirty days. Back down to Stupid Street where the concrete was hard and the nights cold. Well, now that he had taken the time to think things through, being forced to climb that ladder again, rung by rung, made as much sense as setting up post on the local corner, bearing a sign that read "Will work for beer."

Not a chance. It took him thirty days to fall; if all went well it would take him no more than thirty to pop back on top.

The hardest part of this whole scheme might very well be the spending of the money. How could Kent Anthony, computer programmer, step into a life of wealth without raising eyebrows? He would have to divorce himself from his past somehow. Not a problem. His immediate past reeked of every imaginable offensive odor anyway. The notion of divorcing himself from that past brought a buzz to his lower spine. His past was tainted beyond redemption. He would put it as far behind him as possible. Wash it from his memory entirely. Begin a new life as a new man.

In fact, it was in this last stage of the entire plan that he would find himself again. The thought of it pushed him into the certainty that coursed through his bones like charged electrons. After weeks of empty dread, it came like a euphoric drug.

Kent looked over Cliff's shoulder at the wall—at the picture of the white yacht hanging in the shadows. An image of that same boat he'd plastered on the refrigerator at home sailed through his mind. His promise to Gloria. *I swear, Gloria, we will own that yacht one day.*

A lump rose to his throat. Not that she had cared much. She'd been too enamored with her mother's religion to appreciate the finer things. Kent had always hung on to the hope that it would change. That she would drop her silly obsessions and run after his dreams. But now she was gone.

For the first few days the thoughts whispered relentlessly, and he began to construct possible solutions to the challenges. Not too unlike debugging. A natural exercise for his mind. While Cliff busied himself with the code before them, Kent busied himself with another code altogether. This morning alone, he had apologized three times for his drifting mind. Cliff guessed it had to do with the loss of his wife and son. Kent nodded, feeling like a pimp for hiding behind the sentiment.

It was one o'clock before he shut down the Cliff machine. "Okay, Ace. I've got some errands to run over lunch. You should have enough to keep you busy for a couple of days anyway." He stood and stretched.

"I suppose you're right. Thanks for the time. I'll just keep digging. You never know what I'll come up with."

A thought crossed Kent's mind. "Actually, why don't you focus on debugging for a few days and leave the digging. I mean, be my guest, dig all you want, but wandering aimlessly through my code is not necessarily the best use for a mind like yours, pal." He shrugged. "Just my opinion, of course. But if you want to find something, just ask me. I'll save you a mountain of time."

Cliff smiled brightly. "Sure, if you're here. I think that was the concern. What happens if Kent Anthony disappears?"

"Well, a week ago that strategy made sense. But it's now obsolete. I'm here to stay. You tell that to whoever punches your buttons." Kent grinned to make the point stick.

Cliff saluted mockingly. "You got it, sir."

"Good then. Off you go, lad."

Cliff left grinning ear to ear. Kent honestly felt nearly jovial. The drug of his plotting had worked its way right through his veins. It felt as though he had stepped out of some nightmare and found himself at the gates of a new undiscovered world. And he fully intended to discover every corner of it.

He locked his office, made some comment to Betty about how much work there was, and hustled out the back. Normally he would have preferred the front doors, but now was not normally. Now he would have crawled through a trapdoor in the floor if there had been one.

He hurried down the alley to his car and slid onto the leather upholstery before considering his destination. The library. He had some books to check out. No. That would leave a trail. The bookstore, then. He had some books to purchase. With cash. The nearest Barnes and Noble was three miles down Sixth Avenue. He made a U-turn and entered the flow of traffic.

Kent was not one to stop and lend a hand to stranded vehicles. Road kill, he called them. If the morons didn't have the foresight to either have their cars properly serviced or sign up for AAA they surely didn't deserve his extended hand. The dead vehicles were usually old cars stuffed with people from Stupid Street anyway. As far as he was concerned, a little breakdown on the road in heavy traffic was a good indoctrination to responsibility, a rare commodity these days.

Which was why it struck him as strange that the white Acura sidelined ahead on the left-hand side of the divided thoroughfare even caught his attention. And even stranger was the simple fact that once it was in his eyesight, he could hardly remove his eyes from the vehicle. And no wonder. It sat like a beacon of light ahead, glowing white, as if a lightning bolt had lit it up. It suddenly occurred to him that the sky was indeed rather foreboding—in fact downright dark. But the Acura was actually glowing up there, and all the other cars just sped by as if it did not exist. Kent gripped the steering wheel, wooden.

A woman with blonde hair, dressed in jeans and a green shirt, was climbing out. She turned to face his approach, and Kent's heart bolted. He didn't know *why* his heart jumped like that, but it did. Something in her face, possibly. But that was just it; he could hardly *see* her face from this distance.

Then Kent was past the car, torn by indecision. If ever there was a soul who deserved assistance, it was this one. On the other hand, he didn't do roadkill. Thirty yards flew by before he jerked the wheel impulsively and slid to a stop, five inches from the guardrail, cars moaning by on the right.

The instant he stopped, he decided it had been a mistake. He thought about pulling back into traffic. Instead, he slid out of the seat and jogged the forty yards back to the Acura. If the glow that had surrounded the car had ever actually been there, it had taken leave. Someone had pulled the plug. The woman

had lifted the hood so that it gaped, black-mouthed, at him like a steel alliga-
tor. She stood watching his approach, bouncing in his vision.

Kent was ten feet from the woman when recognition slammed into his
mind like a sledge. He pulled up, stunned.

It was the same for her, he thought. Her jaw dropped to her chest, and her
eyes grew wide. They stood fixed to the pavement like two deer caught in each
other's headlights.

"Kent?"

"Lacy?"

They responded simultaneously. "Yes."

Her eyes were like saucers. "Kent Anthony! I can't believe it's actually you.
My . . . my car died . . ."

He grinned, feeling oddly out of sorts. She was prettier than he remembered. Thinner perhaps. Her face was still rather ordinary, but those eyes. They
shone like two beaming emeralds. No wonder he'd taken to her in college. And
age was wearing well on her.

"Lacy Cartwright. How on Earth did you end up stranded on the side of the
road?" *Her car broke down, you idiot. She told you that.*

She broke into a wide grin. "This is weird. I don't know what happened. It
just stopped . . ." She chuckled. "So how in the world are you?"

"Good. Yeah, good," he said, thinking it both a downright lie and the honest truth.

He stood silent for a full ten seconds, just staring at her, at a loss for what to
say next. But then she was doing the same, he thought. *Come on, man. Get a grip.*

Kent finally motioned to the car. "So, what happened?"

She gazed at the tangle of tubes under the hood. "It just died. I was lucky
to pull over without hitting the rail."

The atmosphere was charged with expectancy. High above, a line of lightning crackled through black clouds. "Well, I'm not a mechanic, but why don't
you get in and turn her over and I'll poke around a little."

"Good." She held his eyes for a moment as if trying to read any message
there. He felt a strange tightness squeeze his chest.

Lacy jumped behind the wheel, eyeing him through the windshield. He
dipped his head under the raised hood. Good grief! He was staring at a ghost
from the past.

The engine turned over, and he jerked back, immediately hoping she had not seen his reaction. No sense coming off like a wuss.

The engine caught and rumbled to life.

Kent stood back, studied the running motor for a moment and, seeing nothing extraordinary, slammed the hood shut.

Lacy was out. "What did you do?"

He shrugged. "Nothing."

"You're kidding, right? This thing was dead, I swear."

"And I swear that I did nothing but breathe on it. Maybe I should've been an auto mechanic. I could fix cars by breathing on them." He grinned.

"Well, you always did have a lot of hot air." Lacy shot him a coy look and smiled slyly.

They chuckled, and Kent kicked at the pavement, suddenly shy again. He looked up. "Well, I guess you're fixed up. I heard you'd moved to Boulder."

"Yeah."

"Maybe we should get together."

The smile vanished from her face, and he wondered if she'd heard. "You heard about Gloria, right?" he asked.

"Gloria?"

"Yes. My wife died awhile back."

Her face registered shock. "I'm so sorry! I had no idea."

He nodded. "Yeah. Anyway, I should probably get going. I have to get back to work."

She nodded. "Yeah, I have to get back to Boulder. My washer broke down." She offered no further explanation.

He nodded again, feeling suddenly stranded. "Yeah." She was not moving.

"I'm really sorry about your wife, Kent. Maybe we should get some coffee and talk about it."

"I heard you lost your husband a couple years ago."

She nodded. They were nodding a lot. It was a good way to fill in the blanks after, what? Thirteen years?

"You have a card?" he asked. That sounded dumb. Sounded like he was hitting on her, and he had no intention of hitting on anyone. No desire at all.

"Sure." She reached through the window, withdrew her purse, and handed him a card. Rocky Mountain Bank and Trust. Customer Service.

"I didn't know you were in banking." He glanced up at her. "You know I'm in banking, right?"

"Someone said that. Information Systems, right?"

"Yeah. Good, I'll call you. We'll catch up."

"I'll look forward to it," she said, and he thought she meant it.

"Good." Lots of *goods* and *yeahs* and nodding. "Hope your car runs well," he said and dipped his head to her.

Then he was jogging back to his car. The horizon flashed crooked fingers of lightning, and thunder boomed. The rain was eager, he thought. When he reached his door, Lacy's white Acura sped by and honked. He waved and slipped behind the wheel. Go figure.

❧

Lacy drove west through a hard pour with her gut twisted in knots. The chance meeting with Kent had thrown her completely off center. She sped down the blacktop, fixated on the *whap, whap* of the windshield wipers, slowly exiting the big city. But her heart was back there, on the roadside, gazing into those lost blue eyes.

Kent looked as though he'd stepped out of some lost corner of her mind, a carbon copy of the zany college student who'd managed to capture her heart. Her first love. It had been his sincerity, she'd mused a thousand times. A man as sincere and honest as he was ambitious. The unique blend of those traits had whipped up a potion that had her swooning for the first time in her life. Well, his blue eyes and blond hair had not exactly impeded her swooning, she supposed.

He had lost his wife. Didn't he have a son as well? Poor child.

And under that haunting facade hid a man aching for comfort yet repelled by it at once. She should know. She'd been there. "God, help him," she breathed, and she meant it. She meant not only that Kent would receive help, but that *God* would help him. Because Lacy believed in God. She had fallen to his feet just over a year ago while climbing out of her own despondency, learning that she did not have the world by its tail.

"Father, comfort him," she whispered. The wipers squeaked.

Lacy fought a sudden urge to pull off, whip the car around, and chase Kent down. Of course, that was ridiculous. Even if such a thing were possible, she had no business chasing after an old flame who'd just lost his wife. And since when had she become the chasing type, anyway? *Listen to me, even thinking in terms of chasing! Heavens! I don't mean chasing like some dog in heat, but chasing as in trying to . . . help the man.*

She glanced at the new water pump in the passenger seat and remembered the broken washing machine. Now, if that machine had not broken down precisely when it had, she would have missed him entirely. If the strange service tech had not been as accommodating on the phone, if he'd had a pump in stock, if she had not driven to Denver, if her car had not lost its spark for a moment when it did—any single fluctuation in this endless string of events, and she would not have met Kent.

And on top of it all, Kent had pulled over without knowing whom he would be helping. That much was evident by his shock when he recognized her.

On the other hand, every event that ever occurred did so only after a string of other events lined up perfectly.

Lacy glanced at a brown smudge on her right sleeve, a spot of smeared grease. Had he seen it? She returned to her line of thinking. Almost anything was statistically possible. But the pull in Lacy's heart suggested that today's string of events was not just a random occurrence. It had been somehow orchestrated. Had to be.

On the other hand, stranger things had happened.

Lacy ground her teeth and dismissed the mental volleys. But they did not go so easily; within the minute they were back, nipping at her mind.

In the end she decided that none of it mattered. Kent had her card. He would either call, or he would not call. And that had nothing to do with chance. It had everything to do with his choice. Her heart jumped at the thought.

An obscure memory from her early adolescent years flashed through her mind. She was all dressed up for the prom, clad in a pink dress with white frills and her hair pulled back in a cluster of curls. It had taken her and her mother a good three hours to make everything just so. It was her first date, and Daddy had told her how proud he was of her, looking so beautiful. She sat on the living room couch, holding a white carnation for her date. Peter. But Peter was late. Ten minutes, then half an hour, then an hour. And she just sat there swinging her legs, feeling all gooey inside and trying to be brave while her father stormed on the phone. But Peter never came, and his parents knew nothing about their son's whereabouts. Her father took her out for dessert, but she could not manage eye contact with anyone that night.

A lump filled her throat at the memory. Dating had never gone well for her. Even dating with Kent, who had dropped her on her seat at the slightest hint of commitment. She would do well to remember that.

What had she been thinking, *chasing* after him? She no more needed a relationship now than she needed a bout with lupus.

On the other hand, he might call.

17

Week Eight

Helen tossed and turned, and even in her sleep she could feel her eyes jerking behind closed lids. Slapping feet echoed through her head, sounding like a marathon runner who had taken a wrong turn and ended up running through a tunnel. A tunnel called Kent's life.

The feet beat on—*slap, slap, slap*—without pause. Heavy breathing chased the slapping. The runner pulled deliberately against the stale dark air. Maybe too deliberately, as if he or she were trying to believe that the breathing was all about flooding the lungs with air, when actually it was just as much about fighting off panic. Because steady sounds do that—they fight off uncertainty with their rhythm. But this runner seemed to be losing that battle with uncertainty. The deliberate breaths were sounding a little ragged around the edges.

The slapping feet had made frequent visits to her mind in the last week, and that bothered her because she knew they were saying something. She just hadn't been able to decipher their message. At least not all of it.

She knew they were Kent's feet. That Kent was running. Running from God. The running man. She'd heard of a movie called that once. *The Running Man.* Some gladiator type running for his life through a game show.

Pastor Madison didn't like her calling this a game, but here in her own mind she could call it whatever she wanted. And it felt like a serious game show to her. The stakes were death; the prize was life. But in a cosmic sort of way, that prize wasn't so different from winning a Kenmore refrigerator with built-in ice maker or a '64 Mustang convertible, now, was it?

She took a deep breath and tried to refocus her thoughts. *Lighten up, Helen. Goodness, you're going off the deep end. We're not playing* Wheel of Fortune *here.*

Her mind sank into the dungeon again and listened to those slapping feet.

How long could a person run like that? Another sound bounced around in the dark. A thumping sound. A pounding heart to go along with the heavy breathing and the slapping feet. Which made sense, because her heart would certainly be pounding if she ran.

She imagined herself running like that.

The thought came like a sharp jab to her solar plexus.

She caught her breath.

Now there were only two sounds in the tunnel: the beating feet—*slap, slap, slap*—and the pounding heart—*thump, thump, thump.* The breathing had stopped.

Helen bolted up in bed, suddenly awake, a single thought now whispering through her skull: *That breathing stopped when you stopped breathing, sister! That's you in there!*

She snatched her hands to her chest. Her heart pounded to the same cadence she had heard in her dream. In the tunnel. The only thing missing was the slapping feet. And no matter how weird things were getting, she knew that she certainly had not been running up and down her hall in her sleep.

Helen knew the point of it all, then, sitting in bed feeling her heart throb under her palm. If she was not actually in the game, she was *meant* to be. Her feet were *meant* to be slapping along the floor of that tunnel. This insane urge to walk was not just some senile thing; it was the pull of God on her spirit. *Walk, child, walk. Maybe even run. But at least walk.*

It might be Kent in there running for his life, but she was in there too, breathing down his neck! Praying for him. She was in the game too. And her part was the intercessor. That was it.

Helen threw the sheets off and stood beside her bed. It was 5 A.M. She should walk, maybe. The thought stopped her cold for a moment. She was not a walker, for heaven's sake. The doctor had wanted to put new knees in her legs less than a year ago! What on earth did she think she would do now? Hobble up and down the driveway until the neighbors called the police about the lunatic they saw out their windows? Walking back and forth on her plush carpet in running shoes was one thing. Taking a prayer trek through the streets like some prophet was another thing altogether.

And more important, why on God's green earth would he want her to walk at all? What did walking have to do with this craziness? God certainly did not need on old lady's walking to move his hand.

Then again, neither had he needed old Joshua and his cohorts traipsing around Jericho to tumble the wall, now, did he? And yet he had demanded that. This was not so different.

Well, yes, this *was* different. This was different because this was now and that was then and this was her and that was Joshua!

Helen grunted and made for the bathroom. She was up. She might as well get dressed. And there was another reason why this was different. This was different because this was mad! What would Pastor Madison say? Goodness!

She stopped midstride, halfway to the bathroom. *Yes, but what would God say? Was that God talking to you back there, telling you to walk?*

Yes.

Then walk.

Yes.

It was settled then, in that moment.

Twenty minutes later Helen stepped from her house wearing her white Reeboks and over-the-calf basketball socks below a swishing green dress with yellow sunflowers scattered in a pattern only the original designer could possible identify.

"Oh, God have mercy on my soul," she muttered and stepped from the landing to the sidewalk. She began to walk down the street with no destination in mind. She would just walk and see.

And she would pray.

❧

Kent rolled through the hours with all the constancy of a yo-yo those first two weeks. One moment consumed with the audacity of his ever-clarifying plot, the next blinking against memories of Spencer or Gloria. To say that he was unstable would have brought the textbook definition into clear focus.

The ideas came like weeds, sprouting in his mind as though some mad scientist had spilled super-growth formula on them. It didn't even occur to him until the end of the first week that the twisting and turning up there did not stop when he fell asleep. In fact, his best ideas seemed to sneak their way into his mind then, when he tossed in fitful sleep. In his dreams.

Just as the vagrant had flashed his tongue about and told Kent just what he thought of the situation, other voices seemed to be suggesting other opinions. He could never quite remember their precise words or even the overall context of their suggestions, but he seemed to wake each day with an eagerness to explore a vague notion. And regardless of why his mind seemed to favor the night, Kent did not complain. It was the stuff of genius, he thought.

The meeting with Lacy nagged at him occasionally, but the growing prospects of his new life overshadowed the strange encounter. Several times he pulled her card out, intending to call. But he found things confusing once he attempted to clarify his reason for contacting her. *Oh hi, Lacy. How about a nice romantic dinner tonight? Did I tell you that my wife and son just died? Because that's important. I'm a free man, Lacy.* Gag! He was certainly in no mood for a relationship.

On the other hand, he was starving for friendship. And friendship was relationship, so in that sense he was growing slowly desperate for a relationship. Maybe even someone to tell . . . Someone to share this growing secret with. But that would be insane. Secrecy was his friend here.

Life at the office began to take on its own rhythm, not so different from the one that had once marched him through the days before his world had turned upside down. And the nights. It was the night routine that Kent began to methodically add to his work regimen. He needed his coworkers to be thoroughly accustomed to his late nights at the office again. His whole plan depended on it.

It was impossible to lock or unlock the building without triggering a signal that notified the alarm company of the event. The entries were posted on the branch manager's monitors each morning. So Kent made a point of entering and leaving through the backdoor, creating a consistent record of his work habits, and then offhandedly reporting the progress he'd made the previous night to Borst.

What they could not know was that the debugging he accomplished in those late hours while they slept took only a fraction of the time indicated. He could produce more clean code in one hour than any of the others could in a day. He not only possessed twice the gray matter any of them did, but he was working on his own code.

Not his own code as in AFPS, but his own program as in refining ROOSTER and the way ROOSTER was going to wreak its havoc on the world.

Cliff made a habit of poking his head in each day, but Kent did his best to minimize their interaction. Which simply meant knowing at all times what the zany snowboarder was working on and staying clear of his routines.

"You seem awfully well adjusted for having just gone through such loss," Cliff stated at the end of Kent's first week back.

Kent scrambled for a plausible explanation. "Denial," he said, turning away. "That's what they say, anyway."

"Who says that?"

He had not been to a shrink. "The pastor," Kent lied.

"You're kidding! I had no idea you went to church. I do too!"

Kent began to regret his lie immediately.

"So how long have you been a Christian?"

"Well, actually I'm really not that well connected."

"Sure, I can understand that. They say 80 percent of churchgoers are disconnected beyond Sunday services. So I hear that your wife was a strong believer."

Kent looked up. "Really? And who told you that?"

"I just picked it up somewhere."

"Somewhere like where? I didn't know it was common knowledge around here."

Cliff shrugged uncomfortably. "Well, from Helen, actually."

"Helen? My mother-in-law's been talking to you?"

"No. Relax, Kent. We talked once when she called in."

"And you just happened to talk about me and my wife? Well that's real sweet of you— 'Poor Kent, let's gossip about his faith, why don't we? Or should we say, his lack thereof.'"

"We're Christians, Kent. Some things are not as sacred as others. Don't worry, it goes no further than me."

Kent turned away, angry without knowing exactly why. Helen had her rights. Gloria was, after all, her daughter. He began to avoid Cliff then, at the end of his first week back to work. Although getting away from the pineapple-eating grinner was easier said than done.

It took Borst most of two weeks to buy into Kent's reformed attitude. But a daily dose of soothing accolades administered by Kent greased the wheels to the man's mind easily enough. Kent had to hold his nose while smearing the stuff on, but even that became easier as the days passed.

Borst asked him about the schedule once after Kent had handed him the fix to a bug that Borst himself had attempted and failed to remedy. It had taken Kent exactly twenty-nine minutes the previous night to locate the misplaced modifier responsible.

"You got it, huh? Gotta hand it to you, Anthony. You sure can crank this stuff out." He lifted his greasy head. "You seem to work best at night these days, don't you?"

A flare hissed white-hot in Kent's mind. His heart flinched in his chest, and he hoped desperately that Borst was not catching any of his reaction. "I've always worked best at night, Markus." He'd discovered that Borst liked to be called Markus by his friends. He lowered his eyes. "But since the deaths, I'm not crazy about being alone at night with nothing to do, you know?"

"Yeah, sure. I understand." He waved the pages in the air. "You did all of this last night, huh?"

Kent nodded.

"What time you pull out of here?"

Kent shrugged. "I came back at, oh, maybe eight or so, and left at midnight."

Borst smiled. "Four hours? Like I said, you're good. You keep working like this, and the rest of us will run out of things to do." He chuckled. "Good work." He'd winked then, and Kent swallowed an urge to poke his eye out.

Instead he smiled. "Thank you, sir."

The *sir* brought a flare of pride to Borst's nostrils, and Kent left, determined to use the expression more frequently.

He resumed his friendship with Will Thompson within the first few days. As before, their shallow talk led to nothing of substance, which was fine by Kent.

"I just can't believe you're back after what they put you through," Will told him, walking to lunch the third day. Taking time for lunch sat rancid in Kent's gut, but he was on a mission to appear as ordinary as possible, and the occasional lunch would fit the image well.

"You know, if Spencer had not passed away, I don't think I would be here. But when you lose the ones you love the most, things change, Will. Your perspectives change. I just need to work now, that's all." He looked across the street to Antonio's Italian Cuisine. "Who knows? Maybe once things have settled I'll move on. But now I need stability."

Will nodded. "Makes sense."

Touché, Will. Indeed it makes sense. Everything needs to make sense. You remember that when they question you about me.

Betty Smythe became just another office fixture again, smacking her lips at the front desk, handling all of Borst's important calls and constantly scanning her little world with the peeled eyes of a hawk. It made little difference to Kent, who simply closed his door. But when the poop hit the fan, hers would be the most active mouth, flapping nonstop, no doubt. He wanted her gabbing to favor him, not cast suspicion his way. So he began the distasteful task of working his way into her corner.

A bouquet of roses, for all of her support, started him off on the right foot. The fact that she had not lifted a single finger in support of him didn't seem to temper her appreciation. Then again, judging by the amount of acrylic hanging off the end of her fingers, lifting them would be no easy task.

"Oh, Kent! You shouldn't have!"

He had always wondered if women who carried on with wide eyes about flowers really did find them as stimulating as they let on. He could see a cow slobbering over vegetation, but women were hardly cows. Well, most women weren't. Betty came pretty close, which probably explained why she had just rolled her eyes back as if she were dying and going to heaven over the red blossoms on this particular arrangement of vegetation.

"But I should have," he replied with as much sincerity as he could muster. "I just wanted you to know how much your support has helped me."

A quick flicker in her eyes made him wonder if he had gone too far. If so, she quickly adapted. "You're so kind. It was nothing, really. Anybody would have done the same." She smiled and smelled the roses.

Kent had no idea what she could possibly be referring to, but it no longer mattered. "Well, thank you again, Betty. I owe you." *Gag!*

"Thank you, Kent." Somehow one of the petals had loosed itself and stuck on her upper lip. It looked ridiculous. She didn't seem to notice. Kent didn't bother to tell her. He smiled genuinely and turned for his office.

Todd and Mary were like two peas in a pod—both eager to please Borst and fully cognitive of the fact that they needed Kent to do it. They both trotted in and out of his office like regular pack rats. "Kent, how would you do this?" Or, "Kent, I've done such and such but it's not working quite right." Not that he particularly minded. At times it even made him feel as though nothing had really changed— he had always been at the center of their world.

It was the way they straightened when Borst walked by that brought Kent back to earth. In the end, their allegiance was for Bossman.

Todd actually apologized for his behavior at one point. "I'm sorry for . . . well, you know." He sat in Kent's office and crossed his legs, suddenly a tinge redder in the face. He pushed up his black-rimmed glasses.

"For what, Todd?"

"You know, for the way I acted that first day."

Kent did not respond. Let the boy squirm a little.

"It's hard being caught in the middle of office politics, you know. And technically speaking, Borst *is* our boss, so we don't want to cross him. Besides, he was right. It's really his thing, you know?"

A dozen voices screamed foul in Kent's head. He wanted to launch out and turn this boy. Slap some sense into him. And he could've pulled it off, too. But he only bit his lip and nodded slowly.

"Yeah, you're probably right."

Todd grinned sheepishly. "It's okay, Kent. Borst promised to take care of us."

Todd obviously told Mary about the conversation, because the next time she sat her chunky self in his guest chair, she wore a grin that balled her cheeks. She dove right into a question without referring to the incident, but Kent knew they had talked. Knew it like he knew both she and Todd were, spineless, Twinkie-eating propeller-heads.

During his second week back, Kent began leaving for lunch through the front lobby. Despite his aversion to doing so, he'd done it before so he would do it now. He walked nonchalantly, avoiding eye contact but responding to the occasional call of greeting with as much enthusiasm as he could stomach.

They were all there, like windup dolls, playing their parts. The tellers whispered about their fanciful relationships and counted the money. Zak the security guard paced and nodded and occasionally swung his stick like he'd learned from some Hollywood movie. Twice Kent saw Sidney Beech, the assistant vice president, clicking across the floor when he entered the lobby, and each time he pretended not to see her. Once he saw Porky—that would be Price Bentley—walk across the marble floor, and he immediately cut for the bathrooms. If the bank president saw him, he did not indicate so. Kent chose to believe he had not.

By the end of the second week, the routines had been reestablished and Kent's most recent altercations with the bank all but forgotten. Or so he hoped. Everything settled into a comfortable rhythm, just like the old days.

Or so they thought.

In reality, with the passing of each day, Kent's nerves wound tighter and tighter, like one of those spring-operated toys in the hands of an overeager child. At any moment the spring would break and he would snap, berserk.

But the plan was taking shape, like a beautiful woman walking out of the fog. Step by step, curves began to define themselves, and flesh took on form. The emerging image was Kent's link to sanity. It kept him from going mad during the long hours of pretending. It gave him a lover to fondle in the dark creases of his mind. It became . . . everything.

He was setting them up for one major backstab.

He was going to rob them blind.

18

Week Nine

Dawn had come to Denver with a flare of red in the East. Bill Madison knew because he had watched the sun rise. From gray to red to just plain blue with a little smog thrown in to remind him where he lived.

Helen had called the previous evening and asked him to join her in the morning. They had talked twice on the phone since his last meeting with her, and each time Helen's words had rung in his mind for a good hour or two after the final click of the receiver. The prospect of seeing her again had brought a knot to his gut, but not a bad knot, he thought. More like the twisting you might expect just before the first big drop on a roller coaster.

"And why, precisely, am I joining you?" he'd asked good-naturedly.

"We've got some talking to do," she said. "Some walking and talking and praying. Bring your walking shoes. You won't be disappointed, Pastor." And he knew he wouldn't be. Although he doubted they would really be doing much walking. Not with her bad knees.

He stepped up to her porch at 6 A.M. feeling just a tad foolish with the tennis shoes on. Helen opened the door on his first ring and walked right past him and into the street without uttering a word.

Bill closed the door and scrambled after her. "Hold up, Helen. Good night! What's gotten into you?" He said it chuckling. If he didn't know her, he might guess she'd suddenly become a spring chicken by the way she moved her legs.

"Morning, Bill," she said. "Let's walk for a minute before we talk. I need to warm up."

"Sure."

That's what he said. *Sure.* As if this were just one more day in a long string of days in which they had climbed from bed in the dark to meet for an edge-of-dawn walk. But he wanted to ask her what on Earth she thought she was doing. Walking like some marathoner in a knee-length dress and socks hiked above her calves. It looked ridiculous. Which made him look ridiculous by association. And he had never seen her take such bold strides, certainly not without a noticeable limp

He shoved the thought from his mind and fell in. He was, after all, her pastor, and like she said, she needed shepherding. Although, at the moment, he was following more than shepherding. How could he be expected to feed the sheep if it was ten feet ahead of him?

Bill stumbled to catch up. Not a problem—she would begin to fade soon enough. Until then he would humor her.

They walked three blocks in silence before it began to occur to Bill that Miss Knee-Socks here was not fading. If there was any fading just now it was on his end of things. Too many hours behind the desk, too few in the gym.

"Where we going, Helen?" he asked.

"Oh, I don't know. We're just walking. Are you praying yet?"

"I didn't know I was supposed to be praying."

"I'm not sure you are. But as long as I am, you might as well."

"Uh-huh," he said. Her Reeboks were no longer shiny and white like they had been a week earlier. In fact, they were not the same pair because these were well worn and the other had been almost new. Her calf muscles, flexing with each step, were mostly hidden by a thin layer of fat that jiggled beneath the socks, which encircled her legs with red stripes just below her knees. She reminded him of a basketball player from the seventies—minus the height, of course.

Her fingers hung by her side, swinging easily with each stride.

"You ever wonder why God used a donkey to speak, Bill? Can you even imagine a donkey speaking?"

"I suppose. It is rather strange, isn't it?"

"How about a whale swallowing Jonah? Can you imagine a man living in a fish for three days? I mean, forget the story—could you imagine that happening today?"

He dropped his eyes to the sidewalk and studied the expansion cracks appearing beneath them every few feet. "Hmm. I suppose. You have a reason for asking?"

"I'm just trying to nail down your orientation, Bill. Your real beliefs. 'Cause lots of Christians read those old stories in the Bible and pretend to believe them, but when it gets right down to it, they can barely imagine them, much less believe they actually happened. And they certainly would balk at such events happening today, don't you think?"

She strode along at a healthy pace, and he found himself having to work a bit to match her. Heavens! What had gotten into her?

"Oh, I don't know, Helen. I think people are pretty accepting of God's ability to persuade a whale to swallow Jonah or make a donkey talk."

"You do, do you? So you can imagine it, then?"

"Sure."

"What does it look like, Bill?"

"What does what look like?"

"What does a whale swallowing a full-grown man whole look like? We're not talking about chomping him up and gulping down the pieces—we're talking swallowing him whole. And then that man swimming around in a stomach full of steaming acids for a few days. You can see that, Bill?"

"I'm not sure I've ever actually pictured the details. I'm not even sure it's important to picture the details."

"No? So then what happens when people start imagining these details? You tell them the details aren't important? Pretty soon they toss those stories into a massive mental bin labeled 'Things that don't really happen.'"

"Come on, Helen! You don't just jump from a few details being unimportant to throwing out the faith. There are elements of our heritage we accept by faith. This doesn't necessarily diminish our belief in God's ability to do what he will—including opening the belly of a whale for a man."

"And yet you balked when I told you about my vision of Gloria's death. That was a simple opening of the *eyes*, not some whale's mouth for a man."

"And I did come around, didn't I?"

"Yes. Yes, you did."

She let it go with a slight smile, and he wondered at the exchange. Helen walked on, swinging her arms in a steady rhythm, humming faintly now.

Jesus, Lover of My Soul . . . Her favorite hymn, evidently. "You do this every day, Helen?" he asked, knowing full well she did not. Something had changed here.

"Do what?"

"Walk? I've never known you to walk like this."

"Yes, well I picked it up recently."

"How far do you walk?"

She shrugged. "I don't know. How fast do you think we're walking?"

"Right now? Maybe three, four miles an hour."

She looked at him, surprised. "Really? Well then, what's three times eight?"

"What's eight?"

"No. What's three *times* eight?"

"Three times eight is twenty-four."

"Then I guess I walk twenty-four miles each day," Helen said and grinned satisfactorily.

Her words sounded misguided, like lost birds smashing into the windowpane of his mind, unable to gain access. "No, that's impossible. Maybe a mile a day. Or two."

"Oh, heavens! It's more than a mile or two, I know that much. Depends on how fast I'm walking, I suppose. But eight times three *is* twenty-four. You're right."

Her meaning caught up with Bill then. "You . . . you actually walk . . . eight hours?" Good heavens! that was impossible!

"Yes," she said.

He stopped dead in his tracks, his mouth gaping. "You walk *eight hours* a day like this?"

She answered without looking back. "Don't fall apart on me, Pastor. My walking is certainly easier to accept than Jonah and his whale."

Bill ran to catch up. "Helen! Slow down. Look, slow down for just a minute here. You're actually saying you walk like this for *eight hours* a day? That's over twenty miles a day! That's *impossible!*"

"Is it? Yes, it is, isn't it?"

He knew then that she was pulling no punches, and his head began to buzz. "How? How do you do it?"

"I don't, Bill. God does."

"You're saying that somehow God miraculously allows you to walk twenty miles a day on *your* legs?"

She turned and lifted an eyebrow. "I should hope I walk on my legs. I would hate to borrow yours for a day."

"That's not what I mean." He was not laughing. Bill looked at those calves again, bouncing like a stiff bowl of jelly with each step. Apart from the socks, they looked plain enough to him. And Helen was asserting that she was walking twenty-four miles a day on those damaged knees that, unless his memory had gone bad, just last week favored hobbling over walking. And now this?

"Do you doubt me?"

"No, I'm not saying I doubt you." He didn't know what he was saying. What he did know was that a hundred voices were crying foul in his mind. The voices from that bin labeled "Things that don't really happen," as Helen had put it.

"Then what are you saying?"

"I'm saying . . . Are you sure you walk a full eight hours?"

"Walk with me. We will see."

"I'm not sure I can walk eight hours."

"Well, then."

"Are you sure you don't take breaks . . ."

She lost it then, right on the sidewalk in front of Freddie's Milk Store on the corner of Kipling and Sixth. She pulled up suddenly and planted both hands on her hips. "Okay, look, mister. You're the man of God here! Your job is to lead me *to* him, not away from him. Now, forgive me if I'm wrong, but you're starting to sound as though you're not sure anymore. I'm walking, aren't I? And I've been walking for over a week—eight hours a day, three miles an hour. You don't like it, you can go ahead and put your blinders back on. Just make sure you look straight ahead when you see me coming."

He dropped his jaw at the outburst. Heat flared up his neck and burned behind his ears. It was at times like this that he should be prepared with a logical response. Problem was, this was not about the logical. This was about impossibilities, and he was staring one right in the face. Which made it a possibility. But in reality, he already knew that. His outer self was just throwing a fit, that's all.

"Helen . . ."

"Now, I also had some trouble with this at first, so I'm willing to cut you some slack. But when I give you simple facts, like *I walk eight hours a day,* I don't need you analyzing me like I'm loony tunes."

"I'm sorry, Helen. Really, I am. And for what it's worth, I believe you. It's just not every day this kind of thing happens." He immediately wondered if he did believe her. You don't just believe some old lady who claims to have found kryptonite and discovered that Superman was right all along—it does work! On the other hand, this was not just some old lady.

She studied him for a full five seconds without another word. Then she *humphed* and marched on deliberately.

Bill walked beside her in silence for a full minute, unnerved. A hundred questions coursed through his mind, but he thought it better to let things settle. Unless he had missed something here, Helen was claiming that God had empowered her with some kind of supernatural strength that allowed her to walk like a twenty-year-old. A strong twenty-year-old at that. And she was not just claiming it, she was showing him. She had insisted he come and see for himself. Well, he was seeing all right.

She strode by him, step for step, thrusting each foot out proudly like Moses strutting across the desert with cane in hand.

He glanced at her face and saw that her lips were moving. She was praying. Prayer walking. Like those mission teams that went overseas just to walk around a country and pray. Break the spiritual strongholds. Only in Helen's case, it was Kent who would presumably benefit.

This was happening. This was *really* happening! Never mind that he had never in his life even heard of, much less *seen,* such a thing, this was happening right before his eyes. Like a hundred Bible stories, but alive and well and here today.

Bill suddenly stopped on the sidewalk, aware that his mouth hung dumbly open. He closed it and swallowed.

Helen walked on, possibly not even aware he'd stopped. Her strides showed not a hint of weakness. It was as if her legs did their business beneath her without her full knowledge of why or how they operated. They just did. Her concern was praying for Kent, not understanding the physics of impossibilities. She was a walking miracle. Literally.

Doubt suddenly felt like a silly sentiment. How could you doubt what you saw?

Bill took after her again, his heart now surging with excitement. Goodness, how many men had seen something like *this?* And why was it so hard to accept? Why so far out? He was a pastor, for Pete's sake. She was right. It was his job to illuminate the truth, not doubt it.

He imagined his pews full of smiling church members. *And today, brothers and sisters, we want to remember sister Helen, who is marching around Jericho.*

His bones seemed to tingle. He skipped once to match stride with Helen, and she looked at him with a raised brow.

"You just pray while you're walking?" he asked, and then he immediately held out his hands in a defensive gesture. "I'm not doubting. I'm just asking."

She smiled and chuckled once. "Yes, I pray. I walk, and I pray."

"For Kent?"

"For this crazy duel over Kent's soul. I don't know all the whys and hows yet. I just know that Kent is running from God, and I'm walking behind him, breathing down his neck with my prayers. It's symbolic, I think. But sometimes I'm not even sure about that. Walk by faith, not by sight. Walk in the Spirit. They that wait upon the Lord shall renew their strength; they shall walk and not grow weary. It wasn't literal back then, but now it is. At least it is with me."

"Which suggests that the whole business about Kent is real as well, because now it's not just visions and things in the head but this walking," Bill said. "Do you know how unusual that is?"

"I'm not so sure it's unusual at all. I just think I'm unusual—you said so yourself. Maybe it takes a bit of unusualness for God to work the way he wants to work. And for your information, I knew it was real before this walking thing. I'm sorry to hear that you thought my visions were delusional."

"Now come on, Helen. Did I say that?" He frowned and turned sideways so she could see his expression.

"You didn't need to." She set her jaw and strode on.

"Can I touch them?" he asked.

She scrunched her brow. "Touch what? My legs? No, you can't touch my legs! Heavens, Bill!"

"Not *touch* touch them! Goodness!" He walked on, slightly embarrassed. "Are they warm or anything. I mean, can you feel anything different in them?"

"They buzz."

"Buzz, huh?" He looked at them again, wondering how God altered physics to allow for something like this. They should bring some scientists out here to prove a few things. But he knew she would never allow that.

"What do you mean by *duel?* You said this was about a crazy duel over Kent's soul. That's not exactly out of the textbooks."

"Sure it is. The books may use different words, but it all boils down to the same thing. It is war, Bill. We do not wage war against flesh and blood but against principalities and powers. We duel. And what greater prize than a man's soul?" She faced forward deliberately. "It's all there. Look it up."

Bill chuckled and shook his head. "I will. Just for you, Helen. Someone's got to make sure you don't walk right off the planet."

"So that's your idea of shepherding?" Her eyes twinkled above a smile.

"You asked for it. Like you said, it's my gift. And if God can transform your legs into bionic walkers, the least he can do for me is give me a little wisdom. To help you walk."

"That's right. Just make sure the wisdom is not your own, Pastor."

"I'll try. This is just incredible!"

"You should go back now, Bill." Helen strode forward, down the sidewalk, right down Kipling. "I've got some praying to do. Besides, we don't want to get you stranded out here, now, do we?"

"I shouldn't walk and pray with you?"

"Has God told you to walk and pray with me?"

"No."

"Then go be a pastor."

"Okay. Okay, I'll do that." Bill turned, feeling as though he should say something brilliant—something commemorative. But nothing came to mind, so he just turned and retraced his steps.

∽↬↫

They say that a split personality develops over years of dissociative behavior. Like a railroad track encountering large, gnarly roots that slowly but inevitably heave it up and split it into two wandering rails. But the development of Kent's double life was not such a gradual thing. It was more like two high-speed locomotives thundering in opposite directions with a rope tied to the tail end of each. Kent's mind was stretched there in that high-tension rope.

The persona he presented at the bank returned him to the appearance of normalcy. But during the hours on his own, away from the puppets at work, he was slipping into a new skin. Becoming a new man altogether.

The dreams strung through his mind every night, whispering their tales of brilliance, like some kind of alter ego who'd done this a thousand times and now mentored the child prodigy. *What of the body, Kent? Bodies are evidence. You realize that they will discover the cause of death once they examine that body. And you do need the body—you can't just sink it to the bottom of a lake like they do in idiotic movies, Kent. You're no idiot, Kent.*

Kent listened to the dreams, wide eyed and fast asleep.

He ingested a steady diet of ibuprofen for the pain that had latched on to his neck. And he began to settle himself with the occasional nightcap. Only they were not so occasional after the third day. They were nightly. And they were not just nightcaps. They were shots of tequila. His taste for the juice that had nearly killed him in college came back like a soothing drug. Not enough to push him into oblivion, of course. Just enough to calm his ragged edges.

When he wasn't at work, Kent was either poring over research or thinking. A lot of thinking. Mulling the same detail over in his mind a hundred times. Thinking of every possible angle and searching for any loophole he had not considered.

The Discovery Channel had a daily show called *Forensics*. A downtown library had seen fit to catalog fifty consecutive episodes. It was a show detailing actual cases in which the FBI slowly but methodically honed in on criminals using the very latest technology in forensics. Fingerprints, bootprints, hair samples, phone records, perfume, you name it. If a person had been in a room, the FBI experts could almost always find traces.

Almost always. Kent watched the shows unblinking, his analytical mind tracking all of their weaknesses. And then he would reconsider the smallest details of his plan.

For example. He had already determined that he would have to execute the theft *at* the bank—inside the building. Which meant he would have to get *to* the bank. Question: How? He couldn't very well have a cab drop him off. Cabs kept records, and any break from routine might lead to a raised eyebrow. He had to keep those eyebrows down. So he should drive his car, of course, the way he always got to the bank. Yes, possibly. On the other hand, cars represented physical evidence. They left tracks. They could be seen by passersby or vagrants, like that one he'd seen in the back alley. Then again, did it matter? What would he do with the car afterward? Drive it away? No, he definitely could not drive off. Cars could be tracked. Torch it? Now, there was a thought. He could leave a five-gallon container of gasoline in the trunk, as if it were meant for the lawn mower at home, and rig a loose wire to detonate the fuel. *Boom!* That was ridiculous, of course. Even a beat cop would suspect the torching of a car. Maybe send it over a cliff with a full tank. Watch it burst into flames on the rocks. Of course, cars rarely actually exploded on impact.

Then again, why rid himself of the car at all?

The car detail consumed hours of drifting thought over the days. And it was the least of his challenges. But slowly, hour by hour, the solutions presented themselves to him. And when they did, when he had tested them in his mind and stripped them of ambiguity, Kent found something he never would have suspected at such discoveries. He found exhilaration. Bone-trembling euphoria. The kind of feeling that makes you squeeze your fists and grit your teeth to keep from exploding. He would pump the air with his right arm, the way he had done not so long before, with Gloria and Spencer giggling at his exuberance over the completion of AFPS.

Without exception, these occasions called for a shot of tequila.

Rarely did he stop long enough to consider the madness of his plan. He had grown obsessed. The whole thing, stealing such an enormous sum of money and then vanishing—starting over—was laced with insanity. Who had ever done such a thing? In a line of a hundred thousand children, it would not be *him* but the one whose mother had mainlined heroin throughout her pregnancy who would be most likely to one day attempt such a feat.

Or the man who had lost his wife, his son, and his fortune in the space of a month.

No, it was more, he thought. It was his savage thirst for what was due him. For a life. For revenge. But more than those things. As a simple matter of fact, there was nothing else that made sense any longer. The alternative of trudging along a new career path on his own sat like lead in his gut. In the end it was this thought that compelled him to throw back the last mouthful of tequila and discard any reservation.

Through it all, Kent maintained a plastic, white-collar grin at the bank, ignoring the knots of anxiety twisting through his gut and the anticipation bursting in his chest. Fortunately, he had never been one to sweat much. A nervous sweater in Kent's current state would walk through the days dripping on the carpet and changing identical shirts every half-hour in a futile attempt to appear relaxed and casual.

Helen, his religious whacko mother-in-law, saw fit in her eternal wisdom to leave him alone those first two weeks. Which was a small miracle in itself. Helen's God had performed his first miracle. She did call Kent once, asking if she could borrow some of Gloria's old tennis shoes. Seemed she had taken to exercise and didn't see the need to buy a brand-new pair of Reeboks for sixty bucks when Gloria's were just growing mold in the closet. Why she wanted all four pair, Kent had no clue. He just grunted agreement and told her to come by the next day. They would be on the front porch. When he returned from work, they were gone.

Happy walking, Helen. And if you don't mind, you may walk right off a cliff.

⌒⌒⌒

Kent found his way past the confusion surrounding Lacy Cartwright on a Thursday night fifteen days after their strange meeting, almost three weeks after his decision to rob the bank.

It came at midnight during one of those exhilarating moments just after a key to the entire theft had erupted in his mind like a flare. He thought of Lacy, possibly because the solution igniting his mind's horizon brought his focus to the future. Post-theft. His new life. Not that Lacy would fit into any new life, heavens no. Still, once her image presented itself, he could not shake it free.

He dialed her listed number with an unsteady hand and sat back.

Lacy answered on the fifth ring, just as he was pulling the receiver from his ear. "Hello?"

"Lacy?"

"Who is this?" She was not sounding too pleased about being called at midnight by a stranger.

"Kent. I'm sorry. Is it too late?"

"Kent?" Her voice softened immediately. "No. I was just going to bed. Are you okay?"

"I'm fine. I just thought . . . I just needed someone to talk to." He paused, but she remained silent.

"Listen to me. Sounds stupid, I know—"

"Lighten up, Kent. I've been there, remember? You're no more *fine* than I am a porcupine."

He leaned back against the cushions on the sofa and cradled the cordless phone on his neck. "Actually, things are good. Surprisingly good. I've got no one in the world to talk to, but apart from that rather insignificant detail, I would say that I'm recuperating."

"Hmm. How long has it been?" Her voice sounded sweet and soft over the receiver.

"Couple months." Had he told her about Spencer? Suddenly it was a lump rising in his throat instead of a hard-beating heart. "My son was killed in a hit-and-run four weeks ago." He swallowed.

"Oh, Kent! I'm so sorry. That's terrible!" Her voice trembled with shock, and Kent blinked at that. She was right. It was terrible—mind numbing, really. And he was already forgetting the tragedy of it all. So quickly. That made him what? A monster? "How old was your son?"

"Ten." Maybe this was not such a good idea. She was bringing things back into clear focus.

"Kent, I'm . . . I'm so sorry."

"Yeah." His voice sounded unsteady—choked with emotion. Two thoughts slinked through his mind. The first was that this emotion was redemptive—he did care after all; he was not a monster. The second was that the emotion was actually more self-pity than mourning over loss—lamenting the notion that he was indeed a monster.

"I don't know what to say, Kent. I . . . I think I know how it feels. Have you had any counseling?"

"A therapist? No. But I have a mother-in-law, if that counts."

She chuckled nervously. "What about a pastor?"

"Religious counsel? There was plenty of that to go around at the funeral, believe me. Enough for a few hundred years, I would say." What if she was religious? "But no, not really."

The phone rested silently against his cheek. "Anyway," he continued. "Maybe we could talk sometime."

"We're talking now, Kent."

The comment caught him off guard. "Yes. We are." He felt out of control. She was stronger than he remembered. Maybe the comment about religious counsel had been misplaced.

"But we can talk more whenever you're ready," she said. "I couldn't very well turn down an old friend in need, now, could I?" Her voice was soft again. "Really, call me whenever you want to talk. I know the value of talking things through."

He waited a moment before replying. "Thank you, Lacy. I think I would like that."

They talked for another half-hour, mostly about incidentals—catching up stuff. When Kent hung up, he knew he would call again. Maybe the next day. She was right: Talking was important, and he had some things he wanted to talk about.

19

The first real bump in the road came the following Monday.

Kent sat hunched over a tiny table in the coffee lounge in Barnes and Noble Booksellers after leaving work early to run some "errands"—an activity he knew would quickly outlive its plausibility as a valid excuse for leaving the bank. After all, how many errands could a single man without a life run?

He'd scoured the shelves, found two books, and wanted to make certain they contained the data he was after before making the purchase. *The Vanishing Act* lay at an angle on the green-tiled tabletop before him. The other book, *Postmortem Forensics,* rested open between his hands, spread to a chapter on skeletal remains.

Within five minutes he knew the books were perfect. But he decided to read just a little further in one particular chapter. Like another article he'd gleaned off the Internet suggested, the editor here was confirming that a gunshot wound would not bleed after death. If the pump wasn't pumping—if the heart wasn't beating—the blood would not flow. But he already knew that. It was this bit about the effects of high heat to flesh and skeletal remains that had Kent's heart suddenly drumming steadily.

He flipped the page. Human flesh was rather unpredictable, sometimes flaming to a crisp and other times extinguishing itself midburn. Various accelerants assisted the burning of flesh, but most left a residue easily detected in postmortem forensics. Gasoline, for example, left a detectable residue, as did all petroleum products.

Kent scanned quickly down the page, tense now. What then? If he could be certain of the flesh burning . . . A sentence jumped out at him. "Magnesium is sometimes used by mortuaries to—"

"Excuse me, sir."

The voice startled Kent, and he snapped the book shut. A middle-aged man sat across from him, smiling past wire-framed glasses. His black hair was swept back neatly, glistening atop a small, pointy head. A pinhead. He was dressed not unlike Kent himself: tailored black suit, crisp white shirt, red tie held snugly by a gold tie bar.

But what had Kent's pulse spiking was the fact that the stranger now sat down at Kent's table, elbows down and smiling like he had been here first. That and the man's piercing green eyes. Like snowboarder Cliff's eyes. He sat, stunned, finding no words.

"Hello." The stranger grinned big. His voice seemed to echo low and softly, as if he'd spoken into a drum. "I couldn't help noticing that book. *Postmortem Forensics,* huh? Is that the kind of book that tells you how to carve someone up without getting caught?" He chuckled. Kent did not.

The man calmed himself. "Sorry. Actually, I've always been rather interested in what happens after death. You mind if I look at the book? I might want a copy myself." The man stretched out a big tanned hand.

Kent hesitated, taken back by the man's audacity. He held out the book. Was it possible this man was an agent, somehow on to him? *Relax, Kent. The crime is nowhere but in your mind. He fixed his jaw and said nothing, hoping the man would catch his disinterest.*

The stranger scanned through the book and stopped dead center. He flipped the book around and showed a centerfold of a spread-eagle corpse. "Now where do you suppose this man is?" he asked.

"He's dead," Kent answered, "in a grave somewhere."

"You think?" The man's eyebrow arched. "You think your son is in a grave somewhere as well, then?"

Kent blinked and stared at the man hard. "My son?" Now he was growing angry. "What do you know of my son?"

"I know that he was struck by a car a month ago. He say anything to you before he died? Something that morning before you left, perhaps?"

"Why?" Kent demanded. Then it hit him. "Are you a cop? Is this part of the investigation of my son's death?"

"In a matter of speaking, yes. Let's just say we are reviewing the implications of your son's death. I understand you were angry when you left him."

Linda! They had interviewed the baby-sitter. "I wouldn't say angry, no. Look, mister. I loved my boy more than you'll ever know. We had a disagreement, sure. But that's it." What was going on here? Kent felt his chest tighten. What was the man insinuating?

"Disagreement? Over what?"

The man's eyes stared like two green marbles with holes punched in them, dead center. It occurred to Kent that the eyes were not blinking. He blinked and wondered if the man had blinked in that split second while his own eyes flicked shut. But they did not look as if they'd blinked. They just stared, round and wet. Unless wet meant that he had indeed blinked, in which case maybe the man had blinked. If so, he was timing it pretty good.

The agent cleared his throat and repeated himself. "What was your disagreement over, Kent?"

"Why? Actually we really didn't have a disagreement. We just talked."

"Just talked, huh? So you felt pretty comfortable leaving him in the doorway like that?"

Kent flashed back. "How I felt is none of your business. I may have felt like throwing up, for all you should care. Maybe I'd just ingested a rotten apple and felt like puking on the street. Does that make me a murderer?"

The man smiled gently. His eyes were still not blinking. "Nobody called you a murderer, Kent. We just want to help you see some things."

"Do you mind if I see your credentials? What agency are you with, anyway?"

The man casually reached for his pocket. He found a wallet in his breast pocket and pulled it out.

Kent did not know where the man was headed. Didn't even know what he meant by what he'd said. He *was* aware, however, of the heat snaking up his neck and spreading over his skull. How dare this man sit here and question his motives? He had loved Spencer more than he loved life itself!

"Listen, sir, I don't know who you are, but I would die for my boy, you hear?" He didn't intend for it to come out trembly, but it did. Suddenly tears blurred his vision, but he stumbled forward. "I would lay down my life for that boy in a heartbeat, and I don't appreciate anybody questioning my love! You got that?"

The stranger pulled a card from his wallet and handed it to Kent without moving his eyes. He didn't seem affected by these emotions. "That's good, Kent."

Kent dropped his eyes to the card: "Jeremy Lawson, Seventh Precinct," it read in a gold foil. He looked up. The agent's wire glasses rode neatly on his nose above a smug smile.

"I'm just doing my job, you realize. Now, if you'd rather, I can haul you in and make this formal. Or you can answer a few questions here without coming apart at the seams on me." He shrugged. "Either way."

"No, here's just fine. But you just leave my son out of this. It takes a real sicko to even imagine that I had anything to do with his death." He trembled saying it, and for a moment he considered standing and leaving the cop.

"Fair enough, Kent. And to be straight with you, I believe that you did love your son." He offered no more but sat there, smiling at Kent, unblinking. And then he did blink, just once. Like camera shutters, snapping a shot.

"Then that's that," Kent said. "If you've done your homework, you'll know that I've been through enough these last few months as it is. So if you're finished, I really need to get back to work."

"Well, now, that's just it, Kent. Seems to me there just might be more here than meets the eye."

Kent flushed. "Meaning what?"

"Have you talked to anyone else about this?"

"Talked to anyone else about *what?*"

The agent grinned knowingly and licked his forefinger. He turned the page to the book and glanced at its contents. "Just answer the question, Kent. Have you talked to anyone else? A stranger, perhaps."

Kent felt his hands tremble, and he removed them from the table. "Look. You're speaking a foreign language here. Do you know what I'm saying? I don't have the slightest idea what you mean by any of this. You come in here haranguing me about my son—practically accuse me of killing him—and now you want to know if I've talked to any strangers lately? What on Earth does this have to do with me?"

The cop may very well have not even heard him by his response. "A vagrant, say. Or a homeless man in an alley? You haven't talked to anyone like that recently?"

The man pried his eyes from the book and stared at him, that ear-to-ear grin still splitting his jaw. Kent squinted, sincerely wondering if Mr. Cop here hadn't slipped over the edge. His own fear that this bizarre exchange led anywhere significant melted slightly. What could a vagrant possible have anything to do with . . . ?

Then it hit him, and he stiffened. The cop noticed, because his right eyebrow immediately arched curiously.

"Yes?"

The vagrant in the alley! They had talked to the spineless vagrant!

But that was impossible! That had been his mind playing with images!

"No," Kent said. "No, I haven't talked to any vagrant." Which was true enough. You did not actually talk in your dreams. Then again he *had* seen the vagrant in the alley prior to the dream, hadn't he? The man's summary of life whispered through Kent's mind. *Life sucksssss . . .* But he hadn't actually talked to that vagrant either.

"Why don't you ask me if I've had wine and cheese with the president's wife lately? I can answer that for you, as well."

"I think you did talk to a stranger in an alley, Kent. And I think he may have told you a few things. I want to know what he told you. That's all."

"Well, you're wrong. What? Some fool said he told me a few things, and that makes me a suspect in the crime of the century?" Kent almost choked on those last few words. *Control yourself, man!*

"Crime of the century? I didn't say anything about a crime, my friend."

"It was a figure of speech. The point is, you are groping for threads that simply do not exist. You are badgering me with questions about events that have nothing at all to do with me. I lost my wife and my son in the last few months. This does not automatically place me at the top of some most-wanted list, am I right? So then, unless you have questions that actually make sense, you should leave."

The man's smile left him. He blinked again. For a few seconds the agent held him in a thoughtful stare, as if that last volley had done the trick—shown Pinhead here who he was really up against.

"You are a bright one. I'll give you that. But we know more than you realize, Kent."

Kent shook his head. "Not possible. Unless you know more than I do about me, which is rather absurd, isn't it?"

The man smiled again. He shifted his seat back, preparing to leave. Thank goodness.

He dipped his head politely and offered Kent one last morsel to chew on. "I want you to consider something, Kent. I want you to remember that eventually everything will be found out. You are indeed a brilliant man, but we are not so slow ourselves. Watch your back. Be careful whose advice you take."

With that, the agent stood and strode away. He put his hands deep into his pockets, rounded a bookcase ten yards away, and vanished.

Kent sat for a long time, calming his heart, trying to make sense of the exchange. The man's words nagged him like a burrowed tick, digging at his skull. An image of the man, sitting there with his slicked hair and cheesy grin, swallowed his mind.

Ten minutes later he left the bookstore without buying the books he'd come for.

20

Kent sat in the big tan leather lounger facing the tube Monday night taking stock of things. The Forty Niners led the Broncos sixteen to ten, and Denver had the ball at the fifty yard line, but Kent barely knew it. The roar of the crowd provided little more than background static for the images roaring through his mind.

He was taking stock of things. Getting right down in the face of the facts and drawing conclusions that would stay with him until he croaked.

At least that's how his self-analysis session had started out, back when Denver led six to three. Back before he had gotten started early on his nightcap. Actually he had dispensed with the nightcap routine at the first quarter whistle and settled for the bottle instead. No use kidding around. These were serious matters here.

At the top of his list of deliberations was that cop who had interrupted his reading at Barnes and Noble. The pinhead was on the case. Granted, not *the* case, but the man was onto *him*, and he was the case. Kent took a nip of liquor. Tequila gold. It burned going down, and he sucked at his teeth.

Now what exactly did that mean, *on the case?* It meant that Kent would be a fool to go through with any robbery attempt while Detective Pinhead was around. That's what it meant. Kent took another small taste from the bottle in his hand. A roar blared through the room; someone had scored.

But then, how could anyone know anything about anything other than what had already happened? Not a soul could possibly know about his plans—he'd told no one. He had started the fine-tuning of ROOSTER, but no one else had access to the program. Certainly not some pinhead cop who probably didn't know computer code from alphabet soup.

"We know more than you think we do, Kent."

"We do? And who's we? Well I think you're wrong, Pinhead. I think you know zero.

And if you know ten times that much it's still a big fat whoppin' goose egg, isn't it?"

The simple fact was, unless Pinhead could read his mind or was employing some psychic who could read minds, he knew nothing about the planned robbery. He was bluffing. But why? Why would the cop even suspect enough to merit a bluff? Regardless of why or how, the notion of continuing, considering this latest development, rang of madness. Like a resounding gong. *Bong, bong, bong! Stupid, stupid, stupid! Get your butt back to Stupid Street, fool.*

But he could plan. And he should plan, because who was to say that Pinhead would hang around? For that matter, even with the man on the case, Kent's plan was foolproof, wasn't it? What difference would an investigation make? And there *would* be an investigation, regardless. Oh yeah, there would be one heck of an investigation, all right. You don't just kill someone and expect a round of applause. But that was just it. There would be an investigation, no matter what he did. Pinhead or no pinhead. So it really made no difference whether the cop stayed on the case or not.

An episode of *Forensics* Kent had watched on Saturday replayed through his mind. It featured a case in which some idiot had plotted the perfect murder but had one problem. He'd killed the wrong man. In the end he had attempted the murder again, this time on the right person. He had failed. He was rotting in some prison now.

That was the problem with having the cops already breathing down your neck; they would be more likely to stumble onto some misplaced tidbit that nailed you. To be done right, most crimes had to come out of the blue. Certainly not under the watchful nose of some pinhead who was stalking you.

But this was not most crimes. This was *the* perfect crime. The one all the shows could not showcase because no one knew it had even occurred.

Kent lifted the bottle and noted that it was half empty.

And the cop was not the only one breathing down his neck. Cliff, the mighty snowboarder-turned-programmer, was annoying Kent with his intrusive style of *Let's check your code, Kent.* What if Boy Wonder actually stumbled onto ROOSTER? It would be the end, of course. The whole plan rested squarely on the shoulders of ROOSTER's secrecy. If the security program was discovered, the plot would blow up. And if anybody could find it, Cliff could. Not as a result of his brilliance as much as his dogged tenacity. There was a single link buried in AFPS that led to ROOS-TER: an extra "m" in the word "extremely," itself buried in a routine not yet active. If the "m" were deleted by some spelling-bee wizard intent on setting things straight, the link automatically shifted to the second "e" in the same word. Only someone with way too much time on their hands could possibly uncover the hook.

Someone like Cliff.

Kent went for a chug on the bottle and closed his eyes to the throat burn. The game was in its second half. He'd missed the big showdown at the end of the first. Didn't matter.

"Be real," he mumbled. "Nobody's gonna find no link. No way this side of Hades."

And he knew he was right.

An image of Lacy drifted through the fog in his mind. Now, *there* was a solution to this whole mess. He could discuss the fine points of committing a federal felony with Lacy. Cut her in. An anemic little chuckle escaped his lips at the thought. It sounded more like the burp that followed it.

Fact was, even if he wanted a relationship with a woman, it was simply not feasible. Not with mistress ROOSTER in his life. It wasn't that they wouldn't both share him. It was that they *couldn't.* Assuming they wanted to. Which was yet one more problem: He was thinking of ROOSTER as if it were a real person that possessed a will worth considering. ROOSTER was a link, for heaven's sake! A plan. A program.

Either way, he still could not cohabit with both ROOSTER and any living soul. Period. ROOSTER demanded it. The plan would fall apart.

So then, what on earth did he think he was doing with Lacy?

Good question. He should cut her off.

Cut her off from what? It wasn't as if he had a relationship with her. One freak roadside encounter with a stranger and a phone call hardly made a relationship.

On the other hand, Lacy was no stranger. She stood there by her car in Kent's mind, like a ghost stepping from the pages of his past.

Still, he had no desire for a relationship that could be characterized as anything but platonic. There was Gloria to think of—in the dirt nearly three months. That long? Goodness. And mistress ROOSTER.

Get a grip, Kent. You're losing it.

He lifted the bottle, sipped at the burning liquid, and scratched his chin. Sweat wet the skin beneath two days of stubble. He looked at his shirt. It was the same Super Bowl T-shirt he'd slept in for a week. Not a problem. Now that he was doing his own laundry, changing clothes had lost its appeal. Except for underwear, of course. But he could just throw the underwear in the machine once every other week and stuff them in a drawer without all the folding and sorting mess. Which reminded him; he needed another dozen. The machine could easily hold a month's worth. Once a month was clearly better than once every two weeks.

Kent looked at the tube. The game was nearing an end. Outside, the night was pitch black. He licked the bottle and thought about Pinhead again. A needle of anxiety pricked his skin. It was madness. *When you're ready, just call me,* she'd said in the voice echoing from the past. Lacy.

He made the decision then, impulsively, with two minutes to play and the Broncos now leading twenty-one to nineteen.

He climbed out of the lounger and picked up the phone, his heart suddenly stomping through his chest. Which was absurd because he certainly had no emotions for Lacy that would set off its pounding. Except that he did want to see her. That much he could not deny. The realization only added energy to his heart's antics as he dialed her number.

ᏬᎧᎧᏬ

Lacy had just slipped on her bathrobe when the phone began its ringing. The caller ID showed only that the call was "out of area," and she decided to pick it up on the remote chance it was a call she actually wanted to take.

"Hello."

"Hello. Lacy?"

Kent! Her heart leapt. She would know that voice anywhere.

"Yes?"

"Hi, Lacy. Is it too late?"

"And you are . . . ?"

"Oh, I'm sorry. It's Kent. Geez, I'm sorry. Pretty stupid, huh? Call up and ask if it's too late without introducing myself. I didn't mean to sound . . ."

"What do you want, Kent?"

The phone returned only silence for a few moments. Now why had she come off so curt? And why was her breathing tight? *God, help me.*

"Maybe I should call back at a better time," Kent said.

"No. No, I'm sorry. You just took me by surprise. It's only ten. You're fine."

He chuckled on the phone, and she thought he sounded like a boy. "Actually, I was wondering if I could talk to you," he said.

"Sure. Go ahead." Lacy settled onto a chair by the dinette.

"I mean come up there and talk to you."

Now her pulse spiked. "Up here? When?"

"Well . . . tonight."

Lacy rose to her feet. "Tonight!? You want to come up here tonight?"

"I know it's a bit late, but I really need someone to talk to right now."

It was her turn to freeze in silence.

"Lacy?"

What was she to say to this? *Come on up, Lover Boy.*

His voice came again, softer. "Okay, well, maybe it's not such a good idea . . ."

"No, it's okay." It was? It was nothing of the kind.

"You sure? Maybe we could meet at the Village Inn."

"Sure."

"In an hour?"

The sum of this matter began to spread through Lacy's mind like icy waters. Kent was coming to Boulder tonight. He wanted to talk to her.

"Sure," she said.

"Good. I'll see you in an hour, then."

"Sure."

Silence filled the receiver again, and Lacy suddenly felt like a high school girl being asked out by the captain of the football team. "So, what do you want to talk about?" she asked. It struck her that the question was at once both perfectly legitimate and absurd. On one hand, their relationship should remain strictly platonic, for obvious reasons. Reasons that droned through her head like World War II bombers threatening to unload at the first sign of flak. Reasons like, this man had dropped her once before and if it had hurt then, it might kill her now. Reasons like, he had just lost his wife. He was no doubt rebounding like the world's tightest-wound super-ball.

On the other hand, since when did reasoning direct the heart?

"Nothing," he said.

It was the wrong answer, she thought. Because in matters of the heart, "nothing" was much more than "something."

"Okay, I'll see you there," she said and hung up the phone with a trembling hand.

෴

It took Lacy forty-five of the sixty minutes to prepare herself, which was in itself nonsense because other than changing clothes she had not yet *unprepared* herself from the day's preparedness, which had taken her less than fifteen minutes just this morning. Nevertheless, it took her forty-five, due in part to the fact that the blouse she thought would best suit the occasion needed ironing. Not that this was an occasion as such.

Kent was there, at the Village Inn, sitting in a corner booth nursing a cup of coffee when she arrived. He glanced up as she slid onto the bench opposite him. His eyes brightened, which was a good thing because they appeared a bit red and blurry, as if he'd been crying in the last hour. His breath smelled strongly of mints.

"Hi, Kent."

He smiled wide and extended a hand. "Hi."

She took it hesitantly. Goodness. What was he thinking? This was not a business deal that required a handshake.

Looking at him now under the lights Lacy saw that Kent had seen some abuse lately. Dark circles cupped his eyes, which were indeed rather lethargic looking. The lines defining his smile seemed to have deepened. His hair was as blond as it had been the day he'd told her to take a hike years ago, but now it was disheveled. It was Monday—surely he had not gone to work like this. Something had been pummeling him, she thought, but then she already knew that. He had walked through the valley of death. You always got pummeled in the valley of death.

They sipped at their coffees and talked small talk for half an hour—the weather, the new stadium, the Broncos—all in all, things that neither seemed to have any interest in. Without going into their past, they really didn't have much to talk about. But it hardly mattered; just sitting there across from each other after so many years held its own power, however awkward or halting it might be.

The thought of revisiting their past brought an edginess to her heart. They could always talk about death, of course. It was their common bridge now. Death. But Kent was not thinking death. Something else was running around behind those eyes.

"I met a cop today," he said out of the blue, staring at his coffee.

"A cop?"

"Yeah. I was just sitting there in the bookstore, and this cop sits down and starts giving me the third degree about Spencer. About my boy, Spencer." His face drifted into a snarl as he talked. He looked up, and his eyes were flashing. "Can you believe the audacity of that? I mean—" He glanced out the window and lifted a hand helplessly. "I was just sitting there, minding my own business, and this pinhead cop starts accusing me."

"Accusing you of what?"

"I don't even know. That was just it. He goes on as if I had something to do with . . ." He stopped and swallowed, his Adam's apple bobbing against the emotion boiling through his chest. "With Spencer's death," he finished.

"Come on, Kent! That's absurd!"

"I know. It *is* absurd. Then he just went on, as if he knew things, you know."

"What things?"

"I don't know." He was shaking his head. The poor man sat there like someone strung together by a few brittle strands of flesh. Surely he could not have had anything to do with his own son's death! Could he? Of course not!

"It was like a scene out of *The Twilight Zone.*"

"Well, I'm sure you have nothing to worry about. The authorities do things like that as a matter of routine. It's ridiculous. You'll never hear from the man again."

"And maybe you're wrong," he said. She blinked at his tone. "Maybe I have plenty to worry about. The last thing I need is some pinhead with a badge poking his greasy head into my life! I swear I could tear his head off!"

She stared at him, unsure how to respond. "Maybe you need to lighten up, Kent. You've got nothing to hide, right? Don't let it get to you."

"Yeah, easy for you to say. It's not your neck he's breathing down."

Now she felt her face flush. "And it's not yours, either. The police are just doing their job. They should be the least of your concerns. And just in case you're confused here, I'm not one of them. I work at a bank, remember?"

Kent looked at the ceiling and sighed. "I'm sorry. You're right." He collected himself, nodding as if slowly coming to agreement. Then he closed his eyes and shook his head, gritting his teeth in frustration.

Yes indeed, he had been pummeled lately. She wondered what had really happened to bring him to this strange state.

He was smiling at her, his blue eyes suddenly soft and bright at once, like she remembered them from their previous life. "You're right, Lacy. You see, that's what I needed to hear. You always did have a way with the simple truth, you know."

She gulped and hoped immediately that he had not noticed. It was not his words but the way he had said them that bothered her, as if at that moment he was dripping with admiration for her.

She chuckled nervously. "If I remember correctly, you were never too stupid yourself."

"Well, we had our times, didn't we?"

She had to look away this time. An image of Kent leaning over her as they lay under the great cottonwood behind her dormitory filled her mind. "I love you," he was whispering, and then he touched her lips with his own. She wanted to shake the image from her head, force her heart back to its normal rhythm, but she could only sit there, pretending nothing at all was happening in her chest.

"Yes, we did," she said.

Tension hung in the air as if someone had thrown a switch somewhere and filled the room with a thick cloud of charged particles. Lacy could feel his eyes on her cheek, and she finally turned to face him. She gave him a controlled grin. This was madness! He had lost his sensibilities! Two minutes ago he was ranting about some cop and how he would like to tear the poor fellow's head off, and now he was staring at her like some honeymooner.

Death does that to people, Lacy, she reasoned quickly. *It makes them lose their sensibilities. And you're reading way too much into that look. It's not as bad as it looks.*

And then bad went to terrible. Because then Lacy felt heat swallow her face despite her best efforts to stop it. Yes indeed, she was blushing. As red as a cooked lobster. And he could see it all. She knew that because he too was suddenly blushing.

Panic flashed through her mind, and she impulsively considered fleeing. Of course that would be about as sensible as Kent's tearing a cop's head off. Instead, she did the only thing she *could* do. She smiled. And that just made it worse, she thought.

"It's good to see you again, Lacy." He shook his head, diverted his eyes. "I kept telling myself that the last thing I needed was a relationship so soon after Gloria's death. It hasn't even been three months, you know. But I realize now that I was wrong. I think I do need a relationship. A good friendship, without all the baggage that comes with romance. No strings, you know. And I see now that you can give me that friendship."

He faced her. "Don't you think?"

To be honest, she didn't know what to think. Her head was still buzzing from that last heat wave. Was he saying he wanted nothing but a platonic relationship? Yes, and that was good. Wasn't it?

"Yes. It took me six months to get over John. Not *over*, over, of course. I don't think you ever get *over*, over. But to a point where I could see clearly. Some are faster healers. They're back on their feet in three or four months; some take a year. But all of us need someone to stand by. I don't think I could have made it if I hadn't found God."

If he had been eating a cherry tomato, he might have choked on it at the comment. He coughed.

She ignored him. "Ultimately his is the only relationship that brings peace. I guess sometimes it takes a death to understand that." Kent's eyes were following the rim of his coffee cup. "But, yes, Kent. You're right. It is good to have a friendship that is completely unpretentious."

He nodded.

They talked for another hour, telling for the first time their own stories of loss. Lacy's mind kept wandering back to that heat wave that had fallen over them, but in the end she settled herself with the reasoning that these things happened to people who had walked through the valley. They lost their sensibilities at times.

By the time they shook hands and bid each other a good night, the clock's fat hand was past the midnight hour. By the time Lacy finally fell asleep, it was nudging the second morning hour. Surely it was well after Kent had arrived home and fallen comfortably asleep in his big, empty house, she thought.

She was wrong.

21

Helen Crane lived roughly eight miles from Kent's Littleton suburban neighborhood. Depending on traffic the crosstown jaunt took anywhere between fifteen and twenty minutes in her old yellow Pinto. But today she wasn't in the Pinto. Today she was on Reeboks, and the walk stretched into a three-hour ordeal.

It was the first time her walking actually took her anywhere. The minute she'd stepped off her porch, with the sun starting to splash against the Rockies, she'd felt an urge to walk west. Just west. So she'd walked west for over an hour before realizing that Kent's house lay directly in her path.

The silent urge arose in her gut like steel drawn to a powerful magnet. If Pastor Madison had been correct, she figured her normal pace carried her along at an easy three miles per hour. But now she pushed it up to four. At least. And she felt no worse off for the wear, if indeed there was any wearing going on in these bones of hers. She certainly did not feel fatigue. Her legs tingled at times as if they were thinking of falling asleep or going numb, but they never actually slowed her down.

Three days earlier she had tried walking through her eight hours and she had finally fatigued at the ten-hour mark. The energy came like manna from heaven, daily and just enough. But she had never felt the energy directing her anywhere except along the streets of her own neighborhood.

Now she felt as a salmon must feel when it strikes out for the spawning ground. Her daughter's Reeboks fit perfectly. She had already tossed her own pair in the garbage and switched to a black pair that Gloria had favored. Now she strutted down the sidewalk sporting black shoes and white basketball socks. Once she had looked at herself in the full-length hall mirror and thought the getup looked ridiculous with a dress. But she didn't care—she was a dress person. Period. She would leave fashion statements to the fools who gave a rat's whisker about such matters.

Helen entered the street leading to Kent's home and brought her focus to the two-story house standing at the far end. Not so long ago she had referred to the home as Gloria's home. But now she knew better. Her daughter was skipping across the clouds up there, not hiding behind pulled drapes in that stack of lumber. No, that was *Kent's* house.

That's your house.

The thought made Helen miss a step. She turned her mind to praying, ignoring the little impulse.

Father, this man living in that house is a selfish, no-good hooligan when you get right down to it. The city is crawling with a hundred thousand people more worthy than this one. Why are you so bent on rescuing him?

He didn't answer. He usually didn't when she complained like that. But of course she had no reason to hide her suspicions from God. He already knew her mind.

She answered herself. *And what about you, Helen? He is a saint compared to what you once were.*

Helen turned her thoughts back to prayer. *But why have you drawn me into this? What could you possibly want from my silly walking? Not to complain, but really it is rather incredible.* She smiled. *Ingenious, really. But still, you could certainly do as well without this exercise, couldn't you?*

Again he didn't answer. She had once read C. S. Lewis's explanation for why God insists on having us do things like pray when he already knows the outcome. It is for the experience of the thing. The interaction. His whole endeavor to create man centers around desire for interaction. Love. It is an end in itself.

Her walking was like that. It was like walking with God on Earth. The very foolishness of it made it somehow significant. God seemed to enjoy foolish conventions. Like mud on the eyes, like walking around Jericho, like a virgin birth.

She mumbled her prayer now. "Okay, so he is worthy of your love. Go ahead, dump some of the stuff over him. Let's have this over with. Lay him out. Drop him. You could do that. Why don't you do that?"

He still wasn't answering.

She closed her eyes momentarily. *Father, you are holy. Jesus, you are worthy.*

Worthy to receive honor and glory and power forever. Your ways are beyond finding out. A tingle ran through her bones. This was actually happening, wasn't it? She was walking around physically empowered by some unseen hand. At times it seemed unbelievable. Like . . . like walking on water.

You are God. You are the Creator. You have the power to speak worlds into existence, and I love you with all of my heart. I love you. I really do. She opened her eyes. *I'm just confused at times about the man who lives in that house,* she thought.

That's your house, Helen.

The inner voice spoke rather clearly that time, and she stopped. The house loomed ahead, three doors down, like an abandoned mortuary, haunted with death. And it was not her house. She did not even want the house.

That's your house, Helen.

This time Helen could not mistake the voice. It was not her own mind speaking. It was God, and God was telling her that Kent's house was actually hers. Or was meant to be.

She walked forward, rather tentative now. High above, the sun shone bright. A slight breeze pressed her dress against her knees. Not a soul was in sight. The neighborhood looked deserted. But Kent was in his house, behind those pulled blinds. The silver car parked in the driveway said so.

"Is that my Lexus too?" The corner of her mouth twitched at her own humor. Of course, she did not want the Lexus, either.

This time God answered. *That's your house, Helen.*

And then she suddenly knew what he meant. She stopped two doors down, suddenly terrified. Goodness, no! I could never do that! The walking is one thing, but *that?*

Helen turned on her heels and walked away from the house. Her purpose here was over. At least for the day. An unsteadiness accompanied her strides now. *That's your house; that's your house.* That could mean anything.

But it didn't mean anything. It meant only one thing, and she had the misfortune of understanding exactly the message.

Helen walked for an hour, mumbling and begging and praying. Nothing changed. God had said his piece. Now she was saying hers, but he was not speaking anymore.

She was on her way back home, less than an hour from her house—her *real* house—before she found some peace over the matter. But even then it was only a thimbleful. She began to pray for Kent again, but it was not as easy as it had been on the first part of the trip.

Things were about to get interesting. Maybe crazy.

⤳⤳

The second real bump in Kent's road came two days later, on Wednesday morning, on the heels of the cop-in-the-bookstore bump.

The day started out well enough. Kent had risen early and shaved clean to the bone. He smiled and nodded a greeting to several tellers on his way through the lobby. He even made eye contact with Sidney Beech on his way in, and she smiled. A sexy smile. Things were most definitely returning to normal. Kent whistled down the hall and entered the Information Systems suite.

Betty sat in typical form, tweezers in hand. "Morning, Betty." Kent forced a smile.

"Morning, Kent," she returned, beaming. If he wasn't mistaken there was some interest in her eyes. He swallowed and stepped past.

"Oh, Kent. They're meeting in the conference room down the hall. They're waiting for you."

He spun around. "There's a meeting this morning? Since when?"

"Since Markus got back from San Jose yesterday with new marching orders, he says. I don't know. Something about taking more responsibility."

Kent retraced his steps and entered the hall, trying to calm himself. This was out of the ordinary, and anything out of the ordinary was bad. His plan would work under existing circumstances, not necessarily under ones altered to meet some new marching orders.

Settle down, Buckwheat. It's just a meeting. No need to go in there and sweat all over the table. Kent took a breath and walked into the conference room as casually as possible.

The others rocked their chairs around the long table, wasting time, in good spirits. Borst had taken the head of the table and leaned back. His navy vest strained against its buttons. If one of those popped it might just poke Mary in the eye. She sat adjacent to Borst, leaning admiringly toward him. You'd think the two were best friends by their body language.

Todd sat opposite Mary, his head thrown back midhowl at some brilliant

182

comment Borst had evidently graced them with. It was Todd's hoot that covered the sound of the door opening and closing, Kent guessed. Cliff sat two chairs down from Mary, facing Borst, grinning his usual pineapple-eater smile.

"Kent! It's about time," Borst boomed. The others thought that funny and lengthened their laugh. He had to admit, the jovial atmosphere was almost contagious. Kent smiled and pulled out a seat opposite Cliff.

"Sorry. I didn't know we were meeting," he said.

They gathered themselves and dug in. Borst started by fishing for a few compliments, which the others readily served up. Kent even tossed him one. Some ridiculous comment about how perceptive the supervisor had been to bring in Cliff.

Mostly the discussion centered on preserving control of AFPS. Evidently the main Information Systems division at the administration branch in California was talking about flexing its muscles. Or, as Borst put it, *going for a power grab.*

"That's all it is, and we know it," he said. "They have a dozen greedy engineers up there who feel left out, so now they want the whole thing. And I have no intention of giving her up."

Kent had no doubt that the words were not original with Borst. They were Bentley's. He pictured Porky and Porkier yapping up a frenzy on the flight home.

"Which means we have to run a tight ship; that's all there is to it. They're looking for weaknesses in our operation as we speak. In fact, three of them are flying down next Friday to survey the territory, so to speak."

"That's crazy!" Todd blurted out. "They can't just waltz in here and take over."

"Oh, yes they can, Todd. That's a fact. But we're not going to let them."

"How?" Mary asked, wide eyed.

"Exactly. How? That's what we're going to figure out."

"Security," Cliff said.

It was only then that the meaning of this little discussion came home to Kent. Like a flash grenade tossed into his skull. Whether the delay had been caused by tequila residue or his fascination at watching Borst's fat lips move was a tossup. But when understanding did come, Kent twitched in his chair.

"You have something to say about that, Kent?" Borst asked, and Kent knew they had all seen his little blunder. To exasperate the matter, he asked the one question only a complete fool would ask in the situation.

"What?"

Borst glanced at Cliff. "Cliff said security, and you looked like you wanted to add to that."

Security? Good grief! Kent scrambled for recovery. "Actually, I don't think they stand a chance, sir."

That got a smile from them. *That's our boy, Kent.* All of them except Cliff. Cliff scrunched his eyebrows. "How's that?" he asked.

"How's what?"

"How is it that the guys from California don't have a snowball's chance in hell of taking control of AFPS?"

Kent leaned back. "How are they going to maintain a system they know nothing about?" Of course the whole notion was ridiculous. Any good department could work its way through the program. In fact, Cliff was well on his way to doing just that. He said so.

"Really? I've been here three weeks, and I've found my way around the program well enough. The code's not even under active security measures."

The room fell to dead silence. This was not going well. Tightened security could very well bring his entire plan to its knees. Kent felt a trickle of sweat break from his hairline and snake past his temple. He casually reached up and scratched the area as if a tickle annoyed him there.

"I thought you were going to take care of restricted security," Borst said, staring directly at Kent.

"We have restricted codes at every branch. No one can enter the system without a password," he returned. "What else do you want?"

"That covers financial security, but what about security from hackers or other programmers?" Cliff asked evenly. The newcomer was becoming a real problem here.

All eyes were on Kent. They were asking about ROOSTER without knowing it, and his heart was starting to overreact. He had programmed ROOSTER precisely for this purpose.

Then Cliff threw even the *not knowing* part into question. "Actually it looks like someone started to put a system into place but never finished. I don't know; I'm still looking into it."

The kid was on to ROOSTER! He'd found something that led to the link. It was all Kent could do to stay seated. This was it, then. If he didn't stop them now, it was over!

"Yes, we did start a few things awhile back. But if I recall correctly, we discarded the code long ago. It was barely a framework."

Cliff held Kent in a steady gaze. "I'm not so sure it's gone, Kent. I may have found it."

Kent's heart felt like it might explode. He forced a nonchalant look. "Either way, it was far too clumsy to accomplish anything under the current structure." Kent shifted his gaze to Borst. "Frankly, I think you're approaching this all wrong, Markus. Sure, we can look at tightening security, but that's not going to stop a power grab, as you put it. What you need is some political clout."

Borst lifted his eyebrow, and his forehead rode up under his toupee a fraction. "Yes? And?"

"Well, you have some power now. Probably more than you know. You insist on maintaining control under the fairness doctrine. You were responsible for the program's creation as a dedicated employee. It's simply unfair for the big giant to come sweeping in and take your baby away, thereby minimizing any additional advances you might have realized had it remained under your control. I think you could get a lot of ordinary employees to back you on a position like that, don't you?"

The smile came slowly, but when Borst got it, his mouth spread from ear to ear. "My, you are not so dumb, are you, Kent?" He glanced at the others. "By golly, that's brilliant! I think you are absolutely right. The little man against the big corporation and all that."

Kent nodded. He spoke again, wanting to nail this door shut while the hammer was in his hand. "If the boys in California want AFPS, no security is going to slow them down. They'll just take the whole thing and stomp the living daylights out of anyone who stands in their way. You have to put a political obstacle in their way, Markus. It's the only way." Cliff had lost his plastic grin, and Kent wondered about that. What difference did it make to the newcomer how this went down? Unless he knew more than he was letting on.

"I'm surprised Bentley didn't think of that," Borst wondered aloud. He blinked and addressed the group. "Anyway, I think I should take this to him immediately." He was already on his feet. Like the young eager student off to find his professor. Cliff held Kent's gaze for a moment without smiling. He turned to Borst.

"May I suggest we at least handle the security issue since it has been raised?" Cliff asked.

"Yes, of course. Why don't you take the lead on that, Cliff?" he said. But his mind was already in Bentley's office. "I've got to go."

Borst left, wearing a smirk.

Cliff had found his grin again.

Kent blinked. That last exchange had effectively dropped a bucket of heat on his head. It was still leaking down his spine when the others stood and wordlessly followed Borst's lead, exiting the room.

That was it. Cliff knew something. Kent lowered his head and began to rub his temples. It was unraveling. It was coming apart. In the space of ten minutes his link to sanity had been casually snipped free by some snowboarder from Dallas who knew more than he had any business knowing.

Think! Think, think, think, boy!

Okay, this is not the end. This is just another little bump. A challenge. Nobody is better at challenges than you, boy.

Kent suddenly wanted out of the building. The thought of going back to his office and having Cliff walk in with his grin scared him silly. He wanted to see Lacy.

He wanted a drink.

22

Kent spent most of the afternoon walking through the office trying to hide the pallor of death he knew grayed his face.

He took a late lunch by himself and was about to enter Antonio's when he saw Cliff. At least he thought it looked like Cliff. The junior programmer walked toward the corner across the street, and Kent's heart began to palpitate madly. It was not the sight of the snowboarder that had him suddenly fixed to the concrete; it was the sight of the pinhead walking beside Cliff, yapping with the traitor as if they were old buddies. The cop! It was the pinhead cop with slicked-back hair and wire-frame glasses!

Or was it? And then they were gone.

Kent ordered a salad for lunch and left after eating only the two black olives that came perched on top. Imagine the cop showing up here, of all places. And talking to Cliff! Unless that hadn't been the cop *or* Cliff up there. It was for this conclusion that Kent finally angled, and he angled for it hard. He was seeing things in his anxiety. Boulders were beginning to fall from the sky; only they weren't boulders at all. They were sparrows, and they weren't falling from the sky. They were flying happily about.

Get a grip, Kent.

When he got home that night he made straight for the cabinet and pulled out a bottle of tequila. Three shots and a shower later, he still had not managed to shake the sickness in his chest. His head hurt from the day's brain twisting. Thing of it was, this particular challenge was not his challenge at all. It was Cliff's challenge. If Cliff found ROOSTER, the game was over. And there was nothing Kent could do to change that. Nothing at all.

He had just poured his fourth shot when the doorbell rang for the first time in a week. Kent jerked. The shot splashed over his hand, and he cursed. Fortunately he was near the kitchen sink, and a quick run of water washed the liquor down the drain. Who could possibly be ringing his doorbell at eight in the evening?

The answer should not have surprised him. He swung the door open to a frowning Helen. A large travel bag hung from her shoulder.

"Helen! Come in," he said. *Helen, take a hike,* he thought.

She came in without answering and set her bag on the floor. Kent looked at the black duffel bag, thinking at first that she had lost her interest in running after all and was returning the shoes. But he could see already that there was more than footwear in that bag.

"Kent," Helen said, and she smiled. He thought the smile might have been forced.

"What can I do for you?" he asked.

"Kent," She took a deep breath, and suddenly Kent knew this was not just a courtesy visit. "I need to ask you a favor, Kent."

He nodded.

"If I needed you for something—really needed—would you help me?"

"Sure, Helen. Depending on what it was you needed me for, of course. I mean, I'm not exactly the wealthiest man on the earth." He chuckled, all the while scrambling to guess her next move. She was setting him up; that much was clear. She was going to ask him to help clear out her garage or some other horrendous task he could do without.

"No, it won't cost you a penny. In fact, I don't mind paying rent. And I'll buy half the groceries. That should save you some money."

He smiled wide, wondering where this could possibly be leading. Surely she didn't expect to move in with him. She hated his guts. In a mother-in-law sort of way. No, she was angling for something else, but his mind was drawing a blank.

"What's the matter, Kent? Cat got your tongue? Oh, come on now." She walked past him into the living room, and he followed her. "It wouldn't be so bad. You and me living together."

Kent pulled up, flabbergasted. "What!"

She turned to him and looked him square in the eye. "I'm asking you if I can move in, young man. I have just lost a grandson and a daughter, and I've decided that I simply cannot live on my own in that great big house." She shifted her stare. "I need company," she said.

"You need company?" Heat washed down Kent's back. "I don't mean to be rude or anything, but I'm not exactly good company these days. I'm the devil, remember?"

"Yes. I do remember. Nonetheless, I would be so grateful if you would let me use one of your spare bedrooms downstairs here. The sewing room across from Spencer's room, perhaps."

"Helen, you can't be serious!" Kent rounded the couch and walked away from her. This was absurd! What could she possibly be thinking? She would ruin everything! An image of him sneaking to the kitchen for a drink winked through his mind. She would give him hell. "There's no way it would work."

"I'm asking you, Kent. You're not going to turn out family, are you?"

Kent turned back. "Come on. Stop this, Helen. This is crazy. Just plain stupid! You'd hate it here! We have nothing in common. I'm a *sinner*, for God's sake!"

She didn't seem to hear him. "I can do the dishes too. Goodness, just look at that kitchen. Have you even touched it since I was here last?" She waddled off toward the breakfast bar.

"Helen! No. The answer is no. You have your own home. It's yours for a reason. This is my home. It is *mine* for a reason. You can't stay here. I need my privacy."

"I'm walking every day now, Kent. Did I tell you that? So I'll be gone early in the morning for my walk. You'll be gone by the time I get back, but maybe we can have dinner together every evening. What do you think?"

Kent stared at her, at a loss for words at her insane behavior. "I don't think you're listening. I said no! N-O! No, you can't stay here."

"I know the sewing room is full of stuff right now, but I will move it myself. I don't want to put you out." She walked around the bar and turned the faucet on. "Now, you know I can't stand television. It's the box from hell, you know. But I thought you could watch the one upstairs in your sitting room." She twisted the sink tap and ran water over her wrist, testing its temperature. "And I'm not crazy about drinking, either. If you want to drink any alcohol I'd prefer you did that upstairs as well. But I like music, you know. Heavy music, light music, any music as long as the words—"

"Helen! You're not listening!"

"And you're not listening!" she said. Her eyes seemed to reach out with knives and hold him at the neck. His breathing shut down.

"I said I need a place to stay, dear son-in-law! Now, I gave you my daughter for a dozen years; she warmed your bed and ironed your shirts. The least you can do is give me a room for a few nights. Is it really too much to ask?"

Kent nearly buckled under the words. It occurred to him that his mouth was open, and he closed it quickly. The tequila was starting to speak, moaning lazily through his mind. He thought that maybe he should just pull the plug now. Go out and use that nine-millimeter on his own head. End the day with a bang. At the very least he should be screaming at this old wench who had played mother-in-law in his old life.

But he could not scream because she was holding him in some kind of spell. And it was working. It was actually making him think that she was right.

"I . . . I don't think—"

"No, stop thinking, Kent." She lowered her voice. "Start *feeling* a little. Show some kindness. Let me take a room." Then she smiled. "I won't bite. I promise."

He could think of nothing to say. Except okay. It just came out. "Okay."

"Good. I will bring the rest of my belongings in from the car tomorrow after I've had a chance to clean out the sewing room. Do you like eggs, Kent?"

The woman was incredible. "Yes," he said, but he hardly heard himself say it.

"Oh, but that's right. I will have to leave before you get up. I walk at sunrise. Well, maybe we can have an egg dish one evening."

For a minute they faced each other in silence. Then Helen spoke, her voice soft now, almost apologetic. "It'll be okay, Kent. Really. In the end you will see. It will be okay. I guess you've already learned that we can't control everything in life. Sometimes things happen that we just didn't plan on. You can only hope that in the end it will all make sense. And it will. Believe me. It will."

Kent nodded. "Maybe," he said. "You know your way around. Make yourself at home."

Then he retreated to the master bedroom upstairs, grateful that he had stashed a bottle in the sitting room. It was early; maybe he should call Lacy. Or maybe drive up to see her. The idea touched off a spark of hope. Which was good, because hope had been all but dashed today.

～∞～

Lacy cleaned madly, fighting butterflies all the while and chastising herself for feeling any anxiety at all. So she was about to see Kent again. So he was coming to her condo this time. So he had brought that heat wave with him on Monday night. Her rekindled relationship with him was simply platonic, and she would keep it that way. Absolutely.

"Lacy, I need to talk," he'd said, and by the sound of his strained voice, he did need something. *Lacy, I need.* She liked the sound of that. And it was okay to like the sound of someone's platonic voice over the phone.

Indirect lighting cast a soft hue over the leather sofa angled under a vaulted ceiling. The fireplace sat black and spotless. An eight-by-ten picture of her late husband, John, stood at the hearth's center, and she considered removing it but quickly discarded the notion as absurd. Possibly even profane.

She donned jeans and a canary blouse, retouched her makeup carefully, opting for ruby lipstick and a light teal eye shadow, then made coffee. Her hand spooned the grounds with a slight quiver, and she mumbled to herself. "Lighten up, Lacy."

The doorbell chimed just as the coffee maker quit sputtering. Lacy took a deep breath and opened the door. Kent wore jeans and a white T-shirt that looked as if it might have been left in the dryer overnight. He grinned nervously and stepped in. His eyes were a little red, she thought. Maybe he was tired.

"Come in, Kent."

"Thanks."

He scanned the room, and she watched his eyes in the light. A small cut on his cheek betrayed a recent shave. They sat at the dinette and launched into small talk. How was your day? Good, and yours? Good. Good. But Kent was not looking so good. He was forcing his words, and his eyes jerked too often. He was having a bad day; that much he was not hiding. Better or worse than Monday, she did not know yet, but he was obviously still fighting his demons.

Lacy poured two cups of coffee, and they sipped through the small talk. Ten minutes passed before Kent shifted in his seat, and Lacy thought he was about to tell her why he wanted to see her again so soon. Other than maybe just wanting to see her. Unless her antenna had totally short-circuited over the last decade of marriage, there was some of that. At least some, regardless of all this platonic talk.

He stared at his black coffee, frowning. Her heart tightened. Goodness, he looked as though he might start crying. This was not just a bad-day thing. Something big had happened.

Lacy leaned forward, thinking she should reach out and take his hand or something. But he might misread her intentions. Or *she* might misread her intentions. She swallowed. "What's wrong, Kent?"

He shook his head and lowered it. "I don't know, Lacy. It's just . . ." He slid his elbow on the table and rested his forehead in his palm, looking now as if the blood had been siphoned from his face.

Now Lacy was worried. "Kent. What's going on?"

"Nothing. It's just hard, that's all. I feel like my life is unraveling."

"Your life *has* unraveled, Kent. You just lost your family, for heaven's sake. You're supposed to feel unraveled."

He nodded unconvincingly. "Yeah."

"What? You don't buy that? You think you're the man of steel who can just let these little details run off your big strong shoulders?" *Whoa, a bit strong there, Lacy. He is a wounded man. No need to kill him off with good intentions.*

Kent looked up slowly. There was a look in those eyes that brought a strange thought to Lacy's mind. The thought that Kent might actually be drinking. And maybe not just a little. "It isn't that. I know I'm supposed to be grieving. But I don't *want* to grieve," he growled through clenched teeth. "I want to make a new life for myself. And it's my new life that's driving me nuts. It hasn't even started, and it's already falling apart."

"Nothing's falling apart, Kent. Everything will work out; you'll see. I promise."

He paused and closed his eyes. Then, as if a spark had ignited behind his blue eyes, he suddenly leaned forward and grabbed her hand. A bolt of fire ripped through her heart. "Imagine having all this behind you, Lacy. Imagine having all the money you could dream of—starting over anywhere in the world. Don't you ever wonder what that would be like?"

He glanced at his hand around hers, and he pulled back self-consciously.

"Honestly? No," she answered.

"Well, I do. And I could do it." He gripped his right hand into a fist. "If it wasn't for all these fools who keep sticking their noses in my business . . ." Now it was more rage than anger lacing his voice, and he shook slightly.

Lacy blinked and tilted her head. He was making no sense. "Excuse me. What are we talking about here? *Who* are we talking about? You still work at the bank, right?"

"The cop at the bookstore for one thing. I can't shake him."

"You can't shake him? You've seen him again?"

"No, well yes—or maybe. I don't know if I really saw him again, but he's right there, you know. Riding along in my mind."

"Come on, Kent. You're overreacting now. For all you know, he was some kook pretending to be a cop. You don't know anything about this investigation of theirs."

He snapped his eyes to hers. "Pretending?"

"No, I don't know. I'm just saying *you* don't know. I'm not actually saying he was a kook, but there's no reason to walk around in this fear of yours when you hardly know a thing about the man. You have nothing to hide."

He blinked a few times quickly and bobbed his head. "Yeah. Hmm. Never thought of that." His glassy eyes stared at her cup now. Poor guy was upside down.

"Cliff's driving me nuts. I could kill the guy."

"Cliff, the new programmer? I thought you liked him. Now you're talking about killing the kid?" Lacy stood and walked to the coffee machine. "You're sounding scary, Kent."

"Yeah, never mind. You're right. I'm okay. I'm just . . ."

But he wasn't okay. He was sitting with his back to her, rubbing his temples now. He was coming unglued. And by the sounds of it, not from his wife's death, but from matters that followed no rhyme or reason. She should walk over there and knock some sense into his head. Or maybe go over there and hold him.

Her stomach hollowed at the thought. *A woman does not hold a man in a platonic relationship, Lacy. Shake his hand, maybe. But not hold him, as in, Let me put my hands on your face and stroke your cheek and run my fingers through your hair and tell you that everything—*

Something hot burned her thumb.

"Ouch!" Lacy snatched her hand to her mouth and sucked on the thumb. She had overfilled the cup.

Kent turned to her. "You okay?"

"Yes." She smiled. "Coffee burn." She returned to her seat.

"Helen moved in with me," he said.

Lacy sat back down. "Your mother-in-law? You're kidding! I thought you two were at each other's throats."

"We were. We are. I'm not even sure how it happened—it just did. She's staying in the sewing room."

"For how long?"

"I don't know." He was shaking his head again, and this time a tear had managed to slip from his right eye. "I don't know anything anymore, Lacy." Kent suddenly dropped his head onto folded arms and started to sob quietly. The man was stretched beyond his capacities.

Lacy felt her heart contract beyond her control. If she wasn't careful the tears would be coming from her eyes as well. And then one did, and she knew she could not just watch him without offering some comfort.

She waited as long as her resolve would allow. Then she stood unsteadily from her chair and stepped to his side. She stood over him for a brief moment, her hand lifted motionlessly above his head. His wavy blond hair rested against his head just as it had years ago, halfway down a strong neck.

Lacy had one last round with the inner voice that insisted she keep this relationship purely platonic. She told the voice to stretch its definition of *platonic*.

And then she lowered her hand to his head and touched him.

She could feel the electrical impulse run through his body at her touch. Or was it running through *her* body? She knelt and put her arm around his shoulder. His sobs shook him gently.

"Shhhh." Her cheek was now wet with tears. "It will be okay," she whispered.

Kent turned into her then, and they held each other.

That's all they did. Hold each other. But they held each other for a long time, and when Kent finally left an hour later, Lacy had all but decided that *platonic* was a word best left in the textbooks. Or maybe just erased altogether. It was a silly word.

23

Kent dragged himself to work Thursday morning, swallowing continually against the dread that churned in his gut. It reminded him of the time he'd been audited by the IRS three years earlier. He'd felt like a stranded Jew interrogated by the Gestapo. Only this time things were clearly worse. Then, he'd had nothing to hide beyond the moving deduction he'd possibly inflated. Now he had his whole life to hide.

His eyes had taken to leaking again—as they had those first few weeks after Gloria's death. The tears came without warning, blurring traffic signals and dissolving his dashboard to a sea of strange symbols. A dull ache droned through his head—a reminder of the "nightcaps" he'd indulged himself in after returning from Boulder. If it wasn't for the single thread of hope that strung through his mind, he might have stayed home. Downed some more nightcaps. Of course, he would have to tread lightly now that Helen had managed to work her way into his life. Things seemed to be coming apart at the seams again, and he had hardly begun this mad plan of his.

As it was, those words Lacy had spoken the previous evening triggered a new thought. A most desperate plan, really, but one to which he could cling for the moment. "For all you know he was some kook pretending to be a cop," Lacy had said. It was true that the cop had not shown his badge, and everyone knew that a business card could be had in half an hour at Kinko's. Still, he had known too much to be pretending. That was not it. But the comment had spawned another thought that centered around the word *kook*. And it had to do with Cliff, not the cop.

From all indications, it seemed that Cliff was on to him. Somehow that little snoop had gotten a hair up his nose and decided something needed exposing. So then why not undermine the kid? Showing him to be a kook might be a tad difficult; after all, the guy had already demonstrated his competence as a programmer. But that didn't mean he was squeaky clean. For starters, he was a snowboarder, and snowboarders were not textbook examples of conformists. There had to be some dirt out there on Cliff. Just enough to spin some doubts. Even a rumor with no basis at all. *Did you know that Cliff is the ringleader for the Satanist priesthood that murdered that guy in Naperville?* Didn't matter if there was such a priesthood or a murder or even a Naperville. Well, maybe it mattered a little.

By the time Kent got to work he knew precisely how he would spend his morning. He would spend it dragging Cliff into the dirt. And if need be, he would create the dirt himself with a few clicks of his mouse. Yes indeed, twenty years of hard study and work were gonna pay off this morning.

His ritual *Good mornings* came hard, like trying to speak with a mouthful of bile. But he managed them and rushed into his office, locking the door behind him. He made it halfway to his chair when the knock came. Kent grimaced and considered ignoring the fool—whichever fool it was. It didn't matter; they were all fools. It was probably Cliff the hound out there, sniffing at his door.

Kent opened the door. Sure enough, Cliff stood proud, wearing his ear-to-ear pineapple-eating grin.

"Hey, Kent. What are you doing this morning?"

"Work, Cliff." He could not hide his distaste. The realization that he was sneering at the man flew through his mind, but he was powerless to adjust his facial muscles.

Cliff seemed undeterred. "Mind if I come in, Kent? I've got some things you might want to look at. It's amazing what you can find if you dig deep enough." Cheese.

Kent's right hand nearly flew out and slapped that smiling face on impulse. But he held it to a tremble by his side. Things had evidently just escalated. It could very possibly all come down to this moment, couldn't it? This snowboard sniffer here may very well have the goods on him. Then a thought dropped into his mind.

"How about one o'clock? Can you hold off until then?"

Cliff hesitated and lost the grin. "I would prefer to meet now, actually."

"I'm sure you would, but I have some urgent business to attend to right now, Cliff. How about one o'clock?"

"And what kind of urgent business is that, Kent?"

They stared at each other without speaking for a full ten seconds.

"One o'clock, Cliff. I'll be right here at one."

The programmer nodded slowly and stepped back without answering. Kent closed the door, immediately breathing heavily. He scrambled for the desk, frantic, his knees weak. It was the end. If he had any sense at all he would leave now. Just walk out and leave Niponbank to its own problems. He had not broken any laws yet; his coworkers could do little but gossip. He would become "that poor man who lost his wife and son and then his mind." Too bad, too, because he showed so much promise. Borst's right-hand man. The thought made him nauseous.

This whole notion of stealing twenty million dollars had been foolishness from the beginning. Insane! You just don't think up things like that and expect to pull them off. He grabbed a tissue from a box on his desk and wiped at the sweat wetting his collar.

On the other hand, if he did leave he might very well kill himself. Drink himself to death.

Kent wiped his palms on his slacks and stabbed at the keyboard. A moment later he was into the human resources secure-data files. If anyone caught him in the files without authorization, he would be fired on the spot. He ran a query on Cliff Monroe. A small hourglass blinked lazily on his screen. This exercise now seemed like a stupid idea too. What did he expect to do? Run out into the hall, ranting and raving about the programmer who was really a werewolf? Maybe the bimbos in the lobby would believe him. *Honest, gals! He's a werewolf! Spread the word—quick, before my one o'clock meeting with him.*

A record popped on the screen, showing a home address on Platte Street in Dallas, a social security number, and some other basics. According to the record, Cliff had been employed exactly one week before his transfer to Denver in response to a request placed by Markus Borst. The reason was listed as "Replacement." So Borst had not expected to see him back. *Surprise, Baldy! Here I am!*

The rest of Cliff's record noted a basic education with high scores, and a list of previous employers. The kid had worked with the best, according to his short history. *Well, not for long, fella.*

Kent glanced back at the door quickly. *Here goes nothing.* He deleted the employment history from Cliff's record with a single keystroke. Then he quickly changed the file number so that no corresponding paper file would match this record, and he saved the modifications. In the space of ten seconds he had erased Cliff's history and lost the hard copy file. At least for a while.

He leaned back. Simple enough, if you knew what you were doing. Although the crashing of his heart belied that fact. Now the real test.

Kent picked up the phone and dialed Dallas. He was patched through to a Mary in human resources.

"Good morning, Mary. Kent Anthony here from IS in Denver. I'm checking on the qualifications of an employee. A Cliff Monroe, file number 3678B. Can you pull that up for me?"

He stared at the modified file on his screen.

"Yes, what can I help you with?"

"I'm trying to determine his employment history. Can you tell me where he worked before taking a job with us?"

"Just a second . . ." Kent heard the faint sound of keys clicking. "Hmm. Actually, it looks like he has no history. This must be his first job."

"You're kidding! Isn't that a bit odd for a high-level programmer? Can you tell me who hired him?"

Mary clicked for a minute and then flipped through some papers before answering. "Looks like Bob Malcom hired him."

"Bob? Maybe I should talk to Bob. He works there?"

"Sure. Talk to Bob. Does seem a bit odd, doesn't it?"

"Can you transfer me?"

"Sure, hold on."

It took a full five minutes of refusing to leave a message and holding to finally get the man on the phone.

"Bob Malcom."

"Bob, this is Kent Anthony from Denver. I'm looking into the employment history of a Cliff Monroe . . ." He went through the spiel again and let Bob look around a bit. But in the end it was the same.

"Hmm. You're right. It does say that I hired him, but, you know, I don't remember . . . Hold on. Let me look at my log."

Kent leaned back. He bit at his index fingernail and stared at the screen.

Bob's voice crackled again. "Yep, we hired him. So it says. How long did you say he's been working there?"

Kent scooted to the edge of his seat. "Six weeks."

"On what kind of project?"

"AFPS."

"The new processing system? And you have management control over him?" Suddenly Bob's voice rang with a note of concern.

"No, I'm not his direct supervisor; I'm just running a query to understand his qualifications for a project he's working on for me. And yes, it *is* the new processing system. Is there a problem with that?"

"Not necessarily. But you can never be too careful." He paused as if thinking things through.

It sounded too good to be true. Kent was trembling again, but now with waves of relief at this sudden turn of fortunes. "What do you mean?"

"I'm just saying you can never be too careful. It's odd we sent someone without an employment history to such a sensitive assignment. You never know. Look, I'm not ready to say that Mr. Monroe is anything but what he appears to be; I'm just saying until we know for sure, we should be careful. Corporate espionage is big business these days, and with the implementation of that system of yours up there—who knows? I'll tell you what. Why don't you have Mr. Monroe give me a call?"

No, that wouldn't do. "Actually, Bob, if there's any possibility that what you're saying proves to have merit, I'm not sure we want to tip Mr. Monroe off."

"Hmm. Yes, of course. You're right. We should begin a quiet investigation right away."

"And we may want him recalled in the meantime. I'll check with the department supervisor, but seeing as he's on temporary-replacement assignment anyway, I don't see any sense in keeping him in a sensitive position. AFPS is too valuable to risk, at any level."

"Reassign him?"

"Reassign him immediately," Kent insisted. "Today. As soon as I've talked to Borst, of course."

"Yes. Makes sense. Call me then."

"Good. In fact, maybe you could send him on an errand. Run to the bookstore or something—get him out of here while we sort this out."

"I'll call him as soon as we hang up."

"Thank you, Bob. You're a good man."

Kent hung up feeling as though the world had just been handed to him on a platter. He stood and pumped his fist. "Yesss!" He walked around his office, thinking through his next play. He would tell Borst about the possibility that they had a spy working under their noses. It was perfect! Cliff the kook, a spy.

Twenty-five minutes later it was all over. Kent talked to Borst, who nearly lost his toupee bolting from his seat. Of course, he had to call Bob himself—make sure this removing of Cliff happened immediately, barking orders like he owned the bank or something. Kent watched, biting his cheeks to keep the grin from splitting his face.

The plan proceeded flawlessly. Cliff left on some errand for Bob at eleven, after popping his head into Kent's office to remind him of the one o'clock, clueless as to his impending demise. It was the last they would see of him for at least a few days while Human Resources checked out this whole business. They would discover that Cliff's file had mistakenly been wiped out, possibly, but by then, it would not matter.

Borst changed the access codes to AFPS within the hour. Cliff Monroe was history. Just like that. Which meant that for now, all was back to a semblance of order. As long as ROOSTER had not yet been discovered, there was no reason not to continue.

Actually, there was plenty of reason not to continue. In fact, every reasonable bone in his body screamed foul at the very thought of continuing.

It was noon before Kent found the solitude he needed to check on ROOSTER's status. He virtually dove at the keyboard, punching through menus as if they did not exist. If Cliff had discovered the link, he would have left tracks.

Kent held his breath and scrolled down to the MISC folder containing ROOSTER. Then he exhaled long and slow and leaned back in his chair. The file had been opened one week earlier at 11:45 P.M. And that was good, because that had been him, last Wednesday evening.

A small ball of hope rolled up his chest, ballooning quickly. He closed his eyes and let the euphoria run through his bones. Yes, this was good. This was all he had. This was everything.

The pinhead cop's face suddenly flashed before him, and he blinked it away. The authorities had not made further contact, and he had decided that Lacy was correct about one thing—they were just doing their job. At least that's what he insisted on believing. They simply could not know about ROOS-TER. And without ROOSTER, they had nothing. Nada. This bit about Spencer was absolute nonsense. Why Pinhead had even gone on about everything one day being found out, Kent had no clue. Certainly the man was not a psychic. But no other explanation fit. And psychics were nothing more than con men. Which meant that nothing fit. Pinhead simply did not fit into any reasonable picture.

Once he executed the plan, the point would be moot anyway. Cops would be crawling all over the bank.

He had to do this now, before some other menace cropped up. Before some other propeller-head walked into his life, flashing a pineapple-eating grin. And *now* meant within a week. Or next weekend. Which meant beginning now.

⌘

"You what?"

"I moved in with him."

"You moved in with Kent?" She did not answer. "Why?"

"I had no choice in the matter. Actually, I did have a choice. I could have ignored him."

"*Kent* asked you to move in?"

"No. I meant I could have ignored God. He told me to move in. And don't think I wanted to, either. Believe me, I fought this one."

Bill Madison shook his head slowly. Helen had been walking for over two weeks now. Eight hours, twenty miles a day, without any signs of weakness. It was Jericho all over again, and Bill was not sleeping so much these days. His wife had accused him of being distracted on several occasions, and he had not bothered to deny it. Neither had he bothered to tell her about Helen's little daily ventures out into the concrete jungle. It seemed somehow profane to talk idly about the matter. And he would be less than honest to deny that a small part of him wondered whether she had somehow conjured up the whole thing. A senile intercessor suffering from delusions of walking in God's power. It was not unthinkable. Actually more plausible than believing her.

But that was the problem—he did believe her. In fact he had *seen* her.

"So how did you talk him into that?"

"It wasn't pleasant."

"I'm sure it wasn't." He paused, choosing his questions carefully. They spoke every other day, give or take, and Bill found himself begging time to skip forward to their conversations. Once on the phone, he fought for every minute. Invariably it was she who ended the discussion.

"I'm surprised he didn't flatly refuse."

"He did."

"I see. And still you're there. How is he?"

"He's no nearer the truth than he was a decade ago," she returned flatly. "If I were walking in circles and he was the wall of Jericho, I might feel like we had come to the end of the first day."

"You think it's that far off?"

"No. I'm not *thinking*. It is how I *feel*."

He smiled. "Surely there must be a crack in that armor of his. You've been breathing down his neck as you say, for weeks. You are specifically called to intercede for the man; surely that means God will hear you. *Is* hearing you."

"You would think so, wouldn't you? On the other hand, you are specifically called to pray for *your* loved ones, Pastor. Does God hear my prayers any more than he hears your prayers?"

"I don't know. I would have said *no* a month ago, but I would also have thought you crazy a month ago."

"You still do at times, don't you, Bill?" He couldn't answer. "It's okay. So do I. But you are right; God is hearing me. We are both deriving a lot of pleasure from this little episode now that I've settled into an acceptance of the matter."

"You've always interceded for others, Helen. In many ways this is not so different."

"Yes, in many ways. You are right. But in one way it's very different. I am now walking in faith, you see. Quite literally. I am living intercession, not simply praying. The difference is like the difference between splashing through the surf and diving into the ocean."

"Hmmm. Good analogy. That's good."

"He's drinking, Bill. And he's slipping. Like a slug headed for the dark creases."

"I'm sorry, Helen. I'm sure it must be hard."

"Oh, it's not so hard anymore, Pastor. Actually the walking helps. It's . . . well, it's like a bit of heaven on Earth, maybe. It's the stretching of the mind that wears one thin. Have you been feeling thin lately, Bill?"

"Yes. Yes, I have. My wife thinks I need a break."

"Good. We have too many of the thick headed among our ranks. Maybe one of these days you'll be thin enough to hear."

"Hmm."

"Good-bye, Bill. I have to fix him dinner. I promised I would. We're having egg foo yung."

24

Week Eleven

Kent saw Helen at each evening meal, but otherwise only the spotless kitchen remained as a clue that another person shared the house. By the time he dragged himself from bed each morning, she was gone. Walking, she said, although he couldn't imagine why a woman Helen's age chose 5 A.M. for her daily walk. By the time he wandered home about six, the evening meal was either on the table or simmering on the stove.

He'd peeked into the sewing room once, just to see what she had done with it. The bed had been neatly made with a comforter he'd never seen before; a small pile of laundry rested at the foot, waiting to be put away. Otherwise there was hardly a sign that Helen occupied the spotless room. Only the nightstand beside the bed betrayed her residence there. There, her Bible lay open, slightly yellowed under the lamp. A white porcelain teacup sat nearby, emptied of its contents. But it was the crystal bottle that made him blink. She had brought this one knick-knack from that hutch in her house and set it here beside her bed. Her most prized possession, Gloria had once told him. A simple bottle filled with only God knew what. Kent had closed the door without entering.

He had come home Tuesday evening to the sound of what he would have sworn was Gloria singing. He'd called her name and run to the kitchen only to find Helen bent over the sink, humming. If she'd heard him, she did not show it. He had retreated to the bedroom for a quick snip at the bottle without her knowing.

The meals themselves were a time of clinking and smacking and polite talk, but not once did Helen engage him in any of her religious dogma. She'd made a conscious decision not to, he thought. In fact, by the way she carried herself, on several occasions he found himself wondering if she had succumbed to some new drug that kept her in the clouds. Her eyes seemed to shine with confidence, and she smiled a lot. Possibly she was misreading one of her prescriptions and overdosing.

If so, she had lost neither her wit nor her analytical skills. He had engaged her about her knee-high socks once and found that out immediately.

"Those socks look silly with a dress. You *do* know that, don't you?"

"Yes, I had noticed that. But they keep my legs warm."

"And so would pants."

"No, Kent. You wear the pants in this family. I wear the dress. If you think these socks look silly, think of how a dress would look hanging off your hips."

"But it doesn't *have* to be that way," he said with a chuckle.

"You're right. But to be perfectly honest with you, it's the only way I can get men to look at my legs these days."

He drove up to the house on Thursday, eager to discover what Helen had prepared for dinner. The sentiment caused him to stop with the car door half open. The fact was, he looked forward to walking into the house, didn't he? It was the only thing he really looked forward to now besides the plan. There was always the plan, of course.

And there was Lacy.

They had steak that night.

Kent forged ahead, tiptoeing through the hours, refining his plan, calling Lacy, drinking. Quite a lot of drinking, always late at night, either in his upstairs sitting room or at the office, maintaining his pattern of late nights at work.

They all took Cliff's departure in stride, talking ad infinitum about how the competition had tried to steal AFPS and almost got away with it. The speculation only fueled their perceptions of self-importance. That anyone would go to such lengths to infiltrate their ranks came off as yet one more feather in Borst's cap. The distraction proved a perfect cover for Kent's last days among them.

Step by step, the perfect crime began to materialize with stunning clarity. And that was no illusion. He had breezed through graduate school, testing with one of the sharpest analytical minds this side of Tokyo. Not that he dwelled on the fact; he just knew it. And his mind told him a few things about his plan. It told him that what he was planning was most definitely a crime, punishable by severe penalties. If he did fail, it would be the end of him. He might as well take a cyanide capsule with him in the event things went wrong.

His mind also told him that the plan, however criminal, however heinous, was absolutely brilliant. Crime-of-the-century stuff. Enough to bring a smile to any cop's mouth; enough to boil any breathing man's blood.

And his mind told him that when it was over, if he succeeded, he would be one rich fool, living in a new skin, free to suck up whatever pleasures the world had to offer. His heart pounded at the thought.

There was simply nothing he had overlooked.

Except Lacy. He had overlooked Lacy. Well, not Lacy herself—she was becoming hard to overlook. In fact, it was the difficulty of overlooking her that he had overlooked.

They talked every evening, and he had become increasingly aware of the way his gut knotted each time he thought about picking up the phone to call her. It had been the way she touched him on his last visit, holding his head as though it might break, feeling her breath in his ear. Long-lost memories had flooded his mind.

The following evening's phone call had driven the stake further into his heart.

"You okay, Kent?"

"Yes. I'm better. I don't know how to thank you, Lacy. I just . . ." And then he had started to blubber, of all things. Cried right then on the phone, and he hardly knew why.

"Oh, Kent! It will okay. Shhh, shhh. It will be okay. I promise."

He should have dropped the phone in its cradle then and walked away from her. But he could not. The calls this whole week had been no better. No more tears. But the gentle words, though not overtly affectionate, could hardly hide the chemistry brewing between them.

And now Friday had arrived. Which was a problem, because Lacy didn't exactly fit into his plan, and his plan started tomorrow.

Helen asked him if anything was wrong during the evening meal, and he shook his head. "No, why?"

"No reason, really. You just look troubled."

It was the last she said of the matter, but her words rang annoyingly through his mind. He had expected to be ecstatic on the eve of the big weekend. Not troubled. And yet he *was* ecstatic in some ways. It was the Lacy thing that tore at his heart.

Kent retired to his room and downed three shots before working up the courage to call her.

"Kent! I'm so glad you called! You would not believe what happened to me at work today." Her voice might just as well have been a vise clamped around his heart, squeezing.

"Oh? What happened?"

"They asked me to enter management school. They want to groom me for management."

"Good. That's good, Lacy." He swallowed. It could have been him six years ago, starting his climb up the ladder. And he'd climbed right to the top . . . before they decided to push him over.

"Good? It's *great!*" She paused. "What's wrong, Kent?"

"Nothing. Really, that's great."

"You sound like you just swallowed a pickle. What's wrong?"

"I need to see you, Lacy."

Her voice softened. "Okay. When?"

"Tonight."

"Right now?"

"Yes."

"Is there a problem?"

"No." Kent was having difficulty keeping his voice steady. "Can I drive up?"

She hesitated, and for some reason that worsened the ache in his chest.

"Sure," she said. "Give me an hour."

"I'll see you in an hour, then."

Kent hung up feeling as though he had just thrown a switch to an electric chair. His own electric chair. But by the time he pulled up to her condo, he had resolved the issue. He would do what needed to be done, and he would do it the *way* it needed to be done. He took a slug of tequila from the bottle in the passenger seat and pushed his door open.

God, help me, he thought. It was a prayer.

❧

They sat at her dinette table again, opposite each other, as they had done nearly two weeks earlier. Lacy wore jeans and a white shirt advertising Cabo San Lucas in splashy red letters. Kent had come wearing faded denims and loafers. His blue eyes had not lost their red sheen. The faint, sweet smell of alcohol drifted around him. He had grinned shyly and avoided contact with her upon entering. Not that she had expected a hug or anything. But that said something, she thought. *What it said*, she had no clue.

For ten minutes they made small talk that would have carried more grace on the phone. Then Kent settled into his chair, and she knew he wanted to tell her something.

"Do you ever feel guilty about wanting to move on?" Kent asked, staring at his coffee.

Lacy felt her heart strengthen its pulse. *Move on?* she thought. *You want to move on? I'm not sure I'm ready to move on yet. At least not in a relationship with another man.* "What do you mean?" she asked and lifted her cup to her lips.

"Move on. Get past . . . John." He nodded to the mantel. "Forget about your past and begin over. You ever feel like that?"

"In some ways, yes. I'm not sure I've ever wanted to *forget* John, though. But we do have to get on with life." She looked at those baby blues, and suddenly she wanted him to just come out and tell her that he did want to move on—and move on with her. She would hold him back, of course. But she wanted to be wanted by him.

He was nodding. "Yes. Only . . . maybe even wanting to put the past totally aside. Because as long as you have those memories you can never really be new. You ever feel like that? Even a tiny bit?"

"Probably. I just never thought about it in those terms."

"Well, now that you are, does it make you feel bad? You know, for not wanting to remember the past."

Lacy thought about the question, thinking it a tad strange. "I'm not sure. Why?"

"Because I'm thinking about starting over," he said.

"Oh? And how would you do that?"

The corners of his mouth lifted barely. His eyes brightened. "If I told you, would you swear to secrecy?"

She did not respond.

"I mean, absolute secrecy. Tell no man, ever—or woman, for that matter. Just you and I. Could you swear to that on John's grave?"

Lacy recoiled at the question. John's grave? Kent was still grinning mischievously, and Lacy sat straighter. "Why? I mean, I think so. It depends."

"No, I need a definite yes. No matter what I tell you, I want you to swear to guard it. I need that confidence in you. Can you do that?"

In any other circumstance Lacy would be telling him she couldn't put herself in that situation without knowing more. But that's not what came out of her mouth.

"Yes," she said. And she knew it was the truth. No matter what he said, she would guard it as her own.

Kent watched her carefully for a few seconds. "I believe you," he said. "And if you ever break this promise, you will be putting me in the grave, right beside my wife. I want you to understand that. Acknowledge that."

She nodded, thoroughly confused as to his direction.

"Good." He took a long drink of coffee and set the cup down carefully, dead serious. "I'm going to start over, Lacy. Completely." He waited, as if he'd just revealed a sinister secret and expected her to drop her jaw to the table.

"That's good, Kent."

Kent lowered his head and looked at her, past her arching eyebrows. His lips curled in a wicked grin. "I'm going be rich, Lacy."

She thought he might burst with this thing. And so far, it was nothing worthy of his behavior. Unless it really was about her and he was showing attraction in some strange, deluded manor. *I'm going to get rich, Honey, so you and I can live a new life together.*

"I'm going to steal twenty million dollars."

"Come on, Kent. Be serious."

"I'm as serious as a heart attack, Honey."

She heard his words the way one might see a bomb's distant mushroom cloud, but it took a second for the impact to reach in and shake her bones. Her first thought was denial. But it fled before his glare, and she knew he was just that: as serious as a heart attack.

"You're going to *steal?*"

He nodded, grinning.

"You're going to steal twenty *million?*"

He nodded, still wearing that thin grin. "That's a lot of money, isn't it? It's the amount that I stood to earn from my bonus if Borst and Bentley hadn't pilfered it." He said the names through a sudden snarl. And then, more matter-of-factly, he added, "I'm going to take it."

Lacy was flabbergasted. "But how? From them? You can't just steal twenty million dollars and not expect to get caught!"

"No? I'm not touching Borst and Bentley, at least not at first. Even if they had that kind of money, you're right—it would be suicide to take such a sum from anyone."

He lifted the cup again, slowly, staring into it, and he spoke just before the rim touched his lips. "Which is why I will take it from no one." He drank, and she watched him, caught up in his drama.

She thought he had flipped his lid—all theatrical and making no sense at all. He lowered the cup to the table, landing it without a sound. "I will take it from one hundred million accounts. Next month, one hundred million interbank ATM service fees will be slightly inflated on selected customers' statements. Not a soul will even suspect a theft has occurred."

She blinked at him several times, trying to understand. And then she did. "They will see it!"

"Service fees are not reconciled, Lacy. When was the last time you even checked on the accuracy of those little charges?" He raised an eyebrow. "Hmm?"

She shook her head. "You're crazy. Someone will notice. It's too much!"

"The banks will not know except through the odd customer who complains. When someone complains, what do they do? They run a query. A query that I will be able to detect. Any account queried, regardless of the nature of that query, will receive a correction. In the world of computing, anomalies do occur, Lacy. In this case, the anomaly will be corrected on all accounts in which it is detected. Either way, the transactions will be nontraceable."

"But that's impossible. Every transaction is traceable."

"Oh?" He let it stand at that and just stared at her, his head still angled in a rather sinister manor, she thought.

Lacy stared at Kent and began to believe him. He was, after all, no idiot. She didn't know the inner workings of a bank's finances, but she knew that Kent did. If anybody could do what he suggested, he could. Goodness! Was he actually planning on stealing twenty million dollars? It was insane! Twenty *million* dollars! Her heart thumped in her chest.

She swallowed. "Even if you could pull it off, it's . . . it's wrong. And you know how it feels to be wronged."

"Don't even begin to compare this with my loss," he shot back. "And who is being wronged here? You think losing a few cents will make anyone feel *wronged?* Like, *Oh, my stars, Gertrude! I've been robbed blind!* Besides, you have to know something in order to feel anything about it. And they will not know."

"It's the principle of it, Kent. You're stealing twenty million dollars, for heaven's sake! That's wrong."

His eyes flashed. "Wrong? Says who? What's happened to me—now, *that's* wrong. The way I'm looking at it, I'm just getting centered again."

"That doesn't make it right." So this was what he'd come to tell her. That he was about to become a world-class criminal. Mafia type. And she'd bared her soul to the man.

She frowned. "Even if you pull it off, you'll spend the rest of your life running. How are you going to explain all that money? It'll catch up to you one day."

"No. You see, actually that's what I came to tell you. Nothing will ever catch up to me, because I don't plan on being around to be caught up to. I'm leaving. Forever."

"Come on, Kent. With international laws and extradition treaties, they can track you down anywhere. What are you going to do, hide out in some tropical jungle?"

His blue eyes twinkled. She furrowed her brows.

He just smiled and crossed his legs. "We'll see, Lacy, but I wanted you to know that. Because tonight may be the last time you see me."

Then she understood why Kent had come. He had not come to ask her to share his life; he can come to say good-bye. He was tossing her out of his life as he had done once before. He had bound her to this secret of his—this crime— and now he intended to heave her overboard.

The realization spread over her like a flow of red-hot lava, searing right through to her bones. Her heart seized for a few moments. She knew it! She knew it, she knew it, she knew it! She'd been a fool to let him anywhere *near* her heart.

Kent's face suddenly fell, and she thought he had sensed her emotions. The instinct proved wrong.

"There will be a death involved, Lacy, but don't believe what you read in the papers. Things will not be what they seem. I can promise you that."

She recoiled at his admission, now stunned by the incongruity facing her. *You promise me, do you, Kent? Oh, well, that fills the cockles of my heart with delight, my strapping young monster! My blue-eyed psycho . . .*

"Lacy." Kent's voice jarred her back to the table. "You okay?"

She drew a breath and settled in the chair. It occurred to her that the time she had spent hurriedly doing her face and cleaning the condo had been wasted. Entirely. "I don't know, Kent. Am I supposed to be okay?" She eyed him point-edly, thinking to thrust a dagger there.

He sat up, aware for the first time, perhaps, that she was not taking all of this with a warm, cuddly heart. "I'm sharing something with you here, Lacy. I'm *exposing* myself. I don't just walk around flashing for the public, you know. Lighten up."

"Lighten up? You waltz into my place, swear me to secrecy, and then dump all over me! How dare you? And you just want me to lighten up?" She knew that nasty little quiver had taken to her lips, but she was powerless to stop it. "And don't assume everyone you flash will like what they see!"

Lacy felt a sudden furious urge to reach out and slap him. *Don't be an imbecile, Kent! You can't just run off and steal twenty million dollars! And you can't just run off, period! Not this time!*

And then she did. In a blinding fit of anger she just reached out and slapped him across the cheek! Hard. *Smack!* The sound echoed in the room as if someone had detonated a small firecracker. Kent reeled back, grabbing at the table for support and gasping in shock.

"Whaa—"

"Don't you *what* me, Kent Anthony!" Heat washed down Lacy's neck. Her hand was stinging. Maybe she had swung a bit hard. Goodness, she had *never* slapped a man! "You're killing me here!"

His eyes flashed with anger, and he scowled. "Look. *I'm* the one who's going out on the line here. I'm risking my neck, for Pete's sake. I'm sorry I've burdened you with my life, but at least you don't have to live it. I've lost everything!" His face throbbed red. "Everything, you hear me? It's either this or suicide, and if you don't believe me, you just watch, Honey!" He jerked away from her, and she saw that his eyes had blurred with tears.

Lacy gripped her fingers into a fist and closed her eyes. *Okay, slow down, Lacy. Relax. He's just hurt.* You're *hurt.* She put her palms flat on the table, took several long pulls of air, and finally looked up at him.

He was staring at her again with those blue eyes, searching her. For what? Maybe she had mistaken his signals all along. Maybe those baby blues were looking at her as a link to reality, a partner in crime, a simple companion. God knew he was living in a void these days. And now she knew why—he was stepping off a cliff. He was playing with death. It was why the meeting with the cop had him wringing his hands.

She should be angry with herself more than with him, she thought. He had not misled her; she had simply been on the wrong track. Thinking foolish thoughts of falling in love with Kent again, while he had his eyes on this—this crime of new beginnings. And a death. Good heavens! He was planning on killing somebody!

"I *will* have to live with it, Kent," she said gently. "Whatever happens to you, happens to me now. You see that, don't you? You've climbed back into my heart." She shrugged. "And now you've just made me an accomplice, sworn to secrecy. You can understand how that might upset me a little, can't you?"

He blinked and leaned back. She could see that the thought was running through his mind for the first time. *Goodness. Men could be such apes.*

She rescued him. "But you're right. You're going to live the brunt of it all. So I may not see you again? Ever?"

He swallowed. "Maybe not. I'm sorry, Lacy. I must sound like a fool coming here and telling you all of this. I've been insensitive."

She held up a hand. "No, it's okay. It's not something I asked for, but now that it's done, I'm sure I can handle it." She looked at him and decided not to press the issue. Enough was enough. "And I shouldn't have slapped you."

"No, I guess I had that coming."

She hesitated. "Yes, I guess you did."

He gave off a nervous *humph*, off balance now.

"So, you really think striped pajamas and a buzz cut will disguise you, Kent? Maybe a ball and chain to boot? It'll be a new life, all right. Don't worry. I'll visit you often." She allowed a small grin.

He chuckled, and the tension fell like loosened shackles. "No way, Honey. If you think I'm going to prison, you obviously don't know me like you think you do."

But that was the problem. She did know him. And she knew that one way or another, his life was about to change forever. And with it, possibly hers.

"You're right. Well, I would wish you luck, but somehow it doesn't quite feel right, if you know what I mean. And I can't very well wish you failure, because I don't really go for watching people jerk and foam in electric chairs. So, I'll just hope that you change your mind. In the meantime, my lips are sealed. Fair enough?"

He nodded and grinned.

They drank coffee and talked for another hour before Kent left. He pecked her on the cheek at the door. She did not return the kiss.

Lacy cried a lot that night.

25

Saturday

Stealing twenty million dollars, no matter how well planned, engenders undeniable risks. Big, monstrous risks. Although Kent had rehearsed each phase of the two-day operation a thousand times in his mind, the actual execution would involve dozens of unforeseen possibilities. The least of these was probably the likelihood of a Volkswagen-sized asteroid striking downtown Denver and ending his day along with a few million others'—not much he could do about that. But somewhere between *Armageddon Two* and the real world lay the lurking monsters that seemed to ruin every crook's good intentions.

Kent let the booze knock him out late Friday night. After his little confessional with Lacy he deserved a good, long drink. Besides, with nerves strung like piano wires, he doubted sleep would come any other way. There would be no drinking for the robbery's duration, which meant he would have to lay off for a few days. Or maybe forever. The nasty stuff was beginning to show.

When consciousness returned at six o'clock Saturday morning, it came like an electric shock, and he bolted from bed.

It was Saturday! *The* Saturday. Six o'clock? He was already late! He stared around his bedroom, straining his eyes against a throbbing headache. His sheets lay in a wrinkled mess, wet from sweat.

A chill flashed down his spine. Who did he think he was, off to steal twenty million dollars? *Hello there, my name is Kent. I am a criminal. Wanted by the FBI.* The whole notion suddenly struck him as nonsense! He decided then, sitting in his bed, wet with cooling sweat at a hair past six Saturday morning, to discard the whole plan.

Seven deliberate seconds passed before he rescinded the decision and threw his sheets from his legs. Twenty million good old American greenbacks had his name on them, and he wasn't about to let them go to Borst and Tomato-Head.

The trip to Salt Lake City would take nine hours, which left him two hours to dress, confirm the order for the *fish,* and retrieve the truck.

Kent ran into the bathroom, cursing himself for the alcohol. He dipped his head under the tap, ignoring the pooling water at his beltline. No time for a shower. He wasn't planning on running into anyone who would mind anyway.

He dressed on the fly, pulling on a baggy shirt and khaki slacks. Within ten minutes of his first jolt in bed, Kent was ready to leave. For good. The thought stopped him at his bedroom door. Yes, for good. He had no plans of returning to the house again—a prospect he'd thought might bring on some nostalgia. But scanning the room now, he felt only anxious to leave.

It had to look as if he'd left with the full intention of returning, which was why he took nothing. Absolutely nothing. Not a tube of toothpaste, not an extra pair of socks, not even a comb. It was always something simple that tipped off the investigators. Truly brain-dead criminals like those from Stupid Street might empty their bank accounts the day before planning a getaway. Those with no mind at all might even run around town kissing loved ones good-bye and grinning ear to ear about some secret. *Gosh, I'm sorry, Mildred. I just can't tell you. But believe me, I'm gonna be soakin' up the sun in Hawaii while you're here workin' like an idiot for the rest of your miserable life!*

That pretty much summed up his little confessional with Lacy. Goodness! Kent shivered at the thought, wondering if his little trip to Boulder might be his undoing. If the visit had been a mistake, it would be his last. He swore it then, surveying his room for the last time.

He ran into the sitting room and turned on the television. He left his bed unmade; the toothpaste lay on the vanity, capless and dribbling. A John Grisham novel rested, dog-eared, on the nightstand, bookmarked at the ninth chapter. He ran down to the kitchen and scribbled a note to Helen.

Helen,
I'm headed for the mountains to fish—clear my head. Won't be back 'til late. Sorry about dinner. If I catch anything, we can fry it up tomorrow.
Kent

He reread the note. Good enough.

Kent left through the front door, casually opened the garage and pulled out his fishing tackle. Bart someone-or-other—Mathews, he thought, Bart Mathews—waved from his riding mower three lawns up. Kent waved back, thinking that the gods were now smiling on him. Yes, indeed, Kent Anthony left his house on Saturday with one thing on his mind. Fishing. He went fishing. Kent lifted his rod in a motion that said, *Yes sir, Bart—I'm going fishing, see? Remember that.* He smiled, but his hands were trembling. He tossed the pole in the backseat, on top of a closed box he'd loaded in the wee hours last night.

Kent backed the silver Lexus into Kiowa Street for the last time and sped from suburban Littleton, blinking his eyes against nagging whispers telling him that he was nuts. *Nuts, nuts, nuts.* Maybe he should *un*-rescind the decision to rescind the decision to abort. Now, there was some clear thinking.

On the other hand, how many would-be criminals had found themselves in precisely this situation—on some precipice overlooking the actual drop and thinking the cliff suddenly looked awfully high? And there was no bungee cord to yank him back if he went into freefall, no rip cord to pull in case he decided to bail out. It was straight down to see if you could land just right and roll out of it. The facts said that 99 percent ended up splattered on the rocks below, bird meat. The facts, the facts. The facts also said that every single one of those greenbacks was waiting to go home to Papa. And in this case, he was Papa.

Besides, at some point you suddenly realized you were already there, over the cliff, falling free, and Kent decided he'd now reached that point. He'd reached it two months earlier when all hell first broke loose.

It took him forty-five minutes to reach Front Range Meat Packers. He had selected the company ten days earlier for several reasons. At least that was the story he was telling himself these days. It might be more accurate to say that he had *chanced* upon the company, and then only because of the dreams.

The dreams. Ah, yes, the dreams. Although he could hardly remember the details of the dreams when he awoke, their general impressions lingered through the day. Brilliant general impressions, like the one that suggested he find his truck on the outskirts of town, near the Coors beer-processing plant. It was as if the alcohol delivered him to a deep sleep where things became clear and memories were bright once again. He'd awakened in the middle of a dream once and found himself shaking and sweating because it really felt like someone was in the dream with him, giving him a tour.

The dreams had played on his mind like fingers across a keyboard, stretching out tunes that resonated with his own brilliance. In fact, he'd finally concluded that they were just that: his own brilliance, shocked into high gear by the events that had pushed him. Pure logic found in the quiet of sleep.

And there were several very logical reasons why the Front Range Meat Packers plant met his needs. First, and possibly most important, it was located far off the beaten track in a large warehouse district south of 470. The metal structure evoked images of the Mafia cover operations he'd seen in a dozen movies. It was also closed on the weekends, leaving a hundred short-box refrigerated trucks parked in the sprawling lot, soaking up the sun's rays until Monday. He'd walked through the lot on Tuesday, wearing glasses and sporting a slicked-back hairdo that did a good enough job of changing his appearance, he thought. He had played a meat buyer from startup Michael's Butcher Shop in East Denver, and he'd played the part well. He'd also been given a lesson on exactly why Iveco refrigerated trucks were still the best units on the road. "No chance of the meat spoiling in here. No way," meatpacker Bob "the Cruiser" Waldorf had insisted, stroking a three-inch goatee.

Which was why he needed a truck in the first place. To keep the meat— the *fish*—from spoiling.

Kent now drove up to the warehouse complex and scanned it nervously. The grounds lay deserted. He snaked the Lexus into an alley and rolled toward the adjacent complex. Gravel crunched under tires; sweat leaked down his neck. It occurred to him that the unexpected presence of a single fool here could close down the operation. There could be no witness to his visit.

The adjacent lot housed a hundred ten-by-thirty storage cubicles, half of which were empty, their white-flecked doors rusted, dented, and tilting. It was a wonder the business found willing renters for the other half of the cubicles. That was another reason he had chosen this particular location: It offered a hiding place for the Lexus.

Kent nosed the car up to space 89 and turned the motor off. Silence rang in his ears.

This was it. Technically speaking, up until now he had not actually committed any crime. Now he was about to break into a storage bin and hide his car. Not necessarily something they would fry him for, but a crime nonetheless. His heart pounded steadily. The alley on either side lay clear.

Okay. Do this, Kent. Let's do it.

Kent pulled on leather gloves and stepped from the car. He pried the roll door up with considerable effort. Its wrenching squeal echoed through the concrete cubical, and he winced. Goodness, he could have just as easily put a flashing red light atop the thing. Kmart special. One crime being committed here! Come one, come all.

But no one came. Kent hopped back into the Lexus and pulled it into the space. He grabbed his briefcase and pulled the door closed, wincing again at its screech. Still the alley remained empty. He knelt quickly, withdrew a small rivet gun from his briefcase, popped a rivet on either side of the tin door, and replaced the gun.

He left space 89 and walked briskly for Front Range Meat Packers, scouring the compound in every direction for the one fool who would ruin everything. But the compound sat still and empty in the morning light.

Kent had run through a thousand methods for stealing a vehicle—crime number two in this long string of crimes he was about to commit. It wasn't until Cruiser had offered his explanation for the five trucks outside the main compound's security fence that Kent had landed on the current plan. "See, out of a fleet of 120, those are the only 5 that are inoperable right now."

"What? Breakdowns?" Kent had said, half kidding.

"Actually, truck 24, the one on the end, is in for a routine tune-up. We take good care of our trucks. Always have, always will."

It had been a gift. Kent stood by Cruiser, frozen for a moment, sure that he'd been here before—standing next to Cruiser while the keys to the kingdom were handed over. A déjà vu from one of those dreams, perhaps. There were other ways, of course. But in an operation strewn with complications, he had no intention of turning down the offering. He'd returned Thursday night and broken into the truck with a coat hanger. If they discovered Friday that truck 24 had been left open, they would probably move it. But it was a risk he had taken gladly. The process of breaking into the truck had taken him two full hours. He couldn't very well take two hours in broad daylight struggling on the hood with a coat hanger.

Truck 24 sat, unmoved, and Kent covered the last thirty yards over the graveled lot in a run. He grabbed the truck's door handle, held his breath, and pressed the latch. The door opened. He sighed with relief, tossed his briefcase on the bench seat, and climbed up, shaking like a leaf. A small ball of victory swelled in his chest. So far, so good. Like taking candy from a baby. He was in the cab, and the coast was clear!

One of the primary benefits of spending six years in higher learning institutions was learning how to learn. It was a skill that Kent had perfected. And one of the things he'd learned as of late was how to hot-wire a truck. Specifically an Iveco 2400 refrigerated truck. Not from a book entitled *How to Hot-Wire Your Favorite Truck,* no. But from a book on safeguarding your property, along with an engineering manual, an auto mechanic's electrical guide, and, of course, an Iveco 2400 repair manual—each source lending a few details to his collective learning experience. In the end, he knew precisely how to hot-wire an Iveco 2400. The procedure was supposed to be a thirty-second affair.

It took Kent ten minutes. The Phillips head he'd brought was a tad small and wanted to slip with every rotation. When he finally freed the panel under the dash, the wires were so far behind the steering column that he nearly ripped the skin from his fingers prying them out. But in the end his learning experience proved valid. When he touched the red wire to the white wire, the truck rumbled to life.

The sudden sound startled Kent, and he jerked up, promptly dropping the wires and hitting his head on the steering wheel in one smooth motion. The motor died.

Kent cursed and righted himself on the seat. He gazed about the compound, breathing heavily. The coast was still clear. He bent over and restarted the truck. His hands were sweating in the leather gloves, and he briefly considered pulling them free. But a dozen episodes of *Forensics* crashed into his mind at once, and he rejected the notion.

He shoved the truck into reverse, backed it into the lane, and nosed it toward the complex's exit a hundred yards off. One look and any reasonable person would have known that the driver perched behind the wheel in truck 24, sneaking toward the exit gate, was not your typical driver headed out for deliveries. For one thing, typical drivers don't sit like ice sculptures on the front edge of the seat, gripping the wheel as if it were the safety rail on a roller-coaster ride. For another, they don't jerk their heads back and forth like some windup doll gone berserk. But then, none of that mattered, because there were no reasonable people—or for that matter, *any* people—to see Kent creep from the lot in truck 24.

Within three minutes he was back on the thoroughfare, headed west, anxious and sweaty and checking the mirrors every five seconds, but undiscovered.

He studied the gauges carefully. The company had seen fit to leave truck 24 full of fuel. *Way to go, Cruiser.* Kent flipped on the cooling unit and rechecked the gauges. In fact, he rechecked the gauges fifteen times in those first ten minutes, before finally settling down for the seven-hour drive to Salt Lake City.

Only he didn't really settle down. He bit his nails and walked through every detail of his plan for the thousandth time. Now that he'd actually jumped over this cliff, the ground below was looking a little more rugged than before. In fact, having executed a brilliant plan that left absolutely nothing to chance, it occurred to him that he had virtually *depended* on chance up to this point. The chance that his alarm clock would actually work that morning. The chance that no one would be at Front Range Meat Packers on a Saturday morning, regardless of the fact that they were closed. The chance that the Iveco had not been moved into the secure compound. The chance that he could actually get the Iveco started.

And now Kent began to imagine the road ahead strewn with chances . . . with flat tires and traffic delays and power outages and routine pullovers. With boulders falling from the nearby cliffs and closing the road. Or worse, squashing his truck like a roach. That one would be God's doing—if indeed Gloria had been right and there was a God. Unless it was an earthquake's doing, in which case it would be Mother Nature reaching out to express her opinion of the matter.

Don't, son. Don't do this.

He glanced at the speedometer, saw that he exceeded the posted sixty miles-per-hour speed limit, and eased his foot from the accelerator. Getting pulled over for a speeding ticket, now, that would be a story for Stupid Street.

Kent reached the preselected dirt turnoff thirty minutes later and pulled into a grove of trees blocking the view to the interstate. It took him no more than five minutes to pull out the large magnetic signs he'd hidden in the tall grass midweek and slap them into place along each side of the truck. He studied his handiwork. For the next twenty-four hours, Front Range Meat Packers truck 24 would be known as McDaniel's Mortuary's truck 1. The signs along each side said so. In black lettering that was quaint and unobtrusive but clear and definite, so there would be no doubt.

Kent pulled back onto the highway and brought the truck up to full speed. Yes, he was most definitely over the cliff now. Falling like a stone.

26

Finding the right body, the "fish," and arranging for the pickup had taken Kent the better part of a week. He'd approached the challenge in two parts. First, setting up a plausible body pickup and second, actually finding the body itself.

Although he'd established McDaniel's Mortuary as a legitimate business only two weeks earlier, to look at the ghost company's Web site you would think it was one of the older houses in the West. Of course, local mortuaries would be the first to identify a new player that suddenly appeared in their territories, so he'd been forced to use distance as a buffer against recognition. It wasn't likely that independently owned mortuaries in Los Angeles, for example, would be familiar with funeral homes in Denver.

The company of choice also needed to be large enough to handle transfers to and from other cities on a regular basis. The request for a particular body on ice could not be an unusual occurrence. In addition, the mortuary had to be computerized, allowing Kent some kind of access to its data files.

These first three restrictions narrowed the field of eligible mortuaries from 9,873 nationally to 1,380. But it was the fourth requirement that put the breaks on eligibility for all but three unwitting participants. The mortuary had to be in possession of the right body.

The right body. A body that was six-feet-one-inch tall, male, Caucasian, with a body weight of between 170 and 200 pounds. A body that had no known surviving relatives. And a body that had no identifiable dental records outside of the FBI's main identification files.

In most cases mortuaries hold cadavers no longer than two or three days, a fact that limited the number of available bodies. For a week, Kent ran dry runs, breaking into the networks using the Web, identifying bodies that fit his requirements.

The process was one of downloading lists and cross-referencing them with the FBI's central data bank—a relatively simple process for someone in Kent's shoes. But it was arduous and sweaty and nerve-racking nonetheless. He ran the searches from his system at home, sipping at the tall bottle next to his monitor while he waited for the files to download.

On Tuesday, he'd found only one body, and it was in Michigan. That had put the jitters right though him, and it had taken nearly a full bottle of the hard drink to bring them under control.

On Wednesday, he'd found three bodies, one of which was actually in Denver. Too close to home. The other two were in California—too far. But at least there were three of them.

On Thursday, he'd found no bodies, and he had shattered his keyboard with a fist, a fit he immediately regretted. It ruined both his right pinkie—which had taken the brunt of the contact, somewhere between the letters J and U by the scattered keys—and his night. There were no twenty-four-hour keyboard stores that he was aware of.

Friday he'd found three bodies, to shuddering sighs of relief. Two on the East Coast and one in Salt Lake City. He downed two long slugs of liquor at the find. Tom Brinkley. *Thank you, Tom Brinkley. I love you, Tom Brinkley!*

Tom Brinkley had died of a gunshot wound to the stomach, and according to the records, no one seemed to have a clue about him beyond that. From all indications the man had shot himself, which also indicated to Kent that there *was* at least one other thing known about the man. He was an idiot. Only an idiot would attempt suicide with a bullet through the gut. Nevertheless, that is precisely what the authorities had concluded. Go figure.

Now poor Tom's body sat awaiting cremation in Salt Lake's largest mortuary, Peace Valley Funeral Home. Kent had tagged his "fish" then—processed an order for a transfer of the catch to McDaniel's Mortuary in Las Vegas, Nevada. Reason? Relatives had been located and wished a local burial. *Now I lay my fish to sleep.* The funeral home had informed him by e-mail that the body had already been stripped and prepared for cremation. *Not a problem. Will pick up as is.* It was in a sealed box. Did he want it in a body bag? A body bag was customary. *Not a problem. Will pick up as is.*

He scheduled a "will call" Saturday between 3 and 5 P.M. He would pick up the fish then. Only he knew it was not a fish, of course. It was just one of those interesting quirks that a mind gone over the edge tends to make. It was a dead body, as cold as a fish and possibly gray like a fish, but certainly not a fish. And hopefully not slimy like a fish.

He confirmed the order an hour later from a pay phone. The girl who answered his questions had a bad habit of snapping chewing gum while listening, but otherwise she seemed cooperative enough.

"But we close at five. You get here a minute past, and you won't find a soul around," she warned.

It had taken a mere forty-five minutes with his fingers flying nervously over the keyboard to make the changes to Tom Brinkley's FBI file. The tingles of excitement had shortened his breath for an hour following. Actually *that* had been the first crime. He'd forgotten. Breaking into the FBI files was not a laughable prank. It had not seemed so criminal, though.

Kent let the memories run through his mind and kept his eyes peeled as he negotiated I-70 west. The trip over the mountains was uneventful, unless you considered it eventful to bite your nails clean off every time a patrol car popped up in your rearview mirror. By the time Kent reached the outskirts of Salt Lake, his nerves had frayed, leaving him feeling as though he'd downed a dozen No-Doze tablets in a single sitting. He pulled in to a deserted rest stop, hurried to the back of the truck, and popped the refrigerated box open for the first time.

A cloud of trapped vapor billowed out, cold and white. The cooler worked well enough. Kent pulled himself up to the back bumper and then into the unit and waved his hand against the billows of vapor. The interior drifted into view about him. Metal shelves arose on the right. A long row of hooks hung from the ceiling on the left like claws begging for their slabs of meat. *For their fish.*

Kent shivered. It was cold. He imagined the gum-snapping gal at Peace Valley Funeral Home, clipboard in hand, staring up at those hooks.

"What are those for?"

"Those? Oh, we find that bodies are much easier to carry if you take them from their caskets and hook them up. You guys don't do that?"

No, the hooks would not do. But then, he was not some white-trash bozo from Stupid Street, was he? No sir. He had already planned for this eventuality. Cruiser had told him that all trucks carried thermal blankets to cover the meat in case of emergency. Truck 24's blankets lay in a neat stack to Kent's right. He pulled them off the shelf and strung two along the hooks like a shower curtain. A divider.

"What are those for?"

"Those? Oh, that's where we hide the really ugly ones so people don't throw up. You guys don't do that?"

Kent swallowed and climbed out of the cooler box. He left the rest stop and slowly made his way to the mark on his map that approximated the funeral home's location. To any other vehicle parked beside him at a light, he resembled a mortuary truck on a Saturday run. Right? The magnetic signs were dragging on the street, exposing the meat packer's logo, right? Because that would look obscene. So then why did he have such a hard time looking anywhere but straight ahead at stoplights?

Liberty Valley's wrought-iron gates loomed suddenly on Kent's left, bordered by long rows of pines. He caught a glimpse of the white building set back from the street, and his heart lodged firmly in his throat. He rounded the block and approached the main gate again, fighting the gut-wrenching impulse to drive on. Just keep on driving, right back to Denver. There was madness in this plan. Stealing a body. *Brilliant software engineer loses sanity and steals a body from funeral home. Why? It is yet unknown, but some have speculated that there may be other bodies, carved up, hidden.*

Then the gate was there in front of him, and Kent pulled in, clearing his throat of the knot that had been steadily growing since entering this cursed city.

The long, paved driveway rolled under him like a black snake. He followed a sign that led him to the rear, where a loading bay sat empty. A buzz droned in his head—the sound of the truck's wheels on the pavement. The steady moan of madness. He backed up to the door, pulled the parking brake, and left the engine running. He couldn't very well be seen fiddling with wires to restart it.

He set himself on autopilot now, executing the well-rehearsed plan. From his briefcase he withdrew glasses and a mustache. He fixed them quickly to his face, checked his image in the rearview mirror, and pulled out his clipboard.

A blonde-headed girl with a pug nose pushed open the rear door of the funeral home on his second ring. She was smacking gum.

"You from McDaniel's?"

He could feel the sweat breaking from his brow. He pushed his glasses back up his nose. "Yes."

She turned and headed into the dim storage area. "Good. You almost didn't make it. We close in fifteen minutes, you know."

"Yeah."

"So, you from Las Vegas?"

"Yeah."

"Never heard of McDaniel's. You ever win big money?"

Big money? His heart skipped a beat. What could she know of big money?

She sensed his hesitation and glanced over at him, smiling. "You know. Las Vegas. Gambling. Did you ever win big?"

"Uh . . . No. I don't gamble, really."

Coffins rose to the ceiling on all sides. Empty, no doubt. Hopefully. She led him to a huge side door made of steel. A cooler door.

"I don't blame you. Gambling's a sin." She popped the door open and stepped through. A dozen coffins, some shiny and elaborate, some no more than plywood boxes, rested on large shelves in the cooler. The girl walked over to one of the plain boxes, checked the tag, then slapped it.

"This is it. Grab that gurney there, and it's all yours."

Kent hesitated. The gurney, of course. He grabbed the wheeled table and pushed it parallel to the casket. Together they pulled the plywood box onto the gurney, a task made surprisingly easy by rollers on the shelf.

The girl slapped the box again. Seemed to like doing that. "There you go. Sign this, and you're all set."

Kent signed her release and offered a smile. "Thanks."

She returned the smile and opened the door for him.

Halfway back to the outer door he decided it might be best if she did not watch him load the body. "What should I do with the gurney when I'm done?" he asked.

"Oh, I'll help you."

"No. No problem, I can handle it. I should be able to—I've done this enough. I'll just shove it back through the door when I'm done."

She smiled. "It's okay. I don't mind. I need to close down anyway."

Kent thought about objecting again but decided it would only raise her curiosity. She held the door again, and he rolled the brown box into the sun. From this angle, with the truck parked below in the loading dock, he caught sight of the Iveco's roof. And it wasn't a pretty sight.

He jerked in shock and immediately covered by coughing hard. But his breathing was suddenly ragged and obvious. Large red words splashed across the roof of the Iveco's box: Front Range Meat Packers.

He flung a hand toward the bottom of the truck's roll door, hoping to draw her attention there. "Can you get the door?" If she saw the sign he might need to improvise. And he had no clue how to do that. Stealing bodies was not something he had perfected yet.

But Miss Gum-Smacker jumped to his suggestion and yanked the door up like a world-class chain-saw starter. She'd obviously done that a few times. Kent rolled the gurney down the short ramp and into the truck, gripping the ramp's aluminum railing to steady his jitters. As long as they remained down here, she would not have a chance to see the sign. Now, when he drove off . . . that would be a different story.

It occurred to him then that the casket would not fit on the shelves designed for meat. It would have to go on the floor.

"How do you lower this?" he asked.

She stepped in and looked at him with a raised brow. "You're asking me how to lower a gurney?"

"I usually carry ours—battery powered. All you do is push a button. But this is a new rig. It's not outfitted properly yet." Now, *there* was some quick thinking. Powered gurneys? There must be such a thing these days. She nodded, apparently satisfied, and lowered the contraption. Together they slid the coffin off and let it rest on the floor. Now to get her back into the warehouse without looking back.

"Here, let me help you," he said and walked right past her to the warehouse door, which he yanked open.

She wheeled the gurney up after him and pushed it through the door. "Thanks," she said and walked into the dim light.

"Thank you. Have a great weekend."

"Sure. Same to you."

Kent released the door and heard its lock engage. He glanced around and ran for the cab, trembling. What if she were to come back out? *"Hey, you forgot your clipboard."* Only he hadn't forgotten it. It was in his right hand, and he tossed it onto the bench seat. With a final glance back, he sprang into the truck, released the brake, and pulled out of the loading dock, his heart slamming in his chest.

He'd crossed the parking area and was pulling onto the long, snakelike drive before remembering the rear door. It was still open!

Kent screeched to a halt and ran to the back, beating back images of a shattered box strewn behind the truck. But not this day; this day the gods were smiling on him. The box remained where he'd left it, unmoved. He pulled the door closed, flooded with relief at small favors.

He pulled out of Liberty Valley's gates, shaking like a leaf. A full city block flew by before he realized that the jerking motion under him resulted from a fully engaged parking brake. He released it and felt the truck surge forward. Now, that was a Stupid Street trick if there ever was one. He had to get control of himself here!

Two blocks later the chills of victory began their run up and down his spine. Then Kent threw back his head and yelled out loud in the musty cabin. "Yes!"

The driver in the Cadillac beside him glanced his way. He didn't care.

"Yes, yes, yes!"

He had himself a body. A fish.

27

Helen scanned the note again and knew it said more than it read. This fishing business was hogwash, because it didn't bring a smile to her face as in, *Oh, good. He's gone to catch us some trout. I love trout.* Instead, it brought a knot to her gut, as in, *Oh, my God! What's he gone and done?*

She had felt the separation all day, walking the streets of Littleton. It was a quiet day in the heavens. A sad day. The angels were mourning. She still had energy to burn, but her heart was not so light, and she found praying difficult. God seemed distracted. Or maybe *she* was distracted.

Helen had walked the same twenty-mile route five days now, stopping briefly at the hot-dog stand at Fifth and Grand each day for a drink and a quick exchange with its proprietor, Chuck. She'd suspected from the first words out of Chuck's mouth that he was a man holed up in his religion.

Today she had helped him out of his shell.

"You walk every day, Helen?"

She'd nodded.

"How far?"

"A long way. Longer than I can count."

"More than a mile?"

"I can count a mile, young man."

"Longer?"

"Longer than I can count."

He'd chuckled nervously. "Ten miles?"

She sipped at the lemonade he'd served her. "Longer."

"Twenty?" he asked incredulous.

She shrugged. "I don't know for sure."

"But that's impossible! You walk twenty miles *every* day?"

She looked right into his eyes then. "Yes, I'm an intercessor, Chuck. You know what that is, don't you? I will walk as long as he requires me to."

He glanced around quickly. "You mean you pray?"

"I pray, and I walk. And as long as I'm walking and praying I don't feel strain on my legs at all." She eyed him steadily. "How does that sound, Chuck?"

He stood there with his mouth open, possibly thinking that this kind woman he'd served over the last five days was stark-raving mad. "Sound strange? Well, there's more, Chuck. I see things too. I walk on legs that have no business walking, and I see things." It was the first time she had been so vocal about this business to a stranger, but she could hardly resist.

She pointed to the overcast sky and gave it a faraway look. "You see those clouds there? Or this air?" She swept her hand through the air. "Suppose you could tear away this air and expose what lay behind. What do you think you would find?"

Chuck the hot-dog man was stuck in the open-mouth, wide-eyes look. He did not answer.

"I'll tell you what you would find. A million beings peering over the railing at the choices of one man. You would find the real game. Because it's all about what happens on the other side, Chuck. And if you could tear the heavens apart, you would see that. All this other stuff you see with those marbles in your head are props for the real game." She flashed him a grin and let that sink in. "At least, that's one way of looking at it all. And I think there is a game over your soul as well, young man."

She had left him like that, holding a hot dog in one hand with his mouth gaping as if he were ready to shove it in.

It had been the high point of the day, actually, because she knew Chuck's life would change now. But the balance of her walk had been a somber one.

Back at home, Helen picked up the phone and called Pastor Bill at home.

"Bill Madison here."

"He's gone off the deep end, Bill."

"Helen?"

"Yes."

"What do you mean?"

"Kent's gone off the deep end, and I smell death in the air. I think he may be in trouble."

"Whoa. You think he may *die?* I didn't think he *could* die in this thing."

"I didn't either. But there's death in the air. And I think it's his death, although I don't know that. There was a lot of silence in the heavens today."

"Then maybe you should warn him. Tell him about this. You haven't been . . . you know . . . told not to, have you?"

"No. Not specifically. I've had no desire to tell him, which usually means that I shouldn't. But I think you may be right. I think I will tell him the next time I see him."

They let the phones rest silent for a moment.

"Helen, are you walking tomorrow?"

"Did you awake this morning, Bill?"

"What? Of course I did."

"The answer to your question should be as obvious, don't you think? I walk every day."

He continued after regrouping himself. "Would you mind if I walked with you for a spell tomorrow? Before church?"

"I would like that, Pastor."

"Good. Five o'clock?"

"Five-thirty. I sleep in on Sundays."

⤬

If Kent thought he could have managed it, he would have driven straight back to Denver. But his body was in no condition to pull a twenty-four-hour shift without sleeping. He had to rest somewhere. At least, that was the way he'd planned it on paper.

He pulled into Grady's Truck Stop two hours outside of Denver, near midnight. A hundred sleeping rigs lined the graveled lot to the west of the all-night diner, and he pulled the little Iveco between two large, purring diesels. So far, so good. No flat tires, no routine pullovers, no breakdowns, no boulders from the sky. He could easily be a real driver for a mortuary, handling just one more body in a series of a hundred.

Kent locked the truck up and walked briskly toward the café. The cool night air rushed softly under the power of the towering trucks on all sides. What were the odds of being recognized in such a remote spot? He paused by the front wheel of a black International tractor-trailer and studied the diner thirty yards away. It stood there all decked out in neon like a Christmas tree. Two thoughts crossed his mind simultaneously, and they brought his pulse up to a steady thump.

The first was that the Iveco back there did not have a lock on the rear door. That had been an oversight on his part. He should have bought a padlock. A grisly wino on the prowl would find his little Iveco easy pickings. Only when the vagrant got back to his lair would he and his cohorts discover that the brown box did not contain rifles or beef or a priceless statue or any such treasure, but a cadaver. A smelly old fish. A dead body—not fit for the eating unless you were on an airplane that went down in the Andes and it was either you or the bodies.

The second thought was that entering Grady's diner, all lit up like a Christmas tree, was starting to seem like one of those stupid mistakes a criminal from Stupid Street might make. *"Yes sir, everything was going perfect until I ran into Bill at Grady's Diner, and he asked me what I was doing at one in the morning toting a cadaver around in a meat truck. Imagine, Bill at Grady's Diner! Who would have possibly thought?"*

Anybody with half a brain would have thought, that's who would have thought! He should have brought his own food. Although he *was* two hours out of Denver. Who that he knew could possibly be here at midnight? But that was just the point, wasn't it? What would *he* be doing here at midnight?

Kent slunk back into the shadows and climbed into the cab he'd made home for the last sixteen hours. He lifted a 7-Up can he'd purchased four hours earlier at the Utah border and swallowed the flat dregs in one gulp. There would be plenty of time for food and drink later. Now he needed sleep.

But sleep did not come easily. For one thing, he found himself craving a real drink. Just one quick nip to settle the nerves. Grady's could probably oblige him with at least a six-pack of beer.

"Don't be a fool," he muttered and lay down on the bench seat.

It was then, parked outside of Grady's, two hours from Denver, that the first major flaw in his plan presented itself to him like a siren in the night. He jerked upright and stared, wide eyed, out the windshield.

Helen! Helen had moved in *after* he'd laid out the timetable. When the rest of his plan was put into play, they would question her, and that questioning rang through his head now, clear and concise—and as condemning as a judge's gavel.

"You're saying he left you a note stating he's going fishing on Saturday but he never comes back? Not even on Sunday?"

"Yes, officer. As far as I can tell."

"So he goes fishing—we know that from the neighbor who saw him—and goes straight to the office in his fishing gear thirty-six hours later, without bothering to come home. No pun intended here, but doesn't that smell a little fishy?"

He had decided not to return for the simple reason that he had the body to contend with. He couldn't very well drive up to his house in the meat truck. Neither could he drive around town with a body in the trunk of the Lexus for a whole day. At some point things would be smelling more than just fishy.

But that was before Helen.

An alarm went off in his head. *Stupid, stupid, stupid!* He had to get to Denver. Get home somehow.

Kent brought the truck to life and roared back to the freeway, once again bouncing on the edge of the seat like some kind of idiot.

An hour later, rumbling into the outskirts of suburban Denver, he conceded to the only plan that made sense in the morning's wee hours. A new element of risk threatened now, but nobody ever said stealing twenty million would be light on the risk factor.

Kent slowly wound his way back to the Front Range Meat Packers compound south of 470 and entered the industrial maze of metal buildings. He killed the lights and crept forward, his eyes peeled for motion, his muscles rigid, his fingers wrapped white on the wheel.

Two minutes later, Kent eased the Iveco into its original space and pulled the ignition wires free. The engine sputtered to silence. By the watch on his right wrist, it was two o'clock in the morning.

For five minutes he sat in the silence, allowing the distant highway drone to settle his nerves. He finally climbed from the truck and walked behind. The roll door remained latched. He eased the lever up and pulled the door up. The box lay on the floor, swirling in a cold mist. He closed the door.

It took him another fifteen minutes to repair the cut wire in the steering column and return the cab to its original condition. Satisfying himself that he no longer needed access to the cab, he locked the doors and shut them quietly. Come Monday morning, if Cruiser had an inkling to pull truck 24 in for service, he would hopefully find her just as he'd left her. Now, if the truck would be kind enough to keep his body hidden and free from rot for another twelve hours without its cooling unit in operation, all would be well.

Kent had made it halfway back to the storage unit housing the Lexus before realizing he'd left the McDaniel's Mortuary signs on the truck. He hastily retreated and tore them free, cursing himself for the oversight. If he could have stopped somewhere and flogged the stupidity from his mind he would have done it without consideration. Evidently he was discovering what most criminals discover midcrime: Stupidity is something that comes upon you *during* the crime, not before. Like the rising sun, you cannot escape it. You can only hope to do your dirty deed before it fries you.

Kent headed back to the storage units, hauling his briefcase in one hand and the rolled-up signs in the other. Sweat soaked his shirt, and he let stealth slip a little. You can't very well pretend to be invisible lugging ten-foot rolls of vinyl under your arm. He plopped the load on the asphalt before the storage door, retrieved the rivet poppers from his briefcase, and made quick work of the fasteners he'd installed earlier.

The Lexus gleamed silver in the moonlight, undisturbed. Kent stuffed the signs in the trunk, tossed the briefcase into the passenger seat, and climbed into the familiar cockpit. He made it all the way to the industrial park's entrance before flipping on his lights. It was 2:38 Sunday morning when he finally entered highway 470 and headed for home, wondering what other small mistake he had made back there.

Yet he had made it, hadn't he? No, not really—not at all. Really he had not even started.

Kent left his Lexus on the street where it would be seen—right in front of the red *No Street Parking* sign by his house. The small black letters below promised that violators would be towed, but they'd never actually hauled any car off that he knew of, and he doubted they would begin on a Sunday.

He entered the house, flipped his shoes off at the front door, made a little noise in the kitchen, moved a few items around, and headed for his bedroom. The trick was to clearly show his presence without actually engaging Helen. He did not want to engage Helen. Not at all.

And, considering the old lady's walking obsession, which he assumed was an everyday affair, missing her might not be so difficult. On the other hand, today was Sunday. She might not walk on Sundays. If she did not, she would at least leave for church. He would have to be gone by noon.

Kent locked the door to the master suite, peeled off his clothes, and fell into bed. He slowly drifted into a fitful sleep.

28

Helen slipped out onto the porch after the doorbell's first ring.

"He's here, Bill."

The pastor did not respond immediately.

"Let's walk." She stepped past him and strolled to the street. The silver Lexus sat along the street beside the driveway. She turned left at the sidewalk and walked briskly past it.

"He came home last night."

"He catch any fish?" Bill asked, beside her now.

"Don't know. He's hiding something."

"Hiding what? How do you know?"

"I don't know what he's hiding, but I'm going to find out the minute I get home. They're on pins and needles up there; that's how I know. Death is in the air. I can feel it."

"You mind if we slow down a little, Helen? You're walking pretty fast here."

"We have to walk fast. I'm cutting it short today. Real short. I've got to get back there." She glanced down at her Reeboks and noted they were wearing thin in the toes.

"You want to pray, Bill?"

"Sure."

"Pray, then. Pray out loud."

❦

Kent awoke with a start. Something was wrong. His chest felt as though a jackrabbit had taken up residence there and was testing its thumpers. Only this was his heart—not some bunny. Which meant he'd had another dream.

He could remember nothing—not even why he was in his own bed.

Then he remembered everything, and he leapt from the bed.

Yesterday he had stolen a truck, driven to Utah, stolen a dead body, and returned to Front Range Meat Packers, where the body now lay dead; slowly warming in the back of truck 24. He'd come back to the house because of Helen. Dear Mother-in-law Helen.

It was this last tidbit that had awakened him to the drumming of Thumper's feet—this bit about Helen. He could not allow Helen to see him. And that was a problem because Helen was close. Imminent. Maybe at the bedroom door right now, waiting for the sound of his stirring.

He grabbed the khaki slacks and shirt he'd thrown off last night and pulled them on. For the second morning in a row he faced the task of leaving the room as though he fully intended to return. He made a quick circuit, rubbing some toothpaste on his teeth with his forefinger and tossing the tube in the drawer; throwing the covers loosely over the bed, half made; moving the Grisham novel forward a few pages. And he did all of it without knowing precisely what he was doing.

No matter—Helen was coming.

Kent cracked the door and listened for the sound of movement downstairs with stilled breath. Nothing. Thank God. He slipped into the hall and flew down the steps two at a time. In a matter of sixty seconds flat he managed to pull out the orange juice, slop some peanut butter on a bagel, down half of both, and hopefully leave the general impression that he had enjoyed a leisurely breakfast on a Sunday morning. He snatched up a pen and, taking a deep breath to still his quivering hand, wrote over the note he'd left yesterday.

Hi, Helen.

Sorry I missed you. Had a great day fishing. All too small to keep. If not home by six, don't wait.

Kent

Kent laid the note on the counter and ran for the entrance. The microwave clock read 9:30. He opened the front door carefully, begging not to see Helen's smiling mug. Sunlight stung his eyes, and he squinted. His Lexus sat idle on the street. Helen's yellow Pinto was parked in the garage and a third car, a green Accord, sat in the driveway behind the Pinto.

A friend's car. In the house? No, he had not heard a sound. Helen was out walking with a friend who owned a green Accord. Which meant Helen would be walking down the street with said friend, ready to run off to church. And church started at ten, didn't it?

Kent pulled the door shut and walked for his Lexus, head down, as nonchalantly as possible. If they were down the street, he would ignore them. Had to. Why? Because he just had to. He'd awakened with that realization buzzing through his skull, and it hadn't quieted just yet.

He brought the Lexus to life without looking up. It was when he started the U-turn that he saw them—like two figures on the home stretch of the Boston Marathon, arms pumping. He knew then what it felt like to jump out of your skin, because he almost did. Right there in the tan leather seats of the Lexus. Only his frozen grip on the steering wheel kept him from hitting his head on the ceiling, which was good because they might have seen the movement. You can't just throw your arms up in surprise and then pretend not to see someone—it just doesn't come off as genuine. Kent's foot jerked a little on the accelerator, causing the car to lurch a tad, but otherwise he managed to keep the turn tight and smooth.

He had a hard time removing his eyes from Helen. She and the man were about a block off, leaning into their walk, waving at him now. She wore a yellow dress that fluttered in the breeze, clearly exposing those ridiculous knee-socks pulled up high.

Should he wave back? It was obviously a *Stop-the-car* wave by its intensity, but he could pretend he'd mistaken it for a *Have-a-good-day* wave and return it before roaring off into the sunset. No, better to pretend not to have seen at all.

Kent's foot pressed firmly on the gas pedal, and he left them just breaking into a run. His neck remained rigid. Goodness, what did they know? They pulled up and dropped their arms. *"Sorry, guys, I just didn't see you. I swear I didn't see a thing. You sure it was me?"*

But he wouldn't be asking that question anytime soon, would he? Never. He glanced at the dash clock: 9:35. He had ten hours to burn.

It took Kent a good ten minutes to calm down, nibbling on blunted fingernails, thinking. Thinking, thinking, thinking. In the mirror his face stared back unshaven and wet. He should have cleaned up a little—at least thrown on some deodorant. Only a slob or a man in a great hurry would neglect basic body care. And he was beginning to smell. Kent sniffed at his armpit. No, beginning was far too kind. He reeked. Which would not present a significant problem unless he ran into someone who took note. And even then what could they do? Call the local police and report the reeking swamp thing tooling about town in the silver Lexus? Not likely. Still, it might leave an impression in some clerk's head.

"Did he appear normal to you?"

"No sir, officer, I daresay not. Not unless you consider walking around with radishes for eyes and smelling of rotted flesh at thirty feet normal."

"That bad, huh?"

"That bad."

Kent decided he would drive to Boulder for a burger. He had the time to burn, and on further thought, he needed the miles on his car. It had just gone on a fishing trip.

Two hours later he pulled into a truck stop ten miles south of Boulder, where he managed to splash some water under his pits and purchase a dry sandwich without incident. He spent three hours on the back lot mulling over matters of life and death before pulling out and cruising back toward Denver the long way. And did he use his credit card? No, of course he didn't use his credit card. That would be brain dead. Stupid, stupid. And he was done being stupid.

Darkness had enveloped Denver by the time Kent nosed the Lexus back into the industrial park holding Tom Brinkley's dead body.

Matters were considerably simpler this time around. He shut off his lights, thankful for a three-quarter moon, and idled through the alleys to the back fence. Truck 24 sat faithfully next to its two cousins, and Kent squeezed his fist in satisfaction. "You'd better be there, baby," he whispered, staring at the truck's roll door. "You'd better be right where I left you." This, of course, was spoken to the dead body, hopefully still lying in the plywood box. And hopefully not yet rotting. Things were smelling bad enough already.

Kent backed the Lexus to within two feet of the truck, hopped out, and popped the trunk. He pulled on a pair of surgical gloves, unlatched the Iveco's door, and yanked up. A heavy musty smell filled his nostrils—musty more like wet socks than musty like a dead body, he thought, although he'd never smelled musty like a dead body before. Still, it was not the smell he'd read about.

The back of the truck opened like a yawning jaw, dark to the throat, with a tongue resting still and brown in the middle. Only the tongue was the box. Kent exhaled in relief.

He pulled a crowbar from his trunk and jumped into the truck. The coffin had been screwed shut, making the prying-open part of the plan a little noisy, but within three minutes the lid lay at an angle, daring him to topple it off.

The sensations that struck next had not been well rehearsed. In fact, not planned at all. Kent had his hand under the lid, ready to flip it casually off, when it occurred to him that he was about to stare into the face of the fish. But it wasn't a fish at all. It was a dead body. He froze. And he wasn't going to just *stare*, but he was going to touch and lift and hoist that cold, gray flesh around. A chill cooled his neck.

A few seconds tripped by in silence. He should get the plastic first.

Kent jumped from the truck and grabbed a roll of black plastic from the car's trunk. He climbed back into the truck and stood over the coffin. *Now or never, buddy. Just do it.*

He did it. He kicked the lid off and stared into the coffin.

Tom Brinkley lay gray and slightly swollen with a hole the size of a fist in his gut. His hair was blond, and his eyes were open. For a full five seconds Kent could not move. It was those two eyes staring at him like marbles—glinting with life in the moonlight, but dead. Then the scent wafted past his nostrils. Faint, oh, so very faint but reaching right through to his bones, and his stomach was not responding so happily.

By the looks of it, Tom Brinkley's stomach had not responded so happily, either. It appeared as though he'd used a bazooka to end his life, judging by the size of that hole. His message to the funeral home flashed through his mind. *Not a problem. Will pick up as is.* Now he was staring at *"as is,"* and it *was* a problem.

Kent spun away and grabbed the metal shelving. Goodness, this was not in the plan. *It's just a body, for heaven's sake! A dead thing, like a fish, with a big hole in its stomach. Get on with it!*

And what if he couldn't get on with it? What if he simply did not have the stomach to slump this body around? He stared at the gloves on his hands; they would shield him from any lingering disease. Any danger he imagined was only in his mind. Right?

The thought forced Kent into a state of bumbling overdrive. He grabbed a lungful of air, whirled back to the body, reached into the coffin, and yanked Mr. Brinkley clean out in one smooth motion.

Or so he'd intended.

Problem was, this cadaver had lain dormant for a good forty-eight hours and was not so eager to change its position. They call it rigor-mortis, and the dead man had found it already.

Kent had not aimed his hands as he dived into the casket; he'd just grabbed, and his fingers had closed around a shoulder and a side of ribs, both cold and moist. The body came halfway vertical before slipping from Kent's grip. Mr. Brinkley turned lazily and landed on the edge of the coffin. His stiff upper torso slipped clean out and landed on the truck's floor boards with a loud, skull-crushing thud. Now the body slumped over the casket, belly down and butt up in the moonlight with its hands hanging out of the rear as though paying homage to the moon.

Kent swallowed the bile creeping up his throat and leapt from the truck, grunting in near panic. If there really was a God, he was making this awfully difficult. None of the books had made mention of the clammy, slippery skin. Had he known, he would have brought towels or something. Of course the books had not featured chapters on the preferred methods of lugging around dead bodies. Usually these things stayed peacefully on their tables or in their caskets.

Standing on the ground, he glanced up at the body in the back of the truck. It was gray in the dim light, like some kind of stone statue memorializing butts. Well, if he didn't get that butt into the trunk soon, there'd be a dozen cops shining their flashlights on that monument, asking silly questions. Questions like, *"What are you doing with Mr. Brinkley, Kent?"*

He turned gruffly to the job at hand, clamped his hands around each wrist, and pulled hard. The cadaver flopped out of the box and slid easily enough, like a stiff fish being dragged along the dock. He pulled it halfway out before bending under its midsection. The thought of that hole in Mr. Brinkley's stomach made him hesitate. He should have rolled the old guy in plastic.

The plastic! He'd left it by the coffin. Dumping the body into the Lexus without covering it would most definitely be one of those idiotic things Stupid Street criminals did. If they ever had an inkling to look, forensics experts would have a field day in there. Kent shoved the body back into the truck, snatched the plastic, and spread it quickly along the trunk floor, draping it over the edges. He bent back into the truck again for the wrists and yanked Mr. Brinkley's naked body out again.

In a single motion, refusing to consider what that hole might be doing to his shirt, Kent hoisted the cadaver onto his shoulder, turned sideways, and let Mr. Brinkley drop into the trunk. The body flipped on descent and landed with a loud thump, butt down. The head might have put a dent in the metal by that sound. But it was covered with plastic, so no blood would smear on the car itself. Besides, dead bodies don't bleed.

Sweat dripped from Kent's forehead and splattered onto the plastic. He glanced around, panting as much from disgust as from exertion. The night remained cool and still; the moaning of the distant highway filtered through his throbbing ears. But there were no sirens or helicopters or cop cars with floodlights or anything at all that looked threatening. Except that body lying exposed beside him, of course.

He quickly forced the head and feet into the trunk, careful not to allow contact with the exposed car. The legs squeaked and then popped on entry, and he wondered if that was joints or solid bones. Had to be joints—bones would never break so easily.

The eyes still stared out of Tom Brinkley's skull like two gray marbles. By the looks of it, his nose might have taken the brunt of that face plant in the truck. Kent yanked the black plastic over the body and shut the trunk.

Then there was the matter of the casket. Yes indeed, and he was prepared for that little problem. He pulled a blanket from the backseat, threw it over the car, retrieved the plywood coffin from the Iveco, and strapped it onto the top of his car with a single tie-down. Not to worry—it was not going far.

He quickly tidied the truck, closed the rear door one last time, and drove off, still guided by moonlight alone. He unloaded the casket into an abandoned storage bin, two down from where he'd parked the Lexus earlier. Whoever next braved the cubicle would find nothing more than a cheap plywood casket ditched by some vagrant long ago.

By the time Kent hit the freeway, it was almost 9 P.M.

By the time he made his first pass of the bank it was closer to ten.

He told himself he made the pass to make sure the lot lay vacant. But seeing the bank looming ahead as he made his way down the street, he began reconsidering the entire business, and by the time he reached the parking lot, his arms were experiencing some rigor mortis of their own. He simply could not turn the wheel.

The white moon bore down like a spotlight in the sky, peering steadily between passing black clouds. The bank towered dark against the sky. The streets were nearly vacant, but each car that did drive by seemed somehow intent on the Lexus. Kent imagined that it was because the car's tailpipe was dragging with Mr. Brinkley hiding like a lead weight back there. Or maybe he'd left a finger poking out of the trunk. He took a deep breath to calm himself. No, the tailpipe wasn't dragging or even sagging. And the finger-in-the-trunk thing was ridiculous. The lid would not have closed with anything so thick as a finger sticking out. Hair perhaps? Kent glanced in the side mirrors but saw no hair flapping in the wind.

"Get a grip, man!" he growled. "You're acting stupid!"

Kent drove three blocks past the bank before turning onto a side street to circle around. The objections were screaming now. Taking the truck—that had been nothing. Stealing the body—child's play. This, now *this* was where it all hit the fan. Only a complete imbecile would actually attempt this. Or someone who had nothing to live for anyway. Because attempting this might very well end in death. *You know that, Kent, don't you? You might die tonight. Like Spencer.*

His palms were slippery on the leather steering wheel, and he wondered if forensics could pick that up. He would have to wipe the sweat off the seat as well. He didn't want some ambitious rookie investigator concluding he'd arrived in a state of distress, leaking buckets of sweat all over the seats. Then again, he had lost his wife and child; he had reason to be distressed.

Kent approached the bank from the rear and rolled into his parking spot at the back corner by the alley. *Okay, boy. Just chill. We're just going to walk in there and take a quick look. You come here all the time at night. Nothing unusual yet. You haven't done anything wrong yet. Not much anyway.*

Kent took a deep breath, stepped from the car, briefcase in hand, and walked for the back entrance. His hand shook badly inserting the key. What if they had changed the lock? But they hadn't. It swung open easily to the sound of a quiet chirping. The alarm.

He stepped in and punched in the deactivation code. Now the alarm company knew that Kent Anthony had entered the building through the rear door at 10:05 P.M. Sunday night. No problem—that was part of this little charade. The rear offices were not monitored by video equipment like the rest of the bank; he was a free bird back here.

Kent walked through dark halls, stepping quickly by the light of glowing exit signs. He found his office exactly as he had left it, untouched and silent except for the *whir* of his computer. The exotic fish swam lazily; red power lights winked in the darkness; his high-back leather chair sat like a black shadow before the monitors. Kent's hands trembled at his sides.

Kent flipped the light on and squinted at the brightness. He set his briefcase on the desk and cracked his knuckles absently. By his estimation, he would need five hours in the building to pull this off. The first four hours would be relatively simple. Just walk into the advanced processing system using ROOSTER, execute the little BANDIT program he'd been fine-tuning for the last three weeks, and walk away. But it was the walking away part that had his bones vibrating.

Kent made one last pass through the halls, satisfying himself as to their vacancy. And then it was suddenly now-or-never time, and he walked briskly back toward his office, knowing it had to be now.

It's okay, boy. You haven't done nothin' yet. Not yet.

He withdrew a disk from his briefcase, inserted it into the floppy drive, took one last long pull of air, and began punching at the keyboard. Menus sprang to life and then disappeared, one after the other, a slide show of reds and blues and yellows. He located ROOSTER and executed it without pausing. Then he was into AFPS, through ROOSTER's hidden link, like a ghost able to do anything at will without the mortals knowing.

He'd already determined his will. His will was to confiscate twenty million dollars. And stealing twenty million dollars all came down to a few keystrokes now.

He stared at the familiar screen of programming code for a long minute, his quivering fingertips brushing lightly on the keys, his heart pounding in his ears.

It's okay, boy. You haven't done . . .

Yeah, well, I'm about to.

He entered the command line: RUN a:\BANDIT.

Then do it. Just do it.

He swallowed and depressed the ENTER key. The floppy drive engaged, the hard drive spun up, the screen went blank for a few seconds, and Kent held his breath.

A string of numbers popped up, center screen, and began spinning by like a gas pump meter gone berserk. The search was on. Kent leaned back and folded his hands, his eyes lost to the blur of numbers.

The program's execution was simple, really. It would systematically scan the massive electronic web of banking and identify accounts in which charges had been levied for interbank ATM use. Example: Sally, a Norwest bank customer, uses her cash card at a Wells Fargo cash machine and is charged $1.20 for the use of Wells Fargo's ATM. The fee is automatically taken from her account. Sally gets her statement, sees the charge, and adds it to the line that reads "Service Charges" on her reconciliation form. Case closed. Does Sally question the charge? Not unless Sally is a kook. BANDIT would search for one hundred million such transactions, add twenty cents to the fee charged by the host bank, and then neatly skim that twenty cents off for deposit into a labyrinth of accounts Kent had already established. In Sally's case, neither Norwest nor Wells Fargo would be short in their own reconciliation. They would receive and be charged precisely what they expected: $1.20. It would be Sally who was out twenty cents, because her statement would show a service charge not of $1.20 but of $1.40. The additional twenty cents she paid would be unwittingly donated to Kent's accounts while the balance of $1.20 happily made its way to Wells Fargo. No one would be the wiser.

But say Sally *is* a kook. Say she calls the bank and reports the mistake: a $1.40 charge instead of the customary $1.20 rate advertised in the bank's brochures. The bank runs a query. BANDIT immediately identifies the query, dispatches a gunman to Sally's house, and puts a slug in her head.

Kent blinked. The numbers on the screen continued to spin in a blur.

Okay, not quite. BANDIT would just return Sally her precious hard-earned twenty cents. But it was here, in the method Kent had devised to return Sally her money, that his real brilliance shone. You see, BANDIT would not just return the money lackadaisically and apologize for the blunder. Too many blunders would raise brows, and Kent wanted to keep those eyebrows down. Instead, BANDIT acted like a self-erasing virus, one that detected the query into Sally's account, and did its dirty deed of returning the twenty cents immediately, before the query returned the details of Sally's account to the operator's screen. By the time the banker had Sally's latest bank statement on the screen, it would show that the customary bank charges of $1.20 had been levied. The computer would then spit out a comment about an internal self-correcting error, and that would be that. In reality, there would undoubtedly be some deeper probes, but they would find nothing. The transactions would be executed through the back door and their trails neatly erased, thanks to AFPS. Of course, the safeguard was AFPS itself—those who entered AFPS normally left their prints at every keystroke.

Normally. But not with ROOSTER.

Either way, it really did not matter. The last hour of this operation would neutralize everything. Meanwhile, he had a body rotting in his trunk. Kent let the computer spin while he chewed his fingernails and paced the carpet. He might have shed a full gallon of sweat in those first three hours, he did not know—he hadn't brought a milk jug along to catch it all. But it did a fine job of soaking his shirt clean through.

It took three hours and forty-three minutes for the program to find its intended victims. The clock on Kent's office wall read 1:48 when the program finally asked him if he wished to get it on—transfer this insanely huge amount of money into his accounts and enter a life on the run from the long arms of the United States justice system. Well, not in so many words. There was actually only one word on the screen: TRANSFER? Y/N. But he knew what the program was really asking by that simple word, because he had written that word.

His hand hovered over the Y that would actually alter the accounts and transfer the money into his own—a process he'd calculated to take roughly thirty minutes. He pressed it, conscious of the small click in the key. The words vanished to black, replaced by a single word blinking on and off: PROCESSING.

Kent backed from the desk and let the computer do its deed. *Yes indeed, BANDIT, rob them blind.* His heart beat at twice its customary pace, refusing to calm. And he still had that clammy body to deal with.

Kent crept out to the Lexus, glancing around nervously for the slightest sign of an intruder. Which struck him as ironic because *he* was the intruder here. He popped the trunk and quickly peeled the plastic away from Mr. Brinkley's body. He had to be quick now. It wouldn't do to have a passerby seeing him hauling a flopping body from the trunk. Backing the car into the alley would have been easier, but it also would have left tire tracks that didn't belong. One of those Stupid Street moves.

The cadaver stared up at the moon with its wide, gray eyes, and Kent shuddered. He reached in, swallowing hard, wrapped both arms around the cold torso, and yanked. The body came out like a bloated sack of grain, and Kent staggered under its weight. The head bounced off the rear bumper and came within an inch of leaving a slab of skin on the asphalt, which would have been a problem.

Move it, man! Move it!

Kent hoisted the body and flipped it into the crooks of his arms as he turned. The trunk would have to remain open for the moment. He staggered down the alley, wheezing like ancient bellows now, fighting to keep the contents of his stomach where they belonged. If he'd eaten more over the last day, it might have come up then while he staggered down the alley, eyes half closed to avoid seeing what lay across his arms. Mr. Brinkley bounced naked and gray. Butt up.

The cadaver nearly fell from his grasp once, but he recovered with a lifted knee. He lost his firm grip on the body, however, and had to run the last few yards before the fish slipped all the way out of his arms.

The rear door proved another challenge altogether. Kent stood there, bent over, straining against the dead weight, knowing that if this thing fell it would leave evidence. Dead body evidence.

Problem was, his hands were trembling in their task of keeping Mr. Brinkley from landing on his toes, and the door was closed. He would have to get the body onto his shoulder—free up a hand.

"Oh, man!" He was whispering audibly now. "Oh man, oh man!" The words echoed ghostly down the alley.

It took him three panicked attempts to heave the naked body up by his head, and by the time he finally managed to snake a shoulder under it, his breathing was chasing those words. The body's flesh felt soft on his shoulder, and visions of that hole in the cadaver's gut filled his mind. But Mr. Brinkley's spare tire was sucking up to his right ear, and the realization put him into gear.

Kent opened the door and staggered through, fighting chills of horror. The thought that he'd have to wipe that door handle managed to plant itself firmly in his mind. He had dead flesh on his hands.

He ran for his office with the body bouncing on his shoulder. Groans accompanied each breath now, but then who was listening?

He heaved the body from its precarious perch the second he lurched through his office door. It fell to the gray carpet with a sickening dead-body thump. Kent winced and pushed the door shut. His face still twisted with disgust, he paced back and forth in front of the body, trying to gather himself.

To his right, the computer screen still winked through its dirty deed.

PROCESSING, PROCESSING, PROCESSING . . .

He needed fresh air. Kent ran from the bank and walked back to the car, thankful for the cool air against his drenched shirt.

He removed a green-and-red cardboard box, which had only two weeks earlier held twelve bottles of tequila, from his rear seat and carefully cleaned out the trunk. Satisfied that the Lexus carried no physical evidence of the body, he stuffed the plastic into the box and walked to a tangle of pipes and knobs poking from the concrete halfway down the alley. The smallest of these controlled the bank's sprinkler system. He twisted a valve and shut it down.

From the tequila box Kent removed a pair of running shoes and replaced his own loafers with them. A few stomps down the alley insured they would leave a print. Evidence. He wiped the rear door handle carefully and reentered the bank.

The body lay face up, naked and pasty when he stepped into his office. He shivered. The computer screen still flashed its word: PROCESSING, PROCESSING . . .

Kent stripped off his clothes, until he stood naked except the running shoes. He started to dress Mr. Brinkley but quickly decided that he could not tolerate being naked in the same room with a naked dead man. Granted, he would put up with whatever it took to do this deed, but bending naked over a dead naked body was not in the plan. He would dress first. He snatched a pair of loose jeans and a white T-shirt from the green-and-red box and pulled them on. Then he turned back to the body.

Dressing a dead body proved to be a task best done with a vengeance—anything less had him cursing. The body's stiffness helped, but the dead weight did not. He forced his white boxers over Mr. Brinkley's midsection first, holding his breath for most of the operation. Relieved, he struggled with the slacks, rolling the body around, and tugging as best he could. He had the shirt nearly over the cadaver's chest when a blip sounded at the computer.

Kent snapped his head up. TASK COMPLETE, the screen read. $20,000,000.00 TRANSFERRED.

A tremble seized his bones. He returned to the body, tearing about it now. His watch went on the wrist, his socks and shoes on the feet.

Satisfied, he withdrew his floppy disk from the drive and exited the program. A fleeting thought skipped through his head. The thought that he had just transferred twenty million dollars into his personal accounts successfully. The thought that he was a very rich man. Goodness!

But the overpowering need to flee undetected shoved the thought from his mind. He emptied half the contents from his briefcase into the tequila box. The incriminating half. What remained in the briefcase represented the work of a dedicated programmer including a personal reminder to speak to Borst Monday morning about efficiency issues. Yes sir, show them he fully expected to return to work on Monday, the morning after a casual fishing trip and a late night at the office.

Kent yanked the cadaver, now fully dressed in his clothes, to a standing position so that it leaned against his chair like some kind of wax museum piece. Here rigor mortis was his friend. He had buttoned the shirt wrong, he saw, and the slacks were hitched up high on one side. Mr. Brinkley looked like some kind of computer nerd short the pocket protector. But none of this mattered.

The corpse stared wide eyed at the poster of the white yacht. Now that Kent thought about it, he should have closed those bug eyes like they did when someone died on television.

He backed to the door, surveyed his work, and pulled the nine-millimeter semiautomatic Uncle Jerry had given him from the box. *Okay boy, now you're gonna do this.* He lifted the pistol. Once he pulled the trigger, he would have to fly. No telling how far the report might travel.

But Mr. Brinkley was having none of it. At least not yet. He suddenly slipped to the side and toppled to the floor, stiff as a board.

Kent cursed and bounded over to the body. He jerked Mr. Brinkley upright and planted him in place. "Stay put, you old fish," he mumbled through gritted teeth. "You're dying standing up, whether you like it or not."

He crouched and squinted. The gun suddenly bucked in his hand. *Bang!* The report almost knocked him from his feet. Panicked, he fired twice more, quickly, into the body—*Bang! Bang!* The body stood tall, still staring dumbly forward, oblivious to the bullets that had just torn through its flesh.

Kent swallowed and tossed the weapon back into the box. Shaking badly now, he staggered forward and yanked a two-gallon can from the box. He gave Mr. Brinkley a nudge and let him topple to the floor. He emptied the flammable mixture onto the body and then doused the surrounding carpet. He scanned the office, picked up the box, and backed to the door.

It occurred to Kent, just before he tossed the match, that he was about to go off the deep end here. Right off into some abyss, spread-eagle. He struck the match and let it flare. What on Earth was he about to do? He was about to put the finishing touches on the perfect crime, that's what he was about to do. He was about to kill Kent Anthony. He was about to join Gloria and Spencer in the ground, six feet under. At least that was the plan, and it was a brilliant plan.

Kent backed into the hall and tossed the match.

Whoomp!

The initial ignition knocked him clear across the hall and onto his seat. He scrambled to his feet and stared, unbelieving, at the blaze. A wall of orange flames reached for the ceiling, crackling and spewing black smoke. Fire engulfed the entire office. Mr. Brinkley's body lay like a log, flaming with the rest, like Shadrach or Meshack in the fiery furnace. The accelerant mixture worked as advertised. This cadaver was going to burn. Burn, baby, burn.

Then Kent fled the bank. He burst through the back door, tequila box in hand, heart slamming. His Lexus sat parked around the corner to his left. He ran to his right. He would not need the car again. Ever.

He'd run three blocks straight down the back alleys before he heard the first siren. He slowed by a trash bin, palmed the gun, and ditched the box. Behind him a cloud of smoke billowed into the night sky. He had known the old wood-frame building would go up, but he had not expected the fire to grow so quickly.

Kent looked back four blocks later, eyes peeled and unblinking. This time an orange glow lit the sky. A small smile of wonder crossed his face. Sirens wailed on the night air.

Five minutes later he entered the bus depot on Harmon and Wilson, produced a key to locker 234, and withdrew an old, brown briefcase. The case held eleven thousand dollars in twenty-dollar bills—traveling expenses—a bus ticket, a stick of deodorant, a toothbrush with some toothpaste, and a passport under his new name. It was all he owned now.

This and a few dozen accounts holding twenty million dollars.

Then Kent walked out into the street and disappeared into the night.

29

Helen brought two glasses of ice tea into her living room and handed one to Pastor Madison. Returning to her own home was the one small blessing in this latest turn in events. No need to stay at Kent's if he was gone.

"Thank you, Helen. So . . ."

"So," she repeated.

"So they've concluded the fire resulted from a freak robbery attempt. You read this story?" he asked, lifting the *Denver Post* in one hand.

"Yes, I saw that."

The pastor continued anyway. "They say evidence from the scene clearly shows a second party—presumably a robber. Evidently this guy found the rear door open and entered the bank, hoping for some easy cash. Unfortunately, Kent was there, 'working late on a Sunday night, not unusual for Kent Anthony. The thirty-six-year-old programmer was well known for working odd hours, often into the early hours of the morning.'"

"Hmmm," Helen offered.

"It says that the investigators speculate that the robber stumbled into Kent, panicked, and shot him dead. He then returned and torched the place—probably in an effort to erase evidence of his presence. He's still at large, and the search continues. The FBI has no current suspects. No actual robbery was committed . . . They estimate the fire damage to reach three million dollars, a fraction of what it could have been, thanks to the rapid response of the fire department." He lowered the paper and sipped at his tea.

"And of course, we know the rest, because it's just about the funeral."

Helen did not respond. There was not much to say anymore. Things had dropped off her plateau of understanding. She was guided by the unknown now. By the kind of faith she had never dreamed possible.

"What's happening to his belongings?" Bill asked.

"His will leaves it all to Gloria and Spencer. I suppose the state will get it now—I don't know and quite frankly, I don't care. From what I've seen, there's no use for this stuff in the next life anyway."

He nodded and sipped again. For a while they sat in silence.

"I have to tell you, Helen. This is almost too much for me."

"I know. It seems difficult, doesn't it?"

Bill cocked his head, and she knew he was letting his frustration get the better of him. "No, Helen. This does not *seem* difficult. Not everything is about *seeming* this way or that way. This *is* difficult, okay?" He shifted uncomfortably. "I mean, first Kent's wife dies of a freak disease, and that was unfortunate. I understand these things happen. But then his son is killed in a freak accident. And now we've hardly put away the funeral garb, and *he's* murdered in some freak robbery attempt. Strange enough? No, not quite. Meanwhile you, the mother, the grandmother, the mother-in-law, are walking around—quite literally—talking about some game in heaven. Some master plan beyond normal human comprehension. To what end? They're all dead! Your family is all dead, Helen!"

"Things are not always what . . ."

". . . what they seem," Bill finished. "I know. You've told me that a hundred times. But some things *are* what they seem! Gloria *seems* quite dead, and guess what? She *is* dead!"

"No need to patronize me, young man." Helen smiled gently. "And in reality, she's more alive now than dead, so even there you are less right than wrong. In practical terms, you might be right, but the kingdom of heaven is not what most humans would call practical. Quite the opposite. You ever read the teachings of Christ? 'If a man asks for your tunic, give him your cloak as well.' You ever do that, Bill? 'If your eye causes you to sin, pluck it out.' You see anybody smash their television lately, Bill? 'Anyone who does not take up his cross'—that's death, Bill—'and follow me is not worthy of me . . . Let the dead bury the dead.' And it was God speaking those words, as a guideline by which to live life."

"Well, I'm not talking about the teachings of Christ here. I'm talking about people dying without apparent reason."

Helen searched him deep with her eyes, feeling empathy and not knowing really why. He was a good man. He simply had not yet seen what was to be seen. "Well, I *am* talking about the teachings of Christ, Bill, which, whether you like it or not, include death. His own death. The death of the martyrs. The death of those on whose blood the church is built."

She looked away, and suddenly a hundred images from her own past crashed through her mind. She swallowed. "The reason you look for is here, Pastor." She waved her hand slowly through the air. "All around us. We just don't often see it clearly, and when we do, it is not often as we think it should appear. We're so bent on stuffing ourselves full of life—full of *happiness*—that we lose sight of God. Make up our own."

"God is a God of joy and peace and happiness," he offered.

"Yes. But the Teacher did not have in mind sitcoms that make you laugh or happy sermons about what a breeze the narrow road really is. Heavens, no. What is pure, Bill? Or excellent or admirable? The death of a million people in the Flood? God evidently thought so. He is incapable of acts that are not admirable, and it was he who brought about the Flood. How about the slaying of children in Jericho? There are few Bible stories that are not as terrible as they are happy. We just prefer to leave out the terrible part, but that only makes the good anemic." She turned from him and gazed at the picture of Christ in crucifixion.

"We are encouraged to *participate* in the sufferings of Christ, not to pretend they were feel-happy times. 'Take this in remembrance of me; this is my blood, this is my body,' he said. Not, find yourselves an Easter bunny and hunt for chocolate eggs in remembrance of me. We are told to *meditate* on Scripture, even the half that details the consequence of evil, the conquest of Jericho and all. Not to pretend our God has somehow changed since the time of Christ. Obviously, Paul's idea of admirable and noble is quite different from ours. God forgive us, Bill. We have mocked his victory by whitewashing the enemy for the sake of our neighbor's approval."

He blinked and drew a deep breath. "Imagine me talking like that from the pulpit. It would scare the breath out of most of them." He lowered his head, but his jaw was clenched, she saw. Suddenly those images from her past were crashing through her mind again, and she closed her eyes briefly. She should tell him, she thought.

"Let me tell you a story, Bill. A story about a man of God unlike any I have known. A soldier. He was my soldier." Now the emotions flooded her with a vengeance, and she noted her hands were trembling. "He was from Serbia, you know, before he came to the States. Fought in the war there with a small team of special forces. He served under a lieutenant, a *horrible* man." She shuddered as she said it. "A God hater who slept with the devil."

She had to stop for a few moments. The memories came too fast, with too much intensity, and she breathed a prayer. *Father, forgive me.* She glanced up at the red bottle in her hutch, sitting, calling from the past. From the corner of her eye she saw that Bill was staring at her.

"Anyway, they walked into a small town one day. The commander led them straight to the church at the center. The soldier said that he knew with one look into the lieutenant's eyes that he had come with cruel intentions. It was a gross understatement."

She swallowed and plowed on before this thing got the best of her. "The commander had them gather the townspeople, about a hundred of them, I think, and then he began his games." Helen looked up at the cross again. "The priest was a God-fearing man. For hours the commander played his game—bent upon forcing the priest to renounce Christ before the townsfolk. The horror of those hours was so reprehensible that I can hardly speak of them, Bill. To hear of them I would weep for hours."

Tears slipped from Helen's eyes and fell to her lap.

"The soldier was appalled by what he saw. He tried in vain to stop the lieutenant—almost lost his own life. But in the end the priest died. He died a martyr for the love of Christ. There is a monument to him in the town now. It is a cross rising from a green lawn bearing the inscription, 'No Greater Love Has Any Man.' The day after the priest's death, they collected some of his blood and sealed it into several small crystal bottles, so they would not forget."

She stood and walked to the hutch. She'd told no one other than her daughter of this, but it was time, wasn't it? Yes, it was time she spread this seed. Her breathing was coming thick as she pulled open the glass doors. She placed her fingers around the small bottle and pulled it out. The container was only slightly larger than her hand.

Helen returned to her seat and sat slowly, her mind swirling with the images. "The soldier went back to the village the next day to beg for their forgiveness. They gave him one of the bottles filled with the martyr's blood." Helen held the bottle out on her palm. "Never to worship or to idolize, they told him. But to remind him of the price paid for his soul."

It was not the whole story, of course. If the pastor knew the whole story he would be slobbering on the floor in a pool of his own tears, she thought. Because the whole story was as much her story as the soldier's, and it stretched the very limits of love. Perhaps one day she would tell him.

"The experience profoundly changed his life," she said, looking at Bill. His eyes were misty, staring at the floor. "And ultimately it changed my life, and Gloria's and Spencer's and even yours and countless others. And now Kent's, possibly. But you see, it all began with death. The death of Christ, the death of the priest. Without these I would not be here today. Nor would you, Pastor. It is how I see the world now."

"Yes." He nodded, gathering himself. "You do see more than most of us."

"I see only a little more than you, and most of that by faith. You think I wear the face of God?"

He blinked, obviously unsure if he was meant to answer.

"You see me walking around, disturbed, worried, with a furrowed brow. You think it's the face of God? Of course not! He is furious at sin, no doubt. And his heart aches over the rejection of his love. But above it all he rolls with laughter, beside himself with joy. I see only the hem of his garment and then only at times. The rest comes by faith. We may have different giftings, but we all have the same faith. Give or take. We are not so different, Pastor."

He stared at her. "I've never heard you say those things."

"Then maybe I should have spoken sooner. Forgive me. I can be a bit mule-headed, you know."

He smiled at her. "Don't worry, Helen. If you're a mule, may God smite our church with a thousand mules." They chuckled.

For several minutes they just sat there and thought in silence. Their glasses clinked with ice now and then, but the gravity of the moment seemed to want its own space, so they let it be. Helen hummed a few bars of "Jesus, Lover of My Soul" and stared out to the field beyond her house. Autumn would come someday. What would walking be like then?

"Are you still walking?" Bill asked the question as if it had been the real reason for his visit and he was just now getting around to it.

"Yes. Yes I am."

"The full distance?"

"Yes."

"But how? I thought you were walking and praying for Kent's soul?"

"Well, that's the problem. That's where things don't seem to be what they seem. I'm still walking because I've felt no urge not to walk and because my legs still walk without tiring and because I still want to pray for Kent."

"Kent is dead, Helen."

"Yes. So it seems. But the heavens are not playing along. I walked that first day after the fire, seeking release. It was to be expected, I thought. But I found no release."

She glanced at him and saw that he'd tilted his head, unbelieving.

"And then there's the dream. Someone's still running through my head at night. I still hear his breathing, the soft pounding of feet through the tunnel. The drama is still unfolding, Pastor."

Bill gave her a small, sympathetic smile. "Come on, Helen. I talked to the lead investigator myself two days ago. He told me very specifically that the coroner clearly identified the body as belonging to Kent Anthony. Same height, same weight, same teeth, same everything. FBI's records confirmed it. That body we buried three days ago belonged to Kent. Maybe he needs help in some afterlife, but he is no longer of this earth."

"They did an autopsy, then?"

"An autopsy of what? Of charred bones?"

"DNA?"

"Come on, Helen. You can't actually believe . . . Look, I know this is hard on you. It's been a terrible tragedy. But don't you think this is going a little too far?"

Her eyes bore into his with an unmoving stare. "This has nothing to do with tragedy, young man. Am I or am I not walking eight hours a day without tiring?"

He didn't answer.

"Is it some illusion, this walking of mine? Tell me."

"Of course it's no illusion. But—"

"Of course? You sound pretty sure about that. Why is God making my legs move like this, Pastor? Is it that he has discovered a new way to make the tiny humans below move? 'Hey look, Gabriel, we can just wind them up and make them walk around forever.' No? Then why?"

"Helen . . ."

"I'm telling you, Pastor, this is not over. And I mean, not just in the heavens, but on Earth it's not over. And since Kent was the main object of this whole thing, no, I don't think he is necessarily dead."

She turned away from him. Goodness, listen to her. It was sounding absurd. She had peeked in the coffin herself and seen the blackened bones. "And if you think it makes sense to me, you are wrong. I'm not even saying he *is* necessarily alive. It is just easier to believe he's alive, given the fact that I'm still praying long days for him." She turned back to him. "Does that make sense?"

Bill Madison took a deep breath and leaned back in his chair. "Well, Helen." He shook his head. "I guess so."

They sat in silence for a few minutes, staring off in different directions, lost in thought. His voice broke the stillness.

"It's very strange, Helen. It's otherworldly. Your faith is unnerving. You're giving your life to impossibilities."

She looked up and saw that his eyes were closed. A lump rose in her throat. "It's all I have, Bill. It's all anybody really has. It's all Noah had, building his impossible little boat while they mocked him. It's all Moses had, holding his rod over the Red Sea. It's all Hosea had and Samson and Paul and Stephen and every other character of every other Bible story. Why should it be so different for us today?"

She saw his Adam's apple bob. He nodded. "Yes, I think you're right. And I fear my faith is not so strong."

He was beginning to see, she thought. Which meant his faith was stronger than he realized. It could use a nudge. She'd read somewhere that eagles would never fly if their mothers did not push them from their nests when they were ready. Even then they would free-fall in a panic before spreading their wings and finding flight.

Yes, maybe it was time the pastor got a little shove.

"Would you like to see more than you've seen, Bill?"

"See what?"

"See the other side. See what lies behind what you see now."

He stiffened a little. "What do you mean, *see?* It's not like I can just flip on a light and see—"

"It is a simple question, Bill, really. Do you want to see?"

"Yes."

"And you would be willing to let go a little?"

"I think so. Although I'm not sure how you let go of something you can't see."

"You forget about how important you are, put aside your narrow field of vision; you open your heart to one thing only. To God, in whichever way he chooses to reveal himself, regardless of how it might seem to you. You let go."

He smiled nervously. "Sounds a bit risky, actually. You can't just throw out all doctrine for some experience."

"And what if that experience is God, the creator? What is more important to you, an encounter with God or your doctrine?"

"Well, if you put it that way—"

"As opposed to which way?"

"You've made your point. And yes, I think I could let go a little."

She smiled slowly. "Then let's pray."

Helen watched him close his eyes and bow his head. She wondered how long the posture would hold. "Father in heaven," she prayed aloud and closed her own eyes, "if it would please you, open this child's eyes to see what you have called him to. May he have the power to see how wide and how deep and how high your love is for him."

She fell silent and closed her eyes to darkness. *Please Father, let him feel your presence. At least that, just a taste of you, God in heaven.*

An image of Kent filled her mind. He walked down a long, deserted street, aimless and lost. His hair was disheveled, and his eyes peered blue above dark circles. For a moment she thought it might be his spirit, like some kind of ghost wandering the streets of her mind. But then she saw that it was him, really him, bewildered by the vacancy of the street on which he walked. And he was lonely.

She forgot about the pastor for the moment. Maybe she should walk. Maybe she should just leave Bill and go for another walk—pray for Kent. Yes, at least that. Her heart swelled in her chest. *Oh God, save Kent's soul! Do not hide your face from this man you made. Open his heart to your spirit. Speak words of love to his ears, drop your fragrance in his mind, dance before his eyes, show him your splendor, wrap your arms around him, touch his cold skin with a warm touch, breathe life into his nostrils. You fashioned him, did you not? So now love him.*

But I have.

Helen dropped her head at the words and began to weep. *Oh God, I'm sorry. You have! You have loved him so much. Forgive me!*

She sat bunched in her chair for several long minutes, feeling waves of fire wash through her chest. It was a mixture of agony and desire—a common senti-ment these days. The heart of God for Kent. Or at least a small piece of it. The piece he chose to reveal to her.

She suddenly remembered Bill and snapped her head up.

He sat on the green chair, head bent back like a duckling begging food. His Adam's apple stuck out prominently on his neck, his jaw lay open, his mouth gaped wide, his nostrils flared. And his body shook like a ragged old cloth doll. Something somewhere had been opened. His eyes, maybe.

Helen relaxed and leaned back into her cushions. A smile split her face wide. Now he would understand. Maybe not any details of Kent's plight, but the rest would come easier now. Faith would come easier.

Tears fell in streams down the pastor's cheeks, and she saw that his shirt was already wet. Looking at the grown man reduced to a heap of emotions made her want to scream full throated. It was that kind of joy. She wondered how it was that she had never had a heart attack. How could a mortal, like Bill there, all inside out, endure such ravaging emotion, busting up the heart, and not risk a coronary? She smiled at the thought.

On the contrary, his heart might very well be finding some youth. Her legs had, after all.

Helen began to rock gently. "Do you want to see, Bill?" she whispered.

30

Lacy Cartwright nibbled at her fingernail, knowing it was an unseemly habit and not caring. The truth be known, she had not cared for much during the last week. She glanced at the clock: 8:48. In twelve minutes the doors of Rocky Mountain Bank and Trust would open for customers.

Jeff Duncan caught her eye from across the lobby, and she smiled politely. Now, there was a man who was maybe more her type after all. Not so impulsive as Kent, but alive and well and here. Always here, not running in and out of her life every twelve years. Not pulling some impossible disappearing trick and expecting her to just get on with life. But that was just the problem—Lacy honestly didn't know if Kent had really disappeared or not. And what she did know was giving her waking fits.

Kent had come to her two nights before the big fire in Denver; that much she had not imagined. He had sat across from her and told her that he was going to do pretty much what happened. Or at least what *could* have happened. But reading the papers, what happened was not what *could* have happened at all. In fact, what happened, according to the papers, was precisely what Kent had said would happen. A robbery attempt, a death, and most important, his disappearance. He had neglected to mention that it would be *his* death, of course, but then she doubted he'd planned that much.

Then again, what actually happened was anybody's guess, and she found herself guessing that something else entirely had happened. Maybe Kent had not been surprised by some wandering robber that night, because maybe Kent himself *was* the robber; he'd suggested as much himself. So then what seemed to have happened must not have happened at all. Which was downright confusing when she thought too much about the matter.

Either way, he had left her again. Maybe this time for good. Well, good riddance.

There was one way to determine if that charred body in the Denver bank fire belonged to Kent Anthony or to some other poor soul everyone *thought* was Kent Anthony. If Kent had actually pulled off this incredible theft of which he'd spoken, he had done it brilliantly, because as of yet, no one even suspected there *had* been a theft. On the other hand, no one knew to look, much less *where* to look. All eyes were on the fire damage and the search for a loose murderer, but no one had mentioned the possibility that a robbery *had* actually occurred. And no wonder—nothing had been taken. At least not that they knew.

But she, Lacy Cartwright, might know differently. And if she did discover that Kent was alive and well and extremely wealthy—would she be compelled to tell the authorities? It was the question that had kept her tossing at night. Yes, she thought so. She would have to turn him in.

If he was indeed alive and if he had left even the slightest of trails, she would find it on the computer screen before her, in some log of ATM transaction fees. Fortunately or unfortunately, depending on the hour, eight days of looking had shown her nothing. And slowly, her anger at him rose to a boil.

"Morning, Lacy."

Lacy started and jerked her head up. Jeff smiled broadly at her reaction. "Strung a bit tight this morning, are we?"

She ignored him.

He chuckled. "I guess. Well, welcome back to the land of the living."

The comment momentarily thrust Lacy back into the land of the dead. "Yeah," she responded politely, shifting her eyes from him. Maybe that was the problem here, she thought. Maybe this land of the living here in the bank with all the customers and meaningless talk and overstuffed maroon sitting chairs was more like death, and the land that Kent had trotted off to was more like life. In a way she was a bit jealous, if indeed he was not actually in hell but roaming the earth somewhere.

Jeff leaned on the counter. "You coming to Martha's party this weekend? It might be a good thing, considering the fact that all the top brass will be in attendance."

She pulled herself back to this reality. "And this should bring me to my knees? When is it?" Actually she had no plans to attend the affair and knew precisely when it was, but Jeff was the kind of guy who liked giving out information. It made him feel important, she guessed.

"Friday at seven. And yes, you might consider paying a little homage."

"To them or to you?"

He smiled coyly. "But of course, I'll be there as well. And I'd be disappointed if you were not."

She smiled kindly. "Well, we'll see." Maybe it would be a good idea, after all. Get her mind off this Kent madness. "I'm not crazy about parties doused in alcohol." She studied his face for reaction.

"And neither am I," he said without missing a beat. "But, like I said, the brass will be there. Think of it as a career move. Reaching out to those who determine your future. Something like that. And of course, an opportunity to see me." He winked.

Lacy stared at him, surprised by his boldness.

Jeff shifted awkwardly. "I'm sorry, I didn't mean to be so—"

"No. It's okay. I'm flattered." She recovered quickly and smiled.

"You sure?"

"Yes, I'm sure."

"Well, I'll take that as a sign of promise."

She nodded, unable to answer for the moment.

Evidently satisfied that he'd accomplished his intentions in the little exchange, Jeff stepped back. "I have to get back to work. Mary Blackley is waiting anxiously for my call, and you know Mary. If it's one penny off, she's ready to declare war." He chuckled. "I swear, the old lady does nothing but wait by her mailbox for her statement. I can't remember a month when she hasn't called, and I can't remember a single complaint that has borne true."

Lacy pictured the elderly, hook-nosed lady wobbling through the doors, leaning on her cane. She smiled. "Yeah, I know what you mean. What is it this time? A missing comma?"

"Some ATM fee. Evidently, we're robbing her blind." Jeff laughed and retreated across the floor.

The heat started at the base of Lacy's spine and flashed up through her skull as if she'd inadvertently hit a nerve. *Some ATM fee?* She watched Jeff clack along the lobby floor. The clock above his head on the far wall read 8:58. Two minutes.

Lacy dived for her keyboard, hoping absently that no one noticed her eagerness. She ran a quick search for Mary Blackley's account number, found it, and keyed it in. She ran a query on all service charges. The screen blinked to black, seemed to hesitate, and then popped up with a string of numbers. Mary Blackley's account. She scrolled quickly down to the service charges levied. She lifted a trembling finger to the screen and followed the charges . . . six ATM transactions . . . each one with a fee of $1.20. A dollar-twenty. As it should be. Mary Blackley was chasing ghosts again. Unless . . .

She straightened and ran a search on the first transaction fee. According to the record that popped up, Mary had used her card at a Diamond Shamrock convenience store and withdrawn forty dollars on August 21, 1999, at 8:04 P.M. The servicing bank, Connecticut Mutual, had charged her $1.20 for the privilege of using its system.

So then, what could have prompted Mary to call?

Lacy backed out of the account quickly and walked across the lobby to Jeff's cubicle. He was bent over the keyboard when she stuck her head in and smiled.

"Lacy!" He made no attempt to hide his pleasure at seeing her materialize in his doorway.

"Hi, Jeff. Just walking by. So, you straighten Mary out?"

"Nothing to straighten out, actually. She was not overcharged at all."

"What was her problem?"

"Don't know. Printing mistake or something. She was actually right this time. Her statement did have the wrong fee on it—$1.40 instead of $1.20." He lifted a fax from his desk. "But the statement in the computer shows the correct fee, so whatever happened didn't really happen at all. Like I said, a printer problem, maybe."

Lacy nodded, smiling, and turned away before he could see the blood drain from her face. A customer stepped through the doors, and she made her way back to the tellers' windows, stunned and lost and breathing too hard.

She knew what had happened then with a dreadful certainty. Kent had done that! The little weasel had found a way to take Mary's twenty cents and then put it back as he had said he would. And he had done it without tipping his hand.

But that was impossible—so maybe that was not what had happened at all.

Lacy returned to her station and lifted the closed sign from her window. The first customer had to address her twice before she acknowledged.

"Oh, I'm sorry. What can I do for you today?"

The older woman smiled. "No problem. I know the feeling. I would like to cash this check." She slid a check for $6.48 made out to Francine Bowls across the counter. Lacy punched it in on autopilot.

"God, help me," she muttered aloud. She glanced at Mrs. Bowls and saw her raised eyebrow.

"Sorry," she said.

Mrs. Bowls smiled.

Lacy did not.

31

One Month Later
Wednesday

Kent sat on the edge of the lounge chair, staring at the Caribbean sunrise, his stomach in knots over what he was about to do.

He rested his hands on the keyboard and lifted his chin to the early morning breeze. The sweet smell of salt swept past his nostrils; a tall tumbler filled with clear liquor sparkled atop a silver platter beside the laptop. The world was his. Or at the very least this small corner of the world was.

From his perch on the villa's deck, Kent could see half of the island. Luxurious villas graced the hills on either side like white play blocks shoved into the rock. Far below, sun-bleached sand sloped into emerald seas that slapped gently at low tide. The ocean extended to a cloudless, deep-blue horizon, crystal clear in the rising sun. The Turks and Caicos Islands rose from the Caribbean Sea like brown rabbits on the blue ocean, a fitting likeness, considering the number of inhabitants there who were on the run. Whether fleeing taxes or the authorities or just plain life, there were few destinations better suited to a man on the lam.

But none of this mattered at the moment. All that mattered now was that some satellites had graced him with a clear connection. After all these weeks of lying low, he was rising from the dead to wreak just a little havoc in the lives of those two fools who'd taken him for a sucker not so long ago. Yes indeed. This was all that mattered for the moment.

Kent lowered his eyes to the laptop's screen and ran his fingers over the keys, taking the time to consider. It was a commodity he had plenty of these days. Time.

He'd paid $1.2 million cash for the villa four days earlier. How the builders had managed to erect the house in the first place remained a mystery, but nothing short of a monster sledge hammer swung from heaven would knock this small fortress from its moorings. On either side, tall palms bustled with a dozen chirping birds. He turned back to the living area. Large flagstones led to an indoor dipping pool beside the dining area. With the flip of a single switch the entire front wall could be lowered or raised, offering either privacy or exposure to the stunning scenery below. The previous owners had constructed a dozen such villas, each extravagant in its own way. He'd never met them, of course, but the broker had assured Kent that they were of the highest caliber. Arabs with oil money. They had moved on to bigger and better toys.

Which was fine by him—the villa offered more amenities than he imagined possible in a four-thousand-square-foot package. And it now belonged to him. Every stick of wood. Every brick. Every last thread of carpet. Under a different name, of course.

Kent took a deep breath. "Okay, baby. Let's see what our two porky friends are doing." He began what he called phase two of the plan, executing a series of commands that took him first into a secure site and then to Niponbank's handle. He then entered a request that took him directly into a single computer sitting idle, asleep in the dark corner of its home, as well it should be at 4 A.M. mountain time. Borst and company had moved to a different wing of the bank following the fire, but Kent had found him easily enough. Beginning within the week of the theft, he had made breaking in to both Borst's and big-boss Bentley's computers a regular routine.

There was always the off chance that someone intelligent was at one of the two computers at 4 A.M.—someone with the capability to detect the break-in in real time—but Kent lost no sleep over the possibility. For starters, he'd never known Borst to work past 6 P.M., much less in the wee morning hours. And if he would be in there, poking around his computer at four in the morning, Porky was not so stuffed with intelligence as he was with other things. Such as pure, unadulterated drivel.

Kent entered Borst's computer through a backdoor and pulled the manager's hard drive up on his screen. The directory filled his screen in vivid color. Kent chuckled and sat back, enjoying the moment. He was literally inside the man's office without the other having a clue, and he rather liked the view.

He lifted a crystal glass from the table and sipped at the tequila sunrise he'd mixed himself. A small shudder ran through his bones. A full thirty days had passed since his night of terror in the bank, lugging that ridiculous body around.

And so far every detail of his plan had fallen into place as planned. The realization still made regular passes through his mind with stunning incredulity. To say that he had pulled it off would be a rather ridiculous understatement.

Kent removed his eyes from Borst's directory and looked out at the emerald seas far below. So far he was batting a thousand, but the minute he touched these keys a whole new set of risks would raise their ugly little heads. It was why his gut still coiled in knots while he presented himself to the seascape as a man in utter tranquillity. An odd mixture of emotions to be sure. Fully pleased at himself and thoroughly anxious at once.

The events of the days leading up to this one slipped through his mind. No need to be overzealous here—he still had time to abort phase two.

He'd escaped Denver easily enough, and the bus trip to Mexico City had flown by like a surrealistic scene on the silver screen. Yet once in the massive city, a certain deadening euphoria had taken to his nerves. He'd rented a room in an obscure dump some enterprising soul had the stomach to call a hotel and immediately set about finding the plastic surgeon he'd made contact with a month earlier. Dr. Emilio Vasquez.

The surgeon readily took a thick wad of money and set about giving Kent a new look. The fact that Kent's "new look" should have required four operations instead of the one did not deter Vasquez in the least. It was, after all, his trademark—doing to a man's face in one operation what took most plastic surgeons three months. It was also why Kent had chosen the man. He simply did not have three months. The rest of his plan was begging for its execution.

Four days after the big fire Kent had his new look, hidden under a heavy mask of white gauze, but there, Dr. Vasquez promised him. Definitely there. The twinkle in the surgeon's eyes had worried him. It was the first time he'd considered the possibility that he might spend the rest of his life looking like something out of a horror comic. But done was done. He'd sequestered himself in the hotel room, willing the cuts beneath the facial bandages to heal. It was a time that both stretched his patience and settled his nerves at once.

Kent lifted the chrome platter from the table and stared at his reflection. His tanned face looked like a Kevin, he thought. Kevin Stillman, his new assumed name. The nose was fuller, but it was the jaw line and brow work that changed his face so that he hardly recognized his own reflection. The plastic surgeon had done an exceptional job—although the first time Dr. Vasquez had removed the bandages and proudly shoved a mirror to his face he'd nearly panicked. Then, the red lines around his nose and cheekbones brought to mind frightening images of Frankenstein. Oh, he looked different, all right. But then, so did a skinned plum. He started to drink heavily that night. Tequila, of course, lots of it, but never enough to knock him silly. That would be stupid, and he was over being stupid.

Besides, too much liquor made the computer screen swim before his eyes, and he'd spent a lot of time staring at the laptop those first two weeks. Whereas ROOS-TER allowed him undetected access into the banking system, it was that second program, the one called BANDIT, that had actually done the deed. When he had inserted his little disk into the drive that night at the bank and executed his theft, he'd left a little gift in each target account from which he'd taken twenty cents. And by all accounts the program had executed itself flawlessly. Indeed, BANDIT worked on the same principles as a stealth virus, executing commands to hide itself at the first sign of penetration. But that was not all it did. In the event the account was even so much as queried, it would first transfer twenty cents from one of Kent's holding accounts back into the target account, and then it would immediately remove itself permanently. The entire operation took exactly one and a half seconds and was over by the time the account-information screen popped to life on the operator's monitor. In the end it meant that any queried account would show erroneous charges on printed statements but not in the accounts themselves.

Kent's little virus executed itself on 220,345 accounts in the first two weeks, refunding a total of $44,069 dollars during that time. The virus would lay dormant in the rest of the accounts, waiting until September 2000 to be opened. They would obediently delete themselves if not activated within fourteen months.

It took two full weeks before he felt comfortable enough to make his first trip to the bank in Mexico City. The lines on his face were still visible, but after applying a pound of makeup he succeeded in convincing himself that they were virtually undetectable. And he was at the point of driving himself crazy in the hotel room. It was either risk a few raised brows in the bank or hang himself with the bedsheets.

The banking official at Banco de Mexico had indeed raised his brow when Kent visited under the name Matthew Brown. It was not the way Mr. Brown looked that had him jumping, it was the five-hundred-thousand-dollar cash withdrawal he'd executed. Of course the official had almost certainly reported the unusual amount—even banks that promise discretion keep a log of such transfers.

But Kent hardly cared. The maze of accounts through which the money had traveled over the last two weeks would require pure fortune to unravel. If any man were able to track the funds back to either Kent Anthony or the fire in Denver, they deserved to see him fry.

But that just wasn't going to happen.

That first five hundred thousand dollars brought a thrill to Kent's bones that he had not felt for months. He'd popped the latches of the black case he'd purchased for just this occasion and dumped the cash onto the moth-eaten bedspread in the hotel room. Then he'd stripped the piles of their rubber bands and physically rolled through them, tossing the bills into the air and letting them float lazily to the floor while pumping his fists and hooting in victory. It was a wonder the neighbors did not come pounding on his door. Possibly because there were no neighbors foolish enough to pay five hundred pesos a night to sleep in the miserable dump. He touched every bill, he thought, counting and recounting them all in a hundred different configurations. Of course he'd had little else to do then besides monitor the computer—that was his reasoning. Then he'd discarded his reasoning and celebrated by drinking himself into a two-day stupor.

It was his first alcoholic binge.

He started his well-rehearsed withdrawal plan then, flying first to Jakarta, then to Cairo, then to Geneva, then to Hong Kong, and finally here, to the Turks and Caicos Islands. At each stop he'd traveled under false identification papers, withdrawn large sums of money, and departed quickly. After each visit to a bank he'd taken the liberty of waltzing into its system using ROOSTER and isolating the links to the closed account. Bottom line, even if the local banking officials wanted to know more about the strange man who'd emptied their daily cash reserves with his massive withdrawal, they would find nothing.

He'd arrived a week ago in the islands packing just over six million dollars. All of it in cash, every last dollar untraceable. He'd become Kevin Stillman then and bought the villa. Fourteen million dollars, give or take, still waited around the world, gathering interest.

Yes indeed, to say that he'd pulled it off might very well be the century's greatest understatement. He had *rocked!* A dead man had ripped off twenty million bucks right under the nose of the almighty United States banking system, and not a soul suspected it was even gone!

That had been phase one.

Phase two had started one week after the fire, two days after Kent had received his new face. And it was phase two that was responsible for these raging emotions of insecurity now charging in to disturb the peace.

Maybe he should have been satisfied to take the $20 million minus the $44,069 and call it even. But in reality the thought hardly even occurred to him. This was not simply a matter of his getting what was coming to him; it was also a matter of Borst and Bentley getting what was coming to *them*. Some would call it revenge. Kent thought of it as justice. Putting things back the way they were meant to be. Or at least one version of how they were meant to be.

It was why he had planted a copy of ROOSTER on both Borst's and Bentley's hard drives several nights before executing the theft. And it was why he had made that first visit to their computers one week after the fire.

They already had routine access to AFPS, of course, and now they had untraceable access as well without knowing it. Only it was Kent in there doing the accessing, using their computers from remote stations. And the stuff he was accessing was not the stuff he was supposed to be accessing. Or rather it was not the kind of stuff *they* should be accessing. Naughty, naughty.

Over the course of three weeks, Kent had helped them steal money on seven different occasions. Small amounts of money—between three and five hundred dollars per whack—just enough to establish a trail. That was his little contribution to their burgeoning wallets, although to look at their private balances they certainly needed no help from him. Their contributions had been to keep the money. So far anyway. Whether because they were exceedingly greedy or because they simply did not know, Kent neither knew nor cared.

He considered all of this, set his drink back on the silver tray, and pressed his fingers together contemplatively. It had gone so smoothly that it would slip through the most sensitive digestive system unnoticed.

So then why the jitters?

Because everything up to this point had been a warmup of sorts. And now the computer sat on his table, wanting him to push the final buttons.

Kent grunted and wiped the sweat from his palms. "Well, we didn't come all this way to weasel out in the end, did we?" Of course not. Although it would certainly not hurt. And it would certainly be the wisest course, all things considered. It would . . .

"Shut up!" he snarled at himself.

Kent leaned forward and worked quickly now. He brought up ROOSTER from Borst's hard drive and then entered AFPS. He was into the bank's records.

Now the excitement of the moment brought a quiver to his bones. He brought up Borst's personal account and scanned the dozens of transactions recorded over the last few weeks. All seven deposits accommodated by him were still present. Thank heaven for small favors! He grinned and scanned down.

There were a few other deposits there as well. Large deposits. Deposits that made Kent squint. The bank was obviously paying him for AFPS. Nothing else could possibly account for a two-hundred-thousand-dollar balance.

"Not so fast, Fat-Boy," Kent muttered.

He selected *all* of the deposits with a single click of the mouse, ten in all including his own, and removed them from Borst's account to a holding account he'd built into ROOSTER. The account balance immediately dropped to an overdrawn status. Overdrawn by the $31,223 in checks Borst had written this month. He was spending his hard-earned money quickly. Well, this would give him pause.

And *this . . . will give you a hernia!*

Kent broke into the bank's primary accounting system, selected the primary bank reserves, and transferred five hundred thousand dollars to Borst's account. Using ROOSTER of course. He didn't want the authorities to know what had happened to the money. Not yet.

He posted a flag on the federal account and retreated to Borst's account. In the morning some lucky operator at Niponbank's headquarters in Japan would bring his computer up to find a nasty flag announcing the overnight disappearance of a half-million dollars from the bank's main account. Bells would clang, horns would blow, nostrils would flare. But nobody would discover the fate of the money, because it was as of yet unfindable. That was the beauty of ROOSTER.

Kent squirmed in his chair. Borst's account now showed a very healthy balance of over four hundred thousand dollars. He stared at the figure and considered leaving it. The ultimate carrot for Mr. Borst. Go ahead. Spend it, baby.

He discarded the notion. A plan was a plan. Instead he transferred the money to the same hidden account he'd set up for the other deposits, returning Borst's account to an overdrawn status. The man was going to wake up to the shock of his life.

Kent smirked, exceedingly happy for the moment.

He retreated from Borst's account and ventured into Bentley's. There he repeated the same steps, placing all of the bank president's money into another hidden account prepared for the occasion.

The porky twins were now very, very broke.

It was time to get out. Kent pulled out of the system, broke his connection, and sat back in the lounger. Sweat ran down his chest in small rivulets, and his hands were shaking.

"See how it feels, you greedy pigs," he sneered. And then he lifted his glass and threw back the remaining liquor.

Yes indeed. It was all going exactly as planned. And to this point, not a soul knew a thing.

Except Lacy, possibly. He'd said a bit much to her that night.

Or possibly that pinhead cop.

The emotion hit him then, full force, as if a lead weight had been neatly aimed from heaven and dropped on the half-naked man lounging on the deck so smugly down there. It felt as though a hole had been punched through his chest. A vacancy. The gnawing fear that it had all gone too smoothly. That in the end this dream facing him in the eyes would not be a dream at all but some kind of nightmare dressed up in sheep's clothing. That trying to live now, surrounded by his millions but without Gloria or Spencer . . . or Lacy . . .

He shook his head to clear the thought. On the other hand, there was no evidence at all that Lacy or the cop knew anything. And someday soon, perhaps, there would be another Gloria or another Lacy. Maybe. And another Spencer.

No, never another Spencer.

Kent rose, snatched the glass, and strode for the kitchen. It was time for another drink.

32

Two thousand miles northwest that same evening Lacy Cartwright stood over her stove struggling to flip the massive omelet she'd concocted in the shallow frying pan. She had no idea how she was going to eat the beast, but its aroma was staging a full assault on her senses, and she swallowed her saliva.

Her mind drifted back to the party Jeff Duncan had insisted she attend. The affair had been far too telling. She'd left after an hour of the foolishness and had to fend off a dozen questions the next workday. In the end she had succumbed to a little white lie. She had gotten sick. Which was, after all, true in heart-matters. Because she was still sick over this whole robbery issue. She knew he had done it—knew it like she knew the weasel was sitting on some beach somewhere, soaking up the rays.

She ground her teeth, turned off the stove, and flopped the eight-inch egg patty on a plate. If the idiot was still alive, off living with his millions, she hated him for it. If he was dead, having attempted such a fool thing, she hated him even more. How could anybody be so insensitive?

Lacy sat at the dinette and forked her omelet. She had decided a week ago that she should go to the authorities, even though she had promised not to tell. Give the little information that she had to the lead investigator. *"Hey, FBI man, you ever consider that maybe it was Kent Anthony who was the real robber?"* That would set them on a new track. Problem was, she could not be absolutely certain, which relieved her of any obligation, she thought. So she might very well tell them, but if she did, she would take her time.

Meanwhile, she had to get back to a normal life. The last time she remembered feeling in any way similar to this was after Kent had severed their relationship the first time. For a week she had walked around with a hollow gut, trying to ignore the lump in her throat and furious all at once. This time it was going on three weeks, and that lump kept wanting to lodge itself in her windpipe.

She had loved him, Lacy thought, and lowered her lifted fork. She had actually fallen in love with the man. In fact, to get right down and honest about the matter, she had been crazy about him. Which was impossible because she really hated him.

"Oh, God, help me," she muttered, rising and crossing to the ice box. "I'm losing my mind."

She returned to her seat with a quart of milk and drank straight from the carton. Impossible habit, but seeing as there was no one to offend at the moment, she carried on anyway. Now if Kent were here—

Lacy slammed the carton on the table in a sudden fit of frustration. Milk cleared the spout a full six inches before splashing to the table. Good grief! Enough with this Kent foolishness!

She jabbed at the omelet and stuffed a piece in her mouth, chewing deliberately. For that matter, enough with men, period. Lock 'em all in a bank somewhere and burn the whole thing to the ground. Now, that might be a bit harsh really, but then maybe not.

What in the world would Kent do with twenty million dollars? The sudden chirp of the doorbell startled her. Who could be visiting her tonight? Not so long ago it might have been Kent. Heavens.

Stop it, Lacy. Just stop it!

She walked for the door and pulled it open. A dark-haired man with slicked-back hair and wire-framed spectacles stood there, grinning widely. His eyes were very green.

"May I help you?"

He flipped a card out of his breast pocket. "Jeremy Lawson, seventh precinct," he said. "Do you mind if I ask you a few questions?"

A cop? "Sure," she muttered, and stepped aside.

The middle-aged man walked in and looked around the apartment, offering no reason for his being there.

Lacy shut the door. Something about the cop's appearance suggested familiarity, but she could not place him. "How can I help you?"

"Lacy, right? Lacy Cartwright?"

"Yes. Why?"

"I just want to make sure that I have the right person before I fire away, you know." He was sill wearing the wide grin.

"Sure. Is there a problem?"

"Oh, I don't know really. I'm doing a little looking into a fire down in Denver. You hear about that blaze that burned down a bank about a month ago?"

Whether or not it showed Lacy did not know, but she felt as though her head swelled red at the question. "Yes. Yes, I did read about that. And what does it have to do with me?"

"Nothing, maybe. We're just talking to people who might have known the gentleman who was killed in the fire. Do you mind if we sit, Miss Cartwright?"

Kent! He was investigating Kent's death! "Sure." She motioned to the sofa and took a seat in the armchair opposite. What was she to say?

Now that she looked at him carefully she saw why Kent had referred to him as a pinhead. His head seemed to slope to a point covered neatly in black shiny hair.

"Just a few questions, and I'll be out of your hair," the cop said, that smile stubbornly stuck on his face. He pulled out a small notebook and flipped it open. "I understand that you knew Kent Anthony. You spent some time with him in his last few weeks. Is that right?"

"And how did you discover this?"

"Well, I can't very well spill my trade secrets, now, can I?"

Lacy settled in her chair, wondering desperately what he knew. "Yes, I saw him a few times."

"Did his death surprise you?"

She scrunched her eyebrows. "No, I was expecting it. Of *course* it surprised me! Am I a suspect in the case?"

"No. No, you're not."

"So what kind of question is that? How could I not be surprised by his death unless I somehow knew about it in advance?"

"You may have expected it, Lacy. Can I call you Lacy? He was depressed, right? He'd lost his wife and his son in the months preceding the fire. I'm just asking you if he seemed suicidal. Is that so offensive?"

She breathed deeply. *Calm down, Lacy. Just calm down.* "At times, yes, he was upset. As would be anyone who'd suffered as much as he had. Have you ever lost a wife or a son, detective . . ." She glanced at his card again. "Lawson?"

"I can't say that I have. So you think he was capable of suicide, then? Is that your position?"

"Did I say that? I don't remember saying that. I said that at times he was upset. Please don't turn my words around."

The cop seemed thoroughly undeterred. "Upset enough to commit suicide?"

"No, I wouldn't say that. Not the last time I saw him."

He lowered his voice a notch. "Hmmm. And did you know about his little difficulties at work?"

"What difficulties?"

"Well, if you knew, you would know what difficulties, now, wouldn't you?"

"Oh, you mean the bit about his boss betraying him while he was mourning the death of his wife? You mean that tiny speck of trouble?"

The cop studied her eyes for a moment. "So you did know."

She was matching him tit for tat without really knowing why. She had no reason to defend Kent. He'd dumped her, after all. Now, if Lawson came right out and asked certain questions, she didn't know what she would say. She couldn't very well lie. On the other hand, she had promised Kent her silence.

"You knew him well, Lacy. In your opinion—and I'm just asking your opinion here, so there's no need to jump up and down—do you think he was capable of suicide?"

"Do you suspect he committed suicide? I thought they concluded that a robber had murdered him."

"Yes. That's the official line. And I'm not saying it's wrong. I'm just doing my best to make sure everything fits. You know what I mean?"

"Sure."

"So then, yes or no?"

"Suicide?"

He nodded.

"Capable, yes. Did he commit suicide? No."

The cop lifted an eyebrow. "No?"

"He was a proud man, Detective Lawson. I think it would take the hand of God to bring him to his knees. Short of that, I don't think he was capable of giving up on anything, much less his life."

"I see. And from what I've heard, I would have to agree with you. Which is why I'm still on the case, see?" He stopped as if that should make everything crystal clear.

"No, actually I don't see. Not in the least."

"Well, if it were a suicide there would be no need for further investigation. Suicide might be an ugly thing, but it's usually an open-and-shut case."

She smiled despite herself. "Of course. And being murdered causes guys like you a lot more work."

He smiled. "If he was murdered there would be no need to investigate *him*. We'd be looking for the murderer, wouldn't we?"

"Then it seems to me that you're barking up the wrong tree, Detective Lawson."

"Unless, of course, your friend Kent was not murdered. Now, if he did not commit suicide and he was not murdered, then what are we left with?"

"A dead body?" Mercy, where was he headed?

Lawson shoved his little notebook back into his pocket, having written maybe two letters on the open page. "A dead body! Very good. We'll make a detective out of you yet." He stood abruptly and headed for the door. "Well, I thank you for your time, Miss Cartwright. You've answered my questions most graciously."

He was hardly making sense now, she thought. She stood with him and followed him to the door. "Sure," she muttered. What did he know? Every bone in her body screamed to ask the question. *Did you know we were in love, Officer? Did you know that?* No, not that!

He had his hand on the door before she spoke, unable to restrain herself. "Do *you* think he's dead, Detective?"

He turned and looked her in the eyes. For a long moment they held eye contact. "We have a body, Miss Cartwright. It is burned beyond recognition, but the records show that what is left belongs to Mr. Kent Anthony. Does that sound dead to you? Seems clear enough." He flashed a grin. "On the other hand, not everything is what it seems."

"So why all the questions?"

"Never mind the questions, child. We detective types practice long and hard at asking confusing questions. It throws people off." He smiled warmly, and she thought he was sincere. She returned the smile.

He dipped his head. "Good evening, Mrs. Cartwright."

"Good night," she returned.

He turned to leave and then hesitated, turning back. "Oh, one last question,

Lacy. Kent never mentioned any plans he had, did he? Say some elaborate plan to fake his death or any such thing?"

She nearly fell over at the question. This time she knew he saw her turning red under the gills. He could hardly miss it.

And then he simply flipped a hand to the air. "Never mind. Silly question. I've bothered you enough tonight. Well, thank you for your hospitality. Coffee might have been nice—we detectives always like coffee—but otherwise you did just fine. Good night."

With that he turned and pulled the door closed behind him.

Lacy sidestepped to the chair and sat hard, heat sweeping over her. Lawson was on to him! The detective was on to Kent! He had to be! Which meant that Kent was alive!

Maybe.

❧

Kent drove his new black Jeep down the hill to the town at seven, just as the orange sun sank behind the waves. The sound of calypso drums and laughter carried on the warm breeze. Brent the real-estate broker had recommended the Sea Breeze. "The finest dining south of Miami," he'd said with a twinkle in his eye. "A bit draining on the wallet but well worth it." Kent could use a little draining on his wallet. It was feeling a tad heavy.

He mounted the wooden steps and bounded up the flight. A fountain gurgled red water from a mermaid's lips just inside the door. Like some goddess drunk on the blood of sailors. He turned to the dim interior. Through a causeway a fully stocked bar already served a dozen patrons perched on tall stools. Mahogany stairs wound to the upper level to his right.

"Welcome to the Sea Breeze, sir. Do you have reservations?"

Kent faced the hostess. Her black hair lay long on bare shoulders. She smiled carefully below dark eyes, and an obscure image of red water spewing from *those* round lips slinked though his mind. Miss Mermaid in the flesh. Her nametag read "Marie."

"No. I'm sorry, I didn't realize that I needed reservations."

"Yes. Maybe you could return tomorrow night."

Tomorrow? Negative, Black Eyes. "I'd rather eat tonight, if you wouldn't mind," Kent returned.

Marie blinked at that. "I'm sorry, maybe you didn't understand. You need a reservation. We are full tonight."

"Yes, evidently. How much will a table cost me?"

"Like I said, sir, we don't—"

"A thousand?" Kent lifted his eyebrow and pulled out his wallet. "I'm sure that for a thousand dollars you could find me a table, Marie. In fact for a thousand dollars you could possibly find me the best table in the house. Am I right? It would be our secret." He smiled and watched her black eyes widen. He felt the subtle power of wealth run through his veins. In that moment he knew that for the right price, Miss Mermaid Marie here would lick the soles of his sandals.

She glanced around and smiled. Her breathing had quickened by the rise and fall of her chest. "Yes. Actually we might have an opening. I apologize, I had no idea. This way."

Marie led him up two flights of stairs to a glass-enclosed porch atop the restaurant. Three tables rounded out the room, each delicately laid with candles and flowers and crystal and silver. The musty scent of potpourri hung in the air. A party of well-groomed patrons sat around one of the tables, drinking wine and nibbling at what looked to be some sea creature's tentacles. They looked at him with interest as Marie sat him across the circular room.

"Thank you," Kent said, smiling. "I'll add it to your tip."

She winked. "You are kind, Mr. . . ."

"Kevin."

"Thank you, Kevin. Is there anything else I can do for you at this time?"

"Not at the moment, Marie, no. Thank you."

She turned with a twinkle in her eyes and left the room.

The two waitresses who served him had obviously been told of his generosity and were unabashed in their attempts to please. He ordered lobster and steak and wine, and they were delicious. As delicious as they had been three months earlier when he had ordered the same in celebration with Gloria at the completion of AFPS. He lifted his glass of wine and stared out at the dark seas, crested with moonlit waves. *Well, I did it, Honey. Every bit and more, and I wish you were here to enjoy it with me.*

It settled on him as he ate that the food, though quite good, did not taste any different than it had when he'd paid twelve dollars for it back at Red Lobster in Littleton. The Heinz 57 sauce certainly came from the same vat. In fact the wine probably came from the same winery. Like different gasoline stations selling branded gas that anyone with half a brain knew came from the same refinery.

Kent finished the meal slowly, intent on relishing each bite, and uncomfortably aware that each bite tasted just as it should. Like lobster and steak should. The wine went down warm and comforting. But when he was done he did not feel as though he'd just eaten a thousand dollars' worth of pleasure. No, he'd just filled up his tank.

In the end he tipped heavily, slipped Marie her thousand dollars, and retired to the bar, where tequila was more in order. Steve, the bartender, must have heard of his tipping, because he eased right on over and set up a glass.

"What'll it be, sir?"

"Cuervo Gold. Straight up."

Steve poured the liquor into the glass and started polishing another. "You passing through?"

"You could say that. I own a place up the hill, but yes, I'll be in and out."

The man stuck out his hand. "Name's Steve Barnes. It's good to have you on the island."

"Thanks. Kevin Stillman."

The man hung around and asked a few more questions to which Kent gave short, pert answers. Eventually Steve wandered off to the other customers, who were talking about how some tourist had fallen off a fishing boat and gotten entangled in a net. Kent smiled once, but beyond the hint of humor, he found himself odd man out, and the hole in his chest seemed to widen. Maybe if he pulled out a few hundred and waved it around them. *"Hey guys, I'm rich. Stinking rich. Yes indeed, you may come over and lick my toes if you wish. One at a time, please."*

By the time Kent pulled into his circle drive back at the villa, his mind was numbed by the alcohol. Which was a good thing, he thought. Because something inside his mind had started to hurt, watching those fools carry on down at the pub.

But there was tomorrow, and tomorrow would be a day of reckoning. Yes indeed. Never mind the fifteen hundred bucks he'd just tossed down for dinner. Never mind the foolishness of those still surrounding the bar, gabbing with Steve the bartender.

Kent fell onto the covers. Tomorrow night he would turn the screws.

Sleep came within the minute.

33

Thursday

Markus Borst ran through the bank, huffing and puffing and not caring who saw him in the state of terror that obviously shone from his face like some kind of shiny red Christmas bulb.

He was not accustomed to running, and it occurred to him halfway through the lobby that he must look like a choo-choo train with his short legs pumping from the hips and his arms churning in small circular motions. But the gravity of the situation shoved the thought from his mind before it had time to set up. A dozen eyes glared his way, and he ignored them. What if Price was not in his office? Heaven help him! Heaven *help* him!

He met Mary as he was charging around the corner leading to Price Bentley's office, and she jumped with a cry. "Oh!" A sheet of paper fluttered from her grasp, and she bolted back. "Mr. Borst!"

"Not now!" he said. He rushed past her and slammed through the bank-branch president's door without bothering to knock. There was a time to knock and there was a time not to knock, and this was the latter if there ever was a time for the latter.

Price Bentley sat behind his big cherrywood desk, his bald head shining red under the bright fluorescent tubes above. His eyes widened in shock, and he came halfway out of his seat before his thighs intersected the bottom edge of his desk, propelling him back into his black leather chair. He immediately grabbed his legs and winced.

Bentley cursed. "What in the blazes are you doing, Borst! *Man* that hurt!" He opened his eyes and blinked rapidly at Borst. "Close the door, you fool. And straighten out that thing on your head! You look ridiculous!"

Borst hardly heard him. He slammed the door shut instinctively. "The money's gone!"

"What? Lower your voice and sit down, Borst. Your wig is slipping, man. Fix it."

Borst jerked his hand up to his head and felt the toupee. It had fallen halfway down his right ear. An image of that choo-choo train pumping through the lobby with a hairpiece slipping down one cheek flashed through his mind. Perhaps he'd frightened Mary with it. A flush of embarrassment reddened his face. He yanked the thing off and stuffed it in his breast pocket.

"We have a problem," he said, still breathing hard.

"Fine. Why don't you run through the lobby tooting a horn while you're at it. Sit down and get ahold of yourself."

Borst sat on the edge of the overstuffed chair, facing Bentley.

"Now, start from the beginning."

The branch president was coming across as condescending, and Borst hated the tone. It was *he*, after all, who had brought this whole idea to Bentley in the first place. He'd never had the guts to shove some of the man's medicine back into his face, but sometimes he sure had the inkling.

"The money's gone." His voice trembled as he said it. "I went into my personal account a few minutes ago, and someone's wiped out all the deposits. I'm overdrawn thirty thousand dollars!"

"So there's been a mistake. No need to come apart at the seams over an accounting snafu."

"No, Price. I don't think you understand. This is not some simple—"

"Look, you fool. Mistakes happen all the time. I can't believe you come storming in here announcing your stupidity to the whole world just because someone put a decimal in the wrong place."

"I'm telling you, Price. This is not—"

"Don't tell me what it is!" Bentley stormed. "This is *my* bank, isn't it? Well, when it's your bank you can tell me what it is. And stop calling me Price. Show some respect, for Pete's sake!"

Borst felt the words slapping at his ears as if they had been launched from a blast furnace. Deep in his mind, where the man in him cowered, a switch was thrown, and he felt hot blood rush to his face.

"Shut up, Price! Just shut up and listen. You're an insolent, bean-brained hothead, and you're not listening. So just shut up and listen!"

The president sat back, his eyes bulging like beetles. But he did not speak, possibly from shock at Borst's accusations.

"Now, whether you like it or not, regardless of whose bank this is or is not, we have a problem." Borst swallowed. Maybe he had gone too far with that attack. He shrank back a tad and continued.

"There is no *simple* accounting mistake. I've already run the queries. The money is not misplaced. It's gone. All of it. Including the small deposits. The ones—"

"I know which ones. And you ever talk to me like that again, and we're finished." The president stared at him unblinking. "I can do to you what we did to Anthony with a few phone calls. You'd best remember that."

Borst's ears burned at the insinuation, but the man was right. And there was nothing he could do about it. "I apologize. I was out of line."

Evidently satisfied that Borst was properly chastised, Bentley turned to his terminal and punched a few keys. He squinted at the screen for a moment and then went very still. A line of sweat broke from his brow, and his breathing seemed to thicken.

"You see," Borst said, "it's just gone."

The president swallowed deliberately. "This is not your account, you fool. It's mine. And it's overdrawn too."

"See!" Borst slid to the front of his chair. "Now, what's the chance of that? Both of our accounts wiped out! Someone found the deposits and is setting us up!"

"Nonsense!" Bentley swiveled back to Borst, dropped his head, and gripped his temples. He stood and paced to the window, rubbing his jaw.

"What do you think?"

"Shut up. Let me think. I told you that keeping those small deposits was a bad idea."

"And who says we've kept them? It's been less than a month. They were put there without our knowing; we were going to report them, right? That wouldn't warrant *this,*" Borst said.

"You're right. And you ran a full query, right? There's no trace of where it went?"

"None. I'm telling you, someone took it!"

Bentley sat down, hard. His fingers flew across the keyboard. Menus popped to life and disappeared, replaced by others.

"You won't find anything. I've already looked," Borst said.

"Yeah, well now *I'm* looking," Bentley snapped back, undeterred.

"Sure. But I'm telling you, there's something wrong here. And you know we can't just report it. If there's an investigation, they'll find the other money. It won't look right, Price."

"I told you not to call me Price."

"Come on! We're each a few hundred thousand dollars upside down here, and you're bickering over what I call you?"

Bentley had finished his queries. "You're right. It's gone." He slammed his big fist on the desk. "That's impossible! How's that possible, huh? You tell me, Mr. Computer Wizard. How does someone just walk into an account and wipe it out?"

A buzz erupted at the base of Borst's skull. "You would need a pretty powerful program." He stiffened in his chair. "AFPS could do it, maybe."

"AFPS? AFPS would leave a trail as wide as I-70."

"Not necessarily. Not if you know the raw code."

"What are you saying?"

"I'm not sure. I'm not even sure how it could be done. But if there were a way, it would be through the alteration of the code itself."

"Yeah, well that's not good news, Borst. And do you know why that's not good news? I'll tell you why. Because you, my dear friend, are in charge of that code! You're the brilliant one who pieced this thing together, right? Now either you stole from yourself, and from me, or someone else is using your program to rob you blind."

"Don't be ridiculous! Those monkeys in there wouldn't have the stomach much less the experience to do anything like this. And I certainly did not mess with my own account."

"Well, somebody did. And you'd better find that somebody, or it won't go nicely for you. Do you understand me?"

Borst looked up at the president, stunned by the suggestion. "Well, if it doesn't go nicely for me, you can bet it won't go nicely for you."

"And *that,* my dear, fine-feathered friend, is where you are wrong." Bentley jabbed his desk with his finger, making a small thumping sound each time it landed. "If this goes down, you'll take the fall, the whole fall, and nothing but the fall. And don't think for a minute I can't do it."

"We will deny it," Borst said, dismissing Bentley's threats.

"Deny what?"

"We deny that we know anything about our accounts at all. We ignore all of this and come unglued when the first sign of trouble crops up."

"And like you said, if they run an investigation we could have a hard time answering their questions."

"Yes, but at least it's only an *if.* You have a better suggestion?"

"Yes. I suggest you find this imbecile and put a bullet in his brain."

They stared at each other for a full thirty seconds, and slowly, very slowly, the magnitude of what they might be facing settled on both of them. The macho stuff vacated their minds, replaced by a dawning desperation. This was not a problem that would necessarily go away at the push of a button.

When Borst emerged from the room thirty minutes later, his head was bald and his face was white. But these issues were of little concern to him now. It was the pressure on his brain that had him swallowing repeatedly as he walked back to his office. And nothing, absolutely nothing, he could think of seemed to loosen the vise that now held his mind in its grip.

~~~

Kent awoke midmorning and slogged out to the deck, nursing a bit of a headache. He squinted against the bright blue sky and rubbed his temples. The ocean's distant crashing carried on the wind, but otherwise silence hung heavily in the air. Not a voice, not a bird, not a motor, not a single sound of life. Then he heard the muted thud of a hammer landing on some new home's wood frame down the way. And with that thud the hole in Kent's chest opened once again. A sobering reminder that he was alone in the world.

He glanced at his watch, suddenly alert. Ten o'clock Friday morning. His lips twitched to a faint grin. By now Borst and Bentley would have discovered the little disappearing trick. Now you see it; now you don't. He imagined they'd be sweating all over their desks about now. What they didn't know was that the trick was just beginning. Act one. Strap yourselves in, ladies and gentlemen. This one will rock your socks. Or perhaps steal them right off your feet without your knowing the better.

He swallowed and thought about mixing himself a drink. Meanwhile, he was wealthy, of course. Must not forget that. How many people would give their children to have what he now had? An image of Spencer, riding his red skateboard, popped into his mind. Yes, a drink would be good.

Kent mixed himself a drink and meandered out to the deck. The soft sound of waves rushing the shore carried on the breeze. He had ten hours to burn before placing the phone call. He couldn't sit around drinking himself into a stupor this time. Not with that conversation coming on tonight. He would have to stay clear headed. Then perhaps he should clear his head out there on the waves.

An hour later Kent stood by the pier, gazing down the long row of boats, wondering how much they would bring. A small chill of excitement rippled through his gut.

"Whoa there, mate!" The voice spoke with an Australian accent.

Kent whirled to face an older seaman pushing a dolly stacked with provisions down the plank. "If you'll step aside, son, I'll be by quicker than a swordfish on a line." He grinned, splitting the bristly white hair that masked his face. Years of sun had turned the man's skin to leather, but if the shorts and tank top were any indicator, he wasn't too concerned.

"Sorry." Kent stepped aside to let the man pass and then followed him up the pier. "Excuse me."

"Hold your head, son," the man croaked without looking back. "I've got a bit of a load, as you can see. I'll be with you in a jiffy. Have yourself a beer."

Kent smiled and trailed the man to a large white boat near the end of the pier. *Marlin Mate.* She was a Roughwater, the little silver plaque on her bow said. Maybe fifty feet in length.

"This your boat?" Kent asked.

"You don't hear too well, do you? Hold your head, mate." The seaman hauled the dolly over the gangplank and into the cabin, grumbling under his breath. This time Kent lost his grin and wondered if the old man's head was out to sea. He could certainly use a little fine-tuning in the social-graces department.

"Now there," the man said, coming from the cabin. "That wasn't such a long wait, was it? Yes, this is my boat. What can I do for you?" The sailor's blue eyes sparkled with the sea.

"What does something like this go for?" Kent asked, looking her up and down.

"Much more than you would think. And I don't rent her out. If you want a day trip, Paulie has—"

"I'm not sure you're answering my question. It was quite simple, really. How much would a boat like this one cost me?"

The man hesitated, obviously distracted by the strong comeback. "What's it to you? You plan on buying her? Even if you could afford her, she's not for sale."

"And what makes you think I can't afford her?"

"She's pricey, mate. I've worked her for half my life, and I still hold a decent note on her." Leather Face smiled. He'd misplaced two of his front teeth. "You got five hundred thousand dollars hanging loose in your pocket there?"

"Five hundred, huh?" Kent studied the boat again. It looked almost new to him—if the Australian had owned it for as long as he let on, he'd cared for her well.

"She's not for sale."

Kent looked back to the old man, who had flattened his lips. "How much do you want for her? I pay cash."

The man looked at him steadily for a moment without answering, probably running through those little note balances in his mind.

"Five-fifty, then?" Kent pushed.

Leather Face's baby blues widened. For a long minute he did not speak. Then a smile spread his cracked face. "Seven hundred thousand U.S. dollars, and she's all yours, mate. If you're crazy enough to pay that kind of dough in cash, well, I guess I'll have to be crazy enough to sell her."

"I'll pay you seven hundred on one condition," Kent returned. "You agree to keep her for a year. Teach me the ropes and take care of her when I'm not around."

"I'm no steward, mate."

"And I'm not looking for a steward. You just let me tag along, learn a few things, and when I'm gone you run her all you like."

The old man studied him with piercing eyes now, judging the plausibility of the offer, Kent guessed. "You show me the cash, I'll show you the boat. If I like what I see and you like what you see, we got us a deal."

Kent was back an hour later, briefcase in hand. Leather Face—or Doug Oatridge as he called himself—liked what he saw. Kent just wanted to get out to sea, feel the breeze through his hair, drink a few beers, distract himself for a few hours. Kick back on the deck of his yacht while Borst and Bentley chewed their fingernails to the knuckles.

By midday they were trolling at twenty knots, precisely. A permanent smile had fixed itself on Doug's face as he feathered the murmuring engine through the seawater. Thinking about the cash, no doubt. They sat on cushioned chairs, eating sandwiches and drinking ice-cold beer. The sun had dipped halfway when the first fish hit. Ten minutes later they hauled a four-foot tuna over the side and shoved it into the holding tank. What they would do with such a creature, Kent had no clue—maybe carve it up and fry it on the grill, although he'd never liked tuna. Give him swordfish or salmon, disguised with chicken broth, but keep the smelly stuff. Three more of the fish's cousins joined him in the tank over the next half-hour, then they stopped taking the bait. Doug was talking about how tuna ran in schools, but Kent was thinking the fish had just grown tired of the senseless self-sacrifice.

The perfect day's only damper came on the trip home, when Kent made the mistake of asking Doug how he'd come to own the boat in the first place. The old man had evidently both grown accustomed to Kent and loosened under the influence of a six-pack, and his story ran long. He'd been married twice, he said, first to Martha, who had left him for some basketball player on a beach court in Sydney. Then to Sally, who had borne them three sons and tired of them all after ten years. It was an inheritance of a hundred thousand dollars that had brought Doug to the islands with his sons, in search of a boat with which to begin life anew. He'd purchased *Marlin Mate* then. Two of his sons had left the island within the first year—off to America to find their own lives. The youngest, his little Bobby, had been swept overboard in a storm one year later.

The old man turned away and stared misty eyed to the sea, having dropped his tale like a lead weight into Kent's mind. The beer in Kent's hand suddenly felt heavy. The afternoon grew quiet beyond the splashing wake. Kent imagined a small boy cartwheeling off the deck, screaming for Daddy. A knot rose into his throat.

They docked the boat an hour later, and Kent showed as much interest as he could muster in the procedure. He shook the old man's hand. Did he want to go out tomorrow? No, not tomorrow. Could he take the boat out tomorrow then? Yes, of course. Do what you like, Doug. He thumped the man on the back and smiled. In fact, keep the stupid boat, he thought, but immediately reined in the absurd notion.

"Hey, me and the mates are going to do some drinking tonight. You want to come? There'll be dames."

"Dames?"

Doug flashed a toothless smile. "Girls, mate. Beach bunnies in their bikinis."

"Oh yes, of course. Dames. And where are we having this party?"

"Here on the boat. But not to worry, mate. The first man to puke gets thrown overboard."

Kent smiled. "Well, that's comforting. Maybe. We'll see."

34

Despite his need for a clear mind, Kent downed two stiff drinks before his eight o'clock phone call. It wouldn't do to have his teeth clattering against the receiver, either, and his nerves had tightened as the hour approached.

Darkness had settled over the island. From the villa's deck the sea looked black below, split by a long shaft of white cast by the bright moon. A spattering of lights twinkled along the hillside on either side. It was hard to imagine that across that sea the sun had already risen over a bustling city called Tokyo. He'd seen pictures of the tall, chrome building that housed Niponbank's headquarters, smack-dab in the middle of the busiest part of town, but he could hardly picture the crowded scene now. The serene one before him had lulled him into a foggy state. Or perhaps the drinks had done that.

A small bell chimed behind him, and Kent started. It was time.

He grabbed the cordless phone from the table and stared at its buttons. His heart pounded like a tom-tom in his ears. For the first time in over a month he was about to expose himself. And for what?

Kent cleared his throat and spoke with a gruff voice, the voice he had decided would be his to complete his disguise. "Hello, this is Bob." Too high. He'd done this a thousand times. "Hello, this is Bob."

Get on with it, man.

He punched the numbers in quickly.

An electronic voice answered his call. "Thank you for calling Niponbank. Please press one if you wish to be served in Japanese. Please press two if you wish to be served in English." *Please press three if you are calling to turn yourself in for grand larceny.*

Kent swallowed and pressed two.

It took all of ten minutes to find the right individual. A Mr. Hiroshito—the one banking executive Kent knew who could quickly get him to the real power mongers at the top. He knew Hiroshito because the high-level man had visited Denver once, and the bank had spent a day dancing around him like crows around fresh road kill.

"Hiroshito." The man said his name like it was an order to attack.

Chill, my friend. "Mr. Hiroshito, you don't know me, but you should. I'm—"

"I am sorry. You must have the wrong connection. I will put you through to the operator."

Kent spoke quickly before the man could pass him off. "Your bank is missing one million dollars, is it not?"

The phone filled with the soft hiss of distant static. Kent was not sure if the man had transferred him. "Hello."

"Who is this?"

"I am the person who can help you recover the million dollars that was missing from your ledgers yesterday. And please don't bother trying to trace this phone call—you will find it impossible. Do I have your attention?"

Hiroshito was whispering orders in Japanese behind a muted receiver. "Yes," he said. "Who is this? How do you know of this matter?"

"It is my business to know of such matters, sir. Now, I will lay this out for you as quickly and as plainly as possible. It would be best if you could record what I say. Do you have a recorder?"

"Yes. But I must know who you are. Surely you cannot expect—"

"If you choose to accept my terms, you will know me soon enough, Mr. Hiroshito. That I can promise you. Are you recording?"

A pause. "Yes."

Here goes nothing. Kent took a deep breath.

"Yesterday a million dollars was stolen from Niponbank's main ledger, but then, you know this already. What you don't know is how I know this. I know this because a certain party within your own bank, who shall remain nameless, tipped me off. This is relatively unimportant. What *is* important, however, is the fact that I managed to break into your system and verify the missing balance. I was also able to track the first leg of the outbound transaction. And I believe I will be able to uncover the theft in its entirety.

"Now, before you ask, let me tell you what you are going to ask. Who in the world am I to think I can track what the engineers in your own bank cannot track? I am a number: 24356758. Please write it down. It is where you will wire my fee if I successfully expose the thief and return your money. As I'm sure you can appreciate, I must protect my actual identity, but for the sake of convenience you may use a fictitious name. Say, Bob. You may call me Bob. From now on, I am Bob. I can assure you that Bob is quite proficient at electronic data manipulation. Without question one of the world's finest. You have not heard of him only because he has always insisted on working in complete anonymity. In fact, as you will see, he depends on it. But there is no man better suited to track down your money; that much I can assure you with absolute confidence. Do you understand thus far?"

Hiroshito did not expect the sudden question. "Y . . . yes."

"Good. Then here are Bob's terms. You will grant him unlimited access to any bank he deems necessary for his investigation. He will both return your money and uncover the means with which the perpetrator took your money. You obviously have a hole in your system, my fine friends. He will not only return your money; he will close that hole. If and only if he is successful, you will transfer a 25 percent recovery fee into the Cayman account I recited earlier: 24356758. You will wire the money within one hour of your own recovery. In addition, if he is successful, you will grant him immunity in connection with any charge related to this case. These are his terms. If you accept them, I can assure you he will recover your money. You have exactly twelve hours to make your decision. I will call you then for your decision. Do you understand?"

"Yes. And how is this possible? How can we be sure you are sincere, Mr. . . . uh . . . Bob?"

"You can't. And once you've had time to think about it, you'll see that it does not matter. If I am unsuccessful, you pay nothing. But you must ask yourself how I know what I know. No one knows the workings of electronic high finance like I do, Mr. Hiroshito. I am simply the best. Please take this message to your superiors immediately."

"And how do I know—?"

"You know enough already," Kent interrupted. "Play the tape for the main man. He'll agree to my terms. Good day."

Kent hung up to a stammering Hiroshito and exhaled slowly. His hands were trembling, and he pulled them into fists. Man, that had felt good! He took a long drink from his glass, slammed the tumbler onto the table, and pumped a fist in victory. "Yes!"

Of course it was not victory. Not yet. But it was the deed. It was the plan. The thrill of the hunt, as they say. Within the hour the whole snobby bunch of them would at least suspect that there existed a man who possessed the electronic wizardry to waltz into their systems and do what he willed. A lunatic who called himself Bob. Now *there* was power! Not just being able to *do* it, but being settled in the knowledge that others *believed* he could do it.

Kent made his way to the bathroom on shaky legs. In twelve hours he would have his answer. And if they said no? If they said no, he might very well go in there and take another million. Then call them back and ask them if they might reconsider. *Ha!*

Yes indeed. Now *there* was power!

⌒⌒⌒

Kent attended Doug's party on the *Marlin Mate* later that night for lack of appealing alternatives. Actually, the thought of standing on a swaying boat with twenty people held little appeal itself. Never mind that there would be "dames." Half-naked dames at that. Never mind that there would be booze. It was all sounding rather bleak now. But staying home alone drumming his fingers on the table held even less appeal, so he took the Jeep to the pier and boarded the swaying boat.

The Aussie knew how to party. It was perhaps the only skill he'd mastered aside from skippering. As promised, a dozen girls smelling of coconut oil slithered about the twin decks. At some point, Doug must have dropped the nugget that the blond-haired man sitting quietly on the upper deck was flush with cash, because the women began to mill about Kent with batting eyes and pouting lips.

For the first hour, Kent quite enjoyed the attention. It was sometime near midnight, however, that a thought dawned on him. He was not attracted to these bathing beauties. Maybe the booze had messed with his libido. Maybe the memory of Gloria was simply too fresh. Maybe the hole in his chest had sucked the life right out of him—neutered him. The realization fell over him like a wet blanket.

By the time he dragged himself back up the hill at two in the morning, the booze had robbed his ability to consider the matter any further. It was the last time he would party with Doug and his dames.

When Kent rejoined the land of the conscious it was to a relentless chirp sounding in his ear. A whistle blowing down the alley. He spun around, except that he couldn't spin at all because Mr. Brinkley's dead body was hanging off his shoulders, butt up, gray in the moonlight. He nearly capsized in his lumbering turn.

Tweep, tweep, tweep!

His heart pounded like a drum to that piercing alarm. They had found him! A figure ran through the shadows toward him, his hand extended accusingly, blowing his whistle.

Tweep, tweep, tweep!

He and Mr. Brinkley had been caught with their pants down behind the bank! At least Mr. Brinkley had. The rest of this nonsense about buying a villa and sailing on his yacht had been a dream. He was still back at the bank!

And then the whistle-blower's face emerged from the shadows, and Kent's heart slammed into his throat. It was the vagrant! And it wasn't with a two-dollar tin whistle that he was sounding the alarm; it was with that long tongue of his, sticking out and curled like a bamboo reed.

Kent bolted up, sticky with sweat, breathing hard.

Tweep, tweep, tweep.

He reached over and smacked the alarm beside his bed.

Eight o'clock! He sprang from the bed and splashed cool water over his face. Hiroshito and company were waiting by the phone—at least he hoped they were. Ready to deal. And if not he would go ahead and rock their world a little. Sound his own wake-up call. *Tweep, tweep!* Maybe he'd take five million next time! That would put them on their seats. Of course he'd have to give it all back—this was not like taking twenty untraceable cents from millions of unsuspecting donors; this was plain old larceny. They'd be crawling over this like ants on honey. And they'd eventually find the link. Which was why he had to get on the phone and strike a deal to find their money *his* way before they found it *their* way. Kent to the rescue.

He snatched up the phone and dialed the number. This time it took less than sixty seconds before Mr. Hiroshito's sharp voice crackled in his ear.

"Hello."

"Mr. Hiroshito. It is Bob. You remember me?"

"Yes. I have someone here who would like to speak to you."

Kent sat on the deck chair facing the blue-green sea. "Sure."

Another voice spoke into the phone, this one sly like a loan shark and definitely Caucasian. "Bob? Are you there, Bob?"

"Yes." The man's tone reminded Kent of a bossman smirking on some gangster movie.

"Okay, Bob. I don't know who you are, and frankly, I don't care. But *you* know who we are, and you should know that we don't deal with extortionists and blackmailers. So why don't you just cut the charades and talk to us straight instead of playing peekaboo, okay, pal?"

Kent ground his teeth, flooded with the sudden urge to hurl the phone over the railing. Maybe fly over to Tokyo and smack some sense into Mr. Cheese Whiz. He crossed his legs and breathed deliberately.

"I'm sorry, Mr. . . ."

A pause. "Call me Frank."

"I'm sorry, Frank, but you have this all wrong. I apologize for the mix-up. You must have been out of the room when they played the tape. Nobody as bright as you sound would have the stomach to threaten a man in my position. Listen to the tape, Frankie. I'll call back in ten minutes." Kent hung up.

His chest was thumping. What was he doing? Frank had obviously listened to the tape already—it was why he had used the term *extortion*. Because frankly, when you got right down to it, this was as close to extortion as kidnapping. He had kidnapped their system, and they knew it. And what he was really proposing was that he would turn over the key to their system (that would be ROOSTER) in exchange for immunity. That and $250,000.

Kent retreated to the kitchen and poured a drink, a tequila sunrise minus the citrus and the ice. Cuervo Gold straight up. If ever there was a time he needed a drink, it was now.

When he called ten minutes later, they put him directly through.

"Bob?" It was Frank, and he was not sounding so slick.

"Did you listen to the tape, Frank?"

"Of course I listened to the tape!" the other man yelled. "Now, you listen to me . . ."

"No, you listen to me, Buckwheat! If you think for a minute that I cannot do what I claim I can do, then simply reject my terms. Don't come at me with all this strong-arm baloney. Either you hire me for a 25 percent recovery fee and immunity, or you don't. Is this too difficult to understand?"

"And how do we know that it wasn't *you* who stole the money in the first place?"

"Not a bad idea, Frankie. Except this is no ransom. Or maybe you didn't listen to the whole tape. I've agreed to turn the perpetrators over to you, and that wouldn't be me. More important, your payment of this recovery fee is contingent upon my closing the security breach through which they were able to gain access to your million dollars. You obviously have a gaping hole somewhere in your system. It was one million this time. Who's to say that it won't be ten million the next?"

"I'm not sure whether to take that as a threat or a warning, Bob."

"Take it as a warning. Don't be a fool, Frankie. I'm not your thief. Think of me as your cybercop. I don't come cheap, granted, but then, I only charge if I deliver. Do we have a deal, or don't we? I have other clients waiting."

The phone hissed for a few long seconds. They were talking, and Kent let them talk.

When a voice spoke again, it was Hiroshito's. "We will accept your terms, Mr. . . . Bob. You have two weeks to find the security breach and recover our money. Is there anything that you require of us at this time?"

"No. I will contact you Monday morning with a list of banks to which I need free access. Until then, rest well, my friends, You have chosen wisely."

"I hope so, Bob. This is most unusual."

"We no longer live in a world of stagecoach robbers slinging Winchesters, Mr. Hiroshito. Now it's the keyboard we have to worry about." The phone sat silently in his hand, and he wondered if the Japanese banking executive made any sense of the comparison.

"Good-bye."

"Good-bye."

Kent dropped the phone on the table and breathed deep. He had done it! Hey, a life of crime might not be such a bad thing. *Stick 'em up, baby!*

Of course he would not give Mr. Hiroshito a list of banks to which he needed access, because he had no intention of visiting a list of banks. He would make one stop, and one stop only. And that bank was located in Denver, Colorado.

On Monday he would step back into his old stomping grounds. Back to Stupid Street. The audacity of the plan struck Kent then as he gazed out to the lapping waves far below. It was lunacy! Terrifying, really. Like a killer returning to the scene of the crime just to see if the cops had found anything. *"Hey guys! It's me! So what do you think? Pretty clever, huh?"*

Kent rose unsteadily and made for the bottle on the kitchen counter. This called for another drink. There was no way he was going to return to Stupid Street completely sober.

35

Sunday

Helen walked with Bill Madison under the swaying oaks, five miles from home and going strong. The park rustled with windblown leaves, yellowed in midfall. An overcast sky grayed the early afternoon, but the light was burning bright in her heart, she thought. Brighter by the day. Which meant that something was up.

"I really need to buy some new walking shoes," she said.

Bill strutted by her side, dressed in green sweats and a pair of running shoes he'd purchased for his afternoon walks with her. That day in her living room had changed the pastor's life. The heavens had torn open for him, and he'd become a new man. He'd announced the next morning that he would like to join her in the afternoons when his schedule permitted. In fact, he'd make sure his schedule did permit. The way he told it, if he joined her on the last leg of her journey, he'd be able to keep up just fine. And keep up he had, brimming with an enthusiasm that in fact spilled over to her.

"How many pair have you been through? How long have you been walking now, anyway? Two—three months?"

"Three. I've been walking three months, give or take. And I guess I've gone through about ten pairs of shoes. Same legs though. I haven't traded those in yet."

He chuckled. "No, I guess you haven't."

They walked on for a hundred feet before Helen told him what had been on her mind for the past few miles. "We are nearing the end, I think."

He turned, surprised. "The end? As in the end of the walking?"

"Yes." She smiled. "It's quite something, you know—having the Spirit of God filling your bones like a miracle drug. It gives the notion of walking in the Spirit new meaning."

"Yes, I can see that. You know, when I first saw that vision in your living room, I couldn't get over how clear everything was. All the questions just evaporated. *Poof,* they were gone. God is obviously God, and heaven obviously exists, and every word spoken here on Earth turns a head up there. But I have to tell you, things are not always so clear down here, even after that kind of encounter. Time dims the memory, and what was so bright only a couple of weeks ago starts to cloud a little. That make sense?"

Helen nodded. "Crystal clear."

"Well, if it wasn't for your walking—this incredible thing God has done to your legs—I might honestly think you had lost your mind, praying every day for a dead man."

"We've been over this, haven't we?"

"Yes. But not lately. You still think he's alive?"

"I'm past thinking too clearly, Pastor. There's a word from God—'Lean not on your own understanding, but trust in God'—you know it?"

"Sure."

"I've learned what that means. My own mind tells me all kinds of things that would make a grown man want to climb into a hole. You think the idea of a sixty-four-year-old lady walking in tube socks and a dress, twenty miles a day, praying for a dead man, is not strange? It is quite absurd. So absurd that whole theologies have been constructed to push such events into a different time zone. As if God woke up one day and suddenly realized that the way he'd been doing things all along, with falling walls and talking donkeys and burning bushes, was really quite childish. Men have grown too smart for that, yes?" She chuckled. "So when I get to the end of my walk each day, I still have to pinch myself. Make sure it's all real. Because my mind is not so different from yours, Bill. It wants to reject some things."

"It's good to know that you're as human as I am. Maybe that's one reason God has given you this physical sign. Helps you keep the faith."

"I'm sure it is."

"So you think Kent is still alive, then?"

"We've come back to that question, have we? Let's put it this way, Pastor. Wherever Kent is, he needs my prayers. The impulse to pray has not dimmed."

"Which basically means he must be alive."

"So it seems."

"But it's all coming to an end, you say."

She closed her eyes for a moment and considered the lightness of her spirit. Although she had not had any visions for over a week now, there was an expectancy riding in the air. A lightness. A brightness, hovering just beyond the clouds. How she knew it was all going somewhere rather quickly remained a small mystery. But she did.

"I think so, yes. How it will end, I have no clue. My spirit is light, but that may be for my sake rather than his. I just don't know. One thing I do know, however. When these legs begin to wobble with fatigue, it is the end."

The pastor did what he had often taken to doing these days. He broke into a prayer. "Jesus, we love you. Father, you are sovereign, your ways beyond finding out. Thank you for choosing to dwell in us. You are mighty, you are holy, you are awesome in your power."

No matter how this ended, Helen thought, the little Community Church on the corner of Main and Hornberry was in for a little jolt. Which was not so bad. Not so bad at all.

Kent peered through the oval window to the darkness. A strobe on the airliner's wingtip lit the fuselage every three seconds, and he half expected to see the vagrant clinging to the silver wing on one of those flashes. Welcome to the Twilight Zone. The engine's steady drone dropped in pitch as the lumbering jet descended through the black skies. A sea of pinpricks sparkled ten thousand feet below them. Denver was lit up like a Christmas tree in October.

Kent rattled the ice in his glass and sipped at the tequila. He'd lost count of the little bottles Sally, the first-class bombshell stewardess, had brought him over the last few hours—enough to ease the sense of dread that had lodged itself in his chest somewhere over the Atlantic. It had felt akin to being trapped between a brood of vipers and a cliff overlooking a black void. Denver would be the coiling snakes, of course. They would be hissing and snapping at his heels if he was not careful.

But it was the cliff at his back that had him calling for the small liquor bottles. The dread he'd wrestled with back there on the island, staring at the blue seas those last two days while awaiting his flight stateside. The truth be told, he was growing tired of paradise on the hill before he'd really had a chance to live the good life. A gloom had settled over the villa by midday Friday, and it had refused to budge.

The problem was quite simple, actually: Kent could find nothing that captured his fancy, sitting high on the hill, nestled in his own private Shangri-la. It was all feeling like day-old soda. No matter how often he told himself that he ought to be thrilled with the new yacht—it was a lifelong dream, for heaven's sake—he could not bring himself to crawl down the hill to take her out again. The realization prompted a slowly moving panic that had gnawed at him with building persistence. The kind of panic you might expect after reaching a coveted destination for which you had sold your firstborn only to discover that the condo on the beach was really a roach-infested shack on a muddy river.

By Saturday the villa felt more like a prison than a resort. The tropical sun seemed like a relentless blast furnace, the quiet like a desperate solitude. And all the while he could not find release, a situation that only served to fuel the growing panic. Madness. Madness in paradise: human nature's grand joke. *When you finally arrive, my friends, you will find the Joker, wearing a frown.*

In the end he'd washed it away with tequila. Lots of tequila.

Sunday came slowly, but it came. Kent packed a million dollars in cash about his body and luggage and boarded his flight, indirectly bound for Denver.

The airliner settled onto the asphalt with a squeal of rubber, and Kent closed his eyes. He was Kevin, now. Kevin Stillman. *Remember that, Buckwheat. Kevin, Kevin, Kevin.* His passport said he was Kevin, his business card said he was Kevin, and a dozen accounts scattered to the four corners, each stuffed with cash, all said he was Kevin. Except at the bank—there he would be Bob.

The huge tower clock in Denver International Airport said it was ten o'clock by the time Kent left the rental desk to collect his Lincoln Towncar. It was black, fittingly. An hour later he took a room in the downtown Hyatt Regency ten blocks from the bank, walking through the lobby on pins and needles, fighting off the fear that someone might recognize him. The sentiment was thoroughly unfounded, of course. He looked nothing like the Kent of old. In fact he was *not* the Kent of old. He was Kevin Stillman, and Kevin Stillman had a new face—broader and well tanned, topped with brown hair. He was not the lanky blond some had once known as Kent Anthony. Goodness, if the prospect of being caught in this remote hotel lobby brought sweat to his forehead, what would a walk through the bank do?

He made the call to Japan at eleven that night. Hiroshito was where all hard-working banking executives were expected to be first thing Monday morning Japan time—in his office.

"Mr. Hiroshito?"

"Yes."

"It's Bob. You do remember me?"

"Yes."

"Good, I will need access to the bank president at your main Denver branch at 9 A.M. mountain time. His name is Bentley. Mr. Price Bentley. Will there be a problem with this request?"

Hiroshito hesitated. "Nine? The bank opens at eight. It is short notice."

"Not too short, I am sure. You have the capability of transferring a million dollars in much less time. Surely you have the capability of making a phone call."

"Of course. He will be ready."

"Thank you, sir. You are very helpful." Kent hung up and made for the liquor cabinet. He managed to drift off near midnight, pretty much inebriated.

∽∾∾

The sounds of rush hour filtered through the room's window when he awoke at seven. He was in Denver! Monday morning!

Kent bounded from the bed and showered, his spine tingling with anticipation. He donned a black double-breasted suit, the first he'd worn in six weeks, by his accounting. He'd chosen a white shirt accented by a teal tie—strictly business. Bob was about to do some business.

By the time he reached the towering bank he was sweating profusely. He pulled the Towncar into a space three down from his old parking spot and turned off the ignition. Silence engulfed the cab. To his right the alley gaped with a red brick mouth, blackened slightly. That would be his handiwork. The memories strung through his mind like Polaroids on a string. He dabbed his forehead and wiped at his neck with a napkin he'd taken from the hotel lounge. Couldn't very well go in there looking as though he'd just come from the sauna.

What if, by some strange force at work in their memories, they *did* recognize him? Something about his hairline or his vocabulary or the sound of his voice. What if it struck a bell in their empty noggins, and they actually identified him?

He cleared his throat and tried the voice. "Hello." It came out squeaky, and he tried again, intentionally lowering it. "Hello, there. I'm Bob."

Kent bit his lip, slipped on black glasses, and stepped from the car, closing his hands against a tremble that had taken over his fingers. He straightened his suit and looked up at the rising steps. Customers already streamed in and out of the revolving doors. He took three long, deep breaths and strode forward. *It's now or never, Buckwheat. Buckwheat Bob. Suck it up. Think of what they did to you.*

Kent did that. He clenched his jaw and bounded up the steps, grasping madly at the sudden surge of confidence. He stepped through the revolving doors like a rooster on the hunt and stopped dead in his tracks.

It all crashed down on him with a vengeance: Zak the security guard, pacing with sagging eyes; the long row of tellers, mechanically pushing and pulling slips of paper across the green counter; the tall sailboat suspended in the middle of the lobby; a sea of muted voices murmuring on about dollars and cents; the smell of a dozen perfumes, all mixed into a potpourri of scents.

If Kent's skin had been invisible they would have all seen his heart bounce up into his throat and stick there, a ball of quivering flesh. He suddenly knew with absolute certainty that this was all a mistake. A huge monstrous mistake. He very nearly spun on his heels for a hasty getaway then. But his muscles were not responding so quickly, and he hesitated. And by then it was too late. Because by then Sidney Beech was walking directly for him, smiling as if to welcome him back into the fold.

"May I help you?" she asked, which was not what Sidney Beech normally did with just any yahoo who wandered into the bank. It was his Blues Brothers look, he quickly decided. He still had the shades on, a good thing—if she could have seen his bulging eyes she might have called security instead of wandering over with that grin on her face.

"Excuse me, can I help you with something?"

Kent cleared his throat. *Strictly business, Bob. Don't be a wuss.*

"Yes. I'm here to see a Mr. Bentley. Price Bentley."

She cocked her head, in a polite way of course. "And you are?"

"Bob."

She waited for more.

"He's expecting me," Kent said.

"Bob?"

"Bob."

"I'll let him know you are waiting, Bob. If you'd like to have a seat in our lounge . . ."

"You may tell him that I'm on a tight schedule. I don't intend on lounging around waiting for him."

She lifted an eyebrow, unable to hide a slight grin. "Of course." Sidney motioned for the overstuffed chairs and strutted off toward Bentley's office, to tell him of the kook that had just walked in, no doubt.

Kent meandered over to the ship and studied the structure, feigning interest. Several tellers watched him curiously. Perhaps he should remove the black glasses. And maybe he should have purchased some of those colored contact lenses—his blues eyes might bare his soul.

Sidney was clacking up behind him. This was it then. He let her come.

"Bob?"

He turned and ground his teeth. *Strictly business, Bob.*

"He will see you now." She had lost the grin.

Kent strode for the office without waiting for her to show the way then realized it would be a mistake. How would he know? He turned to her. "This way?"

"Around the corner," she said.

Better. He walked for the office, tall and mean, looking like a cybercop ought to look, gaining confidence with each step.

Kent put his hand on the brass knob, took a single deep breath, pushed the door open without knocking, and stepped in. The oversized branch president sat behind his desk like a bowl of firm jelly. His oblong face had swelled, Kent thought. The man was eating well on his newfound wealth. Bentley's suit buttons still stretched as he sat. He still wore his collar tight so that it pinched off his head to resemble a tomato. His big cherrywood desk still sat neat and stately. The air still smelled of cigar smoke. Only the look in Bentley's eyes had changed from Kent's last visit. And he wasn't sure if the man's eyes bulged from fear or from offense.

"Price Bentley?"

"Yes." The man extended a hand over the desk. His face split with a manufactured grin. "And you must be Bob. I was told you would be visiting us."

"You were, were you?" Kent shut the door behind him. He removed his sunglasses with a casual flip and ignored Bentley's extended hand. "Get on the horn and call Borst," he said. "I need him here too."

That controlled grin flattened to concern. "Borst? What does he have to do with this?"

"What does he have to do with *what*, Bentley?" Kent stared into the man's eyes, and a small tremor of revulsion swept through his bones. "You don't even know why I'm here, correct? Or am I wrong?"

He did not respond.

"Pick your jaw off the table and call him," Kent said. "And tell him to hustle. I don't have all day."

Bentley called Borst and set the phone down. It missed its cradle and clattered to the president's lap. He snatched it up and clanked it in its proper place. "He's on his way."

Kent watched the pathetic man, expressionless.

"Is there anything I can get for you?"

"Do I look like I need something?" Kent placed his hands behind his back and walked past Bentley toward the far window. "What did they tell you?"

The president cleared his throat. "They said you were investigating something for them."

"Investigating, huh? And did they tell you *what* I was investigating?"

The door burst open, and Borst barged in, his face flushed. "Oh. Excuse me. I got here as soon as I could."

"Sit down, Markus." Bentley said, rising. "This is Bob . . . Bob . . . uh . . . I'm sorry, I don't know your last name."

Kent faced them. "Just Bob to you. Morning, Mr. Borst. Good of you to join us." He looked at Bentley and nodded toward the guest chair beside Borst. "You might as well have a seat over by Borst, if you don't mind."

The president lifted an eyebrow. "In the guest chair? Why?"

"Because I told you to sit there. I want you to sit down beside Borst. Is that so difficult to understand?"

Borst turned white. Bentley's face flashed red. "Look, I think you—"

"Frankly I'm not really interested in what you think. I have no intention of standing here in some jaw-flapping contest with you. Now, when I say sit, you will sit. And if I tell you to open up your shirt and expose your hairy belly, you will do just that. Is this a problem? If so, you say so now, and I'll pick up that phone. But if you're interested in keeping the grossly inflated salary you've somehow managed to wrestle out of our Japanese friends, you should do precisely what I say. Are we clear?"

Bentley's tomato head seemed to swell. Kent looked at Borst and winked. "Right, Borst?"

His old boss did not respond. He might have swallowed his tongue, Kent thought.

"Now, if you don't mind, please sit over by your partner in crime there."

Bentley hesitated a moment and then stormed around the desk to sit heavily beside Borst. The large man's expression teetered between rage and fear.

Kent continued. "Now, before I go any further I want both of you to understand a few things. First, I want you to understand that I'm just doing a job here. You two could be the king and his court jester, for all I care. It makes little difference. My job is to uncover the truth. That's it."

Kent paced across the room, keeping them in his sight as he turned.

"Second, you may not approve of my approach, but obviously the people who hired your miserable necks do, or I wouldn't be here. So keep your lips closed unless I ask you to open them. *Capisce?*"

They stared at him, obviously steaming at his audacity. "You see, now, that was a question. It is appropriate to open your lips in a response when I ask a question. Let's try it again, shall we? I say *Capisce,* which is Italian for *understand,* and you say . . ."

The fear had left Bentley's eyes, for the most part. Now it was just a snarl twisting those fat lips. Borst responded first. "Yes."

Bentley dipped his head but did not speak. It would have to do for the moment.

"Good. Now, I know that you're both big shots in this bank. You're used to having a dozen or so employees follow you around eager to shine your shoes if you are so inclined. Am I right? You don't have to answer that one. Either way, I am not one of those people. Do we have this straight, or should I start over?"

Borst nodded. Bentley's lips twitched.

"Good enough. I'm here because someone obviously suspects that you two have been involved in some hanky-panky. Have you?"

The sudden question caught them off guard. Again Borst answered first. "No! Of course not."

"Shut up, Borst!" Bentley had caught his breath. "I don't think we have to answer your questions without our attorneys present, Mister."

"Is that so?" Kent arched an eyebrow. "Has anyone ever told you that your head is rather large, Bentley? Hmm? I mean, not just figuratively, but physically. I look at you, and I think . . ." He lifted a finger to his chin and looked off to the ceiling. ". . . tomato. Yes, tomato. That's what I've been standing here thinking. My, this fellow has a head that really, really looks like a tomato. Well, you listen up, Tomato-Head. There's a little document that you signed when you agreed to your bloated salary. It's called an employment agreement. I think you will find a clause in your agreement that pretty much gives me, the bank that is, full rights to investigate any matter suspect of hanky-panky. I think the word in the agreement is actually *fraud*. Same difference. Now, if you feel at a later date that we have treated you unfairly, you are free to sue to your heart's content. But until then let's keep things in perspective, shall we? Now, please answer my question. Have or have you not, Mr. Price Bentley, been involved in hanky-panky here at the bank?"

"No." He had collected himself during that long diatribe, which was fine by Kent. A bit of a fight would not be so bad.

"No. Very good. Then I'm sure you have some exceptional explanations for my concerns. Let's start with you, Borst. By the way, please remove your toupee. I find it rather distracting."

Borst's face flushed pink, and he looked up with a sheepish smile.

Kent nodded and waved a hand toward the black toupee. "Go ahead. Rip it off, my friend."

His old boss realized then that he was serious, and his jaw fell open. "You . . . you . . . that's absurd!" he sputtered.

"Either way, please remove it. It's keeping me from concentrating on my job here."

Borst spun toward Bentley, who ignored him.

Kent pushed the point. "Hurry, man. We don't have all day. Just pull it off."

Borst reached up and pulled the hairpiece from his bald head. His face now beamed the shade of red found in a grocer's meat department.

"Good. So then, my friend, were you aware that some money is missing from the bank? Stolen electronically?"

Borst's breathing came raggedly now. "No."

"No? That's funny, because it did indeed find its way into your personal account. Odd. And you, of all people, should know that money does not just float around the system of its own accord. In fact, isn't it your job to see that it does not?"

The man did not respond.

"Now would be a good time to move your lips, Borst."

"No. I mean, yes. Sort of . . ."

"Well, which is it? Aren't you in charge of this new funds processing system everyone is raving about? AFPS?"

"Yes."

"And you designed it, did you not?"

"No. No, *that* is not true!"

Bentley spoke again, furious now. "Will you keep your trap shut, Borst!"

Kent smiled. "Fighting among friends. How tragic. Which is it, Bentley? Yes, he did design AFPS, or no, he did not?"

"I barely even knew the program!" Borst blurted. "I oversee programmers, see, so I might not be as proficient about moving money around as you think. I swear I had no idea how that money got into our accounts!"

"Shut up, Borst!" Spittle flew from Bentley's lips as he spoke. "Listen to what you're saying, Meathead!"

Kent ignored the president. "But you *did* know about the money. And you knew about the money in Tomato-Head's account as well, which means he also knew about it. But we'll come back to that. I want to pursue this line of crock you're feeding me on AFPS." He wagged a finger at them. "Didn't you two take credit for its development? Didn't you sign an affidavit claiming primary responsibility for the conception and implementation of the system? I mean, the last I checked, a lot of money was headed your way as a result of the bank's bonus program. Are you telling me there was some hanky-panky in that as well? Why don't you answer that, Bentley?"

The president looked as though he had indeed tied a noose about his neck and cinched it tight. "Of course I signed an affidavit stating I was primarily responsible for the system's development. And I was. Borst was as well. You just have him tied in knots with this dog and pony show of yours. So what do you say we get down to your real concerns, Bob? What exactly are you suggesting we did or did not do?"

"Oh, my goodness. He shows some intelligence at last. Did you hear him, Borst? Didn't that come off quite nicely? I'll tell you what I'm suggesting. I'm suggesting that you and Borst here are hiding some things. For starters, money transfers were illegally issued, neatly depositing several thousand dollars in each of your accounts, and I don't buy Borst's assertion that he had no idea where that money came from. Nobody could be such an idiot. So I guess I'm suggesting, Mr. Price Bentley, that you just got caught with your hand in the cookie jar. For starters, that is."

"And I'll tell *you* that that is the most ridiculous suggestion I've ever heard. You come walking in here, spouting these absurd accusations of fraud. How dare you!"

Kent stared Bentley down for a full ten seconds. He turned to his old boss. "Borst, will you please tell Mr. Bentley here that he's starting to get under my skin. Will you tell him that I already have enough hard evidence to have him put in the slammer for a few years, and if he doesn't back off, I might do just that. And tell him to cool down. He really is looking more and more like a tomato, and I'm afraid I might just walk over there and bite into him by mistake. Go on, tell him."

Borst blinked. He was obviously completely out of his league here. "Come on, Price. Settle down, man."

Bentley snorted, but he did not attack.

"Good." Kent turned back to the president. "Now, I'll tell you what, Bentley. I really did not come all the way from the Far East to slap your wrists over a couple thousand dollars. If that were the case it would be local security in here, not me. No sir. I'm after much bigger fish. But now you've hurt my feelings with this big talk of yours, and I'm not sure I want to bring you in on my little secret anymore. I'm tempted to just walk out of here and file a report that will nail your hide to the wall. And I could do it too."

He drilled Borst with a stare and returned to Bentley. "But I'll tell you what I'm willing to do. I'm willing to let the small deposits slip and tell you what I really need from you if you'll just apologize for your nasty attitude. How's that? You put your hands together as if you're praying and tell me you're sorry, and I'll forgive this whole mess. Both of you."

They looked at him with wide eyes and gaping mouths. Borst put his hands together and looked at Bentley. The president appeared to have frozen solid.

"Come on, Price," Borst whispered.

The humiliation of the moment was really too much for Kent himself. Two grown men, begging apologies without just cause. At least none they knew of. They had nothing to do with those small deposits, and all three of the men in the room knew that. Still, Bentley was no idiot. He could not know *what* "Bob" knew.

It took a good thirty seconds of silence before Bentley slowly clasped his hands as if in prayer and dipped his head. "I'm sorry. I spoke in haste."

"Yes. I'm sorry too," Borst echoed.

Kent smiled. "Well, that's much better. I feel so much better. Don't you?"

They were undoubtedly too stuffed with humiliation to respond.

"Good, then. And please keep this attitude of contrition about you as long as I am present. Now, let me tell you why I'm really here. Last week, someone stole one million dollars from the bank through a series of ghost transactions. Transactions similar in nature to the deposits made to your accounts. And quite frankly, I'm really quite convinced that you two did it. I think you two have a bunch of money stashed somewhere and that you've used some variation of AFPS to do it."

Their faces went white together, slowly, as the blood slowly vacated. Their mouths gaped.

Kent spoke before they could. "Now, I know what you're thinking. You're thinking that I just told you differently not two minutes ago. You're thinking that I just promised to let things slide if you made that silly apology. And you're absolutely right. But I was lying. You two are quite the liars yourselves, aren't you? You really should have seen it coming."

They sat woodenly, thoroughly seized by shock. Kent firmed his jaw and glared at them. "Somewhere in the deepest folds of cyberspace there's a lot of money hiding, and I guarantee it; I'm gonna find that money. And when I do, I'm going to find your grimy fingerprints all over it. You can bet your next twenty years on that. I figure it'll take me about two weeks. In the meantime, I'll get you a number in case your memory improves and you suddenly want to talk sense."

He walked past them to the door and turned back. Borst was moving his lips in horrified silent protest. Bentley's head had swelled like a tomato again.

Kent dipped his head. "Until then, my fat friends. And I don't mind telling you, that apology really was a special moment for me. I will remember it always."

With that Kent shut the door behind him and left, hardly able to contain himself. He slipped on the dark glasses while still in the lobby, nodding to Sidney Beech as he passed. Then he was through the revolving glass doors and facing Broadway.

Man, that had felt good. Time for a drink.

36

The hole in Kent's chest had returned shortly after noon on Monday, just three hours after his little victory over the porky twins. He was not done with them, of course, but it would be two weeks before he walked back into their lives. Two weeks with nothing to do but wait. Two weeks of empty space.

He could return to the island and live it up with Doug and friends. But the idea felt like death warmed over. Why retreat to solitude? Why not try to shake this emptiness by filling his life with a few things here? Maybe he ought to take a drive up to Boulder.

What was he thinking?

Kent decided to catch a flight to New York. He made the decision impulsively, with a slug of tequila burning his throat. Why not? Money was no object. He could hop the *Concorde* to London if he so desired. And sitting around Denver beating back memories of his past would drive him to the grave.

He checked out of the Hyatt, paid cash for a thousand-dollar ticket to New York, and was airborne by four that afternoon.

The Big Apple was just another clogged city, but it did offer its advantages. Bars, for instance. There were pubs and lounges on virtually every corner around Kent's Manhattan hotel. Kent settled for the one in the hotel— O'Malley's Pub—and retired in a daze at 1 A.M. Tuesday morning.

He woke just before noon, lost in a dark room, wondering where he was. New York. He had flown to New York. Only God knew why. To escape Denver or some such nonsense. He rolled over and shut his eyes. He imagined there would be a dozen messages on the phone number he'd called over to Bentley's assistant before leaving Denver. The president and his cohort were probably coming apart at the seams trying to get hold of him. Yes, well he would let them sweat. Let them die a few deaths, see how it felt.

Kent forced himself out of bed at one, determined to find a distraction beyond the bottle. Goodness, he was chugging alcohol as if it were a runner's water. He had to get hold of himself here.

The bellboy told him that the opera was always a stretching experience.

He attended the opera that night. The sound of the lead vocalist's crooning nearly had him in tears. For some ungodly reason the woman became Lacy in his mind's eye, mourning the loss of her lover. That would be him. He could not follow the plot, but that the play was a story of death and sorrow could hardly be missed.

Kent woke Wednesday to a refreshing thought. Refreshing, not in the sense that he particularly enjoyed it, but refreshing in that it pulled him out of the doldrums—like a bucket of ice water tossed into a hot shower. It was a simple thought.

What if they're on to you, my friend?

He bolted up in bed and grabbed the bedspread. What if, back there in Denver, someone had put a few things together? Like that cop who'd interrupted his reading time at the bookstore. What had become of him? Or Bentley himself, sitting there wheezing like a camel, what if he'd seen something in his eyes? Even Borst, for that matter. No, not Borst. The man was too stupid.

He rolled out of bed, his stomach churning. Or what of Lacy? He had actually told her, for heaven's sake! Most of it anyway. Coming here to the United States had been idiotic. And going back to the bank, now, there was a move straight off of Stupid Street. What had he been thinking! Had to get the nasty boys, yes sir. Extract a slice of revenge.

Kent dressed with a tremor in his bones and headed for the bar. Problem was, the bar hadn't opened yet. It was only 9 A.M. Back to the hotel room to down a few of those small bottles in the cabinet. He spent the day watching golf in his hotel room, sick with anxiety and bored to death for the duration.

He managed to slap some sense into himself the next day by reviewing each and every step of his plan. The simple fact of the matter was that it had been rather brilliant. They had buried Mr. Brinkley's charred body, convinced it belonged to Kent Anthony. Unless they exhumed that body, Kent was a dead man. Dead men do not commit crimes. More important, there had been no crime. Ha! He had to remember that. No theft and no thief. No case. And he was the rich fool who had masterminded it all. A very wealthy man, dripping in the stuff.

It was that day, Thursday, in the bustling city of New York, that Kent began to understand the simple facts of a wealthy life. It all started after a two-hundred-dollar lunch down the street from the hotel, at Bon Appétit French Cuisine. The food was good; he could hardly deny that. For the price, it had better be good. But it occurred to him while stuffing some cupcake-looking pastry into his mouth, with his stomach already stretched far beyond its natural limits, that these French morsels, like most morsels, would come out in much worse shape than they went in. And in all honesty, they did not bring him much more pleasure than, say, a Twinkie at twenty cents a pop. It was a little fact, but it left the restaurant with Kent.

Another little fact: No matter how much money he carried in his wallet, individual moments did not change. Hopes and dreams might, but the string of moments that made up life did not. If he was walking down the hall, placing one foot in front of the other, he was doing just that, regardless of what his wallet packed. If he was pushing the call button for the elevator, it was just that, no more and no less, regardless of the number of bills in his back pocket.

But it was that night, approaching the midnight hour while drinking in O'Malley's Pub, that the full weight of the matter presented itself to him in one lump sum. It was as though the heavens opened and dropped this nugget on him like an ingot of lead. Only it didn't come from the skies. It came from the mouth of a fellow drinker, ready to impart his wisdom.

Kent sat next to the man who called himself Bono—after the U2 singer, he said—an ex-Orthodox priest, of all things. Said he left the Greek church because it left him dry. The man looked to be in his forties, with thick eyebrows and graying hair, but it was his bright green eyes that had Kent wondering. Since when did Greeks have green eyes? Together they knocked back the shotglasses. Actually, Kent was putting them away. Bono contented himself with sipping at a glass of wine.

"You know, the problem with those Wall Street yuppies," Bono offered after a half-dozen shots, "is that they all think there's more to life than what the average man has."

"And they'd be right," Kent returned after a pause. "Average is lazy, and lazy is not much."

"Whoa, so you are a philosopher, are you? Well, let me ask you something, Mr. Philosopher. What's better about busy than lazy?"

It was a simple question. Even awkwardly simple, because everyone knew that busy was better than lazy. But at the moment, Kent was having difficulty remembering why. It was possibly the booze, but it was just as possibly that he had never really known why busy was better than lazy.

He did what all good fools do when presented with a question they cannot answer directly. He raised his voice a tad and threw the question back. "Come on! Everybody knows that being lazy is stupid."

"That's what you said. And I asked you, why?"

Bono was no fool. He'd been here before. "Why? Because you cannot excel if you're lazy. You will go nowhere."

"Excel at what? Go where?"

"Well, now. How about life? Let's start with that. I know it's not much, but let's start with excelling at that little event."

"And tell me what that feels like. What does *excelling at life* feel like?"

"Happiness." Kent raised his shotglass and threw it back. "Pleasure. Peace. All that."

"Ahh. Yes, of course. I had forgotten about happiness, pleasure, and peace and all that. But you see, the average man has as much as the Wall Street yuppie. And in the end, they both go into the same grave. That *is* where they go, isn't it?" The man chuckled.

It was then, at the word *grave,* that the buzzing had first started again in Kent's skull. "Well, most have a good eighty years before the grave," he said quietly. "You only live once; you might as well have the best while you do it."

"But you see, that's where you and the yuppies on Wall Street are mistaken," Bono insisted. "It makes a fine fantasy, no argument there. But when you've had it all—and believe me, I have—wine still tastes like wine. You might drink it out of a gold chalice, but even then you realize one day that you could close your eyes and honestly not know whether the cold metallic object in your hand is made from gold or tin. And who decided that gold is better than tin anyway? In the end we all go to the grave. Perhaps it is beyond the grave where life begins. You know anyone who's gone to the grave lately?"

Kent swallowed and flung back another shot. Lately? His vision doubled momentarily. He leveled a rather weak objection. "You're too pessimistic. People are full of life. Like that man laughing over there." He motioned to a man in a far booth, roaring with his head tilted back. "You think he's not happy?" Kent smiled, thankful for the reprieve.

Bono gazed at the man and grinned. "Yes. Today Clark looks quite happy, doesn't he?" He turned back to Kent. "But I know Mr. Clark. He's a pig-head. Recently divorced and rather smug with the notion because he no longer has to deal with his brats. He's got three of them—six, ten, and twelve—and he can hardly stand them. Problem is, he spends most of his waking hours feeling guilty for his remarkably selfish disposition. He's been trying to wash it all away with the bottle for a year now. Trust me. He will leave this place tonight and retreat to a wet pillow, soaked in tears." Bono took a sip from his glass, evidently satisfied for having made his point. "Look under any man's sheets, and you'll find a similar story. I guarantee it, certifiable."

Kent had lost his interest in arguing the point. He was too busy trying to shake loose the fingers of heat climbing into his brain. The man had hit a nerve. Clark there could easily be him, drowning his failure in the bottle, bent upon pleasure and finding none. Except that he did not hate his son, like Pig-Head did. In fact he would have killed for his son—would've gladly given up every red cent for Spencer's life. The thought brought a sliver of light to Kent's mind.

Bono stood. He slid his glass across the counter and exhaled with satisfaction. "Yessiree. I'm telling you, this life is quite pitiful. No man can escape it." He tilted his head and lifted his brows so that his green eyes bulged down at Kent. "Unless, of course, you understand what lies beyond the grave." He smiled wide and slapped Kent on the back. "But then, I'm sure you know all about that, don't you, Kent?" He sauntered from the pub without looking back.

The words echoed in Kent's for an hour, and no amount of tequila quieted them. Kent drank for another hour by himself before wandering back to his hotel suite. Somewhere in that hour he began to miss Gloria. Not just *wish-she-were-sitting-with-me* missing, but *blurry-eyed-I'm-lost-without-her* missing. It was all these thoughts about the grave that the green-eyed Bono had deposited on him; they brought pictures of Gloria calling to him from some great unseen horizon. And what if there was some truth to all her babble of God? That thought shoved a fist-sized lump into his throat.

Well, Gloria was dead. Dead, buried, and beyond the grave, wherever that was. But there was Lacy—she too knew of the grave. And she knew of God. Still, Lacy could never be Gloria. Kent finally drifted off to sleep, his mind all mixed up with pictures of Gloria and Lacy.

37

Rather than take a room in another hotel, Kent found a furnished executive suite upon his return to Denver Friday afternoon. The agent had hesitated when Kent forked over the ten thousand security deposit in cash, but he had taken it, and Kent had moved in, an event that consisted of nothing more than stepping through the door with the keys in one hand and a single garment bag hanging from his shoulder.

The suite reminded him of the kind you see on futuristic shows, stark and shiny, decorated in black and white. The furniture was all metal, glass, or leather—rather cold for his tastes. But at least it was clean. More important, it was fully stocked, from a flat-screen entertainment center to place settings for eight.

Kent mixed himself a stiff drink, pulled an ugly-looking, black, wrought-iron chair out from under the glass table, and flipped open his laptop. The Toshiba had seen its share of activity over the last six weeks. He powered it up and logged on. Communication on the laptop was through a satellite connection—never a land line. He may have executed a few dumb moves here and there, but not when it came to computing. Here, at least, in his thieving and hiding, he had covered his tracks impeccably, thanks in large part to this baby.

The message box he'd left Bentley was indeed overflowing with messages. There were a dozen or so from Bentley, ranging from the earliest nearly a week old, insisting that he meet with them again, to the latest, left on Friday, screaming about lawsuits and counter lawsuits and what else Kent did not know because he spun quickly through the rest of the voice mail. Phase two was unfolding as planned. Let them sweat.

The last message was from an unidentified number, and Kent sat up when the voice spoke low over his speakers. A chill flashed down his spine. He knew the voice!

"Hello, Bob. You don't know me . . ." *Oh yes I do! Yes, I do.* ". . . but I would very much appreciate bending your ear for a few minutes on this case at the bank. Price Bentley told me I could reach you here. I'm a law enforcement officer working a few angles on a related matter. Please call me as soon as possible to set up a meeting. 565-8970. Thanks, pal. Oh, ask for Germy."

A cop! Pinhead? Impossible! Germy? What kind of name was *Germy?* But he could swear he'd heard that voice before. And it was a cop.

Kent placed his hands over his face and tried to think. What if the cop was indeed on to him? But he'd already decided that was impossible. No theft, no thief, no crime, no problem. Only this *was* a problem, because he was sitting alone in his new apartment, sweating like boxer.

He should pretend the message had never come through. And risk raising the cop's curiosity? No. He should call the man and weasel his way out of an appointment.

Kent snatched up the phone and dialed the number. A lady answered. "Seventh precinct, may I help you?"

Seventh precinct! "Yes . . ." His heart was thumping in his ear. "I was told to call a cop at this number. A Germy?"

"Oh, you must mean the new guy: Jeremy. Hold please."

Pinhead!

The receiver barked before Kent could do anything like slam the phone down. "Jeremy here. What can I do for you?"

"Ah . . . Yes. This is . . . Bob. You left a message for me."

"Bob! Yes, of course. Thank you for calling back so quickly. Listen, I just have a few questions about this business at the bank. Do you have any time to grab a cup of coffee? Say tomorrow morning? Ten-ish?"

What could he say? *No, not ten-ish. Ten-ish is when I start on the bottle, see? How about never-ish?*

"Sure," he said.

"Great! It won't take but a few minutes. How about at the Denny's at Broadway and Fifth? You know where that is?"

"Sure."

"Good. I'll see you at ten tomorrow morning."

"Sure."

The phone went dead. Sure? Gulp.

Kent did not sleep well Friday night.

༄

How the time managed to crawl by, Kent did not know, but it did, like a snail inching its way across a nine-foot razor blade. He awoke at five Saturday morning, although opened his eyes might be a better way to characterize the event, because he'd never really fallen asleep. A shower, a cup of coffee, a few shots of tequila for the nerves, and two miles of pacing across the black-and-white-checkered linoleum delivered him reluctantly to the appointed hour. He found himself parked outside of Denny's at ten o'clock without knowing precisely how he'd gotten there.

Kent slipped on his black shades and walked in. It might look ridiculous for a grown man to wear sunglasses indoors, but he'd decided sometime past midnight that ridiculous was better than incarcerated.

Detective Jeremy sat in a nonsmoking booth, staring at Kent as he entered. And it was indeed Pinhead. Complete with slicked black hair and wire-frame glasses. He was grinning wide. *"Hello, Kent. You* are *Kent, aren't you?"*

Kent swallowed and crossed to the booth, mustering every ounce of nonchalance remaining in his quivering bones.

"Bob?" The detective half rose and extended a hand. "Good of you to come."

Kent wiped his palm and took the hand. "Sure." He sat. Pinhead smiled at him without speaking, and Kent just sat, determined to act normal but knowing he was failing miserably. The cop's eyes were as green as he remembered them.

"So, I guess you're wondering why I've asked you to meet me?"

Kent shrugged. "Sure." He needed another word badly.

"Price Bentley tells me that you're investigating a robbery at the bank. You're a private investigator?"

"I suppose you could call me that." *Cybercop,* he almost said, but decided it would sound stupid. "At this point it's strictly an internal matter."

"Well, now, that depends, Bob. Depends on whether it's connected."

"Connected to what?"

"To my investigation."

"And what might that be, Jeremy?" That was better. Two could be condescending.

"That would be the bank fire a month or so ago."

Every muscle in Kent's body went rigid. He immediately coughed to cover. "The bank fire. Yes, I heard about that. To be honest, arson was never my thing."

"Mine neither. Actually I'm following up the murder. Do you always wear sunglasses indoors, Bob?"

Kent hesitated. "I have a light sensitivity in my left eye. It acts up on occasion."

Jeremy nodded, still grinning like a chimpanzee. "Of course. Did you know the victim?"

"What victim?" *That's it—remain cool, Buckwheat. Just play it cool.*

"The gentleman murdered in the bank robbery? You know, the fire."

"Bank robbery? I didn't know there was a robbery."

"So they say. *Attempted* robbery, then. Did you know him?"

"Should I have?"

"Just curious, Bob. No need to be defensive here. It was a simple-enough question, don't you think?"

"What exactly do you need from me, Jeremy? I agreed to meet with you because you seemed rather eager to do so. But I really don't have all morning to discuss your case with you. I have my own."

"Relax, Bob. Would you like some coffee?"

"I don't drink coffee."

"Shame. I love coffee in the morning." He poured himself a steaming cup. "For some it's the bottle; for me it's coffee." He sipped the hot, black liquid. "Ahh. Perfect."

"That's wonderful. My heart is glad for you, Jeremy. But you're starting to annoy me just a tad here. Can we get on with it?"

The detective just smiled, hardly missing a beat. "It's the possible connection that has me worried. You see, whenever you have two robberies or *attempted* robberies in one bank during the span of six weeks, you have to ask yourself about the connections."

"I hardly see the similarity between a common thief who happened upon an open door and the high-tech theft I'm investigating."

"No. It does seem rather unlikely. But I always turn over every stone. Think of yourself as one of those stones. You're just being turned over."

"Well, thank you, Jeremy. It's good to know that you're doing your job with such diligence."

The detective held up his cup as if to toast the notion. "My pleasure. So, did you know him?"

"Know him?"

"The victim, Bob. The programmer who was killed by the common thief."

"Should I have?"

"You already asked that. Yes or no would be fine."

"No, of course not. Why should I know a programmer who works in the Denver branch of Niponbank?"

"He was responsible for AFPS. Were you aware of that?"

Kent blinked behind the shades. *Watch it, Buckwheat. Tread easy.* "It was him, huh? I figured it couldn't have been Bentley or Borst. So they cheated someone for that bonus after all."

"All I know is that it was Kent Anthony who developed the system, pretty much from the ground up. And then he turns up dead. Meanwhile Bentley and company end up pulling down some pretty healthy change. Seems odd."

"You're suggesting Bentley might have had a finger in the programmer's death?" Kent asked.

"No. Not necessarily. He had nothing to gain by killing Kent. I just throw it out there 'cause it's another stone that needs turning."

"Well, I'll be sure to turn over my findings if they seem to shed any light on the fire. But unless Bentley and company are somehow implicated in the fire, I don't see how the two cases tie in."

"Yes, you're probably right." The detective downed his coffee dregs and looked out the window. "Which leaves us pretty much where we started."

Kent watched him for a moment. By the sounds of it, Pinhead was not turning out to be such a threat after all. Which made sense when you thought about it. The theft had been perfectly planned. There was no way that anyone, including Detective Pinhead here, could even suspect the truth of the matter. A small chill of victory ran up Kent's spine.

He smiled for the first time, confident now. "And where would that be? Tell me, where did we start? I'm a bit lost."

"With a crime that simply does not fit the players involved. If Bentley and Borst don't fit, then nothing fits. Because, you see, if you knew the man, you would know that Kent Anthony was not the kind of man who would leave a door unlocked for a pistol-toting thief. He was not nearly so stupid. At least not according to his friends."

"Friends?" The question slipped out before Kent could hold it back.

"Friends. I talked to his girlfriend up in Boulder. She had some interesting things to say about the man."

The heat was suddenly flashing though Kent's skull. "Anybody can make a simple mistake," he said, knowing it sounded weak. He certainly could not defend a man he supposedly did not know. "In my experience the simplest explanation is usually the correct one. You have a body; you have slugs. He may have been an Einstein, but he's still dead."

Pinhead chuckled. "You're right. Dead is dead." He mulled that over. "Unless Kent is not dead. Now, maybe that would make more sense." The man drilled Kent with those green eyes. "You know, not everything is what it seems, Bob. In fact I am not what I seem. I'm not just some dumb, lucky cop."

Kent's face flushed red; he felt panic-stricken. His chest seemed to clog. And all the while Pinhead was looking directly at him. He was suddenly having a hard time forming thoughts, much less piecing together a response. The cop removed his gaze.

"My case and your case could be connected, Bob. Maybe we're looking for the wrong guy. Maybe your high-tech phantom and my dead guy are really the same person! A bit far-fetched but possible, don't you think?"

"No. That's not possible!"

"No? And why is that not possible?"

"Because I already know who did it!"

The cop arched a brow. "Who?"

"Bentley and Borst. I'm putting the finishing touches on the evidence, but within a week I can assure you, fraud charges will be filed."

"So quickly? Excellent work, Bob! But I really think you ought to rethink the matter. With my theory in mind, of course. It would be something, wouldn't it? Kent alive and kicking with a dead man in his grave?" He dismissed the theory with his hand. "Ah, but you're probably right. The two cases are probably not connected. Just turning over every stone, you know."

At the moment Kent felt like taking one of Jeremy's stones and shoving it down the detective's throat. *Try that for a theory, Pinhead!* But he could hardly breathe, much less reach over there and wrestle the man's mouth open.

"Well, I surely do appreciate your time, Bob. Maybe we will meet again. Soon." The detective smiled.

With that he stood and left, leaving Kent soaking under the arms and frozen to his seat.

This was a problem. Not just a little challenge or a bump in the road, but the-end-of-the-world-as-we-know-it kind of problem. Coming here had been a mistake. Coming back to this *country* had been a mistake. Going to the bank—that had been idiotic!

Still, there was no evidence, was there? No, no evidence. It was Pinhead's theory. A stupid theory at that.

Then a simple little picture popped into his mind and crushed what little hope he had left. It was a picture of Lacy, sitting on her couch, hands folded, knees together, facing Pinhead. She was talking. She was telling her little secret.

Kent dropped his head into his hands and tried to still his breathing.

38

Kent stood by the pillar just outside Macy's in a Boulder mall on Monday evening and stared at the woman, his heart beating like a kettle drum, his palms wet with balls of sweat.

Sometime on Saturday, he'd come to a new realization about life. It was a notion so profound that most people never understood it properly. It was the kind of truth one encounters only in moments when he is stretched beyond all limits, as Kent had been after that little encounter with Pinhead. And it was simply this: When you really got right down to it, life sucked.

The problem with most people was that they never really got right down to it. They lived their lives *thinking* of getting right down to it, but did they ever actually get right down to it? No. *"Next year, Martha, I promise, next year we're gonna sell this rattrap, buy that yacht, and sail around the world. Yes sir."* People's dreams acted as a sort of barrier between life and death. Take them away—let people actually live those dreams—and you would be mopping up the suicides by the dumpster full. Just look at those few who did live their dreams, like movie stars or rock stars—the ones who really have the money to get right down to it—and you'll find a trail of brokenhearted people. Brokenhearted because they'd discovered what Kent was discovering: When you really got right down to it, life sucked.

That fact had delivered Kent to this impossible place, standing by the pillar just outside Macy's Monday evening and staring at a woman, his heart beating like a kettle drum, his palms wet with balls of sweat.

Lacy sighed, obviously unsatisfied with the discount rack's selection. She walked toward him. Kent caught his breath and turned slowly away, straining for nonchalance. In the hour that he had been tailing her, she had not recognized him, but then she had not studied him either. Twice she'd caught his eye and twice he had brushed on as though uncaring. But each time his heart had bolted to his throat, and now it was doing the same.

He bent for a *Shopper's Guide* on a bench and feigned interest in its cover. She walked by him, not three feet away. The sweet scent of lilac drifted by his nostrils, and he closed his eyes. It was all insanity, of course, this stalking. Not just because someone might notice the sweating man staring at the beautiful single woman and call security, but because he was indeed *stalking*. Like some kind of crazed loony, breathing heavily over a woman's shoulder, waiting for his chance.

He had driven to Boulder that afternoon, parked his car a hundred yards from Lacy's apartment, and waited. She had returned from work at six, and he had spent a good hour chewing at his nails, contemplating walking up to her door. Thing of it was, Gloria kept traipsing through his mind. For some reason not quite clear to him, he was feeling a strange guilt about Gloria. More so now, it seemed, than when he had spent time with Lacy before the robbery. Perhaps because then he had had no real intentions of pursuing Lacy. Now, though, faced with this crazy loneliness, he was not so sure.

She'd left the condo and driven here. His greatest regret in stalking her was the decision to leave the bottle of tequila in the car. He could have excused himself to the bathroom a dozen times for nips. But returning to retrieve the bottle from the car would take far too long; she might disappear on him, a thought suddenly more unnerving than staying dry for a few hours.

He twisted his head and watched her from the corner of his eye. Lacy wore blue jeans. She seemed to float along the shiny marble floor, her white running shoes gliding along the surface, her thighs firm beside her swinging brown purse. The lime-green sweater was perhaps a cardigan, resting loosely over her shoulders, its collar obscured by her blonde hair. Her lips seemed to pout, smiling on occasion; her hazel eyes darted over the selections; her fingers walked through the clothing carefully.

Kent watched her walk toward the food court. He wiped his forehead with the back of his hand and stepped cautiously after her. She wandered past shiny windows, casually glancing at their displays without bothering to enter. Kent stepped into a sports store, grabbed a beige flannel shirt from the sale rack, and hurriedly purchased it. He went straight to the shop's dressing room and changed into the new shirt before hurrying past a confused salesclerk to catch Lacy. The red shirt he'd worn went in the nearest trash bin. *You see, Lacy, I've learned a few tricks. Yes, sir, I'm a regular sneaky guy. You gotta be sneaky to steal twenty million, you know.*

He found her in the food court. She sat cross-legged, slowly eating an ice cream cone. He watched it all while peeking around a mannequin in Gart Brothers Sporting Goods across the lobby. There was nothing sexual in his desire—nothing perverse or strange or obsessive. Maybe obsessive. Yes, actually it was obsessive, wasn't it? He blinked at the thought and removed his eyes from her. How else could you characterize stalking a woman? This was no date. *Goodness, you're losing it, Kent.*

A wave of heat washed down Kent's back, and he left the mall then, feeling small and puny and dirty for having driven there. For having peeked at her from the shadows. What was he thinking? He could never tell her the truth, could he? She would be compelled to turn him in. It would be over—all of it.

And Gloria! What would Gloria say to this?

She's dead, *bozo!*

He drove back to Denver, wondering why he should not take his own life. Twice he crossed overpasses wondering what a plunge through the rail might feel like. Like an amusement ride, falling weightlessly for a moment, and then a wrenching crash. The grave. The end. Like Bono had said, in the end it's all for the grave anyway.

Kent shook his head and squeezed his eyes against the mist blurring his vision. He grunted to clear his throat of its knot. On the other hand, he wasn't in the grave yet. He had money, more than he could possibly spend; he had freedom from any encumbrances whatsoever. No wife, no children, no debt, no nothing. That was worth a smile at least, wasn't it? Kent smiled, but the image staring back at him from the rearview mirror looked more like a jack-o'-lantern than the face of a contented man. He lost the charade and slouched in his seat.

The evening took a turn for the better near midnight, two pints of tequila later. He lounged with glass in hand on the black-leather recliner facing a black television screen in the sleek apartment. The memory of his little stalking trip to Boulder sat like an absurd little joke on his brain.

Because of some obsession. Some pearls of wisdom from a Greek named Bono. Yes indeed, life sucked.

Well, it would be the last time he stalked anyone, he thought wryly. He would drive off one of those overpasses at a hundred miles per hour in the Lincoln before doing anything so foolish again. He had the world at his fingertips, for Pete's sake! Only an absolute loser would slink back for another peek. *"Peekaboo, I see you. My name's Kent, and I'm filthy rich. Would you like to share my life? Oh, yes, one small nugget for the hopper—my life really sucks, but not to worry, we will soon be in the grave anyway."*

Kent passed out on the leather recliner sometime before the sun rose.

39

Lacy sat alone in Wong Foo's Chinese Cuisine Thursday evening, nibbling at the noodles on her plate. Indirect lighting cast a dim orange glow across her table. A dozen heavy wooden carvings of dragons stared down from the low-hung ceilings. Cellulose walls lent an aura of privacy to the room. Glasses clinked with iced drinks, and voices murmured softly all about her, behind those paper partitions; somewhere a man spoke rapidly in Chinese. The smell of oriental spices circulated slowly.

A man sat alone in a booth ten meters to her right, reading the paper and sipping at noodle soup. They had noticed each other shortly after he had been seated not ten minutes earlier, and his bright blue eyes reminded her of Kent at first sight. He'd smiled politely, and she'd diverted her gaze. Freaks were everywhere these days. *You don't know that, Lacy. He may be a regular Clark Kent.* Actually, all men were pretty much looking like freaks these days.

Lacy dipped her spoon into the hot-and-sour soup and sipped at the liquid. She was having some difficulty shaking Kent's image. *Why* she could not shake his image, she could not fully understand. The first week was understandable, of course. The second, maybe even the third as well. But he had been gone for over a month now, for heaven's sake. And still he left tracks all through her thoughts every day. It was nonsense. Perhaps it was the thought of him living like a king after having the audacity to rub his plans in her face.

She peered at the man reading the newspaper and found him looking at her again. Goodness. She shot him a contemptuous grin this time. *Not too bold there, Lacy. He might get the wrong idea.* Looked like a decent-enough fellow. Blue eyes like Kent's—*See, now, there I go again*—and a face that reminded her of Kevin Costner. Not bad looking actually.

He had his head buried in that paper again, and Lacy steered her mind back to the plate in front of her. She had not heard from the detective again, and neither had she made any attempt to call him, because as the days passed, the notion began to sound somewhat misguided. She certainly had found no absolute collaborating evidence suggesting Kent's theft. And even if she had, she'd made a promise to him. Not that she *should* be bound by any promise after what he had done. There had been four incidents of mismatched bank statements, but no one seemed to give them any mind. Printer error or something. Whatever it was, it had corrected itself.

Yes indeed. The only thing that had not self-corrected was her mind. And she was beginning to think it might need some professional examination. Lacy lifted her fork and savored a bite of gingered chicken. The dragons glared down at her with glassy yellow eyes, as if they knew something she did not.

They were not the only things staring at her, she thought. The pervert was staring at her again. From the corner of her eyes she could see his face turned her way. Her pulsed spiked. Unless he wasn't really staring at her at all and it was just her imagination.

She turned slowly to him. No, it was not her imagination. He yanked his eyes away as her own zeroed in on him. What kind of guy was this? She should possibly leave before he began wagging his tongue at her.

Then his blue eyes rose to meets hers again, and they held for a long second. Lacy's heart paused for that second. And before it restarted, the man rose from his seat and walked toward her.

He's leaving, she thought. *Please tell me he's leaving!*

But he didn't leave. He walked right up to her table and placed a hand on the back of the chair opposite hers.

"I'm sorry, ma'am. I couldn't help but notice you sitting all alone." He smiled kindly, quite handsomely actually. But then Ted Bundy had been quite handsome. His voice came like honey to her mind, which surprised her. A thin sheen of sweat beaded his forehead. She imagined him breathing heavily in the corner. Lacy stared at the stranger without speaking, *unable* to speak really, considering the contradictions this man represented.

He attempted a smile, which awkwardly lifted one side of his face. "I know this may sound unusual, but do you mind if I have a seat?" he asked.

A hundred voices screamed in unison in her head: *Don't be a fool! Go wag your tongue at some streetgirl! Beat it!*

The stranger did not give her a chance to speak her thoughts. He sat quickly and folded trembling hands. She instinctively pulled back, stunned by his boldness. The man did not speak. He breathed deliberately, watching her in awe, with a slight smile curving his lips.

Goodness! What was she thinking, allowing this man to sit here? His eyes were striking enough, like blue sapphires, wide and adoring. *God, help me!*

"Can I help you?" she asked.

He blinked and sat a little straighter. "I'm sorry. This must seem awfully strange to you. But . . . does anything . . ." He fidgeted uncomfortably. "I don't know . . . strike you as odd?"

Lacy was finding her senses, and her senses were telling her that this man rang bells that echoed right through her skull, as if it were churchtime at the cathedral. They were also telling her that this man had a few loose bells himself.

"Actually, *you* strike me as odd. Maybe you should leave?"

That took the curl out of his gimpish smile. "Yeah? Well, maybe I'm not as odd as you think. Maybe I'm just trying to be friendly, and you're calling me odd. Is that what you think of friendly people? That they're odd?"

Tit for tat. He didn't seem so harmful. "People don't normally wander around Chinese restaurants looking for friendly conversation. Forgive me if I sound a bit concerned."

"People aren't usually friendly, is what you're saying. Well, maybe I'm just trying to be friendly. You consider that?"

"And maybe I don't need any new friends."

He swallowed and studied her for a moment. "And maybe you should think twice before rejecting a friendly neighbor."

"So now you're my neighbor? Look, I'm sure you're a wonderful man . . ."

"I'm just trying to be friendly, ma'am. You should never bite the hand that feeds you."

"I wasn't aware that you had fed me."

He reached over, picked up her bill, and slid it into his pocket. "You are aware now."

Lacy leaned back, struck by the absurdity of the exchange. "I don't even know you! I don't even know your *name*."

"Call me . . . Kevin." The stranger smiled. "And honest, I'm just an ordinary guy who looked across the room and saw a woman who looked like she could use some friendship. What's your name?"

She eyed him carefully. "Lacy." The bells were still gonging in her mind, but she could not place their significance. "And you can't tell me that walking up to a woman in a Chinese restaurant and asking to sit isn't rather strange."

"Maybe. But then, they say all is fair in love and war."

"So then that makes this a war? I'm not looking for a fight, really. I've had my share," she said.

"You have? Not with men, I hope."

"You're right. Men don't fight; they just leave." The crazy discourse was suddenly feeling a bit therapeutic. "You the love-'em-and-leave-'em type, Kevin?"

The man swallowed and grew very still. A pause seemed to settle over the restaurant. "No, of course not."

"Good, Kevin. Because if you were the love-'em-and-leave-'em type, I would throw you out the door myself."

"Yes, I'll bet you would." He shifted in his seat. "So we're sworn off men, then, are we?"

"Pretty close."

He eyed her carefully. "So . . . what happened?"

She did not respond.

⌇⌇⌇

Of course Kent knew precisely what had happened. She was speaking about him. He had courted her, earned her trust, and then dropped her on her seat. And now this.

On Monday he had sworn to kill himself rather than stalk her again. On Wednesday he had broken that promise. He had allowed himself to live despite slinking back to Boulder to sneak a peek. She had gone grocery shopping that night, and he had slipped between the aisles on the edge of panic for the duration.

But this . . . He would pay for this madness. But it no longer mattered. He no longer cared. Life had somehow lost its meaning. He had followed her to the restaurant; taken a seat in plain view, and then approached her table. It had felt like stepping out on a tightrope without a net.

And now he'd had the audacity to ask her what happened. His palms were sweating, and he wiped them on his knees. The electricity between them had his heart skipping beats.

She was not responding, and he repeated the question. "So what happened?"

"No offense, *Kevin,* but if you want to befriend a lady at a restaurant, it's not necessarily advisable to strut up and drop the old *So-what's-happened-in-your-love-life-lately?* line. Comes across like something a pervert might say."

That stung, and he flinched visibly. *Whoa boy, don't expose yourself so easily.*

"You look surprised," Lacy said with a tilt of her head. "What did you expect? That I would lie down on a couch and tell you my life history?"

"No. But you don't have to bite my head off. I just asked a simple question."

"And I just more or less told you to mind your own business."

So, she was bitter and letting it ooze from her seams. She was right; he should have expected nothing less. "Okay look, I'm sorry if my introducing myself caused such offense, but maybe—just maybe—not everyone in the world is as cynical as you think. Maybe there are a few decent people around," Kent said, building his volume. Of course the whole thing was a crock, and he knew it as he spoke. He was about as decent as a rat.

She looked at him for a moment and then nodded slowly. "You're right. I'm sorry. It's just not every day that a man walks up to me and plops down like this."

"And I'm sorry. It was probably a dumb thing to do. I just couldn't help noticing you." She was softening. That was good. "It's not every day you come across a beautiful woman sitting alone looking so lost."

Lacy looked to the side, suddenly awash with emotion. He watched it descend on her like a mist. Watched her swallow. His own vision blurred. *Lacy, Oh, Lacy! It's me! It's Kent, and I love you. I really do!* His throat burned with the thought. But he could never go so far. Never!

"I'm so sorry," he said.

She sniffed and wiped her eyes quickly. "No. Don't be sorry. Actually, I think I'm in love with another man, Kevin."

Heat flashed over Kent's skull. Another man?

"I'm not even sure I could befriend you. In fact, I'm crazy about him"

Goodness, this was impossible! "Yes," he said. But he felt like saying no. Screaming, *No, Lacy! You can't love another man! I'm right here, for Pete's sake!*

"I think you should leave now," she said. "I appreciate your concern, but I'm really not looking for a relationship. You should go."

Kent froze. He knew she was right; he should leave. But his muscles had locked up. "Who?" he asked.

She looked at him, startled. "Who?" Her eyes bore into him and for a moment he thought she might lash out at him. "A dead man, that's who. Please go," she said. "Please go now," she insisted.

"A dead man?" his voice rasped.

"Go now!" she said, leaving no doubt as to her intentions.

"But . . ."

"No! Just go!"

Kent stood shakily to his feet, his world gray and fuzzy. He walked past her toward the door, right past the cashier without thinking to pay for their meals, right out into the street, hardly knowing he'd exited the restaurant.

Lacy was still in love with him. With Kent!

And this was good? No, this was bad. Because he was indeed dead. Kent was dead. And Lacy had not shown the least morsel of interest in Kevin, with his surgically altered cheeks and larger nose and sharper chin.

The realization fell on him like a boulder rolled from a cliff. He had truly died that night at the bank! Kent was truly dead. And Lacy was on the verge of death—at least her heart was. Any lingering hopes for love between them were now lost to the grave. End of story.

Kevin would have to find his own way. But Kevin didn't want to find his own way. Kevin wanted to die. Kevin didn't even exist.

He was *Kent! Kent, Kent, Kent!*

But Kent was dead.

It was the low point of his day. It was the low point of his month. It might very well be the low point of his life—although that day Gloria had died and that day Spencer had died, those had been low as well. Which was a problem because before coming here tonight, he had already been sliding along the bottom. Now the bottom was looking like the sky, and this tunnel he was in was feeling like the grave.

Kent's mind drifted to Spencer and Gloria, rotting six foot under. He might have to join them soon, he thought. Life up here above the grass was becoming quite difficult to manage. He trudged down the street thinking of options. But the only two he could wrap his mind around were trudging and dying. For the moment he would trudge, but maybe soon he would die. Either way, that woman back there was dead.

He knew that because he had killed her. Or he might as well have.

40

Kent stormed up Niponbank's sweeping steps Friday morning at ten, grinding his teeth and muttering under his breath. A fury had descended upon him in the wee hours of the morning. The kind that results from stacking up circumstances on the grand scale of life and then stepping back for a bird's-eye view only to see one end of the brass contraption dragging on the concrete and the other end swinging high in the sky. How much could a man take? Sure, on the one hand there was the brilliant million-dollar larceny bit, teetering up there on one side of the scale. But it was alone, hanging cold in the wind, forced into the loft by a dozen inequities piled high on the other side.

Lacy, for example. Or, as Kent saw the image, Lacy's firm jaw, snapping at him, barking for him to go. *"Just go! Now!"* Then there was the cop, an ear-to-ear grin plastered on that pointy head. Pinhead. *"You wanna know what I think, Bob? Or is it Kent?"* And there was Bono, spouting his wisdom of the grave, and Doug the Aussie, smiling toothlessly on the yacht that had killed his last son, and Steve the bartender hovering like a vulture. The images whispered through his mind, weighing the scales heavily, slowly pushing his blood pressure to a peak.

But it was the final few tidbits that had awakened him an hour earlier, panting and sweating on the covers. The ones he'd somehow managed to bury already. Gloria, swollen and purple and dead on the hospital bed; Spencer bent like a pretzel, cold as stone. Borst and Bentley, sitting behind their desks, smiling. *Welcome back, Kent.*

Somehow, all the images distilled down to the one of the porky twins sitting there, wringing their hands in the pleasure of their *deed.*

Which was why he found himself storming up Niponbank's sweeping steps Friday morning at ten, grinding his teeth and muttering under his breath.

He pushed through the revolving door and veered immediately right, toward the management offices. No nostalgia greeted him this time, only an irrational rage pounding through his veins. Sidney was there somewhere, clacking on the marble floor. But he barely registered the sound.

Bentley's door was closed. Not for long. Kent turned the knob and shoved it open, breathing as hard now from his climb up the steps as from his anger. A dark-haired woman sat cross-legged in a guest chair, prim and proper and dressed in a bright blue suit. Both snapped their heads up at his sudden entry.

Kent glared at the woman, stepped to the side, and flung a hand toward the door. "Out! Get out!"

Her jaw fell open and she appealed to Bentley with round eyes.

Bentley shoved his seat back and clutched the edge of his desk, as though poised to leap. His face had drained of color. He moved his lips to form words, but only a rasp sounded.

The woman seemed to understand. She could not possibly know what was happening here, but she wanted no part of it. She stood and hurried from the room.

"Get Borst in here," Kent said.

"He . . . he was already coming. For a meeting." The boy in Bentley was showing, like a man caught with his pants down. But if Kent's previous encounters with him were any indication, the man would gather himself quickly.

Borst walked into the room then, unsuspecting. He saw Kent and gasped.

"Good of you to join us, Borst. Shut the door." Kent closed his eyes and settled his nerves.

His former boss shut the door quickly.

"Why didn't you return my calls?" Bentley demanded. He was finding himself.

"Shut up, Bentley. I really have no desire to subject myself to more of your nonsense. I can take my share of punishment, but I'm no sadomasochist."

"And what if I had information critical to your investigation? You can't expect to walk out of here hurling your accusations and then just leave us hanging dry!"

"I did, didn't I? And short of a signed confession, nothing you could possibly tell me would prove critical to my investigation. Take my word for it. But I'll tell you what. I'll give you a chance now, how's that?"

Bentley stared at him, flabbergasted.

"Come on, out with it, man. What was so important?"

Still nothing. He had the man off center. No sense stalling.

"I didn't think so. Now, go over there and sit next to Borst."

"I—"

"Sit!"

The man jerked from his seat and shuffled over to where Borst sat, still white as a marshmallow on a stick.

"Now, for your sakes I'm going to keep this short. And I don't want to see you two slobbering all over the chairs, so save your comments for the authorities. Fair enough?"

They sat woodenly, unbelieving.

"Let me start at the beginning. I've put my findings in writing to the men who sign your checks, but I figure we have about ten minutes to chat about it before the Japanese come screaming across that phone. You ever hear cursing in Japanese, Borst? It isn't soothing stuff."

Kent took a breath and continued quickly. "For starters, you two had very little to do with AFPS. Its actual development that is. You evidently learned how to use it well enough. But in reality you did not deserve credit for its implementation, now did you? Don't bother answering. You did not. Which is a problem because, in claiming credit for another man's work you violated your employment agreements. Not only ground for immediate dismissal, but also requiring repayment in full of any monetary gain from the misrepresentation."

"That's not true!" Bentley said.

"Shut up, Bentley. Kent Anthony was solely responsible for AFPS, and you two know it as well as you know you're in this, neck deep." He drilled them with his eyes and let the statement settle in the room. "Lucky for you Kent seemed to meet an untimely demise a month after your little trick."

"That's not true! We had nothing to do with Kent's death!" Borst protested. "Taking a little credit is one thing, but we had nothing to do with his death!"

"You take a man's livelihood, you take his pride. Might as well be dead."

"You can't make any of this stick, and you know it!" Bentley said.

"We'll let the Japanese decide what sticks and what doesn't. But I'd spend just a little more time thinking about the million-dollar problem than about the Kent Anthony problem. Pretty clever, really. It took me the better part of a week to crack your little scheme."

A quiver had taken to Bentley's face, now red like a tomato again. "What are you talking about?"

"You *know* what I'm talking about, of course. But I'll tell you anyway. The way I figure it, Borst here developed this little program called ROOSTER. It looks like a security program for AFPS. Problem is, it was never released with the rest of the code. In fact it resides on only two computers throughout the entire system. That's right, the computer on Markus Borst's desk and the one on Price Bentley's desk. Interesting, given the fact that these two yahoos are the ones who ripped off Mr. Kent Anthony of his just reward. But even more interesting when you discover what the program is capable of. It is a ghost link to AFPS. A way into the system that's virtually undetectable. But I found it. Imagine that."

"But . . . But. . . ." Borst was sputtering.

"Shut up, Borst! That ain't the half of it." Kent delivered his indictment in long staccato bursts now. "It's how the program was used that tops the cake. Actually very clever, that one. A run of small, untraceable transfers to see if anyone notices and then hit them with the big one. *Bam!*" Kent smacked his palm with a fist, and they both jumped.

"One million dollars in a single shot, and no one knows where it's gone to. Unless you peek inside the accounts hidden conveniently on Borst's and Bentley's computers! Why lookie here! A million dollars all neatly tucked away for a rainy day. Not a bad plan."

"That's impossible!" Bentley was steaming red and dripping wet. "We did none of that! You can't be serious!"

"No?" The rage Kent had felt first while stomping up the bank's steps roared to the surface. He was suddenly yelling and jabbing his finger at them, and he knew that he had no reason to yell. They were both sitting five feet from him. "No? Well you're wrong, Porky! Nothing, and I mean *nothing,* is impossible for greedy slobs like you! You confiscate another man's fortune and guess what— someday you can expect yours to be confiscated as well!" He breathed hard. *Easy, boy.*

"It's all there, you idiot." He pointed at Bentley's computer. "Every last detail. You can read it like a mystery novel. Say what you want, but the data does not lie, and they already have the data. You two are going down!"

They gawked at him, thoroughly stunned.

"Do you understand this?" Kent asked, stabbing his forehead. "Is this information sinking in, or are you madly trying to think of ways to save your miserable necks?"

They couldn't respond, by the looks of it. Borst's eyes were red and misty. He was badly unraveled. Bentley was leaking smoke out of his ears—invisible, of course, but just as apparent.

Kent lowered his voice. "And let me tell you something else. The evidence is incontrovertible. Trust me; I put it together. If you want to get out of this you're gonna have to convince the jury that some ghost from the past did it all in your place. Perhaps you could blame it on that programmer you screwed. Maybe Kent Anthony's ghost has come back to haunt you. But short of an insanity plea along those lines, you're toast."

They still were not talking. Kent felt like saying more, like slapping them both back to life. But he had said what he'd come to say. It was the card he'd dreamed of playing for many long nights, and now he'd played it.

Kent strode for the door, past Bentley and Borst who sat unmoving. He hesitated at the door, thinking to put an exclamation mark on the statement. Maybe knock their heads together. *Thump! And don't forget it either!*

He resisted the impulse and walked from the bank. It was the last time he would see them. What happened to them now would be up to someone else, but in any scenario, things would not go easy for the porky twins. Not at all.

41

Helen walked alone on Monday, beside herself with contentment, unable to settle the grin bunching her cheeks. Light was crackling around the seams of heaven. She knew that because she closed her eyes and saw it almost without ceasing now. Yesterday, even Bill had seen the phenomenon. Or felt it, really, because it wasn't about physically seeing. It was more like *knowing* God's love, which in itself took a supernatural power. She mulled over one of the apostle Paul's prayers: "And I pray that you may have the power to grasp how wide and long and high and deep is the love of Christ . . ." It was something not easily grasped, that love. Something imagined with a certain degree of confidence, really. Certainly not heard or touched or seen or tasted or smelled. Not usually, anyway.

The light was like that, not easily grasped. But Pastor Bill was getting a grip on things these days. He was getting better at imagining the world beyond what most see and touch and taste. And he was imagining with belief. Faith. Believing having not seen, as the apostle put it.

Helen hummed the hymn "Jesus, Lover of My Soul." It was the martyrs' song, she thought. Everyone she knew who had carried that song had died for God. *Let me to Thy bosom fly . . .*

In all honesty she was not certain why the light was shining so brightly beyond the sky, but she had an idea. Things were not what they seemed. The death of her daughter, Gloria—such a devastating experience initially—was not such a bad thing at all. Neither was the death of Spencer such a bad thing. She had said so to Bill a dozen times, but now Helen was feeling the truth. Their lives were like seeds, which, having died in the ground, were now bearing a splendor unimaginable in their former puny vessels. Like the martyr who had been slain in Serbia. Somehow the seed was bearing fruit decades later in lives not yet born when that priest gave his life. How that fruit actually looked she did not know yet. She could not see as much. But the light spilling out of heaven was being pushed by peals of laughter.

"Good God, take me!" she mumbled and skipped a step. Her heart pounded with excitement. "Take me quickly. Let me join them, Father."

She had heard many times of how the martyrs walked willingly to their deaths, overjoyed and eager to find the life beyond. She herself felt the same way for the first time in her life, she thought. It was that kind of joy. A complete understanding of this life stacked up against the next life. And she would gladly jump into the next if given the opportunity.

Now this death of Kent, it was not quite so clear. He had died; he had not died. He would die; he would live; he would love; he would rot in hell. In the end she might never even know. In the end it was between Kent and God.

In the end Kent was every man. In the end the pounding feet in her dreams were the feet of every man, running from God.

She knew that now. Yes, there was this grand commotion over Kent in the heavens because of the challenge cast. Yes, a million angels and as many demons lined the sky, peering on his every move. But it was the same for every man. And it was not a game, as she had once suggested to the pastor. It was life.

"Glory!" she yelled, and immediately spun around to see if anybody had been surprised by that. She could see no one. Too bad—would've been nice to treat another human to a slice of reality. She chuckled.

Yes indeed. What was happening here in this isolated petri dish of her experience was no different from what happened in one form or another to every last human being who lived on God's green Earth. Different in the fact that she had been enabled to participate with her walkathon intercession, perhaps. Different because she saw more of the drama than most. But no different up there where it counted.

The truth of it all had descended upon her two days earlier, and now she wanted one thing like she had never wanted anything in the sixty-four years her little heart had managed to beat. She wanted to cross that finish line. She wanted to step into the winner's circle. She wanted to walk into glory. If given the choice to live and walk or to die and kneel before the throne, she would scream her answer: "the throne, the throne, the throne!" Jumping like a pogo stick. She would do it in her running shoes and tall white socks, not caring if a park full of baseball players saw her do it.

She wanted it all because now she knew without the slightest sliver of doubt that it was all about God's love—so desperate and consuming for every man. And she also knew that Gloria and Spencer were swimming in God's love and screaming with pleasure for it.

"God, take me home," she breathed. "Take me quickly."

Frankly, she didn't know how Kent could resist it all.

Maybe he wouldn't. Maybe he had.

Either way, the light was bright and crackling around the seams.

"Glory!" she chirped and skipped again.

ᔐᕽ

It struck Kent that Sunday, two days after Lacy had spit him out like raw quinine, that it had been almost two months since he'd become a millionaire. Actually it didn't *strike* him at all, because the thought barely crept through his mind, like a lethargic slug hoping for safe passage. He rolled over and noted that he'd slept on top of the covers again. A dim light glowed around the room's brown drapes, and by the sounds of traffic he knew it was well past morning. Not that it mattered—day and night had lost their significance to him now.

It is said that money cannot buy happiness. It is one of those axioms often spoken but rarely believed for the simple reason that money does indeed seem to bring with it a measure of happiness. At least for a while. Bono's assertion that all paths end in the grave might be true, but in the meantime, surely money might ease the journey. It was the *meantime* part that Kent was having difficulty with. Because for Kent, the conclusion of the matter—the bit about the grave—took up early residence inside him. Like a hole in his chest.

It was all a bit unusual, possibly. Not in the least fair, it seemed. But hollow and black and sickening just the same. And this all without Pinhead the cop entering the picture. Throw his mug into the mix, and it was flogging desperation.

Kent had walked long and slow that Thursday night, away from Lacy. A limousine stuffed with squealing teenagers had nearly run him over at one point. The near-miss had nearly scared him out of his skin. He had hailed a taxi then and returned to the dungeon in Denver. The sun was already graying the eastern sky when he paid the driver.

Friday. Friday had been the big day of living dangerously, taking out his last few breaths of fury on the porky twins and then submitting his findings to the bank. They had delivered his fee as agreed. Bentley and Borst would undoubtedly find their just reward. Revenge is sweet, so they say. Kent didn't know who *they* were, but he knew now that they knew nothing. His victory was hardly more than a distant memory by two o'clock that afternoon.

He spent a good portion of the next two days—or nights, really, because he didn't roll out of bed until 5 P.M.—trying to plot a comeback. Not a comeback to Lacy; she was dead to him. But a comeback to life. He had eighteen million dollars stashed, for heaven's sake. Anybody who had eighteen million dollars stashed without knowing how to spend it was the better part of a moron. The things one could do with such wealth. Granted, Bill Gates might consider the cash chicken feed, but then Mr. Bill was in a different reality altogether. Most normal human beings would have trouble finding ways to spend even one million dollars, short of purchasing some jet or yacht or some other toy that cost the world.

Kent had considered doing just that. Buying another bigger, fancier yacht, for example, and sailing it to a deserted tropical cove. The idea actually retained some luster for the better part of a beer before he discarded it. He had already purchased one yacht, and he had left it behind. Maybe he'd buy a small jet. Fly around the world. Of course he would be landing and partying at all stops, discovering the local flavors and laughing with the natives. On the other hand, most local flavors were available at specialty restaurants around town—no need to traipse around the world. And laughter was not coming so easily these days.

Perhaps he could visit a few great sporting events. Sit in the stadium with the other rich folk who could afford to drop a few C notes for the pleasure of watching men bat, or throw, or bounce a ball around. Yes, and maybe he could take his own ball and play catch with a few celebrities. *Gag.* Thing of it was, three months ago the idea would have thrilled him. Now that he had the money, he could not remember why.

On Monday another emotion found its way into Kent's mind. Panic. An unearthly desperation at the prospect of finding no solution to this dilemma. A day later the panic settled into a dull hopelessness. He stopped feeling then and just continued his trudging through what he now saw clearly as the wastelands of life. Life without Gloria and Spencer. Life without Lacy. Life without Kent. Life without any meaning at all.

Kent climbed from bed on Wednesday and pulled the drapes aside. A light
drizzle fell from a dark, gray sky. Could be morning, could be afternoon, could
be evening. Looked nasty whatever time it was. He dropped the heavy curtain and
trudged to the bathroom, shoulders drooping. The fluorescent bulb blinked
brightly, and he squinted. Toothpaste stains ringed the sink, and he thought he
might be good to clean the bathroom. He'd slept in the apartment for almost two
weeks now without cleaning the kitchen or the bathroom. What would Helen say
to that?

Helen, dear old Helen. A lump rose to his throat at the thought of the woman.
So sincere, so steady, so sweet, so gentle. Well, not always so sweet or gentle, but
sincere and truthful. She'd likely walk in here and land a loud slap on his cheek.

A tear sprang to Kent's eye. What was this? He was actually missing the old
wench? Maybe, maybe not, but either way the tear felt good, because it was his first
tear in five days. Which meant that his heart was still alive in its prison of bones.

But the sink and the kitchen and the rest of it could wait. Helen was not here.
In fact, no one was here. Nor would anyone be here soon. He could buy the place
and burn it to the ground. That would clean it up good. Yes, maybe he'd do that
when this was over.

When what is over, Kent?

He looked up at the mirror and stared at his disheveled reflection. The face
Lacy had rejected. Three days' stubble. Maybe four days'. The face of Kevin
Stillman, still bearing scars from the surgery, if you knew where to look.

When what is over, Kent?

The lump swelled in his throat, like a balloon. Another tear slipped from his
right eye. *I'm sorry, Gloria. God, I'm sorry.* His chest was aching. *I'm sorry, Spencer.*

Yes, and what would Spencer think of you now?

His shoulders shook, and the mirror dissolved in a single sob. *I'm so sorry.*

It's over, Kent.

He sucked at the air and caught his breath. The notion popped in his mind
with sudden clarity. Yes, it was over, wasn't it? There was nothing left to do anymore. He had spent his life. He had drained it of meaning. Now it was time to
step aside and let the others have a try.

It was time to stop trudging. It was time to die.

Yes, it's time to die, Kent.

Yes, let the other fools bloody their fingers climbing up life's cliff. Let them claw over the edge to find the wastelands stretching like a dusty graveyard. In the end it was all the same. In the end it was the grave.

Yes. You've come home, Kent. Welcome home, Kent.

It was the first touch of peace Kent had felt in weeks, and it tingled down his spine. *Now I lay me down to sleep* . . . Right beside the others who wasted their lives climbing this cliff called life and then lay down to die on barren wastelands. Salmon fighting their way up the river. Lemmings rushing to the cliff. Humans dying in the wastelands. It all made sense now.

Kent brushed his teeth. No sense dying with dirty teeth. He dropped the toothbrush half finished and spat the foam from his mouth. He didn't bother running any water to clean the mess.

The easiest way to slip into the grave would be through some sort of overdose; he'd thought so a hundred times. But thinking of it now, it seemed there ought to be more to the matter. It could be a month before they found his rotting body, maybe longer. Maybe he'd do the deed in a place that made a statement. The bank, for instance. Or in the steeple of a church. On the other hand, did he care? No, he did not care at all. He simply wanted out. Done. Over. He wanted to end. Find Bono's graveyard. Find a priest . . .

Confess.

Kent was halfway across the room, headed nowhere, when the thought dropped into his head. He pictured Bono telling him that. *"Confess, my son."* The word hollowed his chest. It seemed to carry a sense of purpose. And a suicide with purpose felt better than a senseless one. It would be something like leaning over that cliff and calling down to the million fools struggling up the stone face. *"Hey, fellas, there ain't nothin' up here but ashes and tombstones. Save yourselves the energy."*

Confess to a priest. Find a church, find a man of the collar, confess the crime, then drift off to the wasteland. Maybe meet Helen's God. The thought brought a tightness to his chest again. *I'm sorry, Helen.* Dear old Helen.

Kent sat on the bed and rested his forehead on his hands. An image of Helen filled his mind, and he swallowed against the knot in his throat. She was pointing to the bare spot above his fireplace—the spot that had once graced a painting of Christ. *"You crucified him, Kent,"* Helen was saying. Only she wasn't yelling it or stuffing it down his throat. She was crying and smiling.

"Yes," he muttered beneath his breath. A tear slipped down his cheek. "And now I'm going to crucify myself, Helen."

42

Helen called Bill at six that morning, pacing in small circles while she waited for him to answer. "Come on, Bill."

The dream had changed last night. The sound of running had quickened; the breathing had come in gasps. She had awakened wet with sweat and rolled from bed, the fingers of panic playing on her spine.

"Get up, Bill. Pick up the phone!"

A groggy voice spoke through the receiver. "Hello."

"Something's up, Bill."

"Helen? What time is it?"

"It's already six, and I should've been walking half an hour ago, but I started praying in my kitchen and I'm telling you, I could hardly stand it."

"Whoa, slow down, Helen. Sorry, I had a late appointment last night."

She stopped her pacing and peered out the window. A fine drizzle fell from a dark gray sky. "I don't know. But it's never been like this before."

"Like what, Helen. What are you talking about?"

"There's electricity in the air. Can't you feel it?" Helen moved her arm through the air and felt her hair stand on end. "Heavens, Bill, it's everywhere. Close your eyes and calm yourself. Tell me if you feel anything."

"I'm not the one who needs calming—"

"Just do it, Pastor."

The phone went dead for a moment before he came back on. "No. I'm sorry. I see only the backs of my eyelids over here. It's raining outside."

"It feels like heaven is about to tear loose, Bill. Like it's a bag of white-hot light, bursting at the seams over here."

He didn't answer right away, and she was suddenly impatient. She should be out walking and praying. The thought brought another shiver to her bones. "Glory," she whispered. Bill's breathing suddenly went ragged in the receiver.

"Helen . . . ?" his voice warbled.

Her pulse quickened. She spun from the window. "Yes? You see something?"

"Helen, I think something is going to happen . . . Oh, my God! Oh, my God!"

"Bill!" She knew it! He was seeing something right now. Had to be! "Bill, what is it? Tell me!"

But he just mumbled on. "Oh, my God. Oh, my God." His voice wavered over the phone, and Helen fought a sudden urge to drop the receiver and rush to his house. He was over there seeing into the other side, and she was standing here on this side, holding this ridiculous phone and wanting to be *over there.*

"Come on, Bill," she suddenly blurted. "Stop mumbling and tell me something!"

That put the pause in him. But only for a moment. Then he started again. "Oh, my God! Oh, my God!" It was not anything akin to swearing. Quite the opposite. This much Helen knew with certainty: Pastor Bill Madison was peeking into the heavens this very minute. And he was desperately yearning for what he was seeing, yes sir. The truth of it oozed from his shuddering voice as he cried to his God. "Oh, my God! Oh, my God!"

He fell silent suddenly.

Helen took a deep breath and waited a few seconds before pressing again. "What was it, Pastor? What did you see?"

He was not talking. Perhaps not listening, either.

"Bill . . ."

"I . . . I don't really know," came the weak reply. "It just came like a blanket of light . . . like last time, only this time I heard laughter. Lots of laughter."

"Ha! You heard it, did you? Well, what did I tell you? You see? Have you ever in your life heard such laughter?"

He laughed a crazy little chuckle. "No. But who is it? Who's laughing? . . . Do you think it's *God?*"

Helen lifted her arm and saw that the hair stood on end. She should walk. She needed to walk *now!* "The laughter is from humans, I think. The saints. And maybe from angels as well."

"The saints are laughing? *Laughing,* huh? And what about God? Did I see him in there?"

"I don't know what you saw, Bill. I wasn't there. But God is responsible for the light, and you saw the light, right? I think he is mostly loving and being loved and laughing—yes, laughing too—and weeping."

"And why, Helen? Why are we seeing these things? It's not common."

"No, it's not common. But it's real enough. Just like in biblical times, Bill. He's nudging our stubborn minds. Like my walking—impossible yet true. Like Jericho. Like two-thirds of the Scriptures, impossible yet true and here today. He has not changed, Bill." She gazed back out the window. "He has not changed."

"Yes. You are right. He has not changed."

"I have to go, Pastor. I want to walk."

"Yes, you should walk. It's supposed to snow today, they say. First snow of the season. You dress warm, okay?"

Snow? Goodness, that would be something, walking in the snow. "I'll be fine. My legs are not so concerned with the elements these days."

"Go with God, Helen."

"I will. Thank you, Bill."

Helen grabbed a light jacket on the way out and entered the gray morning air. Streetlights glowed like halos in a long string down the glistening pavement. One of those Volkswagen bugs drove by, its lights peering through the mist. The sound of its wheels running over the pavement sounded like tearing paper. She pulled on the jacket and walked into the drizzle, mumbling, hardly aware of the wet.

Father, thank you, thank you, thank you. Her body shivered once, as a chill swept through her bones. But it was not the cold; it was that light, crackling just behind the black clouds, that set off the tremor. True enough, she could not actually see it, but it fizzled and snapped and dazzled there, just the same. Her heart ran at twice its customary clip, as if it too knew that a rare power streamed through the air, unseen but fully charged.

Perhaps the prince of this earth wanted to put a damper on things. Soak his domain with a cold, wet blanket in an attempt to mask the light behind it all. But she was not seeing the blanket at all. She was seeing that light, and it felt warm and dry and bright. *Glory.*

Helen glanced at her white running shoes, stabbing forward with each stride. They flung droplets out ahead of her, christening the sidewalk like a priest flinging water on a baby's head. *Blessed be these feet, walking by the power of God.* It might have been a good idea to pull on long pants and a sweater, but she was not following good ideas these days.

She had run out of words in this prayer-walking weeks ago. She might have prayed through the entire Bible—she didn't know. But now it was just her heart yearning and her mouth mumbling. *You made this earth, Father. It's yours. There's no way a few drops will stand in your way! Goodness, you parted a whole sea for the Israelites—surely this here is nothing. In fact, maybe it's your rain. How about that?*

Helen lifted her hands and grasped at the drops, smiling wide. For a brief moment her chest felt as though it might explode, and she skipped for a few steps. Another car with lights glaring whisked by, its tires hissing on the wet street. It honked once and sped on. And no wonder; she surely looked like a drowned rat with her matted hair and drooping wet dress. *Crazy old woman, walking in this stuff. She'll catch her death!*

Now *there* was a thought. *Take me, Father. I'll gladly come. You know that, don't you? Don't get me wrong here. I'll do whatever you wish of me. But you know I'd die to be with you. To be rid of this flesh and this old wrinkled face and this hair that keeps falling out. Not that it's so bad, really. I thank you for it; really I do. And if you'd want me to, I'd bring it with me. But I'll tell you this, my God: I would give anything to be there with you. Take me any way you choose. Strike me dead with a bolt of lightning, roll me over with a monster truck, send a disease to eat away my bones—any way, just bring me home. Like those before me.*

She jumped once and swung her arm—a grandma-style victory whoop. "Glory!" This was how the martyrs had felt, she thought. Marching to Zion!

The sky slowly but barely brightened as the hours faded. Helen walked, scarcely conscious of her route. The path took her due west along side streets. She'd been here before, numerous times, and she knew the four-hour turnaround point well. If she took a loop around the fountain at 132nd and Sixth, she would end up back at home eight hours after her morning departure. The fat Buddha-looking statue at the fountain's center would be wet today, the goldfish swimming at its feet doubly doused.

Helen groaned at the thought of rounding the fountain and heading home. It should have come as a comfort with all the rain drenching her to the bone and the dark sky foreboding a storm, but it didn't. Not today. Today the thought of heading home made her heart sink. She wanted to hike right over the distant, crackling horizon like Enoch and climb under the black clouds. She wanted to find the light and join in the laughter. *Glory!*

The traffic was light, the normal straggle of pedestrians absent, the shops eerily vacant. Helen approached Homer's Flower Shop on the corner of 120th and Sixth. The old man stood under his eaves with folded arms and raised brows as she came near.

"They say snow's coming, you know. You shouldn't be out here."

"I'm fine, old man. This is no time to stop. I'm near the end now." He squinted at the comment. Of course, he could have no idea what she referred to, but then, a little mystery now and then never hurt anybody.

"Don't say I didn't warn you, old lady," he said.

She was even with him now and kept her head turned to meet his stare. "Yes, indeed. You have warned me. Now hear the warning of God, old man. Love him always. With every last breath, love him madly."

He blinked and took a step back. She smiled and walked on past. Let him think that one through. *Love God madly. Glory!*

She'd come to a string of street merchants who'd packed it in for the day, all except for Sammy the cap man who, truth be said, was more a homeless freeloader than an actual merchant, but nobody was saying so. Those who knew him also knew that he had sincerely if unsuccessfully tried at this life's game. Sometimes the ball rolls that way. He'd left a dead wife and a bankrupt estate in his wake. No one seemed to mind forking over a ten-dollar bill for a cheap, two-dollar cap—not when it was Sammy collecting the money. He stood under the eaves beside two large crates filled with his hats.

"What on Earth are you doing out here in the rain, Helen?"

She veered under the overhang. "Morning, Sammy. I'm walking. You have a cap for me today?"

He tilted his head. "A hat. You're soaked to the skin already. You think a cap will help now? Snow's coming, you know."

"Exactly. Give me one of those green ones you had out the other day."

He eyed her carefully, trying to decide if this bit of business was meant in sincerity. "You got a ten on you?"

"No, but I'll have it tomorrow."

Sammy shrugged and dug out a green hat sporting a red-and-yellow parrot on its bill. He handed it over with a smile, playing the salesman's role now. "It'll look great with that yellow dress. Nothing quite so appealing as a woman wearing a hat—dress or pants, rain or shine, it don't matter. It's the hat that counts."

She pulled it on. "Thanks, Sammy," she said and turned up the sidewalk.

Truth be told, she did it for him. What good would a hat do her? Although now that she had stretched it over her head, the bill did keep the drizzle from her eyes. "Glory!"

The horizon fizzled and crackled with light—she could feel it more than see it with her eyes, but it was real just the same. And she knew that if she could reach up there and pull those clouds aside she'd find one giant electrical storm flooded with laughter.

Helen walked on toward the turnaround point, toward the horizon, toward that sputtering light beyond what Homer or Sammy saw. If anybody was watching her on a regular basis they would notice that today her pace was brisker than usual. Her arms swung more determinedly. On any other day she might look like a crazy old woman with outdated fashion sensibilities, out for a walk. Today she looked like an ancient bag lady who'd clearly lost her mind—maybe with a death wish, soaked to the bone, marching nowhere.

Helen walked on, humming now. She stabbed the air with her white Reeboks, stopping on occasion to pump her fist and blurt out a word.

"Glory."

43

Kent drove to the liquor store at three in the afternoon, two hours after he had awakened and discovered he had only half a bottle of tequila left. He had decided it would be with booze and a bullet that his world would end, and half a bottle was not enough. He would drink himself into a state just this side of comatose, place the barrel of the nine-millimeter to his temple, and pull the trigger. It would be like pulling an aching tooth from society's jaws. Just enough anesthetic to numb the nerve endings and then rip the rotting thing out. Except it was his life decaying, not just some bony incisor.

He navigated the streets in a daze, peering lethargically past the drizzle. Sleet and the occasional snowflake mixed with the rain. The sky loomed dark and ominous. Decay was in the air.

He bought three bottles of the best tequila Tom's Liquor sold and tipped Tommy three hundred dollars.

"You sure? Three hundred dollars?" The man stood there with the bills fanned out, offering them back as if he thought they might be contagious.

"Keep it," Kent said and walked out of the store. He should have brought a couple hundred *thousand* from his mattress stash for the tip. See what Tommy would say to that. Or maybe he'd give the rest of the money to the priest. If he could *find* a priest to hear him. One final act of reconciliation for Gloria's sake. For Helen's sake.

He drove back to the apartment and pulled out the pistol. He'd shot it into the dead body at the bank a few times—three times actually, *blam, blam, blam*— so he wasn't terribly surprised to find six bullets in the nine-round clip. But it would only be one *blam* this time. He felt the cold steel and played with the safety a few times, checking the action, thinking small thoughts like, *I wonder if the guy who invented safeties is dead. Yes, he's dead and his whole family is dead. And now he's going to kill me. Sort of.*

Kent turned off all the lights and opened the drapes. The red numbers on the clock radio read 4:29. Snow now drifted silently past his window. The earth was dying slowly, begging him to join her.

It's time to lie down, Kent.

Yes, I will. As soon as I confess.

But why confess?

Because it seems decent.

You're going to blow your brains against the wall by the bed over there! What does decent have to do with that?

I want to. I want to tell a priest that I stole twenty million dollars. I want to tell him where to find it. Maybe he can use it.

You're a fool, Kent!

Yes, I know. I'm sick, I think.

You are human waste.

Yes, that's what I am. I'm human waste.

He backed to the bed and opened a bottle. The fiery liquid ran down his throat like fire, and he took a small measure of comfort in the knowledge that he was going to stop feeling soon.

He sat on the bed for an hour, trying to consider things, but the considering part of him had already gone numb. His eyes had dried of their earlier tears, like ancient abandoned wells. He was beginning to wonder if that voice that had called him human waste was right about blowing off the confession. Maybe he should stick to blowing off his head. Or maybe he should find a church—see if they even heard confessions of a dying man on dark wintry afternoons.

He dragged out the phone book and managed to find a listing of Catholic churches. Saint Peter's Cathedral. Ten blocks down Third Street.

Kent found himself on the road driving past the darkened cathedral thirty minutes later. The sign out front stated that confessions were heard until 7 P.M. each night, excluding Saturdays, but the dark stained-glass windows suggested the men of God had made an early retreat. Kent thought perhaps the sign should read, *"Confessions heard daily from 12:00 to 7:00 except on dark wintry days that depress everyone including priests who are really only men dressed in long black robes to earn their living. So give us all a break and go home, especially if you are suicidal.*

Don't bother us with your dying. Dying people are really just human waste. Priests are just ordinary people, and dying people are human waste." But that would hardly fit on the placard.

The thought drifted through his mind like wisps of fog, and it was gone almost before he realized he'd thought it. He decided he might come back later to see if the lights had been turned on.

Kent went back to his dark apartment and sat on the edge of his bed. The tequila went down smoothly now, not burning so much. It was five o'clock.

44

The Buddha-belly fountain came and went, and Helen did not stop.

It was as simple as that. She had passed the fountain at 11 A.M., and every other day she had turned around at the four-hour mark, but today she didn't want to turn around. She wanted to keep walking.

She could hear the water gurgling a full block before coming up on Mr. Buddha, and the impulse struck her then.

Keep walking, Helen.

I'm four hours from home if I turn now. I should keep walking?

Just keep right on walking.

Past the fountain? To where?

Past the fountain. Straight ahead.

Until when?

Until it's time to stop.

And how will I know that?

You will know. Just walk.

So she had.

That first step beyond her regular turning point felt like a step into the deep blue. Her heart raced, and her breathing thickened, but now it was not due to light spilling from the seams. This time it was from fear. Just plain, old-fashioned fear.

Certain facts presented themselves to her with convincing authority. Like the fact that every step she took west was one more step she would have to repeat later, headed east. Like the fact that it was now starting to snow, just like the weatherman had forecasted, and she wore only a thin jacket that had been soaked before the rain turned to snow. Like the fact that she was a lady in her sixties, marching off in a storm toward a black horizon. Like the fact that she did indeed look ridiculous in these tall, red-striped socks and wet, dirtied running shoes. In general, like the simple fact that she had clearly graduated from the ridiculous to the absurd.

Still she walked on, fighting the thoughts. Her legs did not seem to mind, and that was a good thing. Although they could hardly know that she was taking them farther from their home instead of closer. The first hour of walking into the cold, wind-blown snow had been perhaps the hardest hour Helen had lived in her sixty-plus years. Actually, there was no *perhaps* about it; nothing had been so difficult. She found herself sweating despite the cold. The incredible joy she'd felt when first walking a few hours earlier had faded into the gray skies above.

Still, she had placed one foot in front of the other and plodded on.

The light returned at three. Helen was in midstride when her world turned. When her eyes snapped open and she saw clearly again. That was exactly what happened. Heaven did not open up to her—*she* opened up to heaven. Perhaps it had taken these last four hours of walking blindly without the carrots of heaven dangling out in front to set her mind straight.

Either way, her world turned, midstride, and she landed her foot and froze. A crackle of light stuttered behind the walls of gray in her mind. Tears sprang to her eyes like a swelling tide. She remained still, her legs scissored on the sidewalk like a girl playing hopscotch. Her shoulders shook with sobs.

"Oh thank you, Father! Thank you!" She moaned aloud, overcome by the relief of the moment. "I knew you were there. I knew it!" Then the joy came, like a tidal wave right up through her chest, and she squeezed her hands into fists.

Just walk, Helen. Walk on.

It's been more than eight hours. It's getting dark.

Walk.

She needed no further urging.

I will walk.

She broke into a long stride. *One, two. One, two.* For a moment she thought her heart might burst with the exhilaration that now throbbed through her chest. *One, two. One, two. I will walk on. I will walk on.*

Helen strode down the sidewalk, through the strange neighborhood, toward the ominous horizon, swinging her arms like some marching soldier on parade. Snowflakes lay like cotton on her green hat and clung in lumps to her hair. She left footprints in the light snow covering the sidewalk. *Goodness, just wait until I tell Bill about this, she thought. "I just kept going, Bill, because I knew it was what he wanted. Did I consider the possibility that I had lost my mind? Sure I did. But still I knew, and he showed me just enough to keep me knowing. I just walked."*

Helen had walked another five blocks when the first pain shot up her right thigh.

She had not felt pain during weeks of walking. Now she felt the distinct sensation of pain, sharp and fleeting but unmistakable. Like a fire streaking through the femur toward her hip and then gone.

She gasped and pulled up, clutching her thigh, terrified. "Oh, God!" It was all she could say for a moment.

Walk.

Walk? Her jaw still gaped wide in shock. She rocked back on her good leg. I just had a leg cramp. I had pain! I'm twenty miles from home, and it's ending. It's over!

Walk. The impulse came strong.

Helen closed her mouth slowly and swallowed. She gazed about, saw that the street was clear of gawkers, and gingerly placed weight back on her right leg. The pain had gone.

Helen walked again, tentatively at first but then with gaining confidence. For another five blocks she walked. And then the pain flared through her femur again, sharper this time.

She gasped aloud and pulled up. "Oh, God!" Her knee quivered with the trauma.

Walk. Just keep walking.

"This is pain I'm feeling down here!" she growled angrily. "You are pulling your hand away from me! Oh God, what's happening?"

Walk, child. Just walk. You will see.

She walked. Halting at first until she realized the pain had left, as before.

It roared back with a vengeance six blocks later. This time Helen hardly stopped. She limped for ten yards, mumbling prayers through gritted teeth, before finding sudden relief.

The pain came every five blocks or so, first in her right leg and then in her left leg, and after an hour, in both legs simultaneously. A sharp, shooting pain right up each bone for half a dozen steps and then gone for a few blocks only to return like clockwork. It was as if her legs were thawing after months in the deep freeze and a thousand miles of pain was slowly coming due. Each time she cried out to God, her face twisted in pain. Each time he spoke to her quietly. *Walk. Walk, child.* Each time she put her foot forward and walked on into the falling darkness.

Three things contributed to her relentless journey despite its apparent madness. First was that quiet voice whispering through her skull. *Walk, child.* Second was the light—it had not fled. The blackening skies crackled with light in her mind, and she could not ignore that.

The third thought that propelled her forward was the simple notion that this might very well be the end. *The* end. Maybe she *was* meant to walk right up to the horizon of heaven and enter glory. Like Enoch. There might not be a flaming chariot to whisk her away. That had been Elijah's treat. No, with Helen it would be the long walk home. And that was fine by her. *Glory!*

The sun left the city dark by five-thirty. An occasional car hissed by, but the early storm had left the streets quiet. Helen limped on into the black night, biting her lower lip, mumbling against the voices that mocked her.

Walk, child. Walk on.

And she did walk on. By six o'clock both legs were hurting without relief. The soles of her feet felt as though they might have caught fire. She could distinctly imagine, if not actually hear, the bones in her knees grinding with each step. Her hips joined in the protest soon after. What began as a dull ache around her upper thighs quickly mushroomed to sharp pangs of searing pain throughout her legs.

Walk, child. Walk on.

Still she walked. The snow fell in earnest now, like ashes from a burnt sky. Helen kept her eyes on the ground just in front of her feet mostly, concentrating on each footfall as her destination—one . . . two, one . . . two. When she did look up she saw a dizzying sea of flakes swirling around the streetlights. The night settled quietly. Biting cold now numbed her exposed knees, and she began to shiver. She tucked her hands under her arms in an attempt to keep them warm, but the new posture threw her balance off, nearly sending her to the ground, and she immediately withdrew them. Oh, God! Please, Father. I have lost my mind here. This is . . . this is madness!

Walk, child. Walk on.

So she walked, but barely now, dragging one foot at a time, inching into the night. She lost all sense of direction, fighting through the landscape of her mind, aware of the pain ravaging her bones but no longer caring. At the eighth hour, back there, she had crossed the point of no return. She had stepped off the cliff and now fell helplessly onward, resigned to follow this still small voice or die trying. Either way the crackling light waited. And there would be laughter in the light. The notion brought a smile to her face, she thought, although she could not be sure because her face had gone numb.

The last fifty yards took twenty minutes—or an eternity, depending on who was counting. But she knew they were the last when her right foot landed on a cement rise of some kind and she could not pull herself up or over it. Helen fell to one knee, collapsed facedown, and rolled to her side.

If she'd been able to feel, she might have thought she had ground her legs to bloody stumps, judging by the pain she felt, but she could feel nothing at all. She was aware of snowflakes lighting on her cheek but no longer had the strength to turn away from them.

Then her world faded to black.

45

Desire for death is a unique sentiment, like a migraine sufferer's impulse to twist off his head in the hopes of banishing a throbbing headache. But Kent was still craving death—and increasingly so as the minutes ticked by in his dark apartment.

It might have been some deep-seated desire to delay his death that pushed him back to the church despite the falling snow. But if it was, it did not feel like any desire he'd ever felt. Nevertheless, he would do this one last deed. He would find his priest.

Snow rushed past his headlights, and it occurred to him that coming out for a priest on a night like this was nuts. But then, so was killing himself. He was a nutcase. The church's tall spiral reached into the night sky like a shadowed hand reaching for God. *Reach on, baby. Nothin' but black up there.*

He parked the car and stared at the dark cathedral. A monument to man's search for meaning, which was a joke because even the robed ones knew, way deep inside, that there was no real meaning. In the end it was just death. A dusty graveyard on the top of a cliff.

Get on with it, Kent.

Kent pushed the door open and slogged toward the wide steps.

The lump on the first step caught his attention immediately. A body lay curled like a fetus, covered with snow. Kent stopped on the sidewalk and studied the form. The priest had fallen down on the job—closed the temple up too early and now his God had dashed him on the steps. Or possibly a vagrant had come to find God and discovered a locked door instead. Either way the body did not move. It was the second dead body he'd seen recently. Maybe he should curl up and join this one.

Kent mounted the steps and climbed to the front door. It was locked. His mouth no longer had the will to swear or speak or even breathe, but his mind swore. He slogged down the steps, his mind still swearing long strings of words that no longer had meaning. He veered to the body and shoved it with his foot. *Death becomes me.* The snow fell from the vagrant's face. An old woman, smiling to beat all. A wide grin frozen on that pale face. She'd finally found her peace. And now he was on his way to find his own peace.

Kent turned from the body and walked for the car. An old memory crawled through his mind. It was dear old Helen, smiling with moist eyes in his living room. *You crucified him, Kent.*

Yes, dear Helen. But I will make amends soon enough. Like I told you, I'm going to kill my—

The next thought exploded in his mind mid-street, like a stun grenade. *That was Helen!*

His legs locked under him, stretched out for the next step.

Kent whirled back to the body. Ridiculous! That old woman lying over there was no more Helen than he was *God!* He turned back to his car.

If that wasn't Helen, then Helen has a twin.

He stopped and blinked. *Get a grip, Kent.*

And what if that is *Helen by some freak accident, dead on the step?*

Impossible! But suddenly the impulse to know trumped the rest of it.

Kent spun back toward the form and walked quickly. He bent and rolled the dead body to its back. Only it wasn't dead; he knew that immediately because its nostrils blew a few flakes from its upper lip in a long exhale. He jerked back, startled by the ghostly face smiling under a cap. His heart crashed against the walls of his chest. It *was* Helen!

It was not the grin or the face or even the hair. It was the yellow dress with small blue flowers, all but covered in snow, that made it so. The same yellow flowered dress she had worn to Gloria's funeral. The same yellow flowered dress she had worn to his door that first night moving in. That and the socks pulled to her knees.

He was staring at Helen, crumpled on the steps of this church, wearing running shoes clotted with frozen snow, smiling like she was in some kind of warm dream instead of freezing to death on this concrete slab.

Leave her.

I can't. She's alive.

Kent glanced around, saw that they were alone, and shoved his arms under Helen's limp body. He staggered to his feet with her dead weight hanging off each arm. The last time he'd done this, the body had been naked and gray and dead. He'd forgotten how heavy these things were. Well, the paramedics could deal with the crazy old fool as they saw fit.

Kent was halfway back to his car with Helen in his arms when that last thought crossed his mind. A swell of sorrow swept through his chest, and immediately he wanted to cry. For no reason that he could think of, really. Maybe because he had called her a crazy old fool and, really, she was no such thing. He looked down at the sagging body in his arms. No, this was no fool he carried. This was . . . this was precious. Helen, in all her eccentric craziness, somehow embodied a goodness. A tear came to his eyes, and he sniffed against it.

Get ahold of yourself, fool. And if she is goodness then what does that make you? Human waste.

Yes. Worse.

Yes, worse. Get rid of her.

Kent barely managed to open the passenger door without falling. He slid Helen onto the seat, slammed the door, and climbed in behind the wheel. She had fallen against the door, and her breathing came steadily now. A knot rose to his throat, and he shook his head. Thing of it was, she brought a strange sentiment out of him. One that had his windpipe aching. He missed her. That's what it was. He actually missed the old lady.

He started the Lincoln and pulled into the deserted street. The snow had eased to a powdery mist, visible only around a row of streetlights on the right. A white blanket lay undisturbed over parked cars and bushes and pavement alike. The sedan crept quietly over the snow, and Kent felt the fingers of death curl around his mind. It was death—death everywhere. A frozen graveyard. Kent swallowed hard. "God, let me die," he growled under his breath.

"Uhh . . ."

The groan from his right slammed into his consciousness like a bullet to the brain, and he reacted instinctively. He crammed his foot on the brake and pulled hard on the wheel. The Lincoln slid for the sidewalk, bumped into the curb, and stalled. Kent gripped the wheel with both hands and breathed heavy.

He whirled to the passenger's seat. Helen sat there, leaning against the passenger door with her head resting on her shoulder, cockeyed but wide eyed, and staring ahead past snow-encrusted brows. Kent's breath seemed to freeze in his throat. She was awake! Awake from the dead like a lost soul from the cast of a cheap horror movie.

Slowly she straightened her neck and lifted a hand to brush the snow from her face. Kent stared dumbly, thoroughly confused on how to feel. She blinked a few times in succession, climbing back into the land of the living, still staring out the windshield.

A small grunt came from Kent's throat, and it was this that clued her in to the fact that she was not alone. She turned to him slowly. Now her mouth was open as well. They locked like that for several long seconds, two lost souls gaping at each other in the front seat of a car, lost in a silent snowfall.

But Helen did not remain lost for long. No, not Helen.

She blinked again and swallowed. She breathed out deliberately, like the sigh of one disappointed. Perhaps she had not intended to wake up on the front seat of a car, staring at a stranger.

"Kent? You look different. Is that you?"

Well, then, perhaps not a stranger.

Kent more guffawed than answered. "Helen! What are you doing? You could have killed us!" It was an absurd statement considering his intentions, and having said it, he swallowed hard.

"You are Kent." She said it as a matter of simple fact. Like, "The sun has gone down."

"And how do you know I'm Kent?" He caught himself. "Even if I were?" But he'd already called her Helen, hadn't he? Good grief!

Either way, Helen was not listening. She was lost; he could see that in her eyes. She turned to the windshield without blinking. "Did you see it, Kent?"

He followed her eyes. The street still lay empty and white. Condensation was beginning to gather on the windshield from the hot breath. "See what?"

"See the light. Did you see the light? It was everywhere. It was heaven, I think." She spoke in awe.

The anger flared up his spine, but he bit his tongue and closed his eyes. "Helen . . . you were out cold and hallucinating. Wake up, you old religious coot. There's nothing but cold snow and death out there." Then he turned on her and let his anger swell past his clenched teeth. "I swear, I'm *sick* of all your crazy heaven and God talk!"

If he expected her to shrink, he should have known better. She turned to him with bright eyes. She did not look like an old woman who had just been dragged, half dead, from a snowstorm. "What if there *is* life out there, Kent?" Her lips flared red. "What if, behind this veil of flesh, there is a spiritual reality crackling with light? What if it was all created for a purpose? What if, behind it all, that Creator is craving relationship?" Tears sprang to her eyes.

"What if you were made to love him? What then, Kent?" Her eyes did not blink but turned to pools of tears. One of those pools broke, and a trail of tears ran down her right cheek.

Kent had his mouth opened to retort, to put her back in her place, before he realized he had nothing to say. Not to *this*. What she suggested could not be. He tried to imagine a God desperate for love, like some huge, smiling ball of light with outstretched arms. The image refused to hold shape. And if there was truth there in those words, if somehow there was a Creator who loved him so . . . he would kill himself anyway. He would slit his wrists in agony.

Kent turned from her and clenched his jaw.

"Kent." Her voice warbled soft to him.

Shut up, Helen! Just shut up! His mind screamed obscenities, locked in torment.

"Kent." She was begging. The small, stuffy cabin of the Lincoln seemed to throb with the beating of his heart. He wanted to reach over and slap her, but his hands had frozen on the wheel.

Kent cast her a sideways glance. Helen was trembling and weeping and melting on the seat before him. His heart screamed with pain. Her lips quivered with desire. A pleading smile.

She reached a shaking hand toward him. "Kent. Do you want to see?"

He could barely hear the words from her constricted throat. *"Kent, do you want to see?"*

No! No, no, no, I don't want to see! "Don't be a fool, Helen! You don't just turn on a light to see this God of yours!"

"No. But tonight is different. Do you want to see?"

No, no, no, you old hag! There is nothing to see! Tears blurred his vision.

What was happening to him? An ache tore at his heart, and he whimpered. Time seemed to cease then, in that moment of agony. *Oh, God! Oh, God! Do I want to see? Yes! Yes, I do want to see, don't I?* Kent slowly kneaded his skull with his fingers. He heard the word from his lips like a distant whisper. "Yes."

She touched his cheek.

A strobe exploded in Kent's skull. The horizon detonated with a blinding light, and he jerked upright. Everything stopped then. His heart seized in his chest; his blood froze in his veins; his breath stalled in his lungs. The world ended with one gasp.

And then it restarted with a blur of images that slammed him back in his seat and yanked his jaw open. Torrents of light cascaded into his mind and thundered down his spine. His body convulsed there on the leather Towncar seat as if seized by death throes.

But it was not death. It was life! It was the breath of God! He knew that the moment it touched him. Helen's creator was . . . was *whispering* to him. He knew that too. This raw emotion pounding through his body was just a whisper, and it said, *I love you, my beloved.*

"Oh, God! Oh, God, God!" He was screaming. Laughter drowned out his own cry—a pealing laughter that echoed across the sky. He knew that laughter! Voices from the past—a mother laughing in pleasure; a child giggling in long, high-pitched squeals of delight. It was Gloria and Spencer, there in the light, ecstatic. Kent heard their voices echo through his skull, and he threw his hand to his face and began to writhe in shame.

"Oh, God! Oh, God. I'm sorry!" It was true! The realization pummeled him like a battering ram to the chest. God! Helen's God. Gloria's God. Spencer's God. *The* God!

And he had said, *I love you, my beloved!*

The injustice of it all twisted Kent's mind, and he wormed in agony. The anguish of a mother having smothered her child. The desperation of a husband having tossed aside his bride for the whore. A wish for death.

A new surge of Helen's heaven crashed through Kent's bones, and he trembled under its power. *I love you, my beloved.*

Kent screamed. With every fiber still intact in his throat he screamed out for death, for forgiveness—but his vocal cords had seized with the rest now. They produced nothing more than a long, drawn-out groan. "Uuuuuuhhhhh . . ."

I have died already. I forgive you.

No, no, you don't understand! I am human waste. I do not know how to love. I am death!

You are my lover.

I am your hater! Kent's body buckled, and his forehead hit the steering wheel. Tears ran down his cheeks. The gross incongruity of these words swung like a steel wrecking ball against the sides of his skull.

You are my lover!

The notion that this being of white-hot love could want to love *him!* It could not be! He arched his neck and faced the Towncar's plush ceiling, his mouth stretched wide. It was then that he found his voice again. And he used it to roar, full throated. "Nooooooooo! I caaan't!"

Please love me. The whisper thundered through his body.

You were made to love him, a small voice said. Spencer's voice. Then it giggled.

Yes, Kent. Love him. That was Gloria.

Then Kent fell apart and heaved with sobs on the front seat beside Helen. In one twisted bundle of agony and ecstasy, of deep sorrow and bubbling joy, Kent loved God.

"Yes. Yes, yes, yes." He drank the forgiveness as if an overwhelming thirst had brought him to the edge of death. He gulped at the love like a fish desperate for oxygen. Except this was God filling him with breath, and it brought an unabashed quiver to each fiber of muscle still capable of movement. He reached out with every ounce of his being, every conscious thought, and he begged to be there with him.

For a few moments he *was* there with him. Or a part of God was down here in the Lincoln with him.

And then the light vanished, leaving Kent gasping for breath, draped over the steering wheel. He fell over Helen's lap and sobbed.

She stroked his head gently. Time lost its meaning for a while.

46

"So you saw him?"

Kent sat up, dazed. He looked at Helen and then back out the front windshield, misted now with condensation. "God!"

"Yes. Words just aren't adequate, are they?"

"So that was . . . God?" He knew it was. Without the slightest question.

"Yes."

Kent turned to her slowly. "Is it that way for everybody? How come I've never heard of this?"

"You've never heard about it because you've kept your ears closed. Is it that way for everybody? Yes and no."

He stared at her, wanting her to continue.

"No, not everyone will see what you have seen here tonight. At least not in the same way. But yes, in many ways, it is the same."

She turned to the windshield. "Let me tell you a story, Kent. You remember a story in the Bible about a man named Job?"

"I heard them, Helen. I heard Gloria and Spencer. They were laughing." A smile curved his mouth.

She smiled, bright eyed. "Yes, I know. You remember this man, Job? From the Bible?"

"They're in heaven, Helen," Kent returned, still distracted by the thought. "They're actually in heaven. With *him!*"

"Yes." She nodded. "Kent. I'm asking you a question here. Do you know of Job in the Bible?"

"The man who suffered?"

"Yes. Satan lost his challenge that he could make a righteous man curse God. You remember that?"

"Job remained faithful to God. And in the end he received twice the wealth. Something like that."

"It actually happened. He lost everything. His children, his wife, his wealth." Kent turned to her, blinking.

She faced the dark sky. "Not so long ago, Satan cast another challenge before God. A challenge of reversals. This time he insisted that he could keep an unrighteous man from responding to God's love. *"No matter how you draw him, no matter how you love him, no matter how you lure him,"* Satan said, *"I can keep this man from responding to your love."*

"You're saying this actually happened?"

"Yes." She looked at him and nodded, teary eyed now. "Yes. And God accepted the challenge. The heavens have been lined with a million creatures, intent on that man's every move for months. And today, God has won the challenge." Helen smiled.

"M . . . me?" Kent asked, stunned. *"I was this man?"*

"Yes."

The notion seemed absurd. "This was all engineered, then? How . . ."

"No, not engineered, Kent. You were drawn. In ways none of us may ever fully understand, you were drawn by the father. And you were pulled . . . in a thousand ways you were pulled by Satan. Away from God."

Kent's mind spun back over the last few months and saw a long string of events full of extremes. Death. But in death, laughter, because Gloria and Spencer were laughing up there. Wealth. But in wealth, death. Or very nearly death. A whole reality behind the stage of life.

"He must have switched strategies halfway through," Kent said absently.

"Satan?"

"Yes. Killing off my family didn't work, so he set out to make me rich."

She chuckled. "Yes, you're getting the picture."

He turned to her again. "But why me?"

She sighed and shook her head. A car drove by, its lights glaring like halos in the windshield. The dull thump of rock music for a moment and then silence once again.

"That's just it, Kent. Your case is unique because of what we were able to see. But otherwise it's not so different than the challenge made over the young man or woman behind the wheel of the car that just passed us."

"It's the same for everybody?"

"You think God loves any one man more than he loves another? Does he draw one more and another less? No. Over every man there is cast a challenge. It is as intense for every man. We just don't see it. If we could . . ." She shook her head. "My, my, my."

Kent's chest began to swell, and he thought he might be reduced to tears again. This changed everything. It seemed so obvious now. So right. The meaning of life all bundled up in a few statements and yet so few knew the truth.

"So then behind this . . . this flesh . . . this physical world, there is activity . . . enough activity to blow our minds." He shook his head, overwhelmed by the notion. "We see only the tip of it all. And then only if we open our eyes."

"We fight not against flesh and blood. And we fight a war that is fleeting. Believe me, this life will pass quickly enough, although sometimes not quickly enough, it seems. Then it will be forever. Somewhere."

"Why don't more people know this? Why has no one told me this?"

She turned to him. "You think Gloria never told you this? We prayed every Thursday morning for five years for this day. You were just too wrapped up in this world to notice."

"Yes, you are right. You are so right!"

"Today you start over, Kent."

Lacy!

He grabbed Helen's arm. "We have to get to Lacy!"

"Lacy?"

"Yes. She lives in Boulder." He started the car and pulled out into the street, sliding on the snow. "Do you mind? I need you there. She'll never believe me."

"Why not? It's a beautiful, snowy night for a drive. I was rather hoping for an entirely different destination, but I suppose Boulder will do for now."

47

Lacy answered the door dressed in a plaid flannel shirt that hung below her jeans. "May I help you?"

Kent stood behind Helen for the moment, his heart pounding like a locomotive in his chest. He saw Lacy's eyes shift to him, questioning at first, and then recognizing. "Hello, Lacy," Helen said. "May we come in?"

"You? Kevin, right? I met you in the restaurant. What do you want?"

Helen answered. "We are not who you might think. My name is Helen. Helen Crane. This is my son-in-law, Kent Anthony. I believe you know each other."

Lacy's eyes grew round.

Kent stepped around Helen, steadying a tremble that had parked itself in his bones since his eyes had been opened. "Hello, Lacy."

She stepped back. "That's . . . that's impossible! Kent's dead."

"Lacy. Listen to me. It's me. Listen to my voice." He swallowed. "I know I look a bit different; I've had a few changes made, but it's me."

Lacy took another step back, blinking.

"You hear me?" Kent pushed. "I told you the whole plan on a Friday night, sitting right there," he motioned to the dinette table, "drinking your coffee. Twenty million dollars, right? Using AFPS? You slapped me."

It was too much for her to reject, he knew. She stepped aside as though in a dream. Kent took it as a sign to enter and he did so cautiously. Helen followed and sat on the sofa. Lacy closed the door and stood facing him, unblinking.

The room stilled to silence. What could he possibly say? He grinned, feeling suddenly foolish and small for coming. "So, I don't know what to say."

She did not respond.

"Lacy. I'm . . . I'm so sorry." His vision swam in fresh tears. She was searching her memory banks, trying to make ends meet, reconciling conflicting emotions. But she was not speaking. He saw her swallow and suddenly it was too much for him. *He* had caused this. *He* might have changed, but the remnants of his life lay in ruins. Gutted shells, hollow lies, broken hearts. Like this heart here, beating but broken, possibly beyond mending.

Lacy's jaw clenched, and her eyes swam in pools of tears.

Kent closed his eyes and fought his own tears. Yes, indeed, she was not so happy; that much was obvious.

Her voice came barely above a whisper. "So. It *is* you. Do you know what you've done to me?"

He opened his eyes. She was still staring at him, still clenching her jaw. But some light had come to her eyes, he thought. "Yes, it is me. And yes, I've been a complete idiot. Please . . . please forgive me."

"And you came to me at the restaurant." Her jaw relaxed.

He nodded. "Yes. I'm sorry."

"Good. You should be. You should be terrified about now."

"Yes. And I am." She was going to reject him, Kent thought. She *should* reject him.

Lacy's eyes blazed. "And why did you come? Tell me why you came."

"Because . . ." It was hard, this dealing in love. First God and now her. He blinked. No, not hard at all. Not in his new skin. Hard in his old self, but in this new skin, love was the currency of life.

He said it easily then. "Because I love you, Lacy."

The words seemed to hit her with their own physical force. A tear broke from her eye. "You love me?"

Oh, what had he done to her? "Yes. Yes, I love you," Kent said. He walked right up to her and opened his arms, desperate for her love.

She closed her eyes and let him embrace her, hesitantly at first, and then she slid her arms around his waist and pulled herself into his chest, crying. For a long time they said nothing. They held each other tightly and let their embrace speak.

When Lacy finally spoke it was in a soft, resigned voice. "And I love you, Kent. I love you too."

48

Present Day

Padre Cadione turned from the window, his face wet with tears at the tale his visitor had shared over the last two hours. They had shifted about the office, reposturing themselves as the story sped on, at times leaning against the wall, at times sitting behind the desk, but always intent. The confessor had told the story with exuberance, with many hand gestures, with tears, and often with a contagious grin splitting his face. And now the tale had ended, much to the father's dismay. But had it?

Beyond the window he could see the east guard tower, stoic against the blue sky. Cadione turned back to the man before him. His chest felt as though a vise had screwed down on his heart for the duration. The visitor sat cross-legged now, swinging one leg over the other, his hands folded on his lap.

"This is true? All of it?"

"Every word, Father."

The fan continued its swishing high above, drying the sweat gathered on Padre Cadione's neck. "You believe that God is capable of such a thing today, then?"

"I know it, Father!" The man stood to his feet and spread his hands wide. Cadione leaned back in his chair. "His love is greater than the greatest love man can imagine. The most extravagant expression of love is but a dim reflection of his own! We are made in his image, yes?"

"Yes." The padre could not help but smile with the man.

"You see, then! The greatest passion you are capable of only hints at his love."

"Yes." He nodded. "But how is it possible for a man to experience God in such a way? The experiences you speak of are . . . incredible!"

The visitor dropped his hands. "Yes, but they are real. I know."

"And how do you know?"

The light glinted off the visitor's eyes, and he smiled mischievously. "I know because I am he."

Padre Cadione did not respond immediately. He was who? The man in the story? But that was impossible! "You are *who?*"

"I am he. I am Kent Anthony."

The father's heart missed its rhythm. "Kent? Your file says your name is Kevin. Kevin Stillman."

"Yes, well, now you know the whole story, don't you? There are certain advantages to changing identities, my friend. It is the one thing they permitted me to keep when I confessed. A small consolation. And of course, I had to confess—you understand that, don't you? I *wanted* to confess. But there is no use living in the past. I am a new man. And I rather like the name."

The father's mind spun. "So then, you say that you personally glimpsed heaven? That this whole wager of Lucifer's was over your soul? You say heaven bent over backward to rescue your soul?"

"You think it is presumptuous?" the man said, smiling. "It is no less so than the challenge over your soul, Father. You just do not see it." He lifted a hand to make a point. "And I'll tell you something else. Everything is not what it seems. I knew early on that the vagrant in the alley was a man of dreams, but I did see him once, and I am not sure to this day whether he was real. But he was not an angel, I can assure you."

"You're saying he was sent from hell, then?"

"Can you think of a reason why not? Now, the others—I believe they were from heaven. I cannot be sure, of course. But the Scriptures do say that we entertain angels without knowing, do they not?"

"Others?"

"Cliff. I could find no record of him in the employment files when I looked for him at the end. And the detective. Detective Pinhead. There is no record of a Jeremy Lawson at the Seventh Precinct. I always suspected there was something with those two. Perhaps even Bono at the bar."

A knock rapped on the door.

"That seems . . ."

The man grinned wide. "Impossible? Not all things are what they seem, my friend."

"What happened to the money? To the bankers?"

"Borst and Bentley? Neither work for the bank now. I told the bank everything, of course. Last I heard they were wrapped up in court battles over the bonus money. They cannot win. And no bank will hire dishonest men. I pity them, really. As for the money, I liquidated everything and returned the money to each and every account from which it was taken, twenty cents at a time. Using ROOSTER, of course. Only the authorities and a few officials at the highest level even know what happened. The bank insisted I keep the $250,000 recovery fee. I tried to give it back, but they said I had earned it by exposing Borst and Bentley. And by developing AFPS, of course."

The rap sounded again. "Time's up, Chaplain."

"Come in," Cadione called, keeping his eyes on the man. The pieces to this puzzle locked in his mind, and he stood, frozen by them.

A uniformed guard walked through the door and stopped. "Come on. Let's go." The guard waved a night stick in Kent's direction. "Back to the cell."

The prisoner named Kevin, who was really Kent—Kent Anthony—turned to leave, still smiling at Padre Cadione.

"And what of Lacy?" Cadione asked, ignoring the guard.

Kent smiled. "I'll be up for parole in two years. If all goes well, we plan to be wed then. Maybe you could do the honors, Father."

He nodded. "Yes. And Helen?"

"Yes, Helen. You will have to meet Helen someday, Padre. She was not always the kind of woman she was in this story, you know. Her life story will make you weep. Perhaps someday when we have more time, I will tell you. It will make you see things differently. I promise."

"I would like that," the chaplain heard himself say. But his mind was spinning, and he was finding it difficult to concentrate.

The prisoner turned at the door and winked. "Remember, Father. It is true. Every last word is true. The same challenge has been cast over your soul. You should ponder that tonight before you sleep. We are all Jobs in one way or another."

They led him out, still smiling.

Padre Cadione staggered to his chair and sat hard. It had been a long time since he had prayed more than meaningless words. But that was about to change.

Everything was about to change.

ABOUT THE AUTHOR

Ted Dekker is known for novels that combine adrenaline-laced plot twists with the supernatural and the surreal. He is the best-selling author of multiple titles including *Heaven's Wager, When Heaven Weeps, Thunder of Heaven* and the co-author of the best-selling series *Blessd Child* and *A Man Called Blessed.* Raised in the jungles of Indonesia, Ted now lives with his family in the mountains of Colorado.

Coming in May 2003

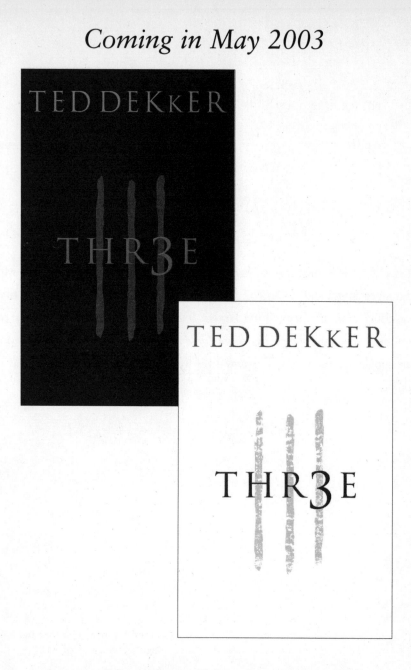

A powerful novel of good, evil, and all that lies
in between. *THR3E* will release in both a black
and white hardcover edition

Also Available from Ted Dekker

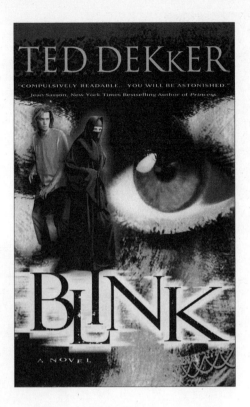

The future changes in the BLINK of an eye...or does it?

Seth Borders isn't your average graduate student. For starters, he has one of the world's highest IQs. Now he's suddenly struck by an incredible power—the ability to see multiple potential futures.

Still reeling form this inexplicable gift, Seth stumbles upon a beautiful woman named Miriam. Unknown to Seth, Miriam is a Saudi Arabian princess who has fled her veiled existence to escape a forced marriage of unimaginable consequences. Cultures collide as they're thrown together and forced to run from an unstoppable force determined to kidnap or kill Miriam.

An intoxicating tale set amidst the shifting sands of the Middle East and the back roads of American, *Blink* engages issues as ancient as the earth itself . . . and as current as today's headlines.

Also Available from Ted Dekker

HEAVEN'S WAGER

He lost everything he ever wanted—and risked his soul to get what he deserved. Take a glimpse into a world more real and vital than most people ever discover here on earth, the unseen world where the real dramas of the universe—and of our daily lives—continually unfold.

WHEN HEAVEN WEEPS

A cruel game of ultimate stakes at the end of World War II leaves Jan Jovic stunned and perplexed. He's prepared for neither the incredible demonstration of love nor the terrible events that follow. Now, many years later, Jan falls madly in love with the "wrong" woman and learns the true cost of love.

THUNDER OF HEAVEN

When armed forces destroy their idyllic existence within the jungles of the Amazon, Tanya embraces God, while Shannon boldly rejects God, choosing the life of an assassin. Despite their vast differences, they find themselves in the crucible of a hideous plot to strike sheer terror in the heart of America.

Also Available from Ted Dekker

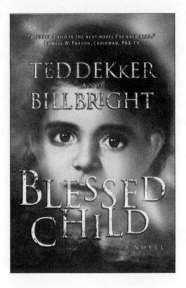

BLESSED CHILD
By Ted Dekker and Bill Bright

The young orphan boy was abandoned and raised in an Ethiopian monastery. Now he must flee those walls or die. But the world is hardly ready for a boy like Caleb. When relief expert Jason Marker agrees to take Caleb from the monastery, he opens humanity's doors to an incredible journey filled with intrigue and peril. Together with Leiah, the nurse who escapes to America with them, Jason discovers Caleb's stunning power. But so do the boy's enemies, who will stop at nothing to destroy him. Jason and Leiah fight for the boy's survival while the world erupts into debate over the source of the boy's power. In the end nothing can prepare any of them for what they will find.

A MAN CALLED BLESSED
By Ted Dekker and Bill Bright

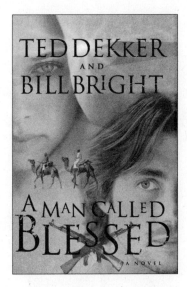

In this explosive sequel, Rebecca Soloman leads a team of Israeli commandos deep into the Ethiopian desert to hunt the one man who may know the final resting place of the Ark of the Covenant. But Islamic fundamentalists fear that the Ark's discovery will compel Israel to rebuild Solomon's temple on the very site of their own holy Mosque in Jerusalem. They immediately dispatch Ismael, their most accomplished assassin, to pursue the same man. But the man in their sights is no ordinary man. His name is Caleb, and he too is on a quest-to find again the love he once embraced as a child. Tensions skyrocket as the world awakens to the drama in the desert. The fate of millions rests in the hand of these three.